# VALENTINE'S
# EXILE

# VALENTINE'S EXILE

## A NOVEL OF
## THE VAMPIRE EARTH

# E. E. KNIGHT

A ROC BOOK

ROC

Published by New American Library, a division of
Penguin Group (USA) Inc., 375 Hudson Street,
New York, New York 10014, USA
Penguin Group (Canada), 90 Eglinton Avenue East, Suite 700, Toronto,
Ontario M4P 2Y3, Canada (a division of Pearson Penguin Canada Inc.)
Penguin Books Ltd., 80 Strand, London WC2R 0RL, England
Penguin Ireland, 25 St. Stephen's Green, Dublin 2,
Ireland (a division of Penguin Books Ltd.)
Penguin Group (Australia), 250 Camberwell Road, Camberwell, Victoria 3124,
Australia (a division of Pearson Australia Group Pty. Ltd.)
Penguin Books India Pvt. Ltd., 11 Community Centre, Panchsheel Park,
New Delhi - 110 017, India
Penguin Group (NZ), cnr Airborne and Rosedale Roads, Albany,
Auckland 1310, New Zealand (a division of Pearson New Zealand Ltd.)
Penguin Books (South Africa) (Pty.) Ltd., 24 Sturdee Avenue,
Rosebank, Johannesburg 2196, South Africa

Penguin Books Ltd., Registered Offices:
80 Strand, London WC2R 0RL, England

First published by Roc, an imprint of New American Library,
a division of Penguin Group (USA) Inc.

First Printing, June 2006
1   3   5   7   9   10   8   6   4   2

Copyright © Eric Frisch, 2006
All rights reserved

ROC REGISTERED TRADEMARK-MARCA REGISTRADA

LIBRARY OF CONGRESS CATALOGING-IN-PUBLICATION DATA:

Knight, E. E.
Valentine's exile : a novel of the vampire Earth / E.E. Knight.
p. cm.
ISBN 0-451-46087-1
1. Valentine, David (Fictitious character)—Fiction. 2. Human-alien
encounters—Fiction.   I. Title.
PS3611.N564V35 2006
813'.6—dc22        2005037232

Set in Granjon • Designed by Elke Sigal

Printed in the United States of America

*To the readers,*
*who carried me and my baby this far.*

*Only solitary men know the full joys of friendship.*
*Others have their family; but to a solitary and an exile*
*his friends are everything.*

—*Willa Cather*
SHADOWS ON THE ROCK

# CHAPTER ONE

*D*allas, March, the fiftieth year of the Kurian Order: Four square miles of concrete and structural steel smoke and pop and sputter as the city dies from the stranglehold of a siege.

Save for the sounds of streetfighting, hard to locate thanks to reflections from the skyscrapers, this city at war seems strangely empty. Scavenging black crows and wary, tail-tucking dogs catch the eye here and there, but human activity is nil. Vague stormlike rumbles mutter in the distance, and sudden eruptions of machine-gun fire from a few blocks away might be jackhammers breaking holes in a sidewalk in a more peaceful time. When men move they move in a rush, pouring from doorways and crossing streets in a quick wave before the whine of shellfire can catch them in the open.

Viewed from above, or on a headquarters map in one of the command bunkers, Big D is now a network of opposing circles.

The largest circle encompasses the great towers of the city center. Linked above the twentieth floor by spiderweb-like cables that allow the sure-tentacled Kurians interbuilding access without mixing with their human herds at street level, they show new holes and pits and hollows from the besiegers' guns and rockets. At street level mounds of debris and rubble stand in concentric rings, defended by batteries of guns manned by everyone from professional soldiers to minor functionaries in what until last year had been the affluent and sprawling North Texas Cooperative.

Surrounding that central axis are an assortment of smaller circles, ringing the central battlements like the chambers in a revolver's cylinder. The closest to the front lines are Texas regulars out of the Pinewoods and the Rio Grande belt; others to the north and east fly the tricolor of the

*Ozarks, and a few smaller ones filling gaps to the rear are clusters of militias made up of men and women freed from the heavy hand of the Cooperative.*

*Northwest of the city rests one of these smaller circles, surrounding an airstrip once called Love Field. The soldiers there are not placed to assault the city. The ad hoc unit occupying the airport grew out of the rising in Little Rock that opened Operation Archangel. They participate in the siege both as a sentimental gesture of gratitude to the Texans who plunged down the Arkansas River to rescue them and as being part of the gun-bristling ring that prevents an organized breakout. Their airfield joins the extreme left of the Ozark troops and the extreme right of the Texans.*

*Their regimental flag, a black-and-blue silhouette of an Arkansas razorback set under the joined Texas and Ozark flags, reads* DON'T FEED ON ME. *Judged from a distance, the forces in this particular encampment, called Valentine's Razors by the veterans, aren't in shape to serve as anything but a supporting unit. Only a few mortars and machine-gun pits fill their lines, more for defense of the camp than for battering those within the city. Instead rolls of concertina wire on the open ground near the airstrip enclose cattle awaiting slaughter for the daily ration, and the airport's garages hum with the sounds of generators and power tools. On the march southwest from the Ozarks the Razors proved invaluable in getting captured Kurian vehicles operational again, and in turning cattle, wheat, pigs, and corn into grist for various regimental kitchens. Their aptitudes reflect the rear-area nature of many of the soldiers in the Razors, united by chance during the uprising in Little Rock.*

*To a general of either side looking at a map and possessed of a modicum of intelligence, military and personal, the Razors are one of the least-threatening circles surrounding Big D.*

*But quality can rarely be judged from a distance.*

*The first clue is in the rifles that each on-duty soldier always has within reach: long, heavy-barreled killers with oversized banana magazines and integral bipods, some with telescopic sights, others with fixtures for high-capacity drum magazines. Souvenirs of the Razors' brief integration into Solon's Army of the Trans-Mississippi, they are the best battle rifles the famous Atlanta Gunworks produces. Thanks to the Type Threes, any soldier is capable of turning into a supporting fire unit in a moment, given a simple wrench and a belt of the proper ammunition.*

*Then there are the "prowlers." The mechanics of the Razors see to it that the best bits and pieces of Quisling wreckage make their way into the regimental motor pool, where they're assembled into armored cars and mortar transports. High-axled, fat-tired, covered with rocket-propelled grenade–stopping webbing, each swamp buggy-cum-armored car bears a pair of angry eyes, and sharp tusks and teeth, somewhere just above and forward of the front tires. A few have front electric winches formed into snouts, and the beds of many of the vehicles sport recoilless rifles, mini-guns, and auto-grenade launchers. Other longer, heavier, double-axled trucks are built to carry troops, loading and unloading from doors in the backs or sides of the transports, and an assortment of trailer-pumps feed the gas tanks from captured gasoline supplies when on the move, or hold a reserve against supply interruptions when encamped.*

*The Razors shouldn't have worked. Soldiers thrown together under the most dire of circumstances couldn't be expected to stand up to a determined assault, let alone hold a precarious position alone in the heart of enemy country. The success of their famous stand on the banks of the Arkansas River might be considered a measure as much of their enemy's incompetence as their own mettle. But some credit must be given to the improvisational skills of the officers who organized the Little Rock Rising.*

*One of those men crosses the outskirts of the airstrip as the sun rises. His mottled dark green-and-gray uniform is thick with "Dallas Dust," an oatmeal-colored mixture of pulverized concrete, ash, and mundane winter dirt. Black hair tied in a pigtail hangs from his scalp, and a thin, white scar on the right side of his face only serves to show off an early spring tan, bronzing indicative of ample melanin in his genes. A short-ened version of his Razor's battle rifle with folding stock and cut-down barrel bumps from its tight sling against leather battle webbing. The assault harness is festooned with everything from a wide-bladed utility parang to a gas mask hood, with flares for a signal gun at his hip and a "camel" water bladder over his shoulder. A veteran of the Razors would note the distinctly nonregulation moccasins on his feet, and infer that the*

*Razors' operations officer, Major Valentine, was back from another of his "scouts."*

ψ

David Valentine breathed in a last snootful of clean air and descended into the muskrat-den reek. He stepped down carefully, holding an uprooted young dandelion in his gun-free hand. The stairwell to the old terminal's sublevel was mostly gone. The entryway had been enlarged, replaced by churned-over earth paved with plywood strips dropping eight feet to the hole in the cinderblock side of the foundation where the basement door used to be.

The entrance to the Razorbacks' headquarters resembled an oversized anthole, if anything. It fooled the eyes that sometimes drifted high above the besiegers' positions.

He rested his gun in a cleaning becket and stood on a carpet remnant in the entryway to let his eyes adjust to the dim light within. Deaf old Pooter, one of the regiment's guinea pigs, rolled up onto his hind legs and whistled a welcome from his chicken-wire cage perched on a shelf next to the door. Valentine tossed him the dandelion.

"They didn't hit us after all," he told Pooter.

Pooter chuckled as a length of milky dandelion stem disappeared into his fast-working jaws.

If the Kurians dusted again, Pooter would expire in a noisy hacking fit, giving the men inside time to ring the alarm, lower the plastic curtains, and put on their gas masks and gloves.

Valentine was tired. He'd spent the last eight hours moving across the forward posts, keyed up for a battle that never came. Probably more than he would have been had there been action, the weird I'm-alive-and-I-can-do-anything exhilaration of surviving combat would have floated him back to the Razors' HQ.

On the other side of the door from Pooter was a sandbagged cubbyhole filled with salvaged armchairs resting among thousands of loosely bound pages from perhaps a hundred different pre-22 magazines and novels. A team of Nail's Bears, Razorback HQ's emergency reserve, lounged within, smoking captured tobacco and reading books or magazine fragments.

Except for one. The Bear Valentine knew as Lost & Found stood just outside the cubbyhole in the deepest shadow of the entrance, an assault rifle resting in his arms like a cradled child, a bucket filled with white powder at his feet.

Valentine took in the HQ air, perhaps ten degrees warmer than the morning chill of the Texas spring outside. The Bear tobacco, a faint fecal smell, brewing coffee, old sweat, drying laundry, gun oil, and a hint of cabbage stewing in salty broth rolled around in his nostrils.

"Morning, sir," Lost & Found said, looking out the door beyond Valentine. He prodded the bucket at his foot.

Valentine dutifully stripped off his combat harness and tossed it in the decontamination barrel. The rest of his clothes followed until he stood naked on the carpet remnant.

He took a handful of the boric acid from the bucket and gave himself a rubdown, concentrating on his shoulder-length black hair, armpits, and crotch. Rednits liked the warmth and tender apertures around hair follicles, and the battalion wasn't losing any more men to nit-fever. Colonel Meadows had enough on his hands with twenty percent of the Razorbacks filling field hospital beds or recovery wards, eating leek-and-liver soup twice daily, getting their blood back up to strength.

Valentine went over to a bank of lockers featuring names written on duct tape plastered on new paint slathered over old rust, and extracted a uniform. Hank had put a fresh one in overnight, while Valentine was forward. Regular soldiers had to make do with the rumpled contents of the slop bins, but the Razorback officers each had a locker for their inside uniforms. When he was properly dressed in the mixed-gray-and-deep-green fatigues of the Razorbacks (Southern Command Mixed Infantry Division, for use of—some said the color scheme was reminiscent of a raccoon's backside) he put on leather-soled moccasins and followed the smell of coffee with his Wolf's nose.

He walked past the headset-wearing HQ radio/field-phone operator, whose gear was swathed in cheesecloth that smelled of kerosene, surrounded by six different No Smoking signs in English, Spanish, and French. The kerosene kept the electicks out.

The little bastards ate electrical insulation and grew into three-inch sticklike bugs whose metallic chitin inevitably shorted out electrical equipment.

The boy with the headset, seventeen but scrawny enough to pass for fourteen, studied the flickering needles of the radio set as though divining runes. Valentine raised an eyebrow to the kid, got a head shake in return, and looked at the clipboard with the most recent com-flimsies. There'd been some chatter out of Dallas the previous day that made GHQ-Dallas Corridor suspect a counterattack in the Razorbacks' area, but nothing had manifested last night.

*Breakfast or a shower?*

Valentine decided to give the boric acid a few more minutes to work and headed for the galley.

In the five weeks they'd occupied the airfield Narcisse and her staff had set up sinks, stoves, and even had a pizza oven going. Companies rotating to or from the forward positions always had a pizza party before creeping out to the strongpoints covering the approaches to Dallas. Narcisse wore no uniform, held no rank, and wandered between the battalion's kitchens and infirmary as the mood struck her, dispensing equal helpings of cheer and food, escorted in her wheelchair by a steadfast rottweilerish mutt who'd wandered into camp on the Razorbacks' trip south from the Ouachitas. The men and women whose job it was to aid and comfort the frontline soldiers obeyed the old, legless Haitian as though she were a visiting field marshall.

Valentine said good morning to the potato peelers, working under faded paint that once demarked a maintenance workshop, rinsed his hands, and poured himself a mug of water from the hot pot. He plopped in one of Narcisse's herbal tea bags from a woven basket on a high shelf, then covered his brew-up with a plastic lid masquerading as a saucer, and took the stairs down to the subbasement and the hooches.

He smelled the steeping tea on the way down the stairs. It tasted faintly of oranges—God only knew how Narcisse came up with orange peel—and seemed to go to whatever part of the body most needed a fix. If you were constipated it loosened you, if you were squirting it plugged you. It took away headache and woke you up in the morning and calmed the jitters that came during a long spell of shellfire.

Valentine had a room to himself down among the original plumbing fixtures and electrical junction boxes. In the distance a generator clattered, steadily supplying juice but sounding as though it was unhappy with the routine. Just along the hall Colonel Meadows occupied an old security office, but Valentine didn't see light creeping out from under the door so he turned and moved aside the bedsheet curtaining off his quarters.

His nose told him someone lay in his room even before his eyes picked out the L-shaped hummock in his wire-frame bed. A pale, boric acid–dusted leg ending in a calloused, hammertoed foot emerged from the wooly army blanket, and a knife-cut shock of short red hair could just be distinguished at the other end.

Alessa Duvalier was back from the heart of Dallas.

Valentine examined the foot. Some people showed the experience of a hard life through their eyes, others in their rough hands. A few, like Narcisse, were bodily crippled. While the rest of Duvalier was rather severely pretty, occasionally exquisite when mood or necessity struck, Duvalier's feet manifested everything bad the Cat had been through. Dark with filth between the toes, hard-heeled, toes twisted and dirt-crusted nails chipped, scabbed at the ankle, calloused and scarred from endless miles on worn-through socks— her feet told a gruesome tale.

A pair of utility sinks held her gear, reeking of the camphor smell of its spell in the decontamination barrel, her sword-concealing walking stick lying atop more mundane boots and socks.

"Val, that you?" she said sleepily from under the blanket, voice muffled by a fistful of wool over her mouth and nose to keep out the basement chill. She shifted and he caught a flash of upper thigh. She'd fallen into his bed wearing only a slop shirt. They'd never been lovers, but were as comfortable around each other as a married couple.

"Yeah."

"Room for two."

"Shower first. Then I want to hear—"

"One more hour. I got in at oh-four."

7

"I was out at the forward posts. Pickets didn't report you—"

She snorted. Valentine heard Hank's quick step on the stairs he'd just come down.

He looked at his self-winding watch, a gift from Meadows when the colonel assumed command of the Razorbacks. The engraved inscription on the back proclaimed forty-eight-year-old eternal love between a set of initials both ending in *C*. "One more hour, then. Breakfast?"

"Anything."

Valentine took a reviving spout-shower that kept Hank busy bearing hot water down from the kitchen. Valentine had been seeing to the boy's education at odd hours, trying to remember the lessons Father Max had issued at thirteen, and had put him in the battalion's books to make it easier to feed and clothe the boy. They shared more than just a working relationship. Both had ugly red-and-white burn scars; Valentine's on his back, Hank's on his semi-functional right hand.

"What's the definition of an isosceles triangle?" Valentine asked as he worked a soapy rag up and down his legs.

"All, no, two sides of equal length," Hank said.

"When all three are the same?"

"Equilateral," Hank said.

Hank also got the questions on degrees of the corners of an equilateral right. Tomorrow Valentine would get him using triangles for navigational purposes . . . it always helped to add practical applicability right away. In a week or so the boy would be able to determine latitude using the sun and a sextant, provided he could remember the definition of a plumb line.

"Haven't seen Ahn-Kha this morning, have you?"

"No, sir," Hank said, reverting to military expression with the ease of long practice.

Valentine hadn't smelled the Grog's presence at headquarters, but Ahn-Kha kept to himself in a partially blocked stairwell when he was at the headquarters. Ahn-Kha was evaluating and drilling some of the newer Razorbacks, mostly Texan volunteers who'd been funneled to them through Southern Command's haphazard field personnel depot north of the city. Southern Command tended to get recruits the all-Texan units didn't want, and Ahn-Kha knew how to turn lemons into lemonade. The first thing Valentine wanted recruits to learn was to respect Grogs, whether they were friends or enemies.

Way too many lives had been lost in the past thanks to mistakes.

Valentine asked Hank to go fill a tray, saw that the light was on in Meadows' office, and poked his head in to see if his superior had anything new on the rumored attack.

"Forward posts all quiet, sir," Valentine reported.

"I'm not forward or quiet," William Post replied. His salt-and-pepper hair showed white traces of boric acid. "Narcisse made her chili last night." Valentine's old subordinate, an ex-Quisling Coastal Marine who'd helped him take the *Thunderbolt* across the Caribbean and back, and was one of the best officers he'd ever known, went back to sorting com-flimsies. Valentine's ears picked up a stifled burp.

"Anything happen here?" *Besides the usual morning gas.*

Meadows had the look of a man just up from a twenty-minute nap that was the only sleep he'd gotten that night. He closed his shirt, his missing-fingered hand working the buttons up the seam like a busy insect. "Not even the usual harassing fire. They're finally running out of shells. Big Wings overhead in the night."

Big Wings were the larger, gargoylelike flyers the Kurians kept in the taller towers of Dallas. Both smarter and rarer than the Harpies Valentine had encountered, they tended to stay above, out of rifle shot, in the dark. Some weeks ago Valentine had seen a dead one that had been brought down by chance, wearing a pair of binoculars and carrying an aerial photograph, grease-penciled icons squiggled all over the photo marking the besieging army's current positions.

"I had the A Company men turn in," Post reported. "The armored cars are still ready to roll, and C Company's alerted. Just in case."

"Thanks, Will," Valentine said. "Colonel, I still think they're preparing a surprise. I'd suggest we keep the line fully manned." Valentine regretted the words before his tongue stilled. Meadows was smart enough that he didn't need to be told the obvious.

"Our sources could be wrong. Again," Meadows said, glancing at the flimsy-basket next to his door. It was piled with messages that came in overnight but weren't important enough to require the CO to be awakened. The belief that an attack was due had been based on Valentine's intelligence, everything from deserter interrogations to vague murmurs from Dallas Operations that the heart of the city was abuzz with activity. There was no hint of reprimand or peevishness in his tone. Meadows knew war was guesswork, and frequently the guesses were wrong.

"Sir, Smoke came in while I was out," Valentine said. "I'll debrief her over breakfast."

Post gave Valentine a playful wink as Meadows read his messages. Duvalier's appropriation of Valentine's bed whenever she was with the Razors inspired a few jokes about Valentine's "operations." Valentine suspected that the best lines originated from Post's salty throat.

"How are the men up the boulevard doing?" Meadows asked.

"The boulevard" was a wide east-west street that marked the forward edge of the Razors' positions. Snipers and machine gunners warred over five lanes of former Texas state route from blasted storefronts.

"Unhappy about being on the line, sir," Post reported. Post had keen antennae when it came to sensing the regiment's mood. More importantly, he cared, and even better, he acted on their behalf. Post was a relentless terror to rear-area supply officers when it came to the well-being of his men. "They only got three days at the airfield." Comparatively fresh companies had been moved up in anticipation of the attack from the relative quiet of the old field.

"Let's rotate them out if nothing happens by tomorrow morning."

"Will do, sir," Post replied.

"I'll see to Smoke now, Colonel, if you don't have anything else," Valentine said.

"Thank her for me, Major. Grab a meal and then hit your bunk." Meadows tended to keep his orders brief and simple. Sometimes they were also pleasant. Meadows picked up the flimsies from his basket, glanced at them, and passed them to Valentine.

Valentine read them on the way back to the galley—or kitchen, he mentally corrected. Shipboard slang still worked itself into his thoughts, a leftover from his yearlong spell posing as a Coastal Marine in the enemy's uniform, and then living in the *Thunderbolt* after taking her from the Kurians.

| | |
|---|---|
| **01:30** | *Potable water line reestablished to forward positions* |
| **02:28** | *OP3 OP11 Artillery fire flashes and sounds from other side of city* |
| **03:55** | *OP3 Barrage ceased* |
| **04:10** | *OP12 Reports train heard north toward city* |

The OP notation was for field phone–equipped forward observation posts. Valentine had heard the barrage and seen the flashes on the opposite side of the city as well, glimpsed from between the tall buildings, making the structures stand out against the night like gravestones to a dead city.

The only suspicious message was of the train. The lines into Dallas had been cut, torn up, mined, plowed under, or otherwise blocked very early in the siege. Readying or moving a train made little sense—unless the Kurians were merely shuffling troops within the city.

Valentine loaded up a tray and employed Hank as coffee bearer, and returned to his room. Duvalier twitched at his entry, then relaxed. Her eyes opened.

"Food," she said.

"And coffee," Valentine replied, after checking to make sure she was decent. Hank being a teenager, he'd waited in the spot with the best viewing angle into the room and bed.

"What's the latest from D?" Valentine asked, setting the tray briefly on the bed before pulling his makeshift desk up so she'd have an eating surface.

"No sign of an assault. I saw some extra gun crews and battle police at their stations, but no troops have been brought up."

Hank hung up Duvalier's gear to dry. Valentine saw the boy clip off a yawn.

"The Quislings?"

"Most units been on half rations for over a month now. Internal security and battle police excepted, of course. And some of the higher officers; they're as fat as ever. I heard some men talking. No one dares report sick. Rumor has it the Kurians are running short on aura, and the sick list is the first place they look."

"Morale?"

"Horrible," she reported between bites. "They're losing and they know it. Deserters aren't being disposed of quietly anymore. Every night just before they shut down power they assemble representatives from all the Quisling brigades and have public executions. I put on a nurse's shawl and hat and watched one. NCOs kept offering me a bottle or cigarettes, but I couldn't take my eyes off the stage."

The incidental noises from Hank working behind him ceased.

"They make the deserters stand in these big plastic garbage cans, the ones with little arrows running around in a circle, handcuffed in front. Then a Reaper comes up from behind one and tears open their shirt. They keep the poor bastard facing the other ranks the whole time so they can see the expression on his face—they're all gagged of course; they don't want any last words. The Reaper clamps its jaws somewhere between the shoulder blades and starts squeezing their arms into the rib cage. You hear the bones breaking, see the shoulders pop out as they dislocate.

"Then they just tip up the garbage can and wheel the body away. Blood and piss leaking out the bottom, usually. Then a political officer steps up and reads the dead man's confession, and his CO verifies his mark or signature. Then they wheel out the next one. Sometimes six or seven a night. They want the men to go to bed with something to think about.

"I've seen some gawdawful stuff, but . . . that poor bastard. I had a dream about him."

"They never run out of Reapers, do they?" Hank put in.

"Seems not," Duvalier said.

Valentine decided to change the subject. "Okay, they're not massing for an attack. Maybe a breakout?"

"No, all the rolling motor stock is dispersed," she said, slurping coffee. "Unless it's hidden. I saw a few entrances to underground garages that were guarded with armored cars and lots of wire and kneecappers."

The last was a nasty little mine the Kurians were fond of. When triggered, it launched itself twenty inches in the air like a startled frog and exploded, sending flechettes out horizontally that literally cut a man off at the knees.

"I don't suppose you saw any draft articles of surrender crumpled up in the wastebaskets, did you?"

She made a noise that sent remnants of a last mouthful of masticated egg flying. "Na-ah."

"Now," Valentine said. "If you'll get out of my bed——"

"I need a real bath. Those basins are hardly big enough to sit in. How about your water boy——"

Hank perked up at the potential for *that* duty.

Valentine hated to ruin the boy's morning. "You can use the womens'. There's piping laid on and a tub."

Such gallantry as still existed between the sexes in the Razors mostly involved the men working madly to provide the women with a few homey comforts wherever the regiment moved. The badly outnumbered women had to do little in return—the occasional smile, a few soft words, or an earthy joke reminded their fellow soldiers of mothers, sweethearts, sisters, or wives.

"Killjoy," Duvalier said, winking at Hank.

⚓

The alarms brought Valentine out of his dreams and to his feet. For one awful moment he hung on a mental precipice between reality and his vaguely pleasant dream—something to do with a boat and bougainvillea—while his brain caught up to his body and oriented itself.

Alarms. Basement in Texas. Dallas siege. The Razors.

Alarms?

Two alarms, his brain noted as full consciousness returned. Whistle after whistle, blown from a dozen mouths like referees trying to stop a football brawl, indicated an attack—all men to grab whatever would shoot and get to their defense stations, plus the wail of an air-alert siren.

But no gongs. If the Kurians had dusted again, every man who could find a piece of hollow metal to bang, from tin can to wheel rim, should be setting up as loud a clamor as possible. No one wanted to be a weak link in another Fort Worth massacre that caused comrades to choke out.

Valentine forced himself to pull on socks and tie his boots, grabbed the bag containing his gas mask, scarves, and gloves anyway, and buckled his pistol belt. Hank had cleaned and hung up his cut-down battle rifle. Valentine checked it over as he hurried through men running every which way or looking to their disheveled operations officer for direction, and headed for the stairs to the control tower, the field's tactical command post. He took seemingly endless switchbacks of stairs two at a time to the "top deck"—the Razors' shorthand for the tallest point of Love Field.

He felt explosions, then heard them a second later. Worse than mortars, worse than artillery, and going off so closely together he wondered if the Kurians had been keeping rocket artillery in reserve for a crisis. The old stairs rattled and dropped dirt as though shaking in fear.

"Would you look at those bastards!" he heard someone shout from the control tower.

"Send to headquarters: 'Rancid,'" Valentine heard Meadows shout. "Rancid. Rancid. Rancid."

Valentine came off the last stairs and passed through the open security door. Meadows and two others of the regiment had box seats on chaos.

Whoever had installed the glass—if it was glass and not a high-tech polymer—had done the job well; still-intact windows offered the tower a 360-degree field of vision. In the distance the crenellated Dallas skyline—one bifurcated tower the men called "the Eye" stared straight at the field thanks to its strange, empty-centered top—broke the hazy morning horizon.

As he went to the glass, noting the quiet voice of the communications officer relaying the "Rancid" alert to Brigade, another explosion erupted in black-orange menace atop the parking garage—the biggest structure on the field.

Valentine followed a private's eyes up and looked out on a sky filled with whirling planes.

Not rickety, rebuilt crop dusters or lumbering old commercial aircraft; the assorted planes shared only smooth silhouettes and a mottled gray-and-tan camouflage pattern reminiscent of a dusty rattlesnake. There were sleek single seaters, like stunt planes Valentine had seen in books, whipping around the edges of the field, turned sideways so the pilots could get a good look at ground activity. Banana-shaped twin-engine jobs dove in at the vehicles parked between the two wings of the terminal concourses, one shooting rocket after rocket at the vehicles while the other two flanked it, drawing ground fire. A pair of bigger, uglier, wide-winged military attack planes with bulging turbofans on their rear fuselages came in, dropping a series of bombs that exploded into a huge snake of fire writhing between the Razors' positions and the southwestern strip.

"Who the hell are these guys?" Meadows said to no one.

The screaming machines, roaring to and fro over the field, weren't the only attackers on the wing. Flying Grogs in the hundreds, many the Harpy-type Valentine had first met over Weening during his spell in the labor regiments, swooped below the aircraft and even the control tower, dispensing what looked—and exploded—like sticks of dynamite at anything that moved. A few bigger wings—the true gargoyles of the kind Valentine had seen lain out—circled above, possibly waiting for a juicy enough target to be worth what-ever they held in saddlebags hung around their thick necks.

The Razors fought back, mostly from their positions in the parking garages and the heavy weapons point around a winged statue depicting "Flight" near the entrance to the terminal build-ings. Small groups of men or single soldiers fired from behind door-ways, windows, or the sandbagged positions guarding the motor pool between the concourses.

Perhaps a gargoyle decided to hit the control tower. Valentine heard a heavy thud among the aerials on the roof, the scrabble of claws.

"Out!" Valentine shouted.

The trio looked up at the roof, apparently transfixed by the harmless scrabbling noises. Meadows' hand went to his sidearm, and the private fumbled with his battle rifle. In seconds they'd be dead, fragmenting brain tissue still wondering at the strange raccoonlike noise—

"Out!" Valentine said again, bodily pushing the private to the stairs with one hand, and pulling the communications officer from her chair with the other. She came out of her chair with her headset on; the headset cord stretched and unplugged as though it were as reluctant to leave its post as its operator. Meadows moved with dramatic suddenness as the realization of what might be happening on the roof arrived, and grabbed for the handle on the thick metal door to the stairway.

"I'll get it," Meadows said. Valentine, keeping touch with both the private and the communications officer, hurried down the stairs.

One flight. Two flights. Meadows' clattering footsteps on the stairs a half floor above . . .

The *boom* Valentine had been expecting for ten anxious seconds was neither head-shattering nor particularly loud, and while it shook peeling paint from the stairs and knocked out the lights, the three weren't so much as knocked off-stride.

Meadows joined them, panting. "The door must have held," he said.

*Or physics worked in our favor,* Valentine thought. An explosion tends to travel along the path of least resistance, usually upward.

"Maybe." Valentine said.

The impact of three more explosions came up through the floor, bombs striking Love Field somewhere.

"Orders?" Valentine asked.

"I'm going back up," Meadows said. "They might think they finished the job with one bomb. The radio antenna's had it for sure, but the field lines might still be functional."

"You two game?" Valentine asked the private—an intelligent soldier named Wilcox who was the military equivalent of a utility infielder; he could play a variety of positions well. Ruvayed, the lieutenant with the headphone jack still swinging at the end of its cord just below her belt, nodded.

Valentine clicked his gun off safety and brought it to his shoulder. "Me first, in case they crawled in."

Meadows brought up the rear going back up the stairs. Valentine reached the security door. Dust had been blown from beneath the door in an elegant spiked pattern, and he smelled smoke and the harsher odor of burning plastic. He turned the handle but the door wouldn't budge.

A kick opened it. The air inside had the harsh, faintly sulfurous tang of exploded dynamite.

As he swept the room over the open sights on his gun, Valentine saw naked sunlight streaming in from a hole in the roof big enough to put a sedan's engine block through. Older air-traffic consoles and the Razors' newer communications gear were blackened and cracked; the transformation was so thorough it seemed it should have taken more time than an instant.

The glass held, though it had cracks ranging from spiderwebbing to single fault lines. The quality of the stuff the old United States used to be able to make made Valentine shake his head in wonder yet again. Outside the planes still turned, swooped, and soared, engines louder now thanks to the hole in the roof.

But he kept his eyes and ears tuned to the new skylight, his cutdown Atlanta Gunworks battle rifle ready. Another tiny plane buzzed by, the noise of its engine rising fast and fading slowly over the other, fainter aircraft sounds. *Who the hell are these guys?*

Meadows pressed binoculars to his eye, scanning the ground in the direction of Dallas. "Not even mortar fire. It's not a breakout."

"Bad intelligence?" Ruvayed asked. "They thought *we* had planes?"

Another ribbon of fire blossomed against the parking garage facing the runway to the southwest. Valentine wondered about Ahn-Kha and Will Post. Both were probably at the hardpoints around the garages . . . why did they keep hitting that side of the airport? It faced the train tracks running out of the city, but the lines were torn up for miles.

Another of the tiny, fast scout planes buzzed low over the overgrown airstrip there. Save for his speed it looked as though he might be on a landing approach. The plane jumped skyward to avoid a stream of tracer.

"I wish we had some ack-ack guns here," Meadows said, binoculars trained up at some big multiengine transport circling the field. "All the high-angle stuff is close in to the city."

"Colonel," Valentine said. "Southwest. Look southwest, hitting hardest there."

"Field phones are shot," Ruvayed reported.

"Wilcox, hustle us up a portable radio," Meadows said. The private disappeared down the stairs.

The colonel searched the southern and western approaches to the airport. "Goddamn."

"I'd like to see what's happening in the garage," Valentine said.

"Go ahead. Pass the word that I'll be on the maintenance frequency, if I can get a radio up here. Send up a couple of messengers."

Valentine handed his gun and ammunition harness to Ruvayed. "Keep an eye cocked to that hole. And watch the balcony," he said. The control tower had an electronics service balcony just below the out-sloping windows. Nothing but birds' nests and old satellite dishes decorated it, but it would be just like the gargoyles to land carrying a couple of sniper rifles.

"Yes, sir," Ruvayed said.

"Tell everyone to keep their heads down, Major," Meadows said. "Maybe this whole attack is a Kurian screwup. The mechanics moved a couple of stripped passenger craft the other day—from a distance it could have looked like we had planes ready to go."

"Yes, sir." Valentine nodded. He turned for the stairs. Meadows didn't care one way or the other about salutes.

"Goes doubly for you," Meadows called after him.

The violent airshow going on outside must have been running short on fireworks; only one more small explosion sounded during the endless turns down the stairs. The elevator to the control tower was missing and presumed scavenged—nothing but shaft ran up the center of the structure.

Valentine double-timed through the tunnel system and up to

the first floor of the terminal. He trotted past empty counters under faded signs and motionless luggage carousels—the only part of the main terminal in use was a small area in front of the bronze Ranger statue (ONE RIOT, ONE RANGER read the plaque) where the consumables for the Razors were delivered every few days.

"Major!" A voice broke through the sound of his footsteps. A corporal with his flak jacket on inside out called from the other end of the terminal, "They're hurtin' on the west approach."

"Thanks. Tell the Bears to find Captain Post and be ready to counterattack if they hit us from the ground. Send messengers and a new field phone up to the top deck. Right away."

The corporal nodded and ran for the stairwell.

Valentine crossed over to the huge parking garages by scuttling under the concrete walkway to the upper deck of the lot. A wheelless ambulance in the center of the parking garage served as an improvised command post for the airport's close-in defense.

The air was full of smoke and a fainter, oilier smell Valentine recognized as burning gasoline.

Wounded men and burned corpses lay all around the ambulance. Captain Martin, a Texas liaison for the Razors, helped the medics perform the gruesome task of triage as he spoke to a pair of sergeants.

Valentine listened with hard ears as he approached. Enhanced hearing, a gift from the Lifeweavers dating back to his time as a Wolf, made each word sound as though it were spoken in his ear. "Everyone to the dugouts but the observers," Martin said. "Yes, treat it like a bombardment. We'll worry about an assault when we see one."

Martin recognized Valentine with a nod. "Weird kinda visit from Dallas. How did they pull this off?"

"I doubt they're from Dallas," Valentine said. "We would have seen them taking off."

More distant explosions—a series of smaller cracks that made up a larger noise like halfhearted thunder.

"I'm putting the men in the shelters," Martin explained.

"Good," Valentine said, not wanting to waste time explaining that he'd already overheard the orders given. "I'd like to take a look at the field south and west of here. Is there still an operational post where I can do that?"

Valentine saw Ahn-Kha approaching from a forward garage stairwell, a man draped on each powerful shoulder. Ahn-Kha's arms, longer than but not quite as thick as his legs, held the men in place in a strange imitation of the classic bodybuilder's pose.

Blood matted his friend's golden shoulder and back fur, Valentine noted as his old companion set the men down near the ambulance.

"He's worth three Texans," Martin observed. Martin was still new enough to the Razors to watch Ahn-Kha as though half fascinated and half worried that the Grog would suddenly sink his ivory fangs into the nearest human. "Ten ordinary men, in other words."

"The observation post?" Valentine reminded the captain, as Ahn-Kha checked the dressings on the men he had just set down. Enormous, double-thumbed hands gently turned one of the wounded on his side.

"Second floor of the garage, back of an old van. It's still wired to the phone network."

Valentine remembered. "I know it. Ahn-Kha!"

The Golden One nodded to one of the Razor medics as she wiped her hands on a bloodstained disinfectant towel and squatted beside the latest additions to the swamp of bleeding men. "Yes, my David?"

"Get your puddler and meet me at OP 6."

Ahn-Kha's "Grog gun" had become famous, a 20mm behemoth of his own design that resembled a telescope copulating with a sawed-off kid's swing set. The other name came from a skirmish the Razors fought outside Fort Worth, where Ahn-Kha reduced an armored car commander to a slippery puddle of goo outside his hatch at six hundred yards.

"Yes, my David." Over seven feet of muscle straightened. "I had to leave Corporal Lopez at the stairwell exterior door. He's dead, or soon will be," Ahn-Kha informed the captain.

"What the hell, Major?" Martin asked. "What's so goddamn important about blowing us off the planet?"

"We'll know sooner than we'd like, I expect," Valentine said.

Another bomb shook dust onto the wounded.

"Christ," Martin said, but Valentine was reminded of something else.

"Make sure the men have their dust gear in the shelters," Valentine said. He ran down a mental list of what else the Razors might need to stop a column, and the two reserve regimental recoilless rifles could be useful. "Get Luke and John operational up here too, with plenty of shells. But the dust gear first." Matthew and Mark were vehicle-mounted, and probably smoldering with most of the other transport between the terminals.

"You'd think we'd be drowning in it. Makes me think—"

"They're probably on their way already."

Valentine offered a salute. Martin's mouth tightened as he returned it—the Texans weren't big on military rigamarole, but there were ordinary soldiers present and the Razors knew a salute from their operations chief meant that the half-Indian major didn't expect you to speak again until you were ready to report on his orders—and hurried to the central stairway.

Valentine went up a floor to the last garage level before the exposed top and hurried to the rusty old van, parked just far enough from the open edge of the parking lot so the sun would never hit it. Though wheelless and up on blocks, missing even its headlamps and mirrors, the Razors kept it clean so that the carefully washed smoked-glass windows at the back and sides wouldn't stand out from the dirt and Texas dust of the nonlethal variety.

Valentine called out his name and entered the van through the open side door. Two Razors looked out on the Dallas skyline and the roads and train tracks running along the western edge of the airfield. Their ready dust-hoods hung off the backs of their helmets like bridal veils. Dropped playing cards lay on the van's interior carpet, the only remaining evidence of what had probably once been plush fixtures for road-weary vactioners.

"I've never seen so many planes in my life, that's for sure," one said to the other, a bit of the Arkansas hills in his voice. Valentine knew his face but the name wouldn't come. "Howdy, Major."

"Hey, Major Valentine," the other said, after relocating a piece of hard candy on a tongue depressor that the soldiers called a "postsicle." Captain Post had a candy maker somewhere in his family tree, and the men liked to suck on his confections to keep the Texas dirt from drying out their mouths. "We got hit after all, huh."

"I'm glad somebody noticed. Did it break up a good card game?"

"Depends. Lewis was winning," the Arkansan said.

"Sorry to hear that, Lewis," Valentine said. He vaguely knew that the tradition of canceling all wins and losses in an unfinished game had sprung up during the siege at Big Rock Mountain the previous year, and was thus hallowed into one of the battalion's unwritten rules.

"What do these aircutters got against the Razors, is what I want to know," Lewis said.

Valentine scanned the approaches to the airfield, then the sky. A larger plane, its wingspan wider than its body length, caught the sun high up.

*Whoever's up there knows.*

φ

The second phase of the attack came within five minutes, as Valentine reported to Meadows through a field phone line patched into the portable radio now installed in the control tower.

"Holy Jesus!" Lewis barked.

The grass between the northwest-southeast parallel runways flanking the field bulged, then dimpled, then collapsed, sending a cloud of dirt to join the smoke still coating the field.

"Between the runways," Ahn-Kha shouted from his position at a supporting column. And unnecessarily, as Valentine locked eyes on the spot and brought up his binoculars.

A corkscrew prow the size of one of the old *Thunderbolt*'s lifeboats emerged into daylight. Striped blacks and browns on a pebbly, organic surface spun hypnotically as it rotated. Brown flesh behind—the snout pulsed, ripples like circular waves traveling backward to the hidden portion of the thing. It rolled like a show diver performing a forward twist and nosed back into the earth. Overgrown prairie plants flew as the giant worm tilled and plunged back into the soil.

"What the devil?" the Arkansan said, watching the creature dig, still spinning clockwise as it reburied itself.

Tiny planes whipped over the inverted $U$ of exposed flesh.

"Tunnels, Colonel, they've tunneled to the airfield," Valentine said into the field phone. He consulted the map of the airfield and its surroundings, pinned to the carpeted wall of the observation van. "We need fire support to grid N-7, repeat N-7."

The tunneling worm's other end finally appeared, another shell-like counterpoint to the prow. Valentine marked an orifice at the very tip this time, though whether it was for eating or excreting he couldn't say.

The two identical warcraft, turbofans bulging above their broad wings, banked in from the west, aiming directly at the parking garages.

Valentine dropped the field glasses and the phone handpiece. Something about the crosslike silhouettes of the aircraft suggested approaching doom.

"This won't be good," Lewis said.

"Out! Out! Out!" Valentine shouted.

Ahn-Kha was already at the van door, perhaps ready to bodily pull the men from the observation post, but the three jumped from the van and ran for the central stairway.

They didn't quite make it.

Valentine heard faint whooshing noises from behind, over the Doppler-effect sound of the quickly growing engine noise. The men flung themselves down, recognizing the rockets for what they were.

The planes had aimed for the floor beneath theirs, as it turned out. Though loud, the only damage the explosions did was to their eardrums. A stray rocket struck their floor of the garage over at the other wing of the structure.

The van caught some of the blast from below. Their carpeted cubbyhole tipped on its side, blown off its blocks.

"Let's see if the phone's still working," Valentine said.

"What if they come around for another pass?" the Arkansan asked, teeth chattering.

"They've got to be out of fireworks by now," Lewis said.

"You alright, old horse?" Valentine asked Ahn-Kha, who was inspecting his puddler.

One business envelope-sized pointed ear drooped. "Yes. The sight may be out of alignment. I dropped it in my haste."

Back at the edge of the garage, in the shadow of a supporting column, Valentine gulped and met Ahn-Kha's eyes before cautiously peeping over the edge of the parking lot wall and surveying the field. A beating sound had replaced the higher-pitched airplane engines.

Helicopters!

Gradually Valentine made out shapes through the obscuring smoke of still-burning jellied gasoline and the more recent rocket blasts. A great, sand-colored behemoth with twin rotors forward, and a smaller stabilizing fan aft thundered out of the west. Smaller helicopters flanked her, like drones looking to mate with some great queen bee.

One of the little stunt planes flew in, dropping a cannister near the holes. It sputtered to life on impact and threw a streamer of red smoke into the sky.

*Where's the damn artillery?*

"Field phone's still good, Major," Lewis said, extracting the canvas-covered pack from the van.

"Spot for the artillery, if it's available," Valentine said, trying to give intelligible orders while racking his brain for what he knew about helicopter function. "Target that cherry bomb by the holes. And send Base Defense Southwest to Colonel Meadows."

"Base defense southwest, yes, sir," Lewis repeated.

Another plane roared by, seemingly inches from the garage, with a suddenness that momentarily stopped Valentine's heart.

"I do not like these airplanes," Ahn-Kha said.

Valentine watched the smaller helicopters shoot off more rockets, but these just sent up more thick clouds of smoke, putting a dark gray wall between the observation point and the holes.

"If we can't see them . . . set up the puddler. Lewis, any word on the artillery?"

"Sounds like they've been hit too, sir," Lewis said, taking his hand away from the ear not held to the phone.

The twin-rotored helicopter blew just enough smoke away with its massive blades so they could get a quick look at it as it landed by the hole.

"That's your target," Valentine said. "See the smaller rotor, spinning at the end of the tail? Aim for the center of that."

Smoke obscured the quick glance, but Valentine had seen something emerge from the hole dug by the worm, a turtlelike shape.

"Our mortars, anything, get it put down on that hole!" *They can shoot a hundred shells a day into the Dallas works, but they can't drop a few on Love Field.*

"Nothing to shoot at, my David," Ahn-Kha said, ears twitching this way and that, telegraphing his frustration. The Grog had his gun resting on his shoulder and its unique bipod. The gun muzzle was suspended by heavyweight fishing line from the bipod arching over it rather than resting atop the supports, allowing for tiny alterations and changes in direction, typical of creative Grog engineering, right down to the leather collar that kept the line from melting. The black-painted line acted as a fore sight when Ahn-Kha wasn't shooting through the telescopic sight.

Valentine felt impotent. "Tell Meadows it's a breakout," he said to Lewis. "I think the Kurians are trying to run for it with the helicopters."

"Why didn't they just land on a street in Dallas?" Lewis asked.

"We've got high-angle artillery there," Valentine said.

"Sir," the Arkansan shouted as the smoke clouds cleared. Some kind of bay doors had opened at the rear of the massive helicopter, which rested on thick-tired multiple wheels. The turtlelike thing, which looked to Valentine like a greenish propane storage tank crawling across the runway without benefit of wheels, tracks, or legs, had turned for the big chopper.

Ahn-Kha's gun coughed and Valentine's nose registered cordite. Ahn-Kha didn't bother to watch the shot. Instead he drew another highlighter-sized bullet from his bandolier and reloaded the gun.

But the smoke was back.

Valentine could just make out the helicopter through the thinning smoke. Explosions sounded from back toward the terminal, as another piece of the Razor military machine was blown up.

Ahn-Kha must have been able to see the rear rotor for a second—he fired again. Valentine marked the strange tanklike thing entering the rear of the helicopter . . . it was like watching a film of a hen laying an egg run backward.

"Where's the fuckin' support?" the Arkansan asked, voicing Valentine's thoughts exactly.

Valentine heard engines on the ground. He looked to the south, where a few of the Razors' strange conglomeration of transport and patrol vehicles—including two prowlers—were barreling past the statue of Flight at the edge of the airport buildings.

"Holy shit, the cavalry!" the Arkansan shouted.

Valentine recognized the salt-and-pepper hair of the man at the minigun in the lead prowler. Captain William Post. It was hard not to join the private in screaming his head off.

The aircraft spotted the vehicles too. A twin-engine airplane swooped in, firing cannon at the column. Valentine saw one big-tired transport turn and plow into the garage.

Ahn-Kha fired again, and the helicopter wobbled as it left the ground, rear doors still closing. The helicopter lurched sideways—perhaps Ahn-Kha had damaged the rear rotor after all.

The pilot managed to get the helicopter, which was skittering sideways across the field like a balky horse, righted.

Light caught Valentine's eyes from above and he looked up to see muzzle flash from a big four-engine aircraft above. Some kind of gun fired on the approaching vehicles.

But the Razors had guns of their own—and someone trained them on the staggering helicopter. Machine guns and small cannon opened up, sending pieces of fuselage flying. Black smoke blossomed from the craft's engine crown, instantly dispersed by the powerful rotors.

Ahn-Kha shot again.

The Razor vehicles had to pay for their impertinent charge. The military turbofan planes swooped in—Valentine grimly noted a desert camouflage pattern atop the craft—and fired from some kind of cannon that created a muzzle flash as big as the blunt nose of the aircraft, planting blossoms of fiery destruction among the Razor attackers.

Post's armored car turned over as it died. Valentine couldn't imagine what the wreck had done to his friend.

Like sacrificing a knight to take the enemy queen, even as the prowlers exploded the double-rotored helicopter tipped sideways, sending its six blades spinning into the smoke-filled sky as it crashed. The helicopter's crew jumped out with credible speed, and Ahn-Kha swiveled his cannon.

"No. I want prisoners," Valentine said.

One of the smaller helicopters swooped in and landed, even as tracer fire began to appear from the positions at the base of the garage, where gun slits had been clawed through the concrete weeks ago.

Ahn-Kha shifted his aim and began to send 20mm-cannon shells into the tail rotor of the rescue helicopter.

The concrete to the left of Ahn-Kha exploded into powdery dust. "Down!" *Was that my voice?* Valentine wondered as he threw himself sideways onto Ahn-Kha. Cannon shells tore through the gap between the floors of the garage, ripping apart the van. The Arkansan fell with a softball-sized hunk of flesh torn away from his neck and shoulder, and Valentine dully thought that he'd have to learn the man's name in order to put it in the report, and then the cannonade was over.

Lewis stared stupidly around, still kneeling next to the van, in the exact same position he'd been in a second ago, still holding the field phone to his ear.

Valentine heard the first *BOOM* of shellfire landing on the field. The artillery had come at last.

φ

Valentine stood between the shell holes on the overgrown, cracked landing strip and surveyed the mess.

What was left of the attackers from the vehicles and the defenders of the garages had encircled the two holes and the downed helicopter. Valentine had seen Post borne away in a stretcher, but couldn't do anything but touch a bloodily peeled hand as the bearers rushed him to the medical unit.

The mysterious air raiders had rocketed their own helicopter before leaving, blowing what was left of the double-rotor airship into three substantial chunks—pilot cabin, part of the cargo area, and stabilizing tail.

The odd, green propane-tank capsule remained in the wreckage. Flames slid off it like oil from Teflon.

The Bears kept watch from the overturned earth of the Kurian wormhole. Valentine had poked his head in—the three-meter-diameter tunnel was ringed with strands of whitish goo about the thickness of his thumb, crisscrossed and spiderwebbed like the frosting dribbled atop a Bundt cake. Whether the digging worm creature (someone called it a "bore worm" but Valentine didn't know if the term came from *Hitchen's Guide to Introduced Species* or if the would-be zooologist had thought it up on the spot). The Bears also watched a pair of wounded prisoners, survivors of the transport helicopter who hadn't made it to the rescuing craft. A medic dressed a cut on one pilot's scalp just below the helmet line. The stranger submitted to the ministrations with something like dull contempt. The aircrew were lean, well-tanned men with oversized sunglasses and desert scarves. Both wore leather jackets with a panel stitched on the back, reading in English and Spanish:

**NONNEGOTIABLE $10,000 GOLD REWARD**
for the safe return of this pilot unharmed and
healthy to Pyp's Flying Circus **YUMA
ARIZONA/AZTLAN**. Negotiable traveling and
keep expenses also paid in trade goods.
**CONTACT PROVOST FT CHICO OR NEW
UNIVERSAL CHURCH—TEMPE
DIRECTORATE FOR INFORMATION
AND DIRECTIONS**

Each also had a patch reading PYP'S FLYING CIRCUS, featuring a winged rattlesnake, flying with mouth open as though to strike.

So the question of *who the hell are these guys* was answered. With another question.

But Valentine's mind was on that tank in the center of the wreckage.

Some of the men theorized it contained a nuclear bomb. Valentine suspected that the contents were a good deal more lethal to the human race long-term.

And everyone was looking at him.

Valentine paced at the edge of the wormhole.

"Nail, I want three Bears ready with demolition blocks. I don't know if it'll dent that thing, but it might rattle them."

Nail was a pigeon-chested Bear with long, sun-lightened blond hair, wearing captain's bars. Nail had been promoted after the fight on Big Rock Mountain, and was the leader of the toughest soldiers in the Razors . . . and probably Texas, in Valentine's opinion—and that meant the world, if you asked a Texan, but Valentine had learned not to argue with Texans in matters of regional pride.

"Ready? Send them forward now."

"No. I'm going to have a talk with them first."

"It's your aura, Val."

Ahn-Kha lifted his improvised cannon. "I'll go along, my David."

Valentine looked around, and pointed to a scrawny, fuzzy-cheeked Razor. "You come too, Appley."

"Yes, sir," young Appley said, uncomprehending but conditioned to respond to orders.

Valentine passed the boy his order book. "If we get some kind of dialogue going, I want you to look like you're taking notes."

"You want me to write down what they say?"

"If you want. Write your mom if you want; I just want you writing when anybody is talking. Can do?"

"Can do!" Appley said. Major Valentine only offered a "can do" to key jobs, and it was the first time the boy had heard the phrase applied to him.

"Great. Follow a little behind."

Ahn-Kha walked beside him. "Why such a youngster?" the Golden One asked, speaking from the side of his mouth—an eerie-looking effort, thanks to his snout and rubbery lips.

"Would you use that boy in an ambush?" Valentine asked.

"Of course not."

"I hope the Kurians think that too."

When he figured he was close enough, Valentine stopped and looked around at his feet. The Kurian vessel reminded him now of a pill rather than a propane tank. Or perhaps a malformed watermelon; the "top" half was a bit bigger than the bottom. Some kind of bright blue sludge clung to the bottom.

"Reminds me of heartroot come to maturity in a drought," Ahn-Kha said. Heartroot was a mushroomlike Grog staple.

Valentine picked up a piece of shattered glass and threw it at the tank. It bounced off. Valentine noted that the blue sludge shrunk away from the vibration. Perhaps a Kurian? They were bluish on the rare instances when they appeared undisguised. But why would it be hiding outside the tank?

"Anyone home?" he yelled.

The blue sludge quivered, shifted up the faintly lined side of the tank vessel. The lines reminded Valentine of the nautical charts and plots he'd seen on the old *Thunderbolt*.

"I've come to negotiate your relocation from Texas," Valentine yelled. He looked over his shoulder; the boy was scribbling. He was also cross-eyed when looking at something up close and Valentine stifled a snicker.

The blue goop bulged, then parted. Valentine startled, and no longer had to fight off laughter when he recognized a Reaper emerging from the protoplasm. The two-meter-tall death machines were living organisms linked to their master Kurian, used in the messy, and sometimes dangerous, process of aura extraction. The Reaper fed off the victim's blood using a syringelike tongue, while the Kurian animating it absorbed what old Father Max had called aural energies. Others called it soul-sucking.

*Is that how they make 'em?*

The Reaper climbed out of the blue sludge and lifted its hood, pulling it far forward over its face to block out the sun. Sunlight didn't kill them, unfortunately, but it interfered with their senses and the connection with the master Kurian.

Valentine silently wished for one of Ahn-Kha's Quickwood spear points or crossbow bolts. Two years ago Valentine had brought a special kind of olive tree–like growth called Quickwood back from the Caribbean. It was lethal to Reapers, but had been consumed in the insurrection in the Ozarks known as Operation Archangel the previous year.

"Look, they shat out a Reaper," Valentine said. The kid laughed, a little too loudly.

Ahn-Kha raised his long gun just a fraction.

Valentine revised his estimate of the interior of the tank. At one Reaper per Kurian, there could only be a dozen or so Reapers inside the tank. The flexible, octopus-crossed-with-bat Kurians could squeeze into nooks and crannies, of course, but the impressively built Reapers could only be packed so tight. And all breathed oxygen. At one Reaper per Kurian—there was a theory that without at least one Reaper to supply it with aura, a Kurian starved to death—that meant a dozen Kurians. Others claimed, with little to back it up but speculation, that the Kurians could "bottle" aura to last until a new Reaper could be acquired. Still others said a Kurian could absorb aura through its touch, a "death grip."

Experience told Valentine that if the third were true, the Little Rock Kurian who had died under his fists hadn't managed it in the last few painful seconds of its life.

"Far enough," Ahn-Kha said as the Reaper approached, raising his gun a little higher.

"*i shall speak for those within, foodling,*" the Reaper said, staying out of grabbing distance. Valentine had to concentrate to hear its low, breathy voice, always averting his gaze from the yellow, slit-pupiled eyes. Reapers had a deceptive stillness to them, like a praying mantis. Their grip was deadly, but their gaze could be just as lethal; the few times Valentine had looked closely into one's eyes he'd been half hypnotized.

Valentine took a step forward. "Use the word 'foodling' again and 'those within' will have to crap out a new negotiator."

The Reaper, apparently as egoless as a Buddhist statue, ignored the threat. "*your terms?*"

"First: You left behind a lot of men in Dallas. Tell them to surrender without another shot fired. No conditions, but officers and military police will be allowed to keep their sidearms, the combatants can keep individual weapons, noncombatants will be under protection of their own people. We're not taking them into custody. They can march wherever they want on whatever supplies they can bring out of Dallas. Second: What's left of Dallas, including artillery and transport, shall be turned over to us, intact. If both those conditions are met, we'll load your tin can on a transport and take you to any border region you like, along with any remaining of your kind that didn't manage to tunnel out of the city."

Valentine knew he had overstepped his authority—in fact this was more like running a track-and-field triple-jump over his authority—but he wanted to make the deal before the Kurians had time to call for some other form of help. For all he knew flying saucers might already be on their way—

"*we no longer control dallas,*" the Reaper said, even more quietly. "*certain handlers remain within, but the skulking soldiers of your breed inside are increasingly obstinate.*"

"Not my problem."

Valentine almost cracked a smile. In their millennia of scheming before taking over the planet in 2022, the Kurians hadn't accounted for human obstinacy. "*we shall consider,*" the Reaper finished, though one of the Kurians within thought up the words.

"Don't consider too long. In fifteen minutes we're going to try high explosives. If that doesn't work we'll start piling tires around your capsule. Then we'll douse everything in gasoline and light it. You'd better have good air-filtration equipment in there; you burn oxygen, same as us, and a good tire bonfire can go for weeks."

The Reaper twitched in the direction of Valentine and Ahn-Kha shouldered his gun, but instead of the expected attack the Reaper lurched back toward the capsule and acted out a strange pantomime, or perhaps a game of charades where "jumping spider" was the answer. It lurched, it spun, it backbent—

Valentine heard his order book hit the ground behind him.

The Reaper fell over, then picked itself up. It returned to its previous position facing the three humans, holding itself stiffly and moving off balance, like a marionette with tangled strings.

"*we agree,*" it said, just before it toppled over again.

ψ

"I'd have given two more fingers to have seen that," Meadows said that night, rattling the ice in his glass. An orderly refilled it from an amber-colored bottle and disappeared back into the throng of officers and civilians at the celebration. The old Sheraton next to the interstate had seen better days—to Valentine it smelled of sweat, sour cooking oil, and roaches—but perhaps never such a universally happy crowd.

Valentine didn't feel like celebrating. William Post, possibly his best friend in the world apart from Ahn-Kha, had been maimed as he led the assault on the helicopters. The surgeons were fighting to save his life along with those of the other wounded.

Luckily that was the only fighting going on. The army of the North Texas Cooperative had marched out of its positions, and then the city, as the sun set.

"You bit off too much, Major Valentine," Brigadier General Quintero growled. Quintero had refused alcohol as well. He reminded Valentine a little of the negotiating Reaper; one side of his body sagged a little thanks to an old shell fragment that had severed muscle in his shoulder. "I can just tolerate those Dallas scoundrels relocating, but I don't like the idea of Texas truckers carrying that fish tank to Arizona."

Valentine liked Quintero, and if the general was speaking to him in this manner he could imagine what had been said to him since the afternoon, when Dallas broke out in white flags and the frontline troops cautiously advanced into the city.

"Could I make a suggestion, General?"

"Eiderdown quilts for the Quislings?" Meadows put in, trying to soften the scowl on Quintero's face.

Valentine ignored the jibe. "Route the Kurian 'fish tank' to Arizona via Dallas, with the drivers in a secure cabin-cage attached to a breakaway trailer. I'll ride shotgun if you need a volunteer. We won't be shy about telling passersby what's in back. Maybe a riot starts and you declare hostilities resumed and renegotiate the surrender more advantageously. Maybe the Kurians get pulped, and those Dallas troops get convinced that the only way they'll ever be safe again is to throw in with us."

Quintero turned it over in his mind, sucking on his cheeks as he thought it through. "You are a mean son of a bitch, Major. Excuse the expression."

"I'm glad you're on our side," Meadows added.

# CHAPTER TWO

*Texarkana, April: The border town has turned into a staging area. Operations in the Texas-Ozark United Free Region move forward as the political leadership convenes in search of a way to govern the aggregation, already being called the TWO-FUR by the willfully dyslexic soldiery.*

*A new name for the region is in the works.*

*The city has become one of those chaotic staging areas familiar to those of long service. Units coming off frontline service bump elbows with freshly organized troops. Equipment and personnel swap by means official and unofficial, and creative middlemen set up shop to service needs ranging from new boots to old wine, aging guns to young women.*

*An old indoor tennis court serves as the local headquarters for the separate commands of the Texas and Ozark forces. There are warehouses and self-storage units nearby to hold gear scraped up by the Logistics Commandos or brought out of the Dallas–Fort Worth corridor. Most importantly of all, a hospital has been upgraded from a bare-bones Kurian health center to a four-hundred-bed unit that can provide care equal to any existing facility outside those patronized by the elite of the Kurian Zone.*

*Churches and temporary schools operate at the edge of "Texarkana Dumps," the current name for the collection of military facilities. Outside the perimeter of the Southern Command's patrols, a tar-paper and aluminum-siding shantytown has sprung up, accommodating refugees from the Kurian Zone as well as the illicit needs of bored soldiers waiting for orders.*

*Even the local wildlife seems to be in a state of leisurely flux. Crows and dogs and a few far-ranging seagulls trot or fly from refuse heap to sewage pit, with the local feral cats sunning themselves on wall top and windowsill after a night hunting the thriving rats and mice.*

35

*The soldiers fresh from the Dallas battlefield feel the same way. Fresh food, sunshine, and sleep are all that are required for blissful, if not purring, contentment.*

ψ

The attenuated Razors' brief period of excited anticipation, carried since getting off the Dallas train and hearing about their billet, ended as soon as they saw the "hotel."

Even in its heyday no one would have called the roadside Accolade Inn worthy of a special trip. The subsequent years had not been kind to the blue-and-white block, four stories of stucco-sided accommodations thick with kudzu and bird droppings. Someone had put in screens and plywood doors, and each room's toilet worked, though the sink fixtures were still in the process of retrofit, having been stripped and not replaced. Neat cots, six to a room, sat against water-stained walls.

"Not bad," a goateed Razor said when Valentine heard him test the john's flush after washing his hands in the toilet tank. "Better than the sisters have at home."

Sadly, the attenuated regiment fit in the hotel with beds to spare. A third of their number were dead or in either a Fort Worth or Texarkana hospital.

The latter was Valentine's first stop after getting the men to the hotel. A First Response Charity tambourine-and-saxophone duo just outside the hospital door accepted a few crumpled pieces of Southern Command scrip with the usual "God Blesses you."

"Continually," Valentine agreed, though over the past year it had been a decidedly mixed blessing. The pair stood a little straighter in their orange-and-white uniforms and reached for pamphlets, but Valentine passed on and into the green-peppermint tiles of the hospital.

He made it a point to visit every man of his command; the routine and their requests were so grimly regular that he began entering with a tumbler of ice—he made a mental note to steal and fill a trashcan with ice before heading back to the Accolade— to spare himself the inevitable back-and-forth trip. But his mind wasn't at ease until he visited the last name on his list, Captain William Post.

Visiting hours were over by the time he made it to the breezy top floor, where Post shared a room with a blinded artillery officer.

"Well, just remember to be quiet," the head nurse said when Valentine showed his ID and signed in on the surgery-recovery floor. Dark crests like bruises hung beneath her eyes.

"Tell it to the FIRCs downstairs," Valentine said, as they started up again with the umpteenth rendition of "Onward Christian Soldiers," one of their supply of three hymns.

Post looked horrible. His cheeks had shrunken in, and the nurse had done a poor job shaving him. A little tent stood over the stump of his left leg and a tube ran from the region of his appendix to a red-filled bottle on the floor. A bottle on a hook attached to the bed dripped clear liquid into a tube in his arm, as though to balance output with input. Post's eyes were bright and alert, though.

His friend even managed a wink when Valentine rattled the plastic, metered hospital tumbler full of ice.

"How's it going?" Valentine asked in a small voice, as if to emphasize the words' inadequacy.

"They got the shrapnel out. Some small intestine came with it. So they say." Post took his time speaking. "No infection." He took a breath. "No infection. That was the real worry."

"God blesses you," the FIRCs chorused downstairs. Valentine agreed again, this time with more enthusiasm.

"You know what? They pulled maggots out of my eyes," Post's roommate said, as though it were the funniest thing to ever happen to anyone. "Got to hand it to flies—they go to work right away. I wasn't laying in the pit but three hours before the medics found me. Flies beat 'em."

"He'll be out tomorrow," Post said quietly, as though he had to apologize for the interruption.

"How much leg is left?" Valentine asked.

"Midthigh," Post said. "At first I thought it was a raw deal. Then I decided the shrapnel could have gone six inches higher and to the right. It's all perspective."

"We'll make a good pair, limping up and down the tent lines," Valentine said.

"You got to admire maggots," the man in the next bed said. "They know they only got one thing to do and they do it."

"I think I'll be spending the rest of the war in the first-class cabin," Post said, using old Coastal Marine slang for a retirement on a wound pension. "I've got to be careful about my diet now. So they say. There's a leaflet around here somewhere."

"Anything I can do for you?"

Later on Valentine spent hours that accumulated into days and weeks thinking back on his offer, and the strange turns his life took from the moment he said the phrase. He made the offer in earnest. If Post had asked him to go back to Louisiana and get a case of Hickory Pit barbecue sauce, he would have done his best to bring back the distinctive blend.

"Get my green duffel from under the bed," Post said.

There were only two items under the wheeled cot, a scuffed service pack and the oversized green duffel. Each had at least three kinds of tagging on it.

Valentine pulled up the bag, wondering.

"There's a leather case inside, little gold fittings."

It was easy to find; everything else in the duffel was clothing. The case felt as though it was full of sand. Valentine lifted it with an effort.

"Open it," Post said.

Valentine saw reams of paper inside. It was like a miniature file cabinet. Three manila folders filled it, marked (in order of thickness, most to least) "Queries/Replies," "Descriptions," and "Evidence." Valentine caught an inky whiff of photocopier chemicals.

Valentine had a good guess about the contents of the briefcase. Post had been looking for his ex-wife almost from the moment they stepped into the Ozarks. Valentine knew the details; Post had talked about her now and then when the mood hit, since the time Valentine met him while posing as a Quisling officer on the old *Thunderbolt*. William Post and Gail Foster had grown up in the Kurian Zone and married young. He joined the Quisling Coastal Marines, became an officer, fought and worked for the Kurians, in an effort to give them a better life. But the man she thought she'd married was no collaborator. As Post's career flourished their marriage dissolved. Gail Post became convinced he'd gone over to the enemy, and left. They'd always talked of trying to make it to the Ozark Free Territory, so Post assumed she'd come here.

Valentine opened the folio marked "Descriptions" with his forefinger. Mimeographed sheets headed MISSING-REWARD had a two-tone picture of a fair young woman with wide-set eyes, photographed full-face and profile. Perhaps her lips were a little too thin for her to be considered a great beauty, but then Kurian Zone identification photographs rarely flattered.

Post was a dedicated correspondent. Valentine guessed there had to be two hundred letters and responses paper-clipped together.

"There's three sheets on top of the Evidence folder. Take them out, will you Dave?" Post said. His head sank back on the pillow as though the effort of speaking had emptied him.

Valentine knew wounds and pain. He took out the pages—bad photocopies, stamped with multiple release signatures—and waited.

"I found her name. She was here."

"That's a damn miracle," Valentine said.

Post nodded. "I had help. Several new organizations were set up after you guys got the Ozarks back to reunite families. Then there was still the Lueber Alliance."

Valentine had learned about LA his first year in the Ozarks. Better than forty years old, it collected information on people lost in the Kurian Zone. Rumor had it the names numbered in the hundreds of thousands.

"Lueber found that first list for me," Post continued.

The page had a list of names, a shipping manifest with train car allocations—thirty to a car, relatively comfortable transport by Kurian standards.

Valentine didn't see a destination for the list. He flipped to the next page.

"That's just an old census. Showed she lived near Pine Bluff before Solon's takeover. Also Leuber."

Valentine had gone to a war college in Pine Bluff when the

commander of Zulu Company offered him a position as lieutenant. He looked at the picture again, trying to associate it with a memory from the town. Nothing.

The third page was the strangest of all. It was a photocopy of a list, and the names were handwritten. Fifty names, numbered 401 to 450. TESTING STATION 9-P was the legend up at the top. Gail's name was in the middle, along with her age. His eyes found it quickly thanks to an X in the column marked "result." All the other names had blanks in the "result" column. Someone had hand-written "She's gone for good" at the top corner, though whether this was a note to Post or not none could say.

"What's this?"

"That's the oddball. Got it about a month ago. It came in an envelope with just my address on it."

Valentine looked at the attached envelope. Post must have received it just before they moved into the Love Field positions. Valentine could remember a change in Post, a resignation, but had attributed it to the strain of the siege.

He examined the document's envelope. Typewritten, obviously with a manual typewriter. Valentine deciphered the stamp—Pine Bluff again. But the post number wasn't the one for the war college. The Miskatonic? The researchers there studied the Kurian Order, probing unpleasant shadows and gruesome corners.

"No cover letter?"

"Nothing."

"How can I help?"

Post took a moment, either to gather thoughts or breathe. "You know people. The"—he lowered his voice, as though fearing comment from the blind man in the next bed—"Lifeweavers. Those researchers. Intelligence. I'd like to know what happened to her after she was taken. No matter how bad the news."

People herded onto trains seldom came to a happy end. Valentine had been in Solon's meetings, heard about "payments" in the form of captives going to the neighboring KZs. "You sure? Maybe you don't."

"She's still alive in my head," Post said.

"Exactly."

Post's lined eyes regained some of their old liveliness. "No, not that way. I always knew she was alive, even when I thought you were just another CM. Can't say how I know. A feeling. I still feel it. You know about feelings like that."

He did. Some inner warning system sometimes let him know when there was a Reaper around—the "Valentingle," his comrades in the Wolves used to call it. First as a joke. Then they learned to trust it.

"I can ask around." Post was right; he had a couple of tenuous contacts at the Miskatonic—the main scholarly center for research into the Kurian Order—and with Southern Command's intelligence. But that was pre-Solon. For all he knew they were dead or lost in the chaos civilians were already calling "the bad spell."

"Let me know the truth, whatever it is, Val."

"Can I have these?"

"Sure. I copied down everything in my journal."

Valentine rested his hand on Post's forearm. "Listen to the doctors and get better. The Razors need you back, even if you're stumping around on a piece of East Texas pine."

"I heard they were breaking up the Razors," Post said.

"From who?"

Post shrugged, and the effort left him red-faced. "Some doctor. Asked me what outfit I was with."

"Probably a rumor. Lots of stuff floating around military hospitals."

"Yeah, like turds in a bedpan," Post's neighbor said.

"A regular Lieutenant Suzy Sunshine, that guy," Post said. Lieutenant Suzy Sunshine was a Pollyannaish cartoon character in one of the army papers—*Freedom's Voice*—who turned any misfortune into a cheerful quip.

"I'll be back tomorrow," Valentine said.

"I'm not going anywhere."

Valentine left, upset enough to forget the ice.

ф

The sun had vanished by the time Valentine returned to the Accolade. The Razors had set up some old car upholstery in the overgrown parking lot, and had gathered to drink and watch the sun go down.

"Bump, Major?" Ruvayed, the communications officer from the control tower, hollered as he passed. She looked off-kilter, like a dog back from the vet—part of her skull was shaved and a dressing blossomed in the bare spot like a white flower. She held out a tall glass.

"I need a major bump," another man added, flat on his back with a tepee of gnawed roasting ears, holding a lit cigar clear of the grass.

"Just have to check in," Valentine said as he passed, regretting the forgotten ice.

Meadows and Nail, the Bear leader, were going over personnel sheets, trying to work out store consumption and medical requirements for the men stabled at the Accolade.

"Wish staff hadn't snatched Styachowski back," Nail said, looking at the broken end of his pencil. "She went through paperwork like quicklime. Hey, Val."

"Maybe we need a piece of that blue blob they pried off the Kurian capsule," Valentine said. "I heard they're keeping it at Brigade. It eats paper."

The "dingleberry" was the only survivor of the Kurian capsule's trip through the defeated Dallas forces. The last Valentine had heard the Dallas Quislings were almost to Houston, being shepherded on blistered feet by mounted Rangers.

"Nail, can I have a moment with the colonel?" Valentine asked.

"Gladly. I'll grab a piece of twilight while I can." Nail drew a utility knife and went to work on his pencil point as he walked out the door.

"How's Will?" Meadows asked.

"Came through fine. I spoke to one doctor and two nurses. He's feeling a little low, but physically he's doing well."

"Send Narcisse over to have a chat with him. She's got a way of putting things in perspective."

"He said there's a rumor floating around that the Razors are through," Valentine said. His voice broke a little as he spoke. The

Razors were a cross to bear, but also a matter of some personal pride.

Meadows sighed and sat down. "I wonder who blabbed. Smoke? I swear her ears detach and walk around on their own."

"No, she's not even in Texarkana. She heard about a Lifeweaver, supposed to be up in Hot Springs, and hopped a train to find him."

"I saw a Lifeweaver once. Or what a Wolf told me was one."

"So the rumor's true?" Valentine asked, wanting to change the subject. Wherever the Lifeweavers helping Southern Command had fled to when the Free Territory fell last year, they were taking their sweet time in getting back, and speculation didn't hurry them along.

"Sorry, Val. Look, the Razors only half existed as far as Southern Command was concerned anyway. They never liked experienced Wolves and a Bear team tied down to a regiment of Guard infantry anyway. That, and the men have specializations that are needed elsewhere."

The truth of his words made it hurt a little less. "When's it going to be announced?"

"Another day or three. We'll have a big good-bye blowout the day after the news; I've arranged for that."

Colonel Meadows understood the men and their needs better than Valentine. In his more introspective moments Valentine admitted to himself that he threw himself so much into the job at hand that he forgot about the stress it put on the tool.

"You can help, Val. In the morning there'll be decorations, then the barbecue starts. I've arranged for Black Lightning to play— according to the Texans they're the best Relief band in Southern Command. Stripper tent, tattoo artists, a back-pay distribution so you'll get the flea marketers in to provide some competition for the Southern Command PX-wagons."

"What do you need from me?" Valentine asked. If he couldn't do anything about the Razors dying, he could at least see to the burial.

"We need a bunch of transfer orders written. I've got a skills priority list; match it up with the men. Wish we had Will. For the party, I mean."

"Seems wrong to have it without him. I just told him the Razors were waiting for his return."

"Sorry about that. I didn't want to tell you until you had a night or two to rest up here."

"I'll sleep tonight. I intend to have a couple of sips of whatever Ruvayed is passing out."

"Consider yourself off duty for the next twenty-four."

Valentine had a thought. "Could you take care of one thing, sir? Pass something up? The general's signature would be helpful."

"What is it?"

"I'd like Post to be able to say farewell to the Razors too."

ψ

Roast pig is a mouthwatering smell, and it penetrated even the back of the ambulance. The vehicle halted.

"What's up your sleeve, Val?" Post asked. No fewer than four nurses and one muscular medical orderly sat shoulder to shoulder with Val, crowded around Post's bed on wheels.

"You'll see."

The doors opened, giving those inside a good view of the Accolade's renovated parking lot. The brush had been chopped away, tents constructed, and paper lanterns in a dozen colors strung between the tent poles and trees. Some nimble electronics tech had rigged a thirty-foot antenna and hung the Razor's porcine silhouette banner—DON'T FEED ON ME read the legend—to top it off.

Bunting hung from the Accolade's windows, along with another canopy of lanterns. Music from fiddles, guitars, and drums competed from different parts of the party. A mass of soldiers—probably a good third of them not even Razors, but men who knew how to sniff out a good party and gain admittance by performing some minor support function—wandered in and out of the various tents and trader stalls.

"Jesus, Val," Post said as Valentine and the orderly took him out of the ambulance. He looked twice as strong as he had on Valentine's visit the previous day—Post made a habit of coming back strong from injury.

"Hey, it's Captain Post!" a Razor shouted.

"Some secret debriefing," one of the nurses said.

"As far as the hospital's concerned none of you will be back for a day," Valentine said. "The only thing I ask is that someone attend Will at all times."

"SOP, Val. I can just holler if I need some water. John, set this thing so I'm sitting up, alright?"

The attendant and a nurse arranged his bed.

"If I'd known this soiree was going full blast," a nurse said, rearranging the cap on her brunette hair, "I would have brought my makeup."

Valentine pulled some bills out of his pocket and passed them to the head nurse. "For additional medical supplies. You can probably find what you need at the PX-wagons. If not, it looked like the strippers had plenty to spare."

"Ewwww," another nurse said.

"Oh, lighten up, Nicks," the head nurse said. "You're on first watch, then. I'll bring you a plate."

The men were already clustering around Post. "Great, great," Valentine heard Post saying. "Food's good. Only problem is, I was wounded in my right leg. They took the healthy one off."

"Just like 'em," one of the more gullible Razors said, before he saw what the others were laughing at.

The male attendant kept various proffered bottles and cups away from Post's mouth. "I want to hear some music," Post said. "Let's get Narcisse's wheelie-stool out and we'll dance."

"Razors!" the men shouted as they lifted the gurney and bore it toward the bandstand.

"That's a nice thing you're doing for your captain, Major," the nurse they called Nicks said. "He's lucky to have you."

"I'm the lucky one," Valentine said.

ψ

Black Lightning lived up to their reputation. Valentine wasn't sophisticated enough with music to say whether they were "country" or "rock and roll" or "fwap" to use early-twenty-first century categories. They were energetic—and loud. So much so that he kept to the back and observed. The crowd listened or danced as the mood struck them, all facing the stage, which was just as well because the men outnumbered the women by six to one or so.

The nurses kept close to Post, who had a steady stream of well-wishers, but seemed to make themselves agreeable to the boys.

Boys. Valentine startled at the appellation. At twenty-seven he could hardly be labeled old, but he sometimes felt it when he passed a file of new recruits. Southern Command had filled out the Razors with kids in need of a little experience—the regiment had never been meant to be a frontline unit in the Dallas siege—and they'd gotten it at terrible cost.

Or maybe it was just that the younger folks had the energy to enjoy the band. Most of the older men sat as they ate or smoked or drank, enjoying the night air and the companionship of familiar faces. A photographer took an occasional picture of those who'd been decorated that morning. Everyone had taken the news of the Razors' breakup well—

"What a surprise. Major Valentine alone with his thoughts," a female voice said in his ear.

Valentine jumped. Duvalier stood just behind him as though she'd been beamed there from the *Star Trek* books of his youth. She wore a pair of green, oversized sunglasses, some cheap kid's gewgaw from the trade wagons, and when the photographer pointed the camera at them, she had a sudden coughing fit as the flash fired.

"Didn't know you were back."

"After all this time, you still haven't figured it out, have you? I don't like my comings and goings to be noticed." Valentine noticed her slurring her words a little. He'd never known Duvalier to have more than a single glass of anything out of politeness—and even that was usually left unfinished.

"I thought you hated parties," Valentine said.

"I do, but I like to go anyway, and hate them with someone."

"You dressed up."

Duvalier wore tight shorts, a sleeveless shirt, and what looked to be thigh-high stockings in a decorative brocade. Her battered hiking boots just made the rest of her look better. "Wishing I hadn't. Some of your horntoads thought I was here professionally."

"Serves you right for getting cleaned up. Any bloodshed?"

"All the ears and noses in your command are accounted for, Major. Colonel Meadows asked me to find you."

"Speaking of finding people, I've yet to find anyone who saw you during our fight at the airfield."

She wrinkled her freckled nose. "I should hope not. Everyone but me was busy being a hero. As soon as the bombs started dropping I hid deep and dark next to a storm sewer leading off-field. You can't outsmart a rocket."

"If they gave out medals for survival you'd have a chestful. Speaking of which, is that the legendary red bra I see peeping out?" He reached for her cutoff shirt—

"Dream on, Valentine." She grabbed his hand and gave his wrist a painful twist, then pulled him toward the barbecue pit, her hand warm in his.

Colonel Meadows was carving pork, heaping it onto plates, and handing them out, at which point Narcisse would slather the meat with barbecue sauce and hand the plates out to the lined-up soldiers. Judging by their sticky lips, most were back for seconds.

"Daveed!" Narcisse said, spinning on her stool. "This recipe I learned on Jamaica—they call it 'jerked.' Have some!"

"In a second, Sissy," Meadows said. "We're getting a drink first. Spell me, Cossack."

A soldier prodding the coals stood up and took the carving knife out of Meadows' hand. Meadows tossed him the apron.

They filled pewter mugs from a barrel at the beer tent—it was poor stuff, as Southern Command had better things to do with its soil than grow hops—and found a quiet spot away from the band. Duvalier followed with a plate at a respectful distance. She had good hearing, if not quite Valentine's Wolf ears, and positioned herself downwind, back to the men but undoubtedly able to hear every word said.

Some fool fired off a blue signal flare to add to the festive atmosphere. It turned the beer black inside the mugs and added deep shadows to Meadows' eyesockets.

"Great party, sir," Valentine said, and meant it.

"We deserve it." Meadows was a *we* kind of officer. He held out his mug and Valentine touched his to it, the faint *klink* sounding a slightly sour note thanks to the pewter.

"An interesting letter in the courier pouch hit my desk the other day. This is as good a moment as any to tell you: They're offering you a Hunter Staff position."

Valentine felt his knees give out for a moment, and he covered with a swig of beer. "Staff?"

"Easy now, Val. It's a helluva honor."

Duvalier brushed past him on the way to the beer tent, and gave his hip a gentle nudge with hers.

"Not that you'll have a lot of time to show off your swagger stick. I hear they work you to death."

Valentine understood that well enough. Southern Commmand operated on a general staff system that selected and then trained a small group of officers in all the subsidiary branches of service: artillery, logistics, intelligence, and so on. The highly trained cadre then served as staff inspectors or temporary replacements or taught until promoted to higher command or, in the event of a crisis, they took command of reserve units.

The Hunters—the Wolves, Cats, and Bears of Southern Command that operated as special forces outside the borders of the Free Territory—had their own identical staff system that trained with the others and then performed similar functions with the smaller Hunter units. A couple of hitches in Wolf and Bear formations was enough for most; the veteran soldiers usually transferred to support units—or the Logistics Commandos if they still had a taste for operating in the Kurian Zone. But most still served Southern Command by belonging to ghost regiments that might be called up.

Captain Moira Styachowski, one of the most capable officers he'd ever met, had been on the Hunter Staff.

Valentine might end up in command of one of those formations. The role was wryly appropriate; he'd been nicknamed "the Ghost" when serving in the Zulus, his first Wolf company.

Meadows broke in on his thoughts. "Valentine, it's official enough so I thought I'd tell you. You're better than two years overdue for a leave. It'll take them a while to get your training schedule worked out. When we're done here you'll be cleared to take a three-months' leave. I'll miss you. It's been a pleasure."

And Valentine would miss the Razors. They seemed "his" in a way none of the other organizations he'd served with or commanded ever had. Seeing them broken up was like losing a child. "Thank you, sir."

He didn't feel like thanking anyone, but it had to be said.

He wandered back among the Razors, accepted a few congratulations with a smile, but all he wanted was quiet and a chance to think. Meadows had tried to add a sparkle to a bittersweet party, but all he'd done was ruin Valentine's enjoyment of the festivities.

*Stow that, you dumb son of a grog.* You're *ruining your enjoyment, not Meadows.*

Back in his days visiting the opulent old theater in Pine Bluff, they'd show movies now and then. He remembered sitting through part of one when arriving early for the evening's movie; the smell of popcorn and sweat on the seats all around him, unable to shut out even the blood from a tiny shaving cut on the man next to him with his inexperienced Wolf's nose.

The early show for the families was a kids' cartoon, full of bright primary colors even on the shabby little projector rigged to an electronic video-memory device. He recalled a bunch of kids' toys in a machine, and a mechanical claw that came down and selected one of the dozens of identical toys now and then. The toys responded to the mystical selection of the claw as though at a religious ceremony.

Life in the creaky, stop-and-start mechanism of Southern Command had never been so elegantly summed up for him. "The claw chooses!" Orders came down and snatched you away from one world and put you in another.

Duvalier proffered a fresh, cool mug filled with colder beer. "Guess that's it for Cat duty, far as you're concerned," she said. Her eyes weren't as bright and lively as usual; either her digestive troubles were back or she'd continued drinking. Valentine sniffed her breath and decided the latter.

The swirl of congratulatory faces wandered off after he took the mug, offered a small celebratory lift of the brew to the north, south, east, and west, and took a sip.

"Did you run down that Lifeweaver?" On second taste, the beer wasn't quite so sharp.

"No. There was a rumor one'd been killed by some kind of agent the Kurians planted last year. Guess Kurs' got their versions of Cats too."

Valentine had heard all sorts of rumors about specially trained humans in Kurian employ. That they could read minds, or turn water into wine, or redirect a thunderstorm's lightning. Everything from mud slides to misaddressed mail was blamed on Kurian agents.

Valentine shrugged.

"They'll get word to us. They always do, one way or another. Right?" Duvalier asked.

The last sounded a bit too much like a plea. Duvalier thought of the Lifeweavers as something akin to God's angels on Earth; the way the Kurians' estranged cousins presented themselves added to the effect. This cool and deadly woman had the eyes of a child left waiting on a street corner for a vanished parent.

"Mystery's their business," Valentine said.

She emptied her mug. "Want to blow this bash?"

The beer worked fast. Valentine already felt like listening to music and discussing the nurses' legs with Post. But he couldn't leave Duvalier tipsy and doubtful.

"Yes," he lied.

Her shoulders went a little further back, and more of the red bra appeared beneath her vest. "Lead on, McGruff," she said.

Valentine was pretty sure it was MacDuff—Father Max made his classes perform two Shakespeare plays a year—but couldn't prick her newly improved mood with something as trivial as, well, trivia.

The men were setting up some sort of chariot race involving wheelchairs, Narcisse, and a Razor with his leg in a cast from ankle to midthigh. By the looks of the clothesline traces and wobbly wheels on the chairs, the soldier's other leg would be in a cast by morning, but Valentine and Duvalier hollered out their hurrahs and stayed to watch. Narcisse's wheelchair overturned at the third turn—she didn't have enough weight to throw leftward to keep both wheels of the chair down in the turn—but she gamely hung on and was dragged through the freshly trimmed parking lot meadow to victory, garlanded by a dandelion leaf in her rag turban.

Duvalier pressed herself up against him as they jumped and cheered her on. As they wandered away from the race, she was on his arm.

"Seems like a staff appointment deserves a special celebration," she slurred as they left the crowd and passed under the Accolade's bunting.

"Careful, now," Valentine said as they made a right turn toward his quarters. "You're evil, teasing me like that."

She looked around and saw that the hall was empty. Then she kissed him, with the same fierce intensity that he remembered from the bloody murder in the Nebraska caboose.

"Let's. Now. *Right* now." She extracted a half-empty flask from within her vest and took a swig.

Valentine had desired her for years, and they'd come close to making love out of sheer boredom once or twice while serving together in the KZ. But the half joking, half flirting they'd done in the past had always been passed back and forth around a shield of professionalism, like two prisoners swapping notes around a cell wall.

"I wanna see what that little Husker cowgirl thought was so special," she said with a facial spasm that might have been a flirtatious eyebrow lift that suddenly decided to become a wink.

*Dumb shit, why did you ever tell her that?*

He pulled her into his room and shut the door behind them.

"Not drunk and not with us about to—" he began, fighting off her fingers as they sought his belt.

"Now who's the tease, huh?" she asked, falling back onto the bed as though he'd kicked her there. "You're a lot of talk and fancy words. Ahn-Kha's got bigger balls than you—"

That struck Valentine as a curious—and stipulatable—argument. They'd both seen Ahn-Kha any number of times, and the Golden One had a testicular sack the size of a ripe cantaloupe.

51

"Ali, I—"

"It's always *I* with you, Val. Ever notice that? I don't even want us to be a *we,* I just want one fuck, one goddamn, sweaty fuck with a guy I halfway care about. I spent eight months on my back for those grunting Quislings. Wasn't like blowing some eighteen-year-old sentry to get through a checkpoint 'cause I had a story about how I gotta get medicine to my sick aunt—I had to eat breakfast with those greasy shits and talk about how great they were and just once I'd like—"

And with that it was like all the air had left her lungs. She leaned over with her mouth open for a moment, a surprised look on her face—then she fled to the bathroom.

Valentine pulled his lengthening hair back from his eyes, listened to the mixture of sobs and retching sounds echoing off the tiles in the washroom, and let out a long breath. At the moment he couldn't be sure that he wouldn't rather face another air pirate raid than go into that room.

But he did so.

The mess was about what he expected. A horrible beery-liquor smell wove itself above and around the sharper odor of her bile, and she was crying into the crook of a vomit-smeared arm at the edge of the toilet.

He picked her up. After a quick struggle he set her in bed and took off her shoes and socks, and gave each rough foot one gentle squeeze.

"No, not now," she said.

"I wasn't."

"I got puke on my good bra."

"I'll rinse it out and hang it up."

"Thanks."

Her freckles looked like wildflowers in a field of golden wheat.

By the time he'd used a washcloth on her face and arm, rinsed out her clothes—and her socks for good measure—she was murmuring at some level of sleep. He put a thin blanket over her and cleaned up the toilet area, using a bowl as a wash bucket.

When that was done she was truly asleep, rolled into the blanket like a softly snoring sausage.

φ

That night Valentine sat in his musty room with its vomit-disinfectant-and-tobacco smell and quieted his mind by laying out the three pieces of paper bearing Gail Foster's name. Black Lightning was still pounding away, the amplified music much reduced by the bulk of the intervening hotel.

He took a yellowed blank sheet of paper from his order book and drew a cross in the center, dividing the paper into four squares. He labeled the top left "Goal" and the top right "Known Known." The bottom left became "Known Unknown." Another scrape or two from his pencil and the bottom right box had the label "Unknown Unknown."

While it seemed like gibberish, the formula had been taught to him in his youth by the old Jesuit, Father Max, the teacher who'd raised him after the murder of his family. Father Max had told him (a couple of times—when Father Max was in his cups he sometimes forgot what he said) that the analytic tool came from a woman who used to work at the old United States Department of Defense intelligence agency.

It divided one's knowledge of a subject into facts you knew, facts you knew you didn't know, and the possibility of important pieces of knowledge out there that you weren't aware of until they rose up and bit you. But by diligent pursuit of the questions in the other two squares you slowly accomplished the goal, and sometimes found out about the third in time to act.

And when an Unknown Unknown showed up you had to be mentally prepared to erase even your Known Knowns.

Valentine had lived in the Kurian Zone, had even spoken to one directly, and all his experiences had left him with was the unsettling conviction that humanity's place in the universe wasn't much different than that of a *Canis familiaris*—the common dog. There were wild dogs and savage dogs and tamed dogs and trained dogs, and dogs knew all about other dogs, or could learn soon enough, but their guesses about the wider world (cars and phones and other phenomena) and a dog's place in it was limited by the dog's tendency to put everything in dog terms.

If he tried to put himself in the place of the practically immortal Kurians, an endless series of doubts and fears popped up. The

Kurians had laid waste to Earth once with a series of natural catastrophes and disease, so what was to stop them from unleashing an apocalyptic horseman or two if mankind became too troublesome? He'd seen on the Ranch in Texas that the Kurians were toying with different forms of life in an effort to find a more pliable source of vital aura than man, in the form of the ratbits. How much time did man have before the Kurians decided to clear off the ranchland that was Earth and raise a different kind of stock? Wouldn't a goatherd who got sick of bites from the billys switch to sheep?

Depressing speculation didn't help find Post's wife. He remembered his promise and picked up the pencil again. Under "Goal" he wrote: "Learn what happened to Gail Foster." He did some mental math as he transcribed Kurian dates (the years started in 2022, and after a brief attempt at calendar reform had reverted back to old-style months and days).

**Known Knowns**
*Gail Foster lived in the Free Territory (Pine Bluff?).*
— *was tested at station 9-P*
— *no other woman on the list had an X under "result."*
— *was shipped somewhere by the Kurians five days later.*

**Known Unknowns**
— *Shipped to where?*
— *Did test indicate a negative or a positive?*
— *Purpose of test?*

He checked the list of names on the Miskatonic paper again and wrote:

Why only females tested? (Fertility? Privacy? Expediency?)

The last was guesswork, for all he knew they tested all women, whether of childbearing age or not. There was the chance that they gave men the same test too, and for reasons of their own performed the tests separately—though the Kurians were not known for breaking up families and couples, it made groups of humans easier to handle.

Statistically, being one out of fifty in the Kurian Zone meant bad news for Gail Foster—formerly Gail Post. In his time under-cover in the Kurian Zone Valentine had seen dozens—strike that, hundreds—of instances where the Kurians had culled humans into a large group and a small group.

The small groups never lasted long.

Were they checking for a disease or infirmity that meant she only had a short time to live? The Kurians used humans the way banks exchanged currency; perhaps a human only counted as a human if it could be expected to survive more than one year.

Valentine looked at himself in the shard of mirror on the wall. The single bare bulb in the wall cut shadows under his eyes and jawline. *You're a glass-is-half-empty kind of guy, Valentine.*

*Maybe she scored supergenius on a test and was being shipped off to learn some kind of Kurian technology. Maybe she had a special skill that would keep her comfortably employed in the Kurian Order to a ripe old age.*

*Or maybe she showed up on some list as a refugee, and was shipped back to her original owners faster than you could say Dred Scott.*

The other thing he'd learned from Father Max was that the first step in discovering a few Unknown Unknowns was to answer the Known Unknowns.

So much to do. He'd have Ahn-Kha take Hank to a boarding school. He didn't want the boy to become just another camp extra until he enlisted at fifteen. He'd have to arrange for transport for both of them, and for himself to Pine Bluff and the Miskatonic.

He had one promise to keep before starting this new page. Even if it was a page he didn't know that he was up to turning. Just as well Post had given him this. At least he had something to do with his leave other than fret.

φ

Hank brought in breakfast. The boy looked as gray and bleary as a Minnesota October, and Valentine smelled more beer and vomit on him.

"How about a little yogurt, Hank?" Val said, holding up what passed for yogurt in Texarkana to the boy. He lifted a spoonful and let it drop with a plop.

"No, sir, I'm—already ate," the boy said, putting his burn-scarred hand under his nose. He fled, and Valentine chuckled into his bran mash.

"Are you up early or late?" Duvalier groaned. She rolled over and looked at the window. "Early."

"No, late. It's almost nine. I think everyone slept in."

She reached down into her covers. "Water?"

Valentine got up and gave her his plastic tumbler full.

"Val, we didn't . . ."

"Didn't what?"

"You know."

"You yodel during sex. I never would have guessed that."

"Dream on, Valentine." She rolled over on her stomach. "God, gotta pee."

She got up and dragged herself into the bathroom.

"This would have been a bad time of the month for us to do *that*," she said from within.

"Do I need to get you anything from supply?"

"No, I mean—fertility and all that."

Valentine wondered for one awful second what his daughter looked like. She'd probably have dark eyes and hair; both he and Malita Carrasca were dark.

"I got basic hygiene first week of Labor Regiment," Valentine said. "Good soldiers don't shoot unless they've taken precautions not to hurt the innocent."

She laughed and then cut it off. "Ow. My head."

Someone pounded on the door hard enough that the hinges moved.

"Come in," Valentine called.

Ahn-Kha stood, blocking ninety-five percent of the light coming through the open door.

"Final review at noon, Major. Colonel's orders. Three generals will be in attendance."

"Thank you. Eat up—" Valentine said, indicating the tray. Narcisse always issued him three times the breakfast he could consume and there was a pile of sliced ham on the tray the height of a New Universal Church Archon's bible.

Ahn-Kha wedged himself between chair and desk.

"Generals, eh?" Duvalier said. "I'm going to make myself scarce. Striped trousers are for clowns."

Valentine looked at his row of battle dress and wondered which one could be pressed sufficiently for the occasion.

None of them, really. Whatever the Razors were all about, whatever was dying that afternoon, wasn't about creased trousers.

φ

"I'm sorry, Valentine," Meadows said out of the side of his mouth as they approached the four generals on the bandstand that last night had barely contained Black Lightning. "He tagged along at the last minute."

Post and some of the other nonambulatory wounded sat behind them on the stand so they could see. The remaining Razors were drawn up in a great U of six attenuated companies in the open parking-lot space in front of the bandstand. Ahn-Kha stood with the senior NCOs, Hank with a group of Aspirants, and Narcisse watched from high on the shoulder of one of his soldier's husbands. In the center, a color guard of Bears took down the Razors' boar-silhouette flag. They did it badly, and the men coming together as they folded it looked like a mistimed football hike. The Bears did everything badly.

Except fight.

They presented the triangular folded flag to Meadows, who accepted it as he would a baby.

Valentine looked at the rows of men for what was probably the last time. They looked hard in their battle dress, hard in the relaxed way that only men who'd seen bloodshed could manage. But Valentine didn't see them as iron-thewed heroes. They were more like blown-glass sculptures, beautiful in their irregularity, their variety of colors, heights, and shapes. And just like the glass vessels, tiny shards of fast-flying shrapnel could convert them into a shattered ruin of gristle, blood, and half-digested food in an eyeblink. He'd seen it more than once, and once was enough for any sane man.

Their delicacy made them all the more precious.

Then he and Meadows turned and walked to the generals. Valentine knew each one by name, but only one from experience.

General Martinez.

The man who'd executed two of his Grogs, and would have killed Ahn-Kha right before Valentine's eyes, was the second-highest-ranking officer gathered at the ceremony, subordinate only to MacCallister, who'd supervised the drive on Dallas–Fort Worth. Valentine knew that he held some rear-area post as a reward for his resistance—such as it was—during Solon's brief reign over the Ozarks.

Old and very bad blood linked Valentine and Martinez. In the crowning irony, Valentine's whole rising in Little Rock and his defense of Big Rock Mountain had taken place under Martinez's command. But only technically; Martinez hadn't moved a man to his assistance when he was most needed.

There were salutes, and when the salutes were done, handshakes.

"Congratulations on your staff appointment, Major Valentine," MacCallister said from beneath a white mustache that mostly hid a missing incisor when he spoke.

"Richly deserved," Meadows put in.

They sidestepped.

Valentine gave Martinez a formal salute, returned equally formally.

"General," Valentine said.

"Major," General Martinez returned. He still looked like a turtle, even in his green-and-brown dress uniform. He didn't offer his hand.

Meadows led Valentine to a chair behind and to the right of the generals. He passed Valentine the Razors' flag.

"You deserve this more than anyone," Meadows said quietly. "They always were yours."

"Co—"

"Shut up, Major. That's an order."

MacCallister said a few words thanking the men for their bravery, devotion, and sacrifice. He read out the Razors' list of regimental achievements and citations, and explained that skilled men were desperately needed elsewhere, and it was his sad duty to order the dissolution of the battered regiment.

"A grateful Free Republic thanks you," General MacCallister said as he dismissed the men. Evidently progress had been made in the governance of the bits of four states that comprised the Freehold.

The soldiers had heard it all before. All of them knew about the Claw, and that the Claw couldn't be questioned. Even if they didn't call it that.

When it was done Valentine was expected at a late lunch with the generals. But there was something he had to do first. He went over to the line of wounded and spoke to each one. He ended at Post's elevated bed. Post looked better by exponents.

"Which nurse did you end up with?" Valentine asked.

"Which didn't he?" one of the men snickered.

"Sort of all of them and none of them, if you follow me, Dave," Post said.

Valentine handed him the folded flag. "I want you to hang onto this until you're better and we link up again."

"Hear you're going to be kind of busy on staff training. Maybe the higher-ups aren't nuts after all." As executive officer for the Razors, Post had spent endless hours in the Byzantine bowels of Southern Command procedures, trying to keep the Razors better supplied and better equipped than a half-forgotten rear-area reserve. "But why me? It's Meadows' flag."

"It's our flag," he said, and hoped Duvalier was lurking somewhere near—perhaps beneath the bandstand. "You're keeping it until I come back from leave. There's a few questions to be asked and a promise to keep."

Post's smile matched the Texas sun in brightness, and exceeded it in size.

"Thank you, sir."

# CHAPTER THREE

*T*he Ark, Pine Bluff, Arkansas: Southern Command collapsed when Solon arrived, not in panic, but in a controlled implosion more reminiscent of a carefully demolished high-rise than a chaotic rout.

Stockpiles of foods, medicines, and especially weapons disappeared into predug and camouflaged caverns. Where caverns weren't available, basements sufficed. One of the most important of the Eastern Arkansas caches resided at SEARK—the Southeastern Arkansas College. Southern Command had several important facilities around Pine Bluff, including the main docks on the lower Arkansas, the old arsenal that produced munitions for the Freehold, the war college at the old University of Arkansas (an agricultural and technical university taught civilians on the same campus) and, in a nondescript building at the edge of campus, a group of scientists devoted to researching the Kurians, known by a few as "the Miskatonic." From machine tools to research archives, key resources were concealed on the overgrown campus of SEARK, or "the Ark." A whole greenhouse on the campus existed just to shelter plant growth that would be used to cover entrances to underground warehouses, and the more burned-out and disused a classroom building looked, the more likely it was that explosives could be found stored in the rusty darkness of the basement.

The Ark deception worked in Pine Bluff. Southern Command, in abandoning the arsenal, blew up piles of junk to make it look as though machinery was destroyed rather than hidden. The Miskatonic turned piles of old phone books into fine white ash in a bonfire outside the institute.

Pine Bluff, in the year after Solon's rule, is only a shadow of the lively riverfront town, with its markets and stores, blacksmiths and *seamstresses. Some of the population still wears the dull yellows and or-anges of Solon's Trans-Mississippi Confederation, others go about like hungry beggars as they look for lost friends and loved ones, searching for familiar faces from the shops and docks.*

*The Ark has a new lease on life thanks to its period as an archive. The Miskatonic has relocated from the burned U of A campus to Mc-George hall, three stories of red brick with freshly painted white pillars around the entrance and new-planted trees relocated from roof and doorstep. If the building's architecture reflected the facts and secrets locked within, it would be a dozen stories tall and carved out of black granite, with horns projecting from the roof and gimlet eyes peering from the gaps in the still-boarded windows. . . .*

ψ

David Valentine stepped off the train even before it came to a full stop and landed neatly on his good leg. He checked in at the Guard Station and reacquainted himself with the modest sights of the hill-circled town, enjoying the sensation of being off the rickety train.

It had been a long trip up from Texarkana, thanks to the stop-and-start nature of nonmilitary travel. He spent a night in Hope, and learned that the famous unification of Texas and Arkansas forces had actually taken place in the nearby crossroads of Fouke. Southern Command, perhaps with an eye toward history, or real-ism about the soldier's eagerness to say they were present at the fa-mous Texas-Arkansas-Fouke, had broadcast the news to the world from a minor general's temporary headquarters in Hope. Valentine spent ten dollars on an afternoon outing from Hope to the spot of the linkup (sandwich lunch included!) and saw the two state flags waving on a small hill next to a creek where beer and whiskey bot-tles from the celebration were still in evidence.

He wandered up and down Pine Bluff's main streets. Occupa-tion seemed to have leeched all the cheery color from the town he remembered from his early days as a Wolf, studying at the academy. Vanished flower boxes, missing chalkwork advertisements on the brickwork, empty display windows where once mannequins had stood displaying everything from rugged smocks to ruffled wedding gowns, even the tired-looking berry bushes and picked-clean fruit trees filling every vacant lot related the occupation's story.

The lots made him think of Razors for some reason. Missing faces, dead or gone. He missed Hank most of all, even more than Narcisse or Ahn-Kha. Both could take care of themselves. But Hank had gone off to school with little enthusiasm. Valentine had tried to ease the parting by giving him his snakeskin bandolier, the same one he'd worn the night of the Rising in Little Rock.

"You deserve a medal, Hank, but this is the best I can do."

Hank ran his good hand across the oversized scales. "For real? For keeps?"

"For exceptional valor," Valentine said.

Hank hooked a finger in one of the loops. "Take a while to grow more Quickwood," Hank said.

"Fill it with diplomas."

At that Hank frowned—the boy saw himself as tried and tested as any of the Razors. In the end Valentine tasked Ahn-Kha with seeing the boy safely seated—and if necessary, handcuffed—at school.

He brought himself back to the present.

Valentine read the lettering next to a white cross painted on a walkway above the street, connecting two buildings at the heart of downtown:

HERE THEY HUNG JAMES ELLINGTON
FOR SPITTING UNDER THE BOOTS OF THE OCCUPIERS AS THEY MARCHED
THEY SAID HE WAS TO BE AN EXAMPLE
THEY WERE RIGHT

One of Valentine's happier memories was of his time spent in Pine Bluff as a student at the war college. Essays on the qualities of Integrity, Professional Competence, The Courage to Act, and Looking Forward; regulations on the care of dependants and children of his soldiers; sound management principles—Southern Command was nothing if not parsimonious—the multitude of identification badges . . .

Or the cheery efficiency of Cadet "Dots" Lambert, juggling student and instructor schedules with teenage energy. Valentine laid down circuitous paths so he could pass her desk and say hi between his early duties with Zulu Company, class, and meals. He'd never worked up the courage to so much as ask her to a barbecue—he'd been a scruffy young Wolf, a breed apart from the well-tailored guards and cadets who undoubtedly dazzled as they whirled the girl around the floor at military mixers that Valentine, with patched trousers, collarless shirts, and field boots always managed to miss.

He hoped Lambert hadn't been hung from the clock tower at the university. Or shipped off in a cattle car.

Which brought him back to his reason for the trip to Pine Bluff. The Miskatonic.

Valentine refreshed himself with a hotdog in heartroot at the diner, then wandered southward along the tracks to the old SEARK campus, now listed on the town map as the "HPL Agricultural and Technical Resource Center." The entire SEARK campus was now surrounded by two rows of fencing topped with razor wire on either side of the streets surrounding the campus, enclosing as it did the war college, cadet school, and military courthouse.

Valentine showed his ID at the gate, surrendered his weapons, and signed in as a visitor.

"Have a fine one," the gun-check said, handing him a locker key on a pocket lanyard.

He heard distant gunfire from the other side of the railroad tracks as he entered, the spaced-out popping of a practice range. The cadets probably had a range day—it was a Friday and it would be just as well to stink them up on a day when they'd be a smelly nuisance to friends and family rather than their instructors—as most of the students looked to be in their late teens or early twenties. They looked so young. Elaborate razor-cut sideburns reminiscent of a bull's horns looked to be the new standard with the boys, and the girls were showing tight ringlet curls dangling from their little envelopelike caps.

Valentine, now closer to thirty than twenty, with three long trips into the Kurian Zone behind him that aged a man more than years or mileage, could shrug and disparage them as children. Except that the children had each been more or less handpicked and was studying morning, noon, and night in an effort to win their first brass tracks. Children didn't make PT at four A.M. and fall asleep on a pile of books at midnight.

There wouldn't be any old instructors to visit—frontline officers took a year or two off to teach, sometimes, but only the cadet school had permanent faculty and Valentine had ventured onto that campus only to take qualification tests. He took the sidewalk bordering the inner fence straight to the Miskatonic.

Their new building looked a good three times the size of the old one. Perhaps Southern Command had finally decided to take the scholars seriously. The Miskatonic researched how the Kurians and other dangerous fauna they'd "brought over" interacted and thought, instead of simply cataloging and quantifying threats.

Valentine had visited the "oddballs" inside now and then as a student at the war college, and had constant contact since in the form of debriefings every time he came back from the Kurian Zone. The debriefings were always by a variegated trio; a young student who served as stenographer, an intellectual-looking questioner, and then an older man or woman who silently listened, almost never asking a question him or herself, but sometimes calling the other two off into another room before the trio returned with a new line of questioning. He'd gotten to know a couple of the "oldsters"—by their faces, anyway—enough so that he hoped he could run down Post's mystery letter.

A pair of workmen bent over an addition to the entryway, adding a small brick blister next to the doorway. Valentine passed through a layer of glass doors. A second layer was in place, but the glass was missing.

The whole institution had a fresh-scrubbed smell to it. Valentine caught a whiff of wet paint from one of the halls.

Six feet of neatly uniformed muscle stood up from his desk. "Can I help you?"

Valentine wondered if the hand casually dangling at the edge of the desk had a sidearm in reach, or was hovering over the alarm button. Two more guards watched from a balcony on the second floor.

Procedures had changed since he was a student. The last time he'd just walked into the building and wandered around until he heard sounds of activity.

Valentine reached for his ID again, feeling a bit like he was still in the KZ. "David Valentine, for a follow-up to my 18 August debriefing."

The soldier made a pretense of checking a list.

"I don't have—"

"Sorry, Corp," Valentine said smoothly. "A few months ago I got a request for another interview. I'm just back from Dallas, and the creeps told me that whenever duties allowed, I was to report. Duties allow, so here I am."

"Could I see the request, sir?"

"It was in the regimental file cabinet, which fell victim to a 122 during the Dallas siege, and was buried with honors by every soldier with a drunk-and-disorderly charge pending. You want to phone the old man and unclog the pipes at your end, or should I hit the Saenger for the afternoon matinee and work on my complaint letter? Maybe I can get reimbursed for my hotel and expenses from your paycheck."

"Sorry, sir," the corporal said. "It's these pointy heads. They'd run this place like a fruit stand. You'd think security was the enemy. Could you wait a moment?"

"Why the new security?"

"Kurian agent. Six men shot each other running him down."

Valentine looked around for a chair in the foyer, but the only two in evidence held up an improvised coffee station for the workmen set up on one of the missing glass door panes. He settled for sitting on a windowsill.

"I'll wait. I think it was signed O'Connor. David O'Connor," Valentine said, dredging the name from his memory.

"Doubt it," the corporal said, a rugged military phone to his ear. "He bought it when they dropped Reapers on the campus."

"My mistake," Valentine said.

"His. He tried to capture one." The corporal connected with someone and turned ninety degrees away from Valentine to speak.

Whatever he heard made the corporal look at Valentine again.

"Yes, Doc." He replaced the receiver. "You want some coffee or anything, Major Valentine?"

"I'm good."

"One of the senior fellows will be right down, Major."

"And he'll hear how polite you've been as you've done your duty," Valentine said.

"Thanks. I mean it."

The two guards looking down from the balcony on the second floor lost interest, and Valentine heard footsteps over more distant construction noises.

A limp-haired woman wearing shapeless scrubs that looked as though they belonged in a hospital emerged from a door behind the security station and came around the desk, giving a friendly nod to the corporal as she passed. She extended her hand and Valentine shook it. She had an easy, confident manner that made Valentine think of the midwife from his youth in the Boundary Waters.

"Gia Dozhinshka," she said. Valentine wondered if he'd been greeted in an Eastern European tongue. "Zhin's the shorthand around here," she continued.

"David Valentine, or just Val. I don't think we've met."

"No, but I summarized your debriefs. Nebraska and the Caribbean, and I read your Wisconsin and Great Lakes material. Call me a fan. Let's go to an interview room. We can sit."

"New digs," Valentine said as they passed through a different set of doors under the balcony at the back of the foyer.

"We hid our low-level archives here when we got the order to bug out. Seemed easier to move Mohammed to the mountain afterward. No one's complaining. Central air, if you can believe it."

"I thought that was a legend outside the hospitals and Mountain Home."

"We've been blessed. That's what it seemed like at first, anyway."

A young woman pushed a cart down the hall. "Interview A, Tess," Zhin called.

They turned a corner and she opened a door to a room that had been subdivided by half-glass walls. Valentine saw two people speaking to a hairy-faced man with the look of a frontiersman, though even with hard ears he couldn't make out any words through the glass. She led him to a warren of enclosed cubicles.

They circumvented most of them and went to a smaller office at the back, where she turned on a light.

"The chairs in this one are better. It's got its own sugar and such for coffee, too. Have to wait on Tess with your files. Anything to drink? Coffee? We have sage tea, courtesy of your Texas friends."

"Water would be good," Valentine said, spotting a cooler.

"Cups are up top. We don't have the kind that go in the little dispenser anymore."

Valentine got his drink and sat down at the bare table. Zhin settled herself opposite him.

"They decided you're worth guarding, it seems."

"We've come up in the world. Curse of being right."

"How's that?"

"A couple of our guys picked up on some strange dealmaking with the Texas-Kansas-Oklahoma Kurians. Solon hiring himself an army—but you know all about that. We figured we were going to get hit, and hard. Southern Command figured they were going to clean out the Grogs up and down the Missouri—Solon sent out a bunch of false intelligence indicating that. We ended up being right."

"But nobody listened," Valentine said.

"We were always outside the whole command structure. We'd give an opinion on this or that. What might work to pierce Reaper cloaks. Is there a way to disrupt the signal between a Kurian and his Reapers. What kind of ailments kill 'em. But since Solon's bid we've got to issue regular reports, assessments, and they're even starting to filter who we talk to and where we go so we don't lose 'assets.' "

"I met one of the filters at the security desk. Seems a reasonable precaution."

The young woman with the cart knocked and entered, pushing a collapsed binder with Valentine's name and some sort of catalog number printed on the outside. *Be interesting to take a look at the supplemental notes in that file,* Valentine thought. Pens, notepaper, and storage bags and jars littered the cart.

"Tess Sooyan, David Valentine," Zhin said, by way of introduction.

The young woman hid behind her hair and glasses. She sat

down in the corner with a pad, leaving the table to Valentine and her superior.

"Used to be if someone saw a weird track or bone they'd bring it to us, and we'd hand out little rewards and so on, even if it was just another Grog skull. But the, oh, what do you want to call them, shifty types—border trash—they avoid us now. All the barbed wire and uniforms scare them away."

"Speaking of shifty . . . I've got a confession. I'm here under false pretenses. I didn't need a follow-up to my last debrief."

Zhin leaned back in her chair. "Oh?"

Tacitly invited to explain, Valentine extracted Post's note. "A friend of mine got this . . . I'm guessing it's from one of your people. He's looking for his wife."

"Probably one of the kids," Zhin said, showing the note to her assistant. "Still in school or fresh out of it, they start here running down public queries. They shouldn't be sending out copies of documents, though. Or passing on opinions."

"That might be Peter Arnham's writing," Tess said at a level just loud enough for Valentine to hear it. "He's on the Missing/Displaced network."

"Can you look into it?" Valentine asked. "My friend's a good man. Badly wounded outside Dallas. He's going to have to put his life back together after all this. It would help if he knew one way or the other."

Zhin put the message in her leather folio. "I'll get a group going on it."

"I'll owe—"

"No, we don't work that way. No favors, no bargains, and you needn't come back with a crate of brandy. If you want, we can put you up for a night or two on campus."

"I know the town. I'd rather not be behind wire. I'll look up the Copley, if it's still around. Maybe try for a bass in the reservoir lake."

She and Tess both made notes. "You might at that. No one was doing much fishing while Solon was running things."

φ

Few pursuits can compare with fishing for a man looking for peace and quiet.

Two days later, enjoying his leave more than he'd enjoyed anything since parting with Malia, Valentine brought in a nice three-pound bass. As he tied up his aluminum shell he mentally inventoried the seasonings he'd picked up at the market after catching that catfish yesterday but had saved at the last minute in the hope of a better future catch: some green peppers, garlic, cloves, and a tiny bottle of what the spice merchant swore up and down was olive oil.

This particular lunker would be worth it.

He'd grill it over charcoal and hickory within the hour, and enjoy it with a syrupy local concoction everyone in town called a coke.

"Hey, Valentine," he heard a voice call. He looked up. "Reservoir Dan," the man who'd rented him the boat and tackle—and who accepted money only for bait " 'cause that's an actual expense" after seeing his Southern Command ID, stood at the pier, stubbing out one of the ration cigarettes Valentine had insisted that he accept. "Got a message for you—hey, you did good."

Valentine held the fish a little higher. "Got it near the stumps on the north side."

"You try that spinner?"

"That's what got him. What was the message?" Dan would go all afternoon about local fishing with the tiniest prompt.

"Some girl on a bike from the Ark. Said they ran your paper down and that you could come by anytime."

"I hope anytime includes after lunch," Valentine said. "Join me?"

"I'll bring the sweet potato pie," Dan said, smacking his lips.

Half a bass and a thick wedge of pie heavier, Valentine caught a lift on a military shuttle horse cart to the SEARK campus. Everything went faster this time, from surrendering his weapon at the gate to admittance to the Miskatonic.

This time Zhin brought him back to her office. The researcher had a deft hand at indoor gardening; assorted spider plants shot out tiny versions of themselves from the top of every file cabinet and bookcase, taking advantage of the window's southern exposure.

A young man she introduced as Peter Arnham, who seemed to prefer rumpled clothes two sizes too big for him, stood up nervously when Valentine entered.

"This isn't a trial, son," Valentine said. "I'm just doing legwork for a man who's missing his."

"I didn't know Hunter Staff Cats—Cats with the rank of major, anyway—did their own legwork," Arnham said.

"I'm not staff yet," Valentine said.

The Miskatonic researchers looked at each other and shrugged. He knew as little about their world as they did his.

"Everyone just sit," Zhin suggested. "This isn't a formal briefing, nothing like it."

They did so.

"Val, you're free to ask Peter here whatever you like. We don't know much about this; we're holding nothing back."

Valentine sensed an edge to her voice that hadn't been there before.

"You think I'm on an assignment?" Valentine asked.

"We know you work with cover stories and so on."

Valentine leaned forward. "No. It's really what I told you. I'm inquiring for a friend, a fellow officer, William Post. This isn't prep for an operation, not by a long shot."

"It's just that the mule list is a bit of a mystery to us too," Zhin said. "We thought maybe someone was finally looking into it."

"Mule list?"

"Just a shorthand we use," Zhin said. "Solon's departure left behind a real treasure trove of documentation—we've never gotten this complete a picture of human resource processing in the Kurian Zone before. We've had to add and train dozens of people just to sift through it all."

Arnham added: " 'Mule list' is a term we use because all these women appear to carry something the Kurians are interested in. We know it's not blood type or anything obvious, like Down's. About all we know is that only women are tested, and that if they come up positive for it they're immediately packed up and shipped off."

"How do you know it's a positive? List I saw just had an X under 'Result.' "

"Intellectual shorthand," Zhin said. "We just call it a positive. That's the kind of optimists we got here." Zhin and Arnham both chuckled.

"Why the 'she's gone for good' note?"

"I thought he deserved to know." Arnham stared levelly at Zhin. "I don't think that sort of thing should be kept a secret. Like I said, all the security shit is hurting us more—"

"Let's keep this on point, Peter," Zhin said.

Zhin turned in her chair to Valentine. "This Gail, your officer's wife, is most likely dead. Everything we know about the mule list says that they're put on priority trains with extra security and shipped out. Handling is similar to what happens when your Wolves or Bears are captured. We know Hunters are interrogated and killed at a special medical facility; that's been established. Doctors working for the Kurians do a lot of pathology on the bodies."

Valentine had heard rumors along those lines before.

"Have you looked into the family background of your mule list? Do they come from Hunter parents?"

"A few," Arnham said. "Not enough for a real correlation."

"What is the test?"

"Don't know. They take a small amount of blood. Like an iron check when you donate."

Valentine had given enough blood in Southern Command's medical units to know what that meant. A drop or two squeezed from a finger cut. "And then?"

"They drop it in a test tube. We know the negatives stay clear."

"How many show up as positives?"

"Less than one percent," Arnham answered.

"About one out of a hundred and fifty or so, looks like," Zhin said, checking another paper.

Valentine wondered if any of his known unknowns were filled in, or if this just represented a new unknown popping up. "But these women present a danger to the Kurians?"

Arnham's lips tightened. "I didn't say that. I said they were treated that way. Look, we're in the dark about as much as you. We're laying it all out there."

He rooted around in his folios and passed a binder to Valentine. Inside were six tabs. Each had a list from a testing station similar to the one he sent Post.

"Your girl's in the yellow-tabbed one," Arnham said.

71

Valentine nodded and flipped to the list. The sheets were the same as the others, a bare list of negatives. Female names, no particular ethnic background to them

Valentine's heart thudded before his brain knew why.

Melissa Carlson.

The rest of the room faded away for a second as the name held his attention. Melissa . . . Molly . . . the woman whose family had helped him in his trip across Wisconsin, who he'd gone to the Zoo in Chicago to save when she caught the eye of a sexually avaricious Quisling *nomenklatura* and murdered him. . . .

"You okay there, Val?" Zhin asked.

No result next to Molly's name. She hadn't been put on a train. Molly's sister Mary was just below her on the list; she'd been tested too, also no *X* in the result column.

But she had been tested. She'd been tested at the same location as Gail Foster. Why was she listed as Molly Carson? She'd married her Guard lieutenant . . . *What was his name . . . Stockton, no, Stockard. Graf Stockard.*

"Fine. You keep the big directories here, right? The Southern Command Military Census?"

"Yes, of course."

"Can I have a browse?"

"Sure. A name ring a bell?" Zhin guessed.

*Not just a bell. A gong and clattering cymbals.*

# CHAPTER FOUR

*C*rowley's Ridge, Arkansas: Running southwest-northeast through the eastern part of the state, straight as though drawn on the map with a ruler, Crowley's Ridge varies from about two hundred to five hundred feet high, up to a dozen miles wide, and several hundred miles long. Once the next thing to terra incognita in Southern Command, with only a few precariously placed settlements hugging the Saint Francis, it is now considered the "civilized" eastern border for the defenders of the freehold.

The northeastern part of the state suffered literally earth-shattering devastation in the New Madrid quake and never recovered. Now the expanse between the Ridge and Memphis is a tangled floodplain for the newly feral Mississippi and its tributaries, like the Saint Francis, briefly bridged by a few pieces of road and a railroad line during Solon's tenure in the Ozarks.

Solon intended for Crowley's Ridge to be his eastern border and set up the outposts, along with a road and rail network to serve them. Southern Command's Guards were only too happy to assume their upkeep when Valentine's Rising and Archangel put Solon's incorporations into receivership. Now this series of Guard Outposts holds the line here, supplying smaller Hunter formations that explore the flat lands extending to the Mississippi and beyond.

Perhaps no area is more patrolled and contested than the corridor that runs along the old interstate that once linked Memphis and Little Rock. A few Kurians maintain their towers on the west side of the river within sight of Memphis, sending their Reapers into the wilderness to hunt refugees, smugglers, or out-and-out brigands, while

*Southern Command sends Cats and Wolves into the corridor to hunt the Reapers.*

φ

*You're not doing this in order to see her,* David Valentine told himself for the umpteenth time. She's smart, a good observer. Perhaps Molly even knew Gail.

*No, her letters trickled off and you want to know why,* a more honest part of Valentine said.

*Shut up the both of you,* someone whose name might be Super-ego interjected.

Valentine got the feeling he was being watched as he walked up the road running along the western side of Crowley's Ridge. Molly Carlson Stockard's name had turned up as residing at a military camp called Quapaw Post, and a quick message to the CO—Valentine justified it as a joint inquiry with the Miskatonic—revealed that she lived at the Post as a "Class A" dependant, which meant she didn't just live on post, but worked there as well.

A forty-mile train ride, ten-mile wagon hitch, and a two-mile hike brought him to this quiet corner of Southern Command, well north of the corridor.

He bore a full set of arms, as any serving officer in Southern Command did, even on leave. The Atlanta Gunworks assault rifle formerly shouldered by the Razors bumped against his back inside an oiled leather sheath to keep the wet and dirt off. The freehold had learned long ago that the more people trained to carry guns there were traipsing around the rear areas, the less likely they were to have to use them, whether threatened by the lawless or by the emissaries of the awful law that was the Kurian Zone.

He had to stop himself from jogging or falling into his old Wolf lope. He wanted to arrive more or less composed, not sweaty and bedraggled. He regretted that he didn't already have his staff crossbar, or he'd probably have been able to requisition a trap or even a motorcycle.

Quapaw Post didn't look like much; one thick concrete shell that probably enclosed a generator, armory, and fuel supply. A pair of identical, cavernous barns and a few wooden barracks, with a tower at the center for fresh water and sentries, rounded out the station. Miles of fencing stood along either side of the road and extended up into the oak-and-hickory-thick hills of the ridge and west into the alluvial flats, where the fields were subdivided into pasture and hay fields. Horses grazed and swished each other in the gauzy sun, and nearer to the road insects harvested the nectar of butterfly weed and wild bellflowers.

Evidently Quapaw Post supported Southern Command horseflesh. Horses on active duty needed a break as often—probably more often—as the men they carried.

Quapaw Post's CO, a captain by the name of Valdez, met him personally at the gate. Valdez varied his Guard uniform in that he wore camp shorts and leather sandals. Valentine got the impression this corner of Southern Command was not frequently inspected.

"A walking major?" Valentine heard the sentry ask his captain.

"Ex-Wolf. I checked him out; he's a good man on leave," Valdez said. "Oh, he can probably hear you by now, Crew."

"Long as it ain't a Bear, is all."

The Captain hallooed a greeting with Valentine a few strides away.

"Welcome to the Quapaw, Major," Valdez said. "You're welcome to my room, as I've got a cot in my office, or there's all kinds of space in the barns."

"If you don't mind flies and horseshi—" the sentry started.

"The barn is fine, Captain," Valentine said. The captain shook his hand and led him past some weedy sandbags to the official starting point of the base, a line of painted rocks. Valentine looked around. "Do you train the mounts here, or just feed them?"

"Both. That widow you asked about, Molly, she's one of our civilian trainers."

"Widow?"

"MIA technically, over six months, so that makes her a widow on the books."

"Does she know I'm coming?"

"I kept my mouth shut. But you know a small post."

"No sense wasting time. I'd like to see her."

"You're invited to a dinner with the other officers. Unless

75

you'll be umm, otherwise occupied." Valdez made a point of nudging a path-bordering rock back into line, where it guarded some fragrant tomato vines.

"Tell your officers to dress down, this isn't an official visit. If they'd rather play cards over beer—"

Valdez brightened. "Your credit's good here, if you want to get in on a game. My kebabs are very popular if you like finger food."

"Sick horses have to go sometime. Glad to see border station duty's still the same." They turned up a little row of what looked like trailers with the wheels removed.

"You will want to get back to the electricity soon enough, I'm sure. Here we are."

Valentine recognized the bunkhouses. Known as "twenty by eights"—though a screened-in porch that could be opened on one end gave them dimensions closer to thirty feet in length—the easily constructed prefab bunkhouses were the backbone of Southern Command's dependant housing.

This one had the screened porch, and a thriving band of hostas living in the semishade under the floor, set a foot off the ground by concrete blocks.

Molly stood on the other side of the screen door. She seemed to shimmer a bit. Perhaps it was the water in his eyes.

A tiny, dark-haired figure clung to one of her legs. A tabby cat watched the drama from the tar-shingle roof.

"David?" she said.

"Hello, Molly." *Say something else!* "How are you?"

"I'll take your rig over to the barn," Valdez put in.

Valentine released his pack, grateful for something to do with his body.

When he'd had the barn office pointed out and said good-bye to the captain, Molly had the screen door open. She stood a few pounds heavier, her eyes were a little more tired perhaps, but her hair shone with its same golden glory. If anything, it was a little longer and fuller, drawn back from her cheekbones into a single braid. Some of the wariness that he'd come to know all too well on their trip back to the Free Territory still haunted her. She wore a civvied version of the old female Labor Regiment top, cheered up by a set of silver buttons, and a simple jean skirt with a built-in apron-pouch. She smelled like lavender.

The child had her creamy skin, or maybe it just looked light set against the boy's dark hair and eyes. If he and Molly had had a child the boy might have ended up looking like that.

"I'm sorry about Graf," Valentine said.

"Thank you. I'm adapting." Her eyes kept striking the scar on his face, then circling away, then coming back to it, alighting just for a flash before looking away.

Valentine was used to the reaction. In an hour or two, or tomorrow, it would just be another part of his face.

"You never told me—"

"This is Edward," Molly said, picking the boy up with an easy grace that suggested that she did it a hundred times a day.

"Edwid," the child agreed.

"Edward, say 'hi' to David."

The child didn't want to say hi and buried his face in his mother's neck.

"I smell like a long trip," Valentine said.

"Is that why you're limping?"

"I fell badly," Valentine sort of lied, leaving out the bullet entering his leg that precipitated the fall.

"He's two and he's got his own mind about people. Six months ago he giggled at strangers and grabbed their fingers."

Valentine did some mental math. If Molly had given birth about two years ago, the baby had been conceived at the end of his summer as a Quisling Coastal Marine in the *Thunderbolt*. Tripping over Post's square liquor bottles in the cabin they shared. The phony marriage to Duvalier. Had Molly's stomach quivered that August night the way it had when—

*Stop that insanity. . . .*

"I want to get cleaned up. Can I do that, and then we'll talk?"

"The only water in here is for the sink. We share flush toilets and showers at the end of the street. There's a hose that works at the stable, too; the vet room has a sluice in the center. Sometimes I'll just hook the hose in the ceiling there after work and shower."

"I'll do that. Back in an hour?"

"Do you want dinner with us?"

"Yes," Valentine said. Probably too eagerly. "If it's not trouble for you and Edward."

"You changed my whole definition of trouble," Molly said, but she smiled when she said it. "No, an extra plate is no trouble at all."

φ

Dinner that night passed in uncomfortable small talk.

The bunkhouse had a tiny folding table that just fit the child's high chair and the two adults. A propane stove—natural gas was obtainable in the Ozarks, almost plentiful compared to some parts of the country—with two burners and an oven made up a tiny kitchen annex. A bead curtain partition separated a couple of twin beds that sat under a few pictures and a black-framed set of military ribbons and decorations.

Molly described, in broad strokes, her marriage to Graf Stockard, and life at home for her father and sister—her mother had finally succumbed to the illness that the doctors described only as "malignant cancer" (were there any nonmalignant varieties, Valentine wondered) while he had been crossing the Great Plains Gulag with Duvalier. She largely skipped over "the occupation," and somehow Valentine couldn't ask her about the testing as the horsemeat stew changed place with a strawberry cobbler on the table, if not in the smears on Edward's face. *Are you keeping your promise to Post or trying to get back into her bed?*

Of course conversing without really talking was an old habit of his and Molly's. They'd been that way ever since the zoo. She grew more animated when she described her duties as a civilian horse trainer.

When they said good night under a moth-shrouded lamp, both bled relief into the chill spring night.

Valentine spent the next day with Valdez, who wanted an opinion on some beadwork one of his men had found in a bush. On the way there he expounded on the virtues of sandals for soldiers, waxing eloquent on both their hygiene and durability benefits. They examined the site where the piece had been found, but neither

Valentine nor any of the men could find tracks, and they returned to Valdez's office in the cool of the concrete redoubt.

"It's pretty dirty," Valentine said, evaluating what he supposed was a bracelet. "The leather's dried. Looks like Grog work, but I'm thinking a crow spotted it somewhere and decided to add it to his collection. Weren't the Grogs in this area during the occupation?"

"Fighting with the TMCC," the sergeant who brought it to Captain Valdez's attention added, referring to the Trans-Mississippi Combat Corps. Valentine had worn their uniform during his ruse in Little Rock.

"How'd it go with the Carlson girl?" Valdez asked after the sergeant had left, with an order to pass news of the find up to the brigade headquarters in Forrest City. He filled two glass tumblers with water and added a splash of something that smelled like it was trying to be gin.

"Why isn't she the 'Stockard girl'?"

"That *chulo* gave up on his family when he ran." Valdez opened an envelope resting in his in box, tossed it back like a fish too small to be kept, and sat down. He waved to a chair against the wall. Valentine pulled it up and thanked him for the drink by raising his glass halfway across the ring-stained desk.

"Ran?"

"Yes. I heard he and a few other cowards ran north into Grog land. He left a note saying that he'd send for her once he was established. I understand the Grogs sometimes employ men as mechanics and so on."

"She told you this?"

"No. As I said, it is a small post."

"Then what do you know about me?"

"From gossip? Nothing. But I've been around enough men to know when one is thinking about losing himself in a woman. You should do whatever you came here to do and leave again."

Valentine at once liked and disliked his temporary host. He liked the open way Valdez offered what could be construed as criticism, and disliked him because the criticism was so near the mark.

That afternoon he kept Molly company while she worked, cooling and calming the horses down after they'd been trotted on a long lead. Edward spent his days in the company of a B-dependant, an older woman who'd lost her husband and two sons to Southern Command's Cause.

They quit early when an afternoon drizzle started up.

Afterward, Molly hung the traces up in the tack room to dry.

"Is Mary still horse crazy?" Valentine asked, smelling the rich, oiled leather and remembering the preteen's currycomb obsession in Wisconsin.

"She discovered boys just before . . . everything."

"Where is she now?"

"They took her away."

"I thought she tested negative," Valentine said, and realized the implications of his words.

"Tested negative? What does that have to do with it?"

"I—"

"A gang of soldiers saw a fourteen-year-old girl they liked in a bread line and just took her." Valentine heard a fly futilely buzzing in a spider's web from the tack room's corner; in the stalls a horse nickered to an associate. Only human ears had the capacity to appreciate the grief in Molly's voice. "They killed her for the fun of it. According to our mouthpiece, they did get a trial and one of them was convicted for murder. Who knows what really happened."

"They do, for a start. I wouldn't mind talking it over with one of them."

"They're probably dead, Dave. Was it always like this in the Free Territory? When you talked about it with me in Wisconsin . . . seems like everyone's either dead or has dead family."

"You're not saying it was better back there?"

"No, not better. Easier. You always had the option of believing all the lies, too. Why are you here, David? It's not the sort of place soldiers spend their leave."

"Let's find somewhere to sit."

"I'll take you to my spot," she said, and extended her hand.

Valentine took it, wondering.

She took him out of the barn and to a portion of fence that projected from a side door. Extra hay bales sat here on wooden pallets, under a wooden awning to keep the rain off, a sort of ramshackle add-on to the aluminum structure that a pair of carpenters had probably put up in a day.

She scooted up onto one of the bales and sat looking at the springtime green of Crowley's Ridge, rising less than a mile away. "I like the view," she said. "Normally I eat with Edward and the other kids, but sometimes Carla takes the kids out for the day to the duck pond. Then I just eat my lunch here."

"Remember that day we sat on the hill and talked about your dad's setup for us?"

She tilted her head back with eyes closed. "Yes. God, I was young."

"You're still young."

"You're not," she said, startling Valentine a little. "Afraid of a little honesty? You're not that earnest young lieutenant anymore. You used to look at me. It gave me—kind of a tickle. Now you stare through me. Through that ridge, as a matter of fact."

"I'm here because your name came up in something we're looking into. A test that you—and your sister—took involving a blood draw."

"That's it?" she asked.

Valentine nodded.

"This has nothing to do with Graf?"

"Should I be asking you about him?"

"He's a good man. Was a good man. Guard duty was his world. When that went away he had nothing."

"He had you and a child."

"A prison camp's not much of a place for either. Don't you want to know about the boob test?"

Valentine wasn't so sure any more. "Why do you call it that?"

"That's what we called it in Wisconsin. They gave all the girls the same thing at about thirteen or fourteen. Just when you got your boobs so we called it the boob test."

"How do you know it's the same?" Valentine asked.

Molly twisted a piece of straw around her finger. "They did the same thing both times. Line up all the girls—well, it was all the women in Pine Bluff, I suppose, since they were just getting us organized. Usual health check with a tongue depressor and ther- mometer and listening to your heart and lungs."

"Okay."

"At the end they took a little wooden stick, smaller than a knit- ting needle, and scratched you with the end. Some gals got a big welt from it. To get released from the exam you had to show your arm. Most of us got a red mark, on some it raised a welt—it didn't on me or my sister—then, for those who didn't react, the nurse drew some blood and dropped it in a test tube."

"I don't suppose you asked—"

"Both times. They said it checked for infection."

"What happened when they put the blood in the test tube?"

"Nothing. It just dissolved."

"Do you remember if there was anyone who had it do any- thing else?"

Molly's face scrunched up. "Not in Wisconsin, but they only checked about eight of us. They plucked out some women from the group in Pine Bluff, I recall. A bunch of others kind of kicked up at that, and the women taken were yelling out messages to friends, but the soldiers said something like, 'They've got it made, they're going to Memphis priority style,' or something like that. Maybe it was just to calm everyone down."

"Memphis?" Valentine said.

"Yes, I'm sure about Memphis. Memphis in style."

"Wait here a moment, okay?"

"Sure."

Valentine trotted up to his pack and extracted Post's flyer. He returned to Molly and showed her the picture.

"Did you see her there?"

"That wasn't the woman I saw taken away. She was sorta black." She looked more closely at the picture. "She's pretty."

"She's my friend's wife. He wants to know what happened to her."

She yanked some more straw out of the bale and tossed it piece by piece into the breeze. "When they take you away it's never good. Never. That guard was just talking for the sake of talk."

"I don't suppose you saw the train leave or the uniforms of the men who took her."

"No. You know how they are with that stuff. Someone disappears through a door or behind a curtain and then they're just gone."

She stood up with a little hop. "Now. Your question's been answered. You can go."

"I wasn't the one who got married and quit writing," Valentine said. He saw her eyes go wet.

"Go join one of the nightly card games with Valdez and the corporals, David. Go and learn about a bad hand. We were a bad hand, that's all. You played it well back in Wisconsin, you did right by me and my family, but it was still a bad hand. Leave me—us—alone."

Valentine stood up too, and regretted it. He was a good six inches taller than Molly and the last thing he wanted to do was physically intimidate her. "What 'us'? You and me or you and your son? I've got a daughter, Molly. She's a thousand miles away and all I know is that she was born, but she's a piece of me. Just like you." He took a step back.

"A piece, you mean."

"Don't! Molly, just don't. It wasn't that way, not with us, not with Mo—Malita. Don't play with words and think that'll change what happened."

An arch collapsed inside her. "Crap," she said, and sniffled.

"You want me to go?"

"Yes. No—no. Do what you have to. You're built for it."

He spoke softly. "What's that supposed to mean?"

"One of the old hands in Weening used to say you Wolves and whatnot, the aliens came and took out your hearts and put in those of horses and pigs and lions or whatever to make you so you could stand up to them. You weren't human anymore, not on the inside."

"We drank some kind of medicine. That's it."

"You can eat with us tonight if you want. Or just leave—I'll understand. That trail you're on's cold enough." She turned and went quickly into the barn, and Valentine got the distinct feeling she didn't want to be followed.

She didn't want anything from him at all.

ɸ

He borrowed a horse from Valdez—"We've got plenty that need exercise; take one!"—and rode the big quarter horse hard down to Forrest City. He posted a letter summarizing the relevant pieces of his conversation with Molly to the Miskatonic and saw to the feeding and care of his borrowed gelding. A few hundred dollars of back pay disappeared into the stalls and markets the next morning, and a hard afternoon's ride later he was back at Quapaw Post.

"What's all this?" Molly said at her screen door. Edward interposed himself in front of his mother.

Valentine set down canvas mailbags, and the child reached out with both hands. He was sophisticated enough to know what a big bag promised.

"Season's Greetings," Valentine said. "It's customary to give a little something in exchange for valuable information."

He reached in and extracted three bolts of fabric. "Denim, of course, and I hope you like that green. You're the kind of blond who can wear green."

A big bag of buttons came next. "Most of them match. I looked. I figured you could trade any you didn't like."

Shoes in various sizes for Edward came next, a heavy slab of bacon in waxed paper, great loops of sausage like ox yokes, some lemons and limes, candied dates, and a black-and-white ceramic cow that had probably once been a cookie jar.

He'd let Molly discover the cookies inside on her own, if Edward didn't first.

"Thought it looked like the cows in Wisconsin."

"Holsteins," Molly said, her hand at her throat.

Tea, powdered sugar, a bottle of brandy, even elastic-banded socks and underwear—luxuries all, smuggled from the Kurian Zone, no doubt, but it was considered bad taste to ask a trader questions beyond quality—all joined the growing pile on the tiny table.

"And some cans of jelly," Valentine finished.

"Jelly!" Edward said.

"You're too . . . too much, David. They were just words, and I was angry."

"I thought it was kind of refreshing. First time we'd been honest with each other since . . . well, your dad's basement."

Molly blushed, but just a little. "We were just about to have macaroni and ration cheese." The tiniest pause after "macaroni" told Valentine all he needed to know about what she thought of Southern Command's "cheese"—an oily yellow concoction that tasted faintly like axle grease. "I can fill another plate."

"Fine."

They ate on the steps of the porch rather than clear off the table. "It occurred to me on the ride back that I didn't know if you could sew," Valentine said. "I recall you were good with leather."

"Not like my mom. But I'm getting better."

One of Molly's civilian neighbors, a tight-faced, tan woman, walked by and took a second look at Valentine. Then she turned her face straight to home with everything but an audible *hmpff*.

After Edward went to bed they talked. Looking back on it Valentine realized that he talked and Molly listened. Beck and leaving the Wolves, Duvalier and training as a Cat, the Eagle D Brand in Nebraska's sand hills, the wild night of fire in the General's hangar, Jamaica, Haiti, ratbits, finding out that he'd be a father one rainy day in the Texas pinewoods. The deaths of M'Daw and and the Smalls, Hank. He raised his shirt and she touched the burns on his back.

He couldn't feel whether her fingertips probed or caressed. The surface nerves were mostly dead.

It felt so good to talk about it, maybe because Molly was a piece of his life dating back to before so much of it had happened.

"I can't sit anymore. There's a beautiful moon," Molly said. "You want to take a walk?"

Valentine wasn't sure he did. Or he wasn't sure of the part of himself that did, anyway. "What about Edward?"

"Mrs. Colbert can listen for him. She hears everything that goes on in the cabin anyway. It's all of eight feet away."

"Anything to help Southern Command's cheese along," Valentine said. "You'd think something that greasy—"

"What is it about soldiers and their bowels?" Molly asked. "You'd think with a woman and a moon and a warm night you'd just—"

Horse hooves clip-clopped through the gravel and turned up the little lane running between the rows of bunkhouses.

Four men on horseback leading a fifth saddled horse appeared. One of Valdez's men walked ahead, and pointed toward Molly's cabin.

Valentine could make out the uniforms even in the dim light. The two in back were Wolves; there was no mistaking the trademark soft buckskins and fringed rifle sheaths. The others wore the plain khaki and the round-brimmed "Smokey" hats of the Rounders, Southern Command's law enforcement branch.

Usually veteran Guards, the Rounders patrolled the roads and bridges of Southern Command keeping the population safe from "bummers"—people in the Ozarks without a stake of one kind or another, who were often conduits of everything from black-market antibiotics to military information—and outright criminals.

The Rounders often brought bad news to the harder-to-reach families as well. *Rounder on the doorstep* was a phrase that meant misfortune to most people living outside the towns.

"Rounders," Molly said, echoing his thoughts.

The horses stopped in front of her cabin and Edward appeared, seeking the comfort of her hem. She picked her son up.

Valentine went to the screen door of the tiny porch.

"You Major Valentine?" a man with jowls spilling over his frayed collar asked as he approached.

The Wolves stayed on their horses. One looked halfway familiar to Valentine—then it came to him; he'd been a Wolf at his Invocation, though the name escaped him. The Wolves' hands were conspicuously off their weapons.

"Could you step outside, sir?" The jowly man's laminated name tag said Goebbert.

"What's this about?"

"Just step outside, please, sir."

They ignored Molly and her wide-eyed child. As Valentine came out the Wolves got off their horses.

"You're a hard guy to find, Valentine," the other Rounder put in. He had cockeyed ears, like a hound listening to a raccoon on the roof. He handed a pair of handcuffs to Goebbert.

"Sir, please turn around and put your hands behind you."

Valentine's heart fired like a triphammer. *What the hell?*

"What's this about?" Valentine repeated, sounding a lot less like a major this time.

"You're under arrest for murder," Goebbert said.

"Murder?" Valentine felt sweat everywhere.

Goebbert grabbed him firmly by the wrist. "Sorry, Major, orders."

They patted him down. Valentine winced as the hard hands traveled over the old scar tissue on the backs of his legs.

"David, what's going on?" Molly asked from her porch. She held Edward sideways, putting her body in between her son and the four strangers.

"It's got to be a mistake," Valentine said, looking again at the Wolf. Hammond, that was his name. The other young Wolves called him "Lightning" because he had a little tuft of blond hair in his brown.

"Might be," Goebbert said. "But we have to take you to court. Okay, Jim, he's in custody. Make a note of the time."

"Hammond, what is this?" Valentine asked.

Hammond might have smiled—his walrus mustache changed shape—though Valentine wondered why he would look pleased to be recognized by someone being arrested for murder. "We just got orders to make sure you come in. These boys were scared you'd get wind and take to the hills."

Molly had doubt in her eyes; she squinted against it as she might protect herself against dust.

"Molly, I'm not a fugitive. I wasn't hiding with you."

"Enough, Major," Goebbert said. "We've got to get you away. Help him mount, Hammond."

"Put him up backward. Fugitive mount," Uneven Ears said. "They say he's tricky."

The Wolves helped him mount. Sitting backward on the saddle made the night even more surreal. "My gear's in the barn—"

"It'll come along," the other Wolf put in.

"Where are you taking him?" Molly blurted, perhaps too emotionally, for Edward started to cry.

"Crowley Garrison Station, then on to Fort Allnutt, ma'am," Goebbert replied. Valentine craned his neck around and saw Goebbert shaking his head at his fellow Rounder.

David Valentine rode out of Quapaw Post backward. The soldiers came out of their cabins to see the "rogue parade," wondering faces glowing in the moonlight like jack-o'-lanterns.

They showed their paperwork at the gate, and carried out his gear on the Wolves' horses. Valentine, facing backward on his mount, carried only the memory of the fear in Edward Stockton's eyes. And the doubt in Molly's.

# CHAPTER FIVE

*The Nut, May: The Nut was an Arkansas State Medium Security Correctional Facility known as Pine Ridge before the Kurian Order, and would probably have remained another overgrown jumble of fence and concrete were it not for Mountain Home, the nearby town that fate selected to be the capital of the Ozark Free Territory (2028–2070).*

*There are any number of legends as to how Mountain Home ("Gateway to the Ozarks") became the seat of the Free Territory and the headquarters of Southern Command. The more colorful legends involve a poker game, a fistfight, a bad map, a general's mistress, or a souvenir shot glass, but the most likely story concerns Colonel "Highball" Holloway and her wayward signals column.*

*The colonel and her sixteen vehicles were one of hundreds of fragments fleeing the debacle south of Indianapolis that marked the end of the United States government as most Americans recognized it. While topping a hill northeast of Mountain Home two of her trucks collided, and Colonel Holloway established her signals company in the nearby town of Mountain Home. USAF General J. N. Probst, in charge of a substantial shipment of the first ravies vaccine, heard Holloway's test transmissions and rerouted his staff to make use of the army's facilities. Soon the fragments of everything from National Guard formations to a regiment of Green Berets were being inoculated and reorganized around Mountain Home. Civilians flocked to the protection of the military guns and vehicles, and a government had to be established to manage them. Some chafing in the first years as to whether Southern Command ran the Ozark Free Territory or the Ozark civilians ran Southern Command settled into the American tradition of military subordination to civilian au-*

*thority—provided the civilians abided by the Constitution and held reg-*
*ular elections.*

*In those chaotic years the only law was martial—unless one counts*
*the occasional lunchtime trial and afternoon hanging of looters and*
*"profiteers" by horse- and bike-mounted posses. Military justice required*
*an incarceration facility, and as the only other prison nearby was being*
*used to house ravies sufferers in the hope of finding a cure, Pine Ridge*
*became Fort Allnutt, named for its first commander.*

*Sometime after his death it became "the Nut."*

*The Nut is an asterisk-shaped building that might pass as a college*
*dormitory were it not for the bars on the windows. Double lines of fenc-*
*ing separate it from the fields—the prisoners grow their own crops and*
*raise their own livestock, and the better behaved they are the more time*
*they get outside the wire—and subsidiary buildings have sprung up*
*around it. Two technical workshops, a health clinic, the guard dorm,*
*and the courthouse that doubles as an administrative center surround*
*the six-story concrete asterisk. Finally there's "the Garage," an alu-*
*minum barn that houses a few wrecks used for spare parts. The Garage*
*is where condemned men are hung, traditionally at midnight on their*
*day of execution.*

ψ

Valentine was proud of his memory, but in later years he never recalled his arrival at the Nut with any real clarity. Mostly he remembered a military lawyer reading the charges against him to a
gray and grave presiding officer: torture and murder of prisoners
under his supervision during the rising in Little Rock the wild
night of what was occasionally being called Valentine's Rising.

Six men had died at the hands of the women he'd freed from
the Kurian prison camp. They were guards who had used dozens
of women under their supervision as sort of a personal harem.
Valentine had never known their names and it was strange to hear
them read out in court with all the formality that legal proceedings
required—one wasn't known by any name other than "Claw."

Southern Command rarely tried its officers for the execution of
armed Quislings—men caught fighting for the vampires were disposed of under a procedure informally called "bang-and-bury."

Two generations of bitter feelings between the sides, and the Kurian habit of sending their own armed prisoners straight to the Reapers, had hardened both sides.

"The court finds cause for a trial." Valentine remembered that phrase. The judge declared that Valentine should be kept within Fort Alnutt until the date of his trial, set for the end of the month: May twenty-third, to be precise.

This rapidity struck Valentine as strange; his knowledge of Southern Command jurisprudence was based on one bad hearing after the destruction of Foxtrot Company at Little Timber Hill and the occasional *Southern Command Bulletin* article, and it was rare to be tried within six months of one's arrest.

And with those words he went dumbly through the sanitary procedures at the jail entrance, climbed into shapeless baby-blue scrubs with large yellow *X*s sewn onto the back, each leg, and the chest pocket, and went to his cell.

His cell he remembered. As a major he got his own room in what his guard escort told him was the nicer wing of the Nut. There was a door with a small glass window rather than bars, and windows that would open to admit a breeze, though the sturdy metal frame was designed so that he couldn't crawl out.

The room had five one-foot-square green linoleum floor tiles across, and nine deep. The bolted-down bed bore a single plastic-wrapped mattress and a depressed-looking pillow in a cotton case that smelled like bleach, as did his combination sink and toilet. His ceiling had a brown-painted light fixture but no bulb: "They don't waste fluorescent tubes on cons, so the sun decides 'lights out,' " the guard said. "Hot chow in the cafeteria twice a day, and we bring out a soup and bread cart to the exercise yard for lunch. Questions?"

"How do I get a shave?" Valentine asked, rubbing his three-day beard.

The guard, whose name tag read Young, but looked as though his first name should be "Gus" or "Mick" or something else hearty and friendly, stuck his thumb in a belt loop. "There's two razors in the showers. You have to use them under supervision. Be sure to put it back in the blue cleanser—"

"I'm not a suicide."

"Didn't say you were. We keep an eye on sharp edges here. Lots of the guys just grow beards until trial."

Valentine looked at what appeared to be a hundred keys at the guard's waist. "Is there a library?"

"Mostly paperbacks held together with rubber bands, and porn. There's a bookcase or two for the highbrows. We've got a store with the *Provisional Journal* and *Serial Digest* for sale; you can earn money in the fields or with janitorial work. Kitchen's full up now."

"Thank you." The formal politeness came out despite the circumstances.

"No problem, Major Valentine. Good luck with the trial. There's a packet of rules and instructions under your pillow. We do an hourly pass through if you need anything."

"A lawyer would be nice."

"You'll have a meeting tomorrow or the next day."

His uniform "scrubs" were poorly finished on the inside. Loose threads tickled whenever he walked. By the time he finished biting off the stray threads with his teeth it was time for dinner.

Officers awaiting trial had a small cafeteria to themselves. Valentine ended up being at the end of the blue-and-yellow file escorted by Young and another guard to the central cafeteria.

Dinner, plopped onto a tray and eaten with a bent-tined fork and a spoon that looked as though it dated from the War of 1812, consisted of an unappetizing vegetable goulash with ground meat.

Two clusters of officers ate together at opposite sides of the cafeteria. A narrow man with long, thinning, butterscotch hair in the smaller of the two cliques looked up at Valentine and made a motion to the seat next to him, but Valentine just dropped into the seat nearest the end of the food service line—and immediately regretted it. He felt alone and friendless, as though already dead, forgotten and entombed in this prison. After dinner some of the men smoked, and Valentine went to the slitlike barred windows and enjoyed the breeze created by the kitchen extractor fans. The Ozarks were black in the distance, the sun masked by haze.

"Shooter or looter?" a reedy voice said.

*Didn't even hear him come.* Valentine felt thick and tired, brain too apathetic to even function—if he didn't know better he'd suspect one of the mild Kurian sedatives had been put in the food.

He looked at the man, short and close to bald, with an ivory mustache and growing beard, smoking a cigarette from a whittled holder. The eyes were crinkled and friendly.

"Pardon?"

"Shooter or looter, boy? You're the new squirrel in the nut. What they got you in for?"

Valentine tried to make sense of the metaphor and gave up. "Murder. Quislings."

"Then you're a shooter. That's those three over there." He turned his chin in the direction of the group with the long-haired man. "I'm Berlinelli. Malfeasance in the performance of my duties."

"Meaning?"

"Looter. I was doing what a lot of other guys were doing, on a larger scale. Siphoning gasoline and diesel out of captured trucks and selling it."

"I thought everyone in prison was innocent," Valentine said, a bit startled at the man's frankness.

"If you're a snitch it's no hair lifted. I'm pleading out."

"I haven't even talked to my lawyer yet. I need to write some letters. You wouldn't know where I could get paper, would you?"

"Who's running your floor?"

"The guard? Young, I think."

"He's a decent guy. Just ask him." He tapped his wooden cigarette holder on the windowsill and winked. "Got to get back to my tribe. It's Grogs and Harpies in here; we don't mix much."

"Thanks for crossing no-man's-land."

"Just a little recon. Mission accomplished."

Valentine asked Young about paper and a pen as they locked him back in his cell. The long-haired man was two doors down.

"Ummm," Valentine said. "Corporal Young?"

"Yes, Major?"

"Could I get some paper and a pencil? I need to write a few people and let them know where I am." And he should write Post and give him the findings of the aborted investigation, which amounted to a few more facts but zero in the way of answers.

"Sure. It's a standard SC envelope; just don't seal it. Censors. I'll slip them under the door gap tonight on my rounds."

"Right. Thank you."

Young unlocked Valentine's door. Valentine couldn't help but glance at the fixture of a secondary bar, a bolt that could be slid home and twisted, fixed to the metal door and the concrete with bolts that looked like they could hold in Ahn-Kha.

"Major Valentine," Young said. "I heard about you on my break today. The fight on that hill by the river in Little Rock. It's . . . ummm . . . a privilege."

Valentine felt his eyes go a little wet. "Thank you, Corporal. Thanks for that."

A sticklike insect with waving antennae was exploring his sink. Valentine relocated it to the great outdoors by cupping it between his palms.

He gave the insect its freedom. He used to be responsible for the lives of better than a thousand men. Now he commanded an arthropod. As for the general staff training . . .

"What the hell?" he said to himself. "What the hell?"

φ

He met with his military counsel the next day right after breakfast—some sort of patty that seemed to be made of old toast and gristle, and a sweet corn mush. The officer, a taciturn captain from the JAG office named Luecke who looked as though she existed on cigarettes and coffee, laid out the charges and the evidence against him. Valentine wondered at the same military institution both prosecuting and defending him, and, incidentally, acting as judge. Most of the evidence was from two witnesses, a captured Quisling who'd been in the prison camp and a Southern Command nurse lieutenant named Koblenz who'd been horrified at the bloody vengeance wreaked by the outraged women.

Valentine remembered the latter, working tirelessly in the overwhelmed basement hospital atop Big Rock Mountain during the siege following the rising in Little Rock. He'd countersigned the surgeon's report recommending a promotion for her.

He'd sign it again, given the opportunity.

"They've got a good case. Good. Not insurmountable," Luecke said.

"And my options are?" Valentine asked.

"Plead guilty and—see what we can get. Plead 'no contest'—get a little less. Plead innocent and fight it out in front of a tribunal." She turned the cap on her pen with her fingers but kept her eyes locked on his as though trying to get a read.

"When you say 'not insurmountable' you mean?"

"Good. I like a fighter. For a start you're a Cat. We're hip-deep in precedent on Cats not getting prosecuted for collateral casualties. We can blame the women for getting out of hand—"

"I'm not hiding behind the women. Try again."

The pen cap stopped twirling for a moment. "If it were just the Quisling we could toss a lot of dust around. Lieutenant Koblenz will be tough; her statement is pretty damning." The cap resumed its Copernican course.

"She must have presented some case of charges for them to hunt me down so fast."

"She didn't file them. They talked to every woman who survived that camp and the battle. All the others couldn't remember a thing."

"Then who's behind this?" Valentine asked.

"Your former commander, General Martinez. I should say General Commanding, Interior, I suppose. He got promoted."

Valentine's head swam for a moment. When he could see the tired brown eyes of his counsel again he spoke. "He's got a grudge against me. I gave evidence at a trial—not sure if it can even be called that."

"Interesting. Tell me more."

Valentine tried to sum the story up as concisely as he could. He had come out of Texas with his vital column of Quickwood and was ambushed by "redhands"—Quisling soldiers who wore captured uniforms from Southern Command stockpiles. He had a pair of Grog scouts—they were smarter than dogs, horses, or dolphins and were far more capable fighters. The Grogs survived with a handful of others, and with a single wagonload of Quickwood made it to General Martinez, more by accident than design, at his refuge in the Ouachitas. Martinez had two of his Grogs shot at once, and it was only by putting a pistol to the general's head and arresting him for murder that Ahn-Kha survived.

The trial ended in a debacle and Martinez's camp was divided; many of the best soldiers decided to quit the place with Valentine. Ultimately they made it to Little Rock where the rising took place.

Captain Luecke remained poker-faced throughout the story, and only moved to set her pen down. "I don't know much about General Martinez, or what happened during the Kurian occupation," she said. "I spent it aspirating mosquitoes in a bayou. I'm going to ask for a delay in your trial date so I can prepare a defense, if you agree. Fair warning: It'll mean a lot more time for you in here."

She was a cold fish, but she was a very smart cold fish. As she packed up Valentine was already missing the smell of tobacco and coffee.

"Captain?" Valentine said.

"Yes, Major?"

"I'm not sure I want to fight this. I let prisoners get tortured and murdered right under my nose."

She sat back down. "I see. Guilty, then?"

"I . . ." The words wouldn't come. *Coward. You're quick to condemn others.*

"You don't have to decide this second. Can you do something for my satisfaction?"

"Yes."

"Give me the names of some of those women. And no, we're not going to point fingers and say 'they did it.' I just want to hear from all sides about what happened that night."

Valentine thought back to the too-familiar faces of the siege, especially those stilled in death. And not always faces: Petra Yao was only identified by the jewelry on the arm they found; Yolanda, who had to wear diapers thanks to the mutilation; Gwenn Cobb who walked around with her collar turned up and her shirt tightly buttoned afterward—rumor had it they'd written something on her chest with a knifepoint; the Weir sisters, who never talked about it except for their resulting pregnancies; Marta Ruiz, who hung her head and grew her hair out so it covered her eyes. . . .

*Christ, those cocksuckers should have gotten worse.*

Valentine felt the old, awful hurts and the heat of that night come back. The thing, the shadow, the demon that sometimes wore the body of "the Ghost" flooded into his bloodstream like vodka until his face went red and his knuckles white.

There were things a decent man did, whatever the regulations said, and let any man who hadn't been there be damned.

"Still want to plead guilty?" she asked.

Valentine tried lowering his lifesign. That mental ritual always helped, even when there weren't Reapers prowling. "Prepare your case."

φ

The men in the exercise yard kicked up little rooster tails of fine Arkansas dust—Valentine hadn't seen its like even in Texas; soft as baby powder and able to work its way through the most tightly laced boot—as they walked or threw a pie-tin Frisbee back and forth.

He got to know his three fellow "shooters" there. They took their sourdough bread and soup out as far from the prison as possible and sat next to the six-inch-high warning wire that kept them ten feet from the double roll of fence.

Colonel Alan Thrush was the highest-ranking, not distinguished-looking or brimming with the dash one expects from a cavalry leader. He had short legs and the deft, gentle hands of a fruit seller. "Caught a company of Quislings doing scorched earth—with the families inside—on a little village called McMichael." McMichael had risen against the Kurians in response to the governor's famous "smash them" broadcast shortly after Valentine's move on Little Rock. "Left them for the crows in a ditch."

Unfortunately, his men left the customary set of spurs on the forehead of the Quisling officer in charge, and the commander of a column of infantry following made the mistake of pointing out his handiwork to a pink-cheeked reporter who neglected to mention the charred corpses in McMichael.

Colonel Thrush intended to fight out his court-martial. He said so, slurping a little beet soup from his pannikin.

Valentine was the only major.

Captain Eoin Farland was a clean-faced, attractive man whose wire-rimmed glasses somehow made him even better-looking. A reserve officer who'd been put in charge of a fast-moving infantry company in Archangel, he'd been far out on the right flank on the drive to Hot Springs. His men recaptured a town, stayed just long enough to arm the locals, and when he asked the local mayor what to do with six captured Quislings who had gunned down a farmer hiding his meager supply of chickens and rice, the mayor said, "Shoot them."

"So I did. I'd seen it done before in the drive, especially to Quisling officers."

"But he put it in his day report. Can you believe that?" Thrush laughed. "Shoot, bury, and shut up."

"Says the man who left bodies in a ditch," Farland said.

"Not better, that's for sure," the thin man with the long, honey-colored locks said. Valentine had learned that his last name was Roderick, that he held the rank of lieutenant though he looked on the weary side of forty, and nothing about the charges against him. Every time anyone asked, he shrugged and smiled.

"Are you asking for court-martial?" Valentine asked Farland.

"No. I'm pleading guilty. They've got my paper trail. Something's holding up the show, though, and my trial date keeps getting postponed."

"As does mine," Thrush said.

"What's gonna happen is gonna happen," Roderick said. "I'm asking for lobster and real clarified butter for my last meal. How about that? Better get it."

"Shut up," Thrush said.

"You start planning yours too, Colonel."

$\psi$

Valentine only got one piece of mail his first week in the Nut. It came in an unaddressed envelope, posted from Little Rock, and bore a single line of typescript:

**HOW DO YOU LIKE IT?**

φ

"You've got a visitor, Major," Young said after the sun called lights out the next day. Valentine wondered if the guard ever got a day off. He'd seen him every day for a week.

Something felt wrong about moving across the prison floor in the dim light. Sounds traveled from far away in the prison: water running, a door slamming, Young's massive ring of keys sounding like sleigh bells in the empty hallway.

Valentine expected to be taken to some kind of booth with a glass panel and tiny mesh holes to speak through, but instead they brought him to a big, gloomy cafeteria on the second floor of the asterisk. Light splashed in from the security floods outside.

Young made a move to handcuff him to a table leg across from a brown-faced man in a civilian suit. Valentine was jealous of the man's clean smell, faintly evocative of sandalwood—in the Nut one got a new smock once a week and clean underwear twice.

Valentine wondered at the smooth sheen of his visitor's jacket. The civilian's gray suit probably cost more than everything Valentine owned—wherever they were storing it now.

"Don't bother, please," the man said, and Young put the handcuffs away. "It's an unofficial meeting. Won't you—"

Valentine sat down. He noticed his visitor nibbled his fingernails; their edges were irregular. Somehow it made him like the man a little better.

"Major Valentine, my name's Sime."

He said the name as though it should provoke instant recognition. Valentine couldn't remember ever having heard it.

Neither man made an offer to shake.

Sime tipped his head back and spoke, eventually. "I'm a special executive of our struggling new republic. Missouri by birth. Kansas City."

"How did you get out?" Valentine asked. Jesus, that used to be

99

the first question he'd ask those fleeing the Kurian Zone in his days as a Wolf. Old habits died hard.

"My mom ran. I was fourteen."

"What's a 'special executive'?" Valentine asked.

"I'm attached to the cabinet."

"That superglue is tricky stuff."

"Quick but dusty, Major."

"You are going to come to the point of this?"

"Tobacco? Maybe a little bourbon?" Sime made no move to produce either, and Valentine wondered if some assistant would emerge from the shadows of the big, dark room.

"No, thanks."

"Trying to make things more pleasant for you."

"You could get me a bar of that soap you used before meeting me."

"How—oh, of course. Ex-Wolf. I'm very sorry about all this, you know."

Valentine said nothing.

Sime leaned forward, placing his forearms on the table with interlaced, quick-bitten fingers forming a wedge pointed at Valentine. "Are you a patriot, Major?"

"A patriot?"

"Do you believe in the Cause?"

Had the man never read his service file? "Of course."

"Body and soul?"

This catechism was becoming ridiculous. "Get to the point."

Sime's eyes shone in the window light. "How would you like to do more to advance the Cause than you've ever done before? Do something that would make the rest of your service—impressive though it is—look like nothing in comparison?"

"Let me guess. It involves the charges against me disappearing. All I have to do is go back into the Kurian Zone and—"

"Quite the contrary, Major. It involves you pleading guilty."

A moment of stunned silence passed. Valentine heard Young shift his feet.

Valentine almost felt the edge of the sword of Damocles hanging above. "That helps the Cause how?"

"Major Valentine. I'm personally involved in—in charge of, in a way, some very delicate negotiations. A consortium of high-level officials in the Kurian Zone—"

"Quislings?"

Sime wrinkled his nose and opened and shut his mouth, like a cat disgusted by a serving of cooked carrots.

"Quislings, if you will," Sime continued. "Quislings who run a substantial part of the gulag in Oklahoma and Kansas. They're offering to throw in with us."

"I see why you use good soap."

"Stop it, Major."

Valentine turned toward Young.

"Listen!" Sime said, lowering his voice but somehow putting more energy into his words. "We're talking about the freedom of a hundred thousand people. Maybe more. An almost unbroken corridor to the Denver Protective Zone. Wheat, corn, oil, livestock—"

"I see the strategic benefits."

Sime relaxed a little. Valentine felt nervous, his dinner of doubtful meatloaf revisiting the back of his throat. "Still don't see how my pleading guilty helps."

"These Quislings are afraid of reprisals. Maybe not to them, but to some of the forces they command. The Provisional Government organizing the new Free Republic wants to show them that we're not going to permit atrocities."

"Show? As in show trial?"

Sime turned his head a little, as though the words were a slap. He looked at Valentine out of one baleful eye.

"You have me. You also have this: plead guilty, and it comes with an offer. You'll get a harsh sentence, most likely life, but the government will reduce it and you'll serve somewhere pleasant, doing useful work. Five years from now, after we've won a significant victory somewhere, your sentence will quietly be commuted to celebrate. You could return to service or we could arrange a quiet little sinecure at a generous salary. When was your last breakfast in bed? I recommend it."

"I have the word of a 'special executive' on that? I've never heard that title before."

"Consider it as coming from your old governor's lips. He knows what you did in Little Rock. I'm speaking for him and for the other members of the Provisional Government."

Valentine took a deep breath.

"Do this, Major, and it'll be the best kind of victory. No bloodshed."

"That's the carrot; where's the stick?"

"You haven't given me an answer yet."

"Let's say I fight it out."

"Don't."

"Let's say I do anyway," Valentine said.

Sime looked doubtful for the first time. "The Garage." The air got ten degrees warmer in the dark of the cafeteria.

"Will you accept a counteroffer?"

"I'm a negotiator. Of course."

"Do you know Captain Moira Styachowski?"

"I know the name from your reports. She served with you on Big Rock."

"Get her in here. I hear that same offer from her, and I'll take it."

"Ah, it has to come from someone you trust. I feel a little hurt, Major. Usually my title—"

"I've had a gutful of titles in the Kurian Zone. You can keep them."

"I'll see what I can do. If she's on active service I might not be able to get her."

"She's the only—no. If you can't get her, get Colonel Chalmers. I've dealt with her before."

Sime extracted a leather-bound notepad and wrote the name down. "She's with?"

"A judge with the JAG."

"Very well. Thank you for your time, Major."

"I have nothing but time."

"Don't be so sure. Take my deal." Sime looked up and waved to Young.

φ

The next day rain tamped down the dust on the exercise yard. The shooters and the looters stayed on opposite sides of the pie slice between the frowning brown wings D and E, trying to keep their pannikins full of lukewarm lentils out of the rain as they sat on long, baseball-dugout-style benches.

"Anyone got an offer from a civilian named Sime?" Valentine asked.

Farland and Thrush exchanged looks and shrugged. Roderick sucked soup out of his tin.

"We're getting pushed back again," Farland said. "God, it's like getting a shot when the doctor keeps picking up and putting down the big-bore needle."

Roderick stopped eating and stared. "I had rabies shots. Harpy bite."

"He said all this is more or less of a show. To convince some gulag Quislings that Southern Command won't just shoot them dead if they join us."

"News to me," Thrush said. He returned his pannikin to the slop bin and returned, twitching up his trousers with his deft little hands before he sat. It took Valentine a moment to remember when he'd last seen that gesture—Malia Carrasca's grandfather in Jamaica would go through that same motion when he sat. "You know, they might be firing smoke to get you to plead out."

"They've tried murderers before," Farland said. "My uncle served with Keck's raiders before they hung Dave Keck. But he killed women and children."

"And Lieutenant Luella Parsons," Roderick said. "When was that, fifty-nine?"

"She shot the mayor of Russelville," Farland put in. He wiped raindrops from his glasses and resettled them.

"Yeah, but she claimed he was working for them. Said she saw him talking to a Reaper."

"I heard they tried General Martinez himself for shooting a couple of Grogs," Roderick said.

"That makes sense," Thrush said. "If you ask me, it's a crime not to shoot 'em."

"Actually it was," Valentine said. "I was there. The two Grogs he shot were on our side."

"First I've heard of it. Were the charges dropped?" Farland asked.

Valentine shook his head.

"You made a powerful enemy, Major," Thrush said. "Martinez had a lot of friends in Mountain Home. He had the sort of command you'd send your son or daughter off to if you wanted to keep 'em out of the fight."

"Technically I was under him during Archangel. His charges are why I'm here, or that's what my counsel says."

"Bastard. Heard he didn't do much," Farland said.

"I wouldn't know. I was over in Little Rock."

Roderick grew animated. "Heard that was a hot one. You really threw some sand in their gears. What was her name, Colonel . . ."

"Kessey," Valentine put in. "She was killed early on in the fighting. Bad luck."

"What are you going to plead, Valentine?" Thrush said.

"Five minutes, gentlemen," a guard yelled, standing up from his seat next to the door.

Everyone was wet. Were they all bedraggled sacrificial sheep? "Haven't made up my mind yet."

ψ

Valentine grew used to the tasteless food, and the boring days of routine bleeding into one another and overlapping like a long hospital stay. He took a job in the prison library, but there was so little work to do they only had him in two days a week. He could see why men sometimes marked the days on the wall in prison; at times he couldn't remember if a week or a month had passed.

The weather warmed and grew hot. Even the guards grew listless in the heat. Young brought in two of the pamphlets produced about the fight in Little Rock and had Valentine sign them.

"Turns out I had a cousin in that camp your Bears took. One's for him and one's for his folks."

Part of his brain considered escape. He tried to memorize the schedule of the guard visits to his hallway, tried to make a guess at when the face would appear in the shatterproof window, but their visits were random.

Also, there was the Escape Law. Any person who broke free while awaiting trial automatically had a guily verdict rendered *in absentia*.

He slept more than he was used to, and wrote a long letter to the Miskatonic about the mule list. He labored for hours on the report, knowing all the while that it would be glanced at, a note would be added to another file (maybe!) and then it would be filed away, never to see the light of day again until some archivist went through and decided which documents could be kept and which could be destroyed.

He suggested that further investigation into the mule list was warranted. Anything important enough for the Kurians to put this kind of effort into—and apart from feeding and protecting themselves, the Kurians had few pursuits that Valentine was aware of—might prove vital.

Valentine signed it. His last testament to the Cause?

ɸ

Letters arrived in a strung-together mass. Outrage and gratitude from Post, who was on the mend in a convalescent home and had installed Narcisse in the kitchen; wonder from Meadows; a few postcards from his former Razors who had heard about his imprisonment one way or another.

One offered to ". . . come git you Sir. Just send word."

Nothing from Ahn-Kha, which worried Valentine a little. The Golden One could read and write English as well as anyone in his former command, and better than many.

Valentine heard footsteps in the hallway pause, and then a knock at the door.

"Visitor, Major."

This time Corporal Young took him down to a regular visiting room, carrels with glass between allowed for conversation through small holes in the glass—or plastic, Valentine thought when he saw all the scratches. There were fittings for phones but it looked as though the electronics had been taken out.

He waited for a few minutes and then they brought in Moira Styachowski.

She wore good-fitting cammies with her Hunter Staff crossbar on her captain's bars. The only female Bear he'd ever met looked about as healthy as she ever did—just a little pale and exhausted.

"So they got you after all," Valentine said.

"I might say the same about you," Styachowski said in return, then her eyes shifted down. "I'm sorry, I shouldn't have said that. Dumb thing to joke—"

"Forget about it, Wildcard."

She smiled at the handle issued to her the night he'd been burned in the Kurian Tower of Little Rock. "You know who's behind this, right?"

"Yes, that Sime . . ."

"No, the charges. It's Martinez."

"My counselor told me. Seems like a sharp woman."

Styachowski looked down again.

"What?" Valentine asked.

"I was told, Val, in language that was . . . umm, remarkable for its vigor, to come here and tell you to work with Sime on this. The 'vigor' of the language employed made me ask a few questions of a friend at GHQ. So, for the record, take the deal."

Valentine lowered his voice. "Off the record?"

She leaned forward. "It's a setup for the benefit of some Oklahoma Quislings. According to my source at GHQ, Sime said, 'They need to see a few hangings to convince them.' Don't look like that. You've got your deal from Sime."

"Sime says. He's powerful enough to make it happen? Even with a Jagger judge?"

"The representatives"—she said the word with the inflection a bluenose might use to describe workers in a bordello as 'hostesses'—"are here and your trials are due to start. Luckily you were the last one arrested. The others will go first. They'll get their hangings."

"Is there anything you can do?" Valentine asked. So goddamn helpless in here. He felt an urge to lash out, punch the Plexiglas between himself and Styachowski. Perhaps even hit Styachowski, for nothing more than being the bearer of bad news. But the mad flash faded as quickly as it rose.

"I don't have much experience in this. A couple of classes on military law and that farce we had near Magazine Mountain sums up my experience."

"What about the newspapers? Your average townie thinks every Quisling should wind up in a ditch."

"Military trials aren't public. I'll see if I can talk to your counsel. If it makes you feel any better, Ahn-Kha is here. I set him up quietly in the woods nearby. I sent word to that Cat you're partial to but I haven't heard back."

"Who's your source at GHQ?"

Styachowski hesitated. "The lieutenant general's chief of staff, a major named Lambert. Says she remembers you from the war college, by the way."

*Dots.* Valentine had a feeling back then that she was destined to rise. She practically ran the war college as a cadet.

"Thank her," Valentine said.

"Val, if there's anything else I can do . . ."

"You've already exceeded expectations," Valentine said. "Again. Good-bye."

She visibly gulped. "You did right by those women." Styachowski got up and left, a little unsteadily.

Young escorted him back to his room/cell. "We turned away a visitor for you yesterday, Major. Guards say she was a bit of a meal. Red hair."

*So Smoke had drifted into the vicinity after all.*

"Turned away?"

"You're to get no visitors except by judge's order. Sorry."

"Is that usual?"

"Not for anyone in Southern Command. Sometimes we try Quislings, redhands, men caught as spies. They're kept I-C if it's thought they know something damaging if it gets out, but you guys are the first of ours."

"Should the lack of precedent worry me?"

"I only work here, Major. But, to tell the truth, it worries me."

ψ

Thrush got his trial the next day. He ate his dinner alone and the "shooters" didn't see him until breakfast (reconstituted eggs that tasted like bottom sand). He wasn't inclined to talk about the proceedings.

"My counsel keeps objecting and getting overruled," Thrush said. "Six witnesses for the prosecution. My defense starts today. There was wrangling over the witnesses, my counsel only got two in."

"Do you have any family or friends in the audience?" Valentine asked.

Thrush scowled, pushing his utensils around on his tray. "There's an audience alright. You never saw such a bunch of hatchet faces. Tight-ass Kansas types. I wouldn't be surprised if they are Quislings."

"I'm going to ask for noseplugs if they're there at my trial," Roderick said.

ψ

Valentine never saw Thrush again after that meal. Young, wary and somber, told him the verdict and sentence. Valentine wasn't surprised by the verdict but he was shocked at his reaction upon hearing the punishment. The Garage. Death by hanging. Thrush's sentence rang in his ears, rattled around in his head like a house-trapped bird frantic but unable to escape: Death by hanging.

Death by hanging. The Garage. Death by hanging.

Farland went next. The morning of his trial he was almost cheerful. "Hey, I've admitted it. I did wrong and I'll take what's coming, serve time and address cadet classes about humane treatment of prisoners if they want. The court's gotta see this as a case for mercy, right?"

His guilty plea just meant he had to spend less time in the courtroom before hearing his sentence. The trial was over and done with in thirty minutes.

This time, when Valentine asked, Young just shook his head. The guard had a hard time meeting Valentine's eyes.

In the yard that day Roderick didn't eat, he just rocked back and forth on his heels, whistling. Valentine felt he should know the tune but couldn't identify it.

" 'There's No Business Like Show Business,' Val," Roderick supplied.

"Roderick, what did you do that got you in here?"

Roderick shrugged. "Guess it doesn't matter now, since none of us will be telling tales. Rape and murder of a Quisling prisoner. She was sweet and creamy, and I figured they do it plenty to our people. She had the softest-looking brown hair, partly tied up in this red bandanna. Funny. If her hair didn't catch my eye, she would have just been another prisoner walking by. But I had the boys pull her out of line."

"They reported you?"

"No. I felt guilty about it afterwards. Talked it over with a chaplain. He turned me in. Guess I don't blame him. There's got to be a difference between us and them, or what's the point? I'm almost so I want their brand of hemp medicine." He made a hanging motion at his neck with his finger, both gruesome and funny at the same time.

Roderick's words stayed with him for hours. Roderick deserved his fate—if the men saw their officers behaving that way, they'd degenerate into a sexually charged mob the next time . . . *but wait.* How different were their crimes, really—save that Valentine amassed a higher body count? Eight men had died in horrible pain.

In the afternoon he met with Captain Luecke in a little, white-painted room with a big table. She looked a little haggard.

"I was handling Farland's case as well. I thought it was just going to be plea negotiations. I heard something about Sime making you an offer."

"What happened to Thrush?"

"He moved onto death row. They hung him at midnight last night. In front of the witnesses." She took a long drag at her cigarette, and the shaking in her fingers stilled for a moment as the nicotine hit her bloodstream. "Farland will go tomorrow night. Our guests can't afford to stay long. Do Sime's deal."

"Or end up like Thrush and Farland?"

"Maybe they're having you go last for a reason. After a few hangings, the bastards might be willing to see a little mercy."

" 'Blessed are the merciful, for they shall obtain mercy,' " Valentine quoted.

"This last week has been strictly Old Testament, Valentine. Like Leviticus."

"How did your checking on Martinez go?"

"It was quite revealing. I'm glad I wasn't at that trial. Were there really bullets flying in through the windows?"

"The prosecuting officer almost got raped."

Luecke sent a funnel of smoke at the ceiling lights. "There were times I thought a lynch mob coming for some overeager scalp-taker wouldn't be altogether a bad thing. But to see it in real life—"

"It worked out in the end. My defense?"

"You don't have one. Every witness I wanted to call met with the same response from the judge: *Major Valentine is on trial, not General Martinez. Denied.* Valentine, honestly, take Sime's deal. If anyone has the pull to get you off the hook, it's him."

"Pull? What kind of justice system is this?" Valentine asked.

Luecke lit another cigarette from the butt of her first as she took a last drag. "A kind I've never seen before. Take Sime's deal."

"If I don't?"

"I'll do my best. I have a feeling it won't be good enough."

"Can you get me a visitor? There's—"

"Sorry, no. Maybe after sentencing."

"That'll do me so much good," Valentine said.

"You're frustrated. I understand. Go back to your room and think it over. Sime's offer is our only hope."

"Our? You're not going to be standing in the Garage with a rope around your neck by the end of the week."

She crushed her cigarette. "You think I don't feel for the people I defend? It's a rotten world. A lot of the men who wind up here just got an extra spoonful of rottenness. Maybe they were born with it, or maybe it got fed to them in little mouthfuls over their lives. In either case, I do what I can for them."

Valentine put his head in his hands. *Keep it together, Ghost.* "I'm sorry. You've done more for me than I should expect, considering."

"If it makes you feel any better, Val, I did turn up one thing. I couldn't see much of it, but Southern Command did investigate Martinez. There's some kind of intelligence file that I saw cross-referenced in the docs. Whatever they were looking into came up negative, so the file got sealed. You wouldn't know anything about that, would you?"

"All I know is he shot two of my complement. And that he kept a few thousand men drunk and hiding in the hills when Southern Command needed them."

"We'll talk tomorrow morning. It looks like your trial is going to be on Thursday."

*Two days.*

"Thank you, Captain. You should eat—you don't look so good."

She pulled out a cigarette. "I'm paving my own trip to the Garage with these. See you in sixteen hours."

φ

Valentine spent the next day in a kind of weary anxiety. They would try Roderick in the morning—he was not going to contest the proceedings, so it would go quickly—and then Valentine's trial would begin in the afternoon. He tried to write letters and found himself unable to find words, went through the motions of his job rebinding books at the prison library in a funk, unable to finish anything. He and Luecke met again, but found they had little to say to each other. She simply asked if he'd take Sime's deal. He shrugged and said that he hadn't made up his mind yet, and she said she had the statement for the tribunal ready if he did decide to plead guilty.

Valentine believed any speech she might make would be scrimshaw on a casket. What would happen to him would happen regardless. The only words that would count would be those that would place him in prison, or send him to the Garage.

The hours slipped away until sundown, and the prison slowly bled off the heat it had soaked in during the day. Valentine lay in his cot, arms and legs thrown wide to allow the perspiration to disperse.

There was a knock at the door and Valentine heard keys rattle.

"Room search," Young said.

Valentine knew the routine. They took him to a holding cell—this one had real bars—while two guards searched his room. The process usually took a half hour or so.

This time it took an hour. Were they worried he'd constructed some kind of weapon to use in court?

When they returned him to his cell Valentine noticed the usual cart outside, piled with his linens. Young looked at the other guard. "I'll take it from here, Steve-o."

"You sure?" the guard asked.

"I'm sure. Enjoy your dinner."

Steve-o, the other guard, extended his hand. "Good luck, Major Valentine."

"You mean good luck tomorrow, don't you?" Young said.

"Yeah. That's what I meant."

Valentine shook the hand.

"Just wanted to say I done it," Steve-o said. He wandered down the hall, whistling "There's No Business Like Show Business." Maybe he'd picked the tune up from Roderick.

"You've got a letter," Young said. He looked again at the envelope. "It says that it's not to be delivered to you until after your trial. But we had to check it anyway. No reason we couldn't check it before."

"Of course," Valentine said, wondering.

"Here you go. I get the feeling it's not from a friend."

Valentine saw the same plain envelope and paper. He opened the tri-folded message.

**ENJOY THE HANGING. WISH I COULD BE THERE.**

Young cleared his throat. "Kind of funny, this person being so sure of your verdict."

"Funny is right," Valentine agreed.

Young extracted a multitool pocketknife, unfolded a screwdriver, and cleaned a black mark from beneath his thumb. A red-painted key jangled from the ring on the knife; Valentine saw it glitter in the dim light coming in from his window. "I've never had a problem with my job before, Major. Most people wind up here, well, they deserve it. The ones that don't get spat back out, usually along with some who do. Better that way than the other. But in sixteen years I've never seen anything like this."

Young pointed to a laundry bag on his bed. "Fresh linens for your bed and a new smock," he said. "Girl in the laundry is new. I think she doesn't read so good. If they screwed up, I'll be back in an hour and fifteen minutes and I'll get you a new set of clothes." He placed the knife in his pocket. "Well, I got to get down to the yard. We got sick dogs tonight and until the vet is done looking at them, it's the two-legged animals that got to walk between the wire. I know the night before a trial is always slow. Hope you get some sleep, eventually."

As he turned, Valentine heard the pocketknife bounce off his boot and hit the floor. It slid under his cot.

"Damn cheap service trousers! Cotton my ass. More like knitted lint," Young said, and slammed the door behind himself—slammed it so hard it didn't close properly. Valentine didn't hear the dead bolt shoot home.

Valentine waited one amazed second, then put his slip-on shoe in between the door and the jamb so it wouldn't close accidentally. He checked his laundry bag. A complete guard uniform, right down to polished shoes and belt, hat, and hankerchief was inside. Valentine read the stitched-on name tag: YOUNG.

"Thank you, Corporal Young."

He got into the uniform. It was a bit roomy, but he didn't look ridiculous once he punched a new hole in the belt with the knife's awl. It was a handy little tool: two kinds of screwdriver, two blades, a saw/fish scaler, a can opener, a file, an awl, and a clipper—though the last didn't look up to the job of cutting the wire in the yard.

He put wadded-up papers—one of them was the mystery note—around his feet so they fit better in the size-twelve shoes.

It occurred to him that if he were to pass as Young at a cursory glance he'd need to be heavier. He wound a sheet around his midsection and put the belt back on at its worn notch.

Feeling hot with excitement he stepped into the hall, trying to walk with his head turned down and handkerchief wiping his nose. He'd never seen cameras in the hall of this part of the prison but he wanted to be safe.

He left the room behind with no regret. When was the last time he slept in the same spot so many days in a row? His cabin in the *Thunderbolt*, most likely.

He walked down the hall in the direction of the edge of the asterisk. Then he stopped in front of a door two down from his. Roderick's.

The man was guilty of an atrocious crime. But if the system was gamed—

Valentine looked through the window. The cot was empty—had Young arranged for two escapes? Then his eyes picked up a figure in the gloom behind the sink/toilet.

Roderick had cheated the hangman.

What looked like a twisted-up sheet was knotted around the sink tap. Roderick was in a sitting position, butt off the floor and held up by his sheet, face purple and tongue sticking out as stiffly as his legs.

He turned away from the window, and looked at the dim hallway light to get the image out of his retinas.

Every other time they'd brought him through the center of the asterisk, but there was a fire exit sign above a heavy door. While he knew some of the routes through the center of the building, there was too much chance of meeting another guard. Valentine tried the red key on the heavy lock, Roderick's purple tongue filling his vision every time he didn't concentrate, and the fire escape door opened. For an aged guard Young thought things through well enough. He listened with hard ears, and heard footsteps somewhere on the floor below.

Valentine slipped off the guard shoes, wincing at the sound of paper crinkling—the tiniest sounds were magnified when one was trying to keep silent—and padded down the stairs to the bottom level.

He searched the door frame leading outside.

The door to the exterior had an alarm on it. Valentine flipped up a plastic access cover and saw a keypad with a green-faced digital readout. Someone had written 1144 on the interior. Valentine passed a wetted thumb over the ink and it smeared easily—it was still fresh. He punched the numbers into the keypad and then hit a key at the bottom marked ENTER.

Nothing changed color.

Every nerve on edge, Valentine pushed open the crash door.

"Thank God for minimum security," he whispered. A real prison would have had at least two more layers of doors.

He put the shined shoes back on. While rugged enough for street wear, he wondered how long they'd last if he had to hike out. His good boots were in storage somewhere in the bowels of the prison complex.

The night air felt cool and clean, but the best thing about it was the amount. Free sky stretched overhead as far as even Cat eyes could see. Valentine drank in the Arkansas night like a shot of whiskey, and even the memory of Roderick's tongue faded . . . a little.

Keeping to the shadows, he walked around the edge of the building. Every now and then he stopped and pulled on a window as though checking to see if it was locked, all the while making for the pathway from the center of the asterisk to the gate in the double wire.

A few lights burned in the subsidiary buildings and the courthouse. Valentine stepped onto the path leading to the gate and strode toward the gate.

He heard high, feminine laughter from the gatehouse.

Valentine sneezed repeatedly into his handkerchief as he stepped into the flood of light around the twin vehicular gates. Valentine had seen the gatehouse in operation often enough; people were supposed to travel through the inside but guards desiring access to the area between the double row of fencing usually just had them open the gates.

Cap pulled low on his head, he looked into the window. Then stopped.

Alessa Duvalier sat on some kind of console, legs prettily crossed though she was in what Valentine thought of as her traveling clothes—a long jacket was folded carelessly next to her, her walking stick, which concealed a sword, next to it.

"... so the blonde gives birth and asks the doctor, 'How can I be sure it's mine?' " They laughed.

"Shit, how did someone as ugly as Young end up with you?"

"Kindness," Duvalier said. "He's a very kind man."

"If you ever want to trade him in on a newer model . . ." the young guard said. He sputtered with laughter as he waved casually at Valentine—not taking his eyes off Duvalier—and Duvalier said, "Oh, let me!" She thumped something without waiting for permission and the twin gates hummed as they slid sideways on greasy tracks. Valentine nipped out of sight of the gate and walked quickly down the road.

Valentine heard a thump from behind, a door open, and then quick footsteps as Duvalier caught up.

She pulled him off the road and gave him a brief embrace, nuzzling him under the chin with her nose. "I can never leave you alone, can I?"

"My luck always turns whenever you're not around," Valentine admitted.

"If they arrested everyone who ever quietly shot a Quisling . . ." she said.

"Let's not mention arrests or prisons for a while, alright? As of this moment I'm a fugitive from justice subject to the Escape Law."

"It's not so bad. My whole life, I've been a fugitive from just about everything," she said.

"What's the plan?" Valentine asked.

"That's your end. But I've got a start under way. Oh, that Corporal Young's a good man. We need to burn those clothes."

"You've got replacements?"

"They're with Ahn-Kha."

She turned him into the woods and an owl objected, somewhere. Valentine heard the soft flap of bats above, hunting insects in the airspace between branches and ground.

They stopped to listen twice, then found a burned-out house. A transport truck with a camouflaged canvas-covered back sat in front of it. Valentine marveled at it. The ruins of the garage held a small charcoal fire and a very large, faun-colored Grog.

"My David," Ahn-Kha said. "We have escaped again."

"If we're still at liberty in twenty-four hours I'll call it an escape. Where'd you get the truck?"

"Styachowski requisitioned us a transport," Duvalier said.

Valentine stripped out of his uniform, and Duvalier flitted about gathering up the guard's clothing.

Ahn-Kha handed him a too-familiar dun-colored overall.

"Labor Regiment?" Valentine said.

"It goes with the truck," Duvalier said. "The big boy looks like he could do a hard day's work with a shovel."

"And you?"

She covered her fiery red hair with a fatigue cap. "I'm management. You two look like the all-day lunch-break type. Besides Val, you're the suckiest kind of driver."

"Where do we go?" Ahn-Kha asked. "My people will gladly shelter us at Omaha."

"We'd have to cross half of Southern Command. No, let's go east."

Duvalier climbed into her own overall and zipped it up over freckled shoulders. "East? Nothing there but river and then the Kurians. Until the Piedmont."

"I have an old friend in the Yazoo Delta. And I've got a mind to visit Memphis."

"Memphis? The music's to die for, but the Kurians see to it that you do the dyin'." She sprinkled something that smelled like kerosene out of a bottle onto the clothes and tossed them on the charcoal. They began to burn with admirable vigor.

"Ali, I've got my claws into a job. I'm wondering more and more about Post's wife, Gail."

"She's gotta be dead if she was shipped."

"No, she was some kind of priority cargo. I'll explain later. We need to go to the area around Arkansas Post on the river. Can you manage that?"

"Says the guy who just broke out of a high-security lockup thanks to me!" Duvalier chided.

"Medium security," Valentine said.

She tossed her bundle of traveling clothes and sword stick into the back of the truck. "How do I look?"

"You're better suited singing in the Dome than for the Labor Regiment," Valentine said.

"Gratitude! The man's got a vocablarney like a dictionary and he doesn't know the meaning of the word!"

"Please," Ahn-Kha said. "We had best be going."

☥

The truck bumped eastward along the torn-up roads. A substantial piece of Consul Solon's army had been borrowed from the area around Cairo, Illinois, and points east, and they had employed a spikelike mechanism called a paveplow to destroy the roadbeds as they went home.

Patching was still being done, so most vehicles found it easier to drive on the gravel shoulder.

Duvalier drove, Ahn-Kha rode shotgun—with his formidable gun pointing out through the liftable front windscreen to rest on the hood—and Valentine bounced along in the back, feeling every divot the worn-out shock absorbers struck and hanging onto the paint-and-rust frame for safety.

About noon he felt the truck lurch to a stop.

"Just a road check," Duvalier said through the flap separating the driver from the cargo bed. "Rounders."

Valentine's stomach went cold. There was an old riot gun in the back, but he couldn't shoot his fellow citizens, even if it meant being rearrested.

"Afternoon, digger," Valentine heard a voice say from up front. "Transport warrant and vehicle check. Jesus, that's some big Grog. He trained?"

"He's a citizen. Sick relief to Humbolt Crossing," Duvalier said, cool as ever. "There's the medical warrant. We've got an unidentified fever in the back, so you want to keep clear."

"Do we?" another voice said. "We'll have to risk it. Orders to check every vehicle. We had a breakout at the military prison in Mountain Home."

"Someone important, I take it," Duvalier said.

"David Valentine, part-Indian, black hair, scar on right side of face."

Duvalier again: "Never heard of him. He run over a general's dog?"

Valentine heard footsteps approaching the bed. There was nowhere for him to hide inside. He might be able to cut his way onto the roof. He reached for the knife, opened the saw blade . . .

"Killed some Quisling prisoners, they say."

"He use too many bullets?" Duvalier said.

"Whoa, Sarge, we got someone back here."

Light poured into the back of the truck, hurting Valentine's eyes and giving him an instant headache. The hole was only big enough to put his head through.

Valentine heard a harsh whisper from Duvalier.

"Well, well, well," one of the Rounders said.

"He doesn't look too sick," the one with sergeant's tabs agreed. "Wouldn't you say, slick."

*That's it. Trapped. Back to trial.*

"No."

"This look like our Quisling killer to you?"

The other squinted. "No, Sarge. Five-one and Chinese, three gold teeth; no way this is our man."

"I should get my eyes checked," the sergeant said, writing something down. "I need to erase, because I see a six-six black individual with a big tattoo of Jesus on his chest. Oh, crap, this stop form looks like shit now." He tore a piece of printed paper off his pad, wadded it in one massive hand, and tossed it over his shoulder.

"Anyway, it ain't our killer."

"No, that's not David Valentine," the sergeant said, winking.

"Too bad, in a way," the other said. "Old friend of mine, Ron Ayres, fought under him in Little Rock. I'd buy this Major Valentine a drink, if I could."

"So you've told me. About a hundred times," the sergeant said, closing the back flap.

Valentine listened to the boot steps return to the front of the vehicle.

"Okay, get your sick man outta here before we all catch it," the sergeant said. "I'd turn south for Clarendon about three miles along; there's an old, grounded bus shell with RURAL NETWORK

PICKUP J painted on it alongside the road. No roadblocks that way to slow up your sick man, and I think this thing can make it through the wash at Yellow Creek."

"Thank you, Sergeant."

"Thank you for having such a pretty smile. Pleasant journey."

*And thank you, old friend of Ron Ayres,* Valentine thought.

# CHAPTER SIX

*T*he Lower Mississippi, July: *The river has reverted to feral since the cataclysm of 2022, a continent-crossing monster unleashed. The carefully sculpted and controlled banks of the twentieth and early twenty-first century are gone, or survive as tree-lined islands surrounded by some combination of marsh, lake, and river.*

*Even on the best and sunniest days, the Mississippi can only manage a rather lackluster blue between banks lined with opportunistic shellbark hickory, willow, and river birch. It is more frequently a dull navy, muddy brown at the edges, striped in the center by wind and broken by swirls or flats created by snags, shallows, and sandbars. Below the Missouri and Ohio joins, the flooded river is sometimes three miles wide, and moves at a steady four miles an hour toward the Gulf of Mexico, carrying with it rich loads of silt—some insignificant fraction of which will be dredged up and placed into the vast rice paddies around the partially flooded Crescent City. The rest accumulates here and there, gradually changing the course and shape of the Father of Waters.*

*The days of tugs churning up- or downriver with a quarter mile of linked barges are gone, along with many of the navigational aids. Barge traffic now looks more like a truck convoy, with various sizes of small craft and tugs pushing a few barges along the river in a long, thin column, led and flanked by small powerboats checking the navigability of the ever-changing river. The Memphis–New Orleans corridor is especially well guarded against quick strikes or artillery attacks by the roving forces of Southern Command, always on the lookout for a chance to seize a few bargeloads of grain, rice, or beans. If they are very lucky, sometimes they free a load of human currency from the Kurian trade system.*

*Of course the Kurians fight back, in a manner. Booby-trapped barges, or "Q-craft," loaded with mercenaries give the raiders an occasional unpleasant surprise.*

*There is one long stretch of river, flanked by a northward bend on one end and a southward hook downriver, that causes the barge captains to press close to the unfriendly western side. This is the "Tunica Sands," a stretch of river between Tunica and Memphis avoided by all the river rats as though it was cursed ground. Ten great, weed-choked casino barges on the eastern bank are now landlocked thanks to silt deposits all around their keels. Like a latter-day leper colony, the entire area is surrounded by fencing and watch posts.*

*Only the sick, under Reaper escort, go in. Only the Reapers come out again.*

ψ

The big Cat hadn't changed much in the eight years since Valentine had last seen him. A little less hair perhaps, a little more waistline certainly, but he was still the big, half-aquatic athlete of the Yazoo swamps with a satchel full of apples. Everready had taught Valentine how to lower lifesign and move without being noticed over the course of one impossibly hot summer, and the fact that he'd survived to return proved the effectiveness of his tutor's methods.

The New Orleans Saints ball cap was gone, though. Now he wore a black, broad-brimmed hat that made him look like a missionary. Strung Reaper teeth rattled at his neck, and layers of bullet-stopping Reaper robe hung off his body in an oversized tunic that no sane man dared call a dress.

Finding him had been surprisingly easy. While casting about for a way to get across the Mississippi they came upon a "summer out" Wolf patrol in charge of monitoring river traffic. The Wolf patrol relied on Everready for information on the opposite bank in the Yazoo Delta between Vicksburg and Memphis, and the trio crossed the river in a birch-bark canoe with a guide who rested and camped with them at the rendezvous until the legendary Cat appeared to trade supplies for data.

Everready had no young Wolves to train this year, further evidence of the still-echoing disruption of Solon's occupation, and the continuing absence of the Lifeweavers. "Good to have you back, David," he said, upon greeting them. "Even an old swamp-hound gets lonely now and then."

So he was willing, after concluding his exchange with their Wolf guide, to take Valentine and company into Memphis.

"Only four ways into that town, barring being brought in in handcuffs and bite-guard," Everready said in their first camp on the trip north.

They looked like four spirits around their Yazoo swamp campfire, the humans under individual shrouds of mosquito netting, while Ahn-Kha followed the Grog manner by pasting his sensitive face and ears under a layer of mud.

"There's the river," Everready explained. "They check everybody at the river, and they're damn good at spotting fake documents, and most visitors are kept to the Riverfront anyway. Then there's the wall. There are gaps at the rock wall, of course, but the smugglers have gone to a lot of trouble to open them and watch 'em, and they won't let you through for free. Then there are the road gates, but it's the same problem, another document check. Most people who come to trade do it at Little City around Memphis, then the middlemen the Memphis authorities know and trust go through the gates with their goods."

"That's three ways in," Ahn-Kha said.

Everready shifted an apple stem to the other side of his mouth. "Yes, sir, Mister Grog, that's only three ways. The fourth is a bit tricky—it's up along the Tunica Run. Tunica's a dumping ground for those that got the ravies bug—Memphis buys 'em cheap off their fellow Kurians and dumps them in Tunica so there's always a feed on for their Reapers. Every now and then they release a batch on the west side of the river to give the Free Territory folks a little trouble, too."

Everready cracked his knuckles. "If you're careful, really careful, you can move north through the ravies colony. It's really just a big wall there, and one gate. They watch the gate and patrol the wall, but not too heavily. Ravies types aren't into engineering ways over or under the wall. Too busy chasing their own tails."

"So what's in Memphis that's worth all that security?" Duvalier asked. Valentine thought she looked like a silent-film starlet, with face glowing in the firelight behind the layer of netting.

"The banks," Everready said.

Her voice rose a notch. "Banks? There aren't banks any more."

"Yes, there are," Everready said. "Only kind of banks that matter to the Kurians. Big marshaling yards for the transhipment of humans."

"Tell her why," Valentine said.

"Logistics," Everready said. "Memphis is only a day's rail from every big city on the eastern seaboard, plus parts of the Midwest and Texas—the parts your boys haven't took yet, that is. It's why ol' FedEx was headquartered there, too. Some Kurian in Kansas buys tractors from Michigan; he sends authorization to the bank in Memphis to ship up three hundred folk or whatever the price was. They're on the next train to Detroit. Those yards are a sight to see. Let me ask you the same question. What's so important in Memphis that you're willing to risk going in?"

"We're looking for someone," Valentine said.

"Unless he got a job in one of the camps—"

"She," Duvalier corrected.

Everready shrugged. "Unless she got a job in one of the camps—wait, is she a looker?"

"She's attractive enough, but there's more to it," Valentine said.

"What do you mean, more?"

Valentine tried to explain the mule list to Everready as concisely as possible. The old Cat thought it worth another apple; he carved off slices for the other three and then gnawed at the remaining wedge himself.

The fruit tasted like candy to Valentine.

"There's this big ol' boy named Moyo who runs all the girls inside the wall. Always has his men checking inbound shipments for beauty. He's got a regular harem; half the large-scale pimps south of the Ohio buy from him. He employs bounty hunters to comb the hills east of here to bring in folks to swap out when one of his men spots a pretty girl. Kurians don't really care—what's the difference between one dollar coin and another? Moyo does a lot of high-priority transshipping. He'd be the first place I'd look for more on this mule list of yours, if it really is all women."

After that he and Valentine spent a few minutes looking at maps—Everready chuckled that he hardly used the maps anymore, he knew the ground between Memphis and Vicksburg so well— and planning the hike north.

"We should jog east a bit at the Coldwater. I got a store of captured gear you three can draw from." Everready flicked his fingers at Valentine's disintegrating guard shoes, and Valentine wondered if he was going to get the old lecture about how there's no reissue on feet.

"How's Trudy?" Valentine asked, jerking a netting-shrouded chin at Everready's ancient carbine. The well-oiled stock glowed in the firelight.

"Still saving my life."

"And the Reaper-teeth collection?"

"Seventy-one and counting."

"All from fair fights, right?"

Everready made a move to box his ears. "Valentine, how you think I got this old? Only time I even get into a scrap with a Reaper is when they's so disadvantaged it's hardly a fight a'tall."

ψ

Valentine woke to the smell of chickory coffee.

Everready and Duvalier were the only ones up. Ahn-Kha lay in a snoring heap, wrapped around his gun like a snake that had swallowed a bullock before retiring to a too-small tree.

He listened to the conversation as he shifted around, feeling for creepy-crawlies. He missed his old hammock.

"I didn't know Cats got as old as you. I thought we were all done by thirty."

"For a start, I stay in territory I know better than they do. I don't make a lot of trouble, I'd rather let my eyes and ears do the work."

"Don't the Lifeweavers ever have you—"

"I think they've forgotten about ol' Everready. But that's fine with me. I like to fight with my own set of priorities. I suppose that's how I ended up in this swamp."

"Seems lonely. Do you go into Memphis often?" she asked.

"No, they know my face there. Not that I wouldn't mind visiting the pros down at the Pyramid. Your pretty face makes me feel twenty years younger."

"Wish I could help—but . . ."

Valentine wondered what the silence portended.

"You're lucky. He's a good man. But be careful working with someone you got that kind of feeling for. The moment will come, maybe you'll have just a split second to move, and you'll move wrong 'cause of your feelings. You'll both wind up dead."

Valentine kept absolutely still.

Everready went on: "Don't look like that. Just one ol' hound's opinion. If I knew what I was talking about I'd have some hardware on my collar and be giving orders, right?"

"Let's see about breakfast."

"I'll check the crawfish traps. Better use the big pot. That Grog can eat."

Valentine waited to open his eyes until he felt the tip of Duvalier's boot. "You can wake up Ahn-Kha," she said. "When he stretches in the morning his gas drops the birds."

ψ

Everready's cache showed his usual craftiness. He kept medical supplies, preserved food, and weapons in several spots between the Yazoo and the Mississippi; the problem was keeping the gear away from scavengers. Humans could use tools and animals could smell food through almost any obstacle. In the Coldwater Creek cache he had solved the problem by burying his supplies behind a house and then placing a wheelless, stripped pickup body over it.

Ahn-Kha stood watch in a high pine while they excavated the cache.

"The engine block's still in this so she's a heavy SOB," Everready explained, retrieving a wire-cored rope from the house's chimney. The rope he fixed to the trailer hitch. Then he tied his Reaper-robe top around the base of a tree, looped the rope around it, and fixed it.

"Here you go, young lady," he said, handing the line to Duvalier.

She hardly had to lean as she applied a transverse pull to the center of the rope. The truck pivoted a few feet, exposing some of the dirt and a few hardy creepers beneath the pickup bed. Everready tightened it again and she slid the pickup body another meter toward the tree.

"Why the material around the tree?" Valentine asked.

Everready checked under the dashboard on the passenger side and then pulled out a folding shovel with a gloved hand. "So the bark doesn't strip. You'd be surprised how clever some scavengers are."

The heavy-duty garbage bags within had further items wrapped up inside them: a few guns thick with protective grease, boxes of ammunition, a large box of red pepper—ideal for throwing off tracking dogs—and a pair of shin-top-high camouflage-pattern boots.

"You and I have about the same size foot, I think," Everready said as Valentine grabbed up the snakeproof boots like a miner spotting a golden nugget. "There are some good socks rolled up in that coffee tin. An extra pair should make up the difference." Valentine smiled when he looked in the tin. It also contained a half-dozen old "lifetime" batteries with a logo of a lightning-bolt-like cat jumping through a red circle. Everready liked to leave the twelve-volt calling cards in the mouths of his kills.

He brought up a cardboard box full of a dozen familiar blue tins.

"Spam?" Valentine asked.

"Naw. This was part of a larger shipment going to the resistance farther east. I took a small expeditor's fee for getting the pony train there. There's plastic explosive inside the cans, you just got to pop the lid—there's even a layer of pork at the top." He passed up another bag. "Three kinds of detonators. One looks like a wind-up alarm clock, one's in this watch but you have to hook it to the batteries in this flashlight, and the others are straight fuses made to look like shoelaces, while the detonators are made to look like nine-volt batteries. Your armorers are clever."

Everready unrolled a chamois and handed a 9mm Beretta up to Duvalier. "This is a nice little gun, young lady."

"I'll take that Mossberg twelve-gauge," she said, pointing at a cluster of long guns. "Folding stock. Dreamy."

"Don't you think you'll stand out a bit in Memphis?"

"Not after I rope it up inside my coat."

"Your duster's going to look strange in this heat," Valentine said.

"Not if I'm mostly naked under it."

"Hope you're not looking for trouble in Memphis. Hard to get into. Harder to get out of. Valentine, since you're going to be posing as a reel looking to add a few new faces to his line, you'll want something with a little flash. I took this off a wandering guitar man in a swap meet card game."

He picked up a sizeable clear plastic food-storage container and broke the seal. A long, silver-barreled automatic pistol rested inside with a shoulder holster and spare magazines. The gun was nickel-plated and would reflect light from miles away—no wonder Everready stuck it in a hole. "You don't mind .22, do you?"

"For this kind of job I'd prefer it. It's quiet."

"Only took you four years and some to add that word to your vocabulary," Duvalier observed.

"And what else?" Everready said in his old talking-with-milk-chinned-young-Wolves tone.

"It's light so you can carry a lot, and it's a nice varmint round for when you get hungry."

"Exacto! Now let's get you a longarm. Where did I put that sumbitch?" He rooted through the guns and found a zipped-up case. "Here we are."

He extracted a gleaming bullpup battle rifle. "This here is real US Army Issue," he said, as another man might speak of a Rothschild vintage or a Cuban cigar. "Took this off some half-assed commandos outta Jackson eight years back. Called a Tacsys U-gun, 'u' for universal. There's four interchangeable barrels and actions so she can shoot 9mm, 5.56, 7.62 with a sniper barrel, or you can open her up and feed her shotgun shells. Used to have a silencer, but I rigged it to a rifle I lost. Sorry. Nice little four-power scope up top. Wish I could give you the grenade launcher for it."

Valentine checked the customizable sling. "This is great. But you keep Trudy?"

"A man doesn't give up on the girl he loves for a hotter model. Even if she's sporting polycarbon rifling.

"Good gear means flash in the KZ. Don't have the full manual but there's a card in the case that you should be able to figure out."

"Speaking of flashing, he could use a change of clothing," Duvalier said, already cleaning her Mossberg.

"Clothes will be a little harder, but I think I've got an old officer's trench coat in here. Very nice waterproofing and only one small, stain-free hole."

φ

"You ready for this, Valentine?" Everready asked. "All your shots up to date?"

They rested atop a stripped Kenworth parked outside Tunica, within heavy-duty fencing and mounds of rubble blocking the roads south of the city, out of the line of sight of the nearest sentry tower, spaced miles apart on this, the less-critical south side of Tunica.

"So we just have to move slowly?" Valentine asked, loading the U-gun.

"Not so much slow as smooth," Everready said. "No sudden moves. I'm not saying a cough will set them off. Just that it could."

"Ahn-Kha, you'll be okay here for a few days?" Valentine asked.

"There is food and water. I will stay in the cab of this fine vehicle at night, and under those trees in the day. Are they less active at night?"

"Depends," Everready said. "If a few start prowling around, sometimes others join them. Then you get a mob mentality. They go off easier in groups."

Duvalier climbed up and hung off one of the rearview mirror posts and looked north into town. The mirrors themselves were gone. "I see one," Duvalier said. "By the traffic light that's touching the road."

Valentine saw it too. A distant figure staggered back and forth across the street, leaning forward as though trying to tie his shoes as he walked.

"Poor souls," Valentine said.

Everready slowly slid off the top of the truck. "Lots more, closer to the old casinos. That's where the missions organize themselves. That one's probably lost and hungry.

"Okay, kiddies, got your iodine?"

Valentine and Duvalier touched their breast pockets and nodded. Valentine had a big bottle, half full, courtesy of Everready's stockpile, and Duvalier had a stoppered hip flask holding the other half.

"You get bit, first thing you do is get clear and iodine it good. Even if you've had your shots the damn thing mutates sometimes, and who knows what strain is in there. Plus it'll save you an infection. Lots of these have hepatitis along with their other problems."

They started down the old road. "And don't shoot unless it's life or death. It'll just get 'em screaming, and between the shots and the screams you'll have a hurtin' of psychos on you before you know it."

Everready set an even pace, the old Cat rocking a little back and forth, like a ship rolling on the ocean. Valentine walked behind, U-gun across his chest in its hands-free sling. Behind him he heard the steady footsteps of Duvalier, pacing her feet to Everready's rhythm.

Valentine had only had one brief brush with ravies sufferers, on the Louisiana border. Southern Command generally shot those who succumbed to the disease once their minds went and they didn't understand what was happening anymore. He'd never seen the aftereffects before.

Seen? Smelled, more like.

Tunica had once been a pretty town, Valentine suspected, fragrant of the magnolias and dogwoods beloved by the residents. Now it smelled like a pig farm. Everready paused at the edge of what had been a park running through the center of town. The three of them stood opposite an old bronze statue of three weary-looking soldiers, the two on the ends supporting a wounded comrade in the center. Everready used the rifle of the one on the left to climb atop the bronze shoulders.

"The kudzu's been cut back from here," Duvalier said. The growth choked most of the rest of the park.

"Probably the Mission people," Everready said, covering his eyes as he looked around. Valentine heard cats spitting at each other somewhere in the park. "See those basins? Food and water. And there they are. Over by the pharmacy."

Valentine saw two heads bobbing among the growth. Both men, with stringy-looking beards. They moved like sleepwalkers, the second following the first.

"Careful now," Everready said. "If anyone hears an engine let me know; my ears aren't what they used to be. Memphis dumps off fresh cases in the center of town sometimes."

They crossed over to one of the main streets. Valentine saw that what he had thought were only two individuals were six; hollow-eyed, tight-cheeked, and knob-kneed. Some shorter women and even a child followed the first two.

Everready walked slowly and smoothly, like a man treading across a pool. Piles of feces lay scattered in the streets and alleys, drying in the summer sun. Valentine saw rats in the alleys, sniffing at the odious piles. Cats filled every shady windowsill and step, watching the rats. A pair of kittens watched them from beneath a wheeled Dumpster.

Valentine put his finger on the U-gun's trigger guard as the slow-moving train of people—or what had once been people—approached.

The two files passed each other, the ravies victims' faces spasming in a parody of vocalization, black-toothed mouths opening and shutting but no sound in their throats but dry wheezes. They looked sunburned and leathery. A few wore stained gray cotton smocks with URM stenciled on the chests and backs.

The little girl seemed a bit more animated than the rest; she pointed and waved.

Everready ignored her.

"URM?" Valentine asked when the group had passed.

"United Relief Missions. Old school Christians. Down at the riverfront. Memphis lets them operate sort of as independents because they keep these folks alive, or what passes for it."

"Looks like they feed themselves, too," Duvalier said, pointing at the corpse of a cat with her walking stick. The cat's midsection had been torn out.

"Wish it would rain," Everready said. "The town's a little better after a good rain."

They crossed a street, and Valentine saw a heap of bodies, mostly nude, on the steps of what looked like a neo-Georgian city hall. One kicked and another rolled over.

"Like hogs in a wallow. The cement gets cool at night," Everready said.

They passed through streets of homes, trees buzzing with cicadas, perhaps one house in three burned to the ground and the others crawling with cats and inhabited by crows. Valentine saw a larger flock gather and disperse around the crotch of a tree, and found the scavengers feeding on a corpse hanging in a backyard tree like a body draped over a saddle.

"That's Reaper work," Valentine said. "Last night, by the look of it."

"Uh-huh," Everready agreed. "When pickings are slim in Memphis they come down here to feed. Memphis buys ravies cases cheap from all across the country and dumps them here, sort of a walking aura reserve. I'm told they stay alive for years—till an infection gets them."

"I didn't know they still used it except to cause us trouble," Valentine said.

"I've heard of them dosing each other's populations when they feud. Or to put down revolts. See, nobody in the KZ gets inoculations except for Quislings."

"How much farther?" Duvalier asked. "This smell is getting to me. I'm getting sick. Seriously, Val . . ."

Everready pulled a little tin from his belt and set it on a stone-and-bar wall in front of one of the houses. He dabbed something from a green bottle on his finger. "Just camphor," he said, and wiped it under her nose. "Breathe through your mouth."

"Better," Duvalier said.

Another pair of rail-thin shamblers wandered near the corpse in the tree. Valentine could have counted their ribs. "I don't like how that one is looking around."

"Smells blood. Blood smell sets them off," Everready whispered, not taking his eyes from them as he mechanically repocketed his first-aid tin. "Best not to move, just stand here. Like those statues at the memorial."

Two crows held a tug-of-war over a piece of viscera.

"Oh God—" Duvalier said.

Valentine could never decide which sound hit his ears first after Duvalier's retch. The wet splash of vomit was certainly louder, heard with his right ear. The high-pitched wailing from the left startled him more, bringing back all the emotions of his first small-unit action as a junior Wolf lieutenant. Perhaps they arrived simultaneously.

Valentine clutched Duvalier's hand and pulled her to her feet. Her walking stick clattered to the ground and Everready grabbed it, unslinging Trudy and running with the carbine in one hand and the stick in the other.

"Follow me!" Everready called. "Don't shoot, you'll just draw more!"

Duvalier came off her feet again, wet-mouthed, unable to control her stomach. Valentine released his weapon and picked her up in a fireman's carry.

He followed Everready up a short slope to an intersection.

"Let me down, I'm okay," Duvalier said.

Valentine went to one knee. He looked back and saw a dozen or so figures running in a more or less arrow-shaped formation. At this distance their bare feet were so dirty that most looked as though they were wearing black shoes and socks.

Kudzu-covered, tree-filled service stations and fast-food restaurants lined the road leading toward the casinos, according to an ancient brown sign. Everready almost leaped across the highway toward a small doughnut shop. A shriek from the direction of the Mississippi let them know that trouble would soon be running in from a second direction.

"Why not the bank?" Valentine yelled. A little way up the road a stout-looking brick structure promised safety—for money or those fleeing psychotics—from behind a wall of scrub pine.

"Too big. Can't stop them from getting in."

Valentine heard footsteps just behind. So sick but able to run so fast . . .

He dropped behind Duvalier and turned, holding the U-gun by barrel and grip. A swift-running young screamer got the butt in his face as he reached for Valentine. He went down, rolling. Valentine shifted his grip and employed the gun in a credible backhand.

The screamer didn't get up again.

There was no glass in the door or the windows. Everready vaulted over the counter and entered the cooking line. The display cabinet held nothing but empty trays and an oversized wasp nest.

Valentine ran around a permanently parked car and entered the formerly white doughnut stop. Duvalier had tears in her eyes as she covered the front of the store with her pump-action.

"In here. Help me with this!" Everready called.

They fled into the cooking line, and Everready and Valentine moved a fryer to block the path to the narrow kitchen. The lighting seemed wrong—Valentine looked up and saw a hole in the roof. Weather or animal activity had enlarged it to the size of a picture window.

Everready emptied the damp mess resting within a plastic garbage can and wedged it above the fryer as Valentine heard screams from within the doughnut shop.

"Nice scouting," Valentine said, pointing to the hole in the roof.

"Hope they don't climb up there," Duvalier said, shifting her shotgun muzzle from the barricade to the roof hole.

Everready put his back to the fryer. Its rear was festooned with smeared warnings. "Planning nothing, never been in here to scavenge. I'd be shocked if there wasn't a hole in the roof of most of these places."

Pounding and screaming came through from the other side of the fryer, horribly loud, horribly near. Valentine fought the urge to run to the other end of the kitchen.

"Valentine, help me hold this—no, the plastic can, they're try-

ing to crawl over! Girl, check the back, there might be a door!"
Everready said.

Duvalier hurried to the other end of the kitchen and disappeared around a corner. Two shotgun blasts followed immediately.

"Oh shit," Everready swore.

Duvalier flew back into the kitchen, her coat billowing and bringing the smell of cordite as she turned and braced herself against a tall refrigerator. "There's a door. Or there isn't—that's the problem."

"How many?" Valentine asked.

"How many are there?" she shot back.

"Thousands," Everready said.

"Sounds about right," Duvalier said.

They came, more like a single organism comprised of screaming heads and waving arms than a series of individuals, filling the kitchen with noise. Valentine brought his U-gun to bear, feeling the pounding on the other side of the fryer against his back.

"The roof!" Valentine shouted, firing. "Go, Ali!"

"I can jump better than either of you. I'll cover you."

More appeared and Valentine didn't wait to argue. He stood on a prep table and tossed his weapon up through the hole, hoping he didn't overthrow and land it in the parking lot. He grabbed an electrical conduit pipe and pulled himself up, got his foot into a light fixture, and climbed. The roof was thick with growth, and disturbed butterflies hurried into the sky.

Everready passed up his gun to Valentine, and Valentine heard Duvalier's Mossberg.

"Forget the packs!" she shouted.

Everready made it to the roof with less difficulty than Valentine.

Duvalier crouched to spring up through the hole in a single leap and they were on her. She spun like a dynamo, slamming one against the fryer, even now moving from the pressure at the other side, screaming as another sank its teeth into her shoulder.

"Goddamn!" Everready swore as yet another grabbed her.

Though mad, though they felt no pain, her attackers weren't Reapers. She pushed one off, kicked another, punched a third, pale limbs and coat a whirling blur of motion. Everready shot a fourth with his carbine.

Valentine dropped back through the hole.

"No!" Everready shouted.

Valentine picked up her sword cane and used it as a club, swinging at the heads and arms coming around the fryer.

"Jump!" Valentine yelled as Everready shot another one down. Valentine struck a ravie on the floor as it clawed at her ankle; his kick broke its jaw.

Duvalier crouched and jumped, and went up through the hole like a missile.

Valentine drew the blade from Duvalier's sword stick. Using the wooden tube in his other hand, he battered his way back toward the office. He felt hands clutch at his canvas boots and broke the grip—if they were snakeproof they'd probably be ravies-resistant—then cracked one across the jaw.

"Val, where are you going?" Duvalier shouted.

"Lemme at that bite, girl!" he heard Everready say.

"Diversion!" he shouted.

Screaming his own head off, Valentine rushed into the office. The back wall had bloody splatters and buckshot holes. A staggered ravie, holding himself up on the desk, received Valentine's boot to his chest, throwing him back onto one coming through the door. Valentine pinned the fresher one like a bug on a piece of Styrofoam with the sword point and vaulted through the door, running.

"Olly olly oxen free!" Valentine shouted, banging a Dumpster with the wooden half of Duvaliers sword cane. "Come out, come out, wherever you are. London Bridge is falling down!" He hurried around into the next parking lot, banging on empty car hoods.

Ravies turned and began to run toward him, screaming. *Fine, better the oxygen flowing out of their pipes than into their bloodstreams.*

"Meet me by the casinos tonight!" Valentine shouted to the pair on the roof. He saw Everready applying a dressing and the iodine bottle to Duvalier's shoulder.

"Come out, come out, wherever you are!" Valentine called again. "Hey diddle diddle, the freak and the fiddle—"

The doughnut shop began to empty, and other ravies hurried up from the direction of the riverfront.

*Just about. Just about!*

"Ring around the rosy!"

The last few around the doughnut shop turned toward him.

"Warriors, come out to play-yay!" Valentine didn't know what childhood game the last one signified, but an old Wolf in Foxtrot Company used to employ the taunt on hidden Grogs, clinking a pair of whiskey bottles together.

He ran.

The ravies followed, screaming.

φ

Ten minutes later and a mile away . . .

His bad leg ached, but he had to ignore it. Ignore everything but the staggered line of ravies running behind him. Valentine turned another corner, his third right through the suburban streets in a row. The pursuers were screaming less, growing weaker—which was just as well; he didn't know how long he could hold out.

*Two more blocks, one more.* He summoned the energy for one final sprint to the last turn, running with the sword cane like a baton in a relay race. His speed came at the cost of a deep, deep burn in his legs and lungs—

And there they were, a few stumbling ravies in a line, following the ones ahead of them, emitting an occasional strangled yelp. The very end of the long file of pursuers, formed into a wagon-train-like circle around six square blocks of Tunica suburbs.

Valentine marked the crash scene he'd seen the first time he ran down this street, impossibly compact cars piled into each other in a rear-end collision, looking like the skeletons of two mating turtles. He staggered behind the cars and sank to his knees, desperately trying to control his panting.

He peered between the cars, looking for his pursuers.

They followed his path onto the tree-limb-littered street, caught sight of their fellows, and ran to catch up to them.

Valentine was too tired to smile.

137

He crept through the underbrush of a lawn, counted twenty of the pack chasing their own tails. Already some were giving up, dropping to their knees and scratching at the accumulated leaves and pine needles in frustration.

Then he noticed the bite—or was it a cut? Must have happened in the doughnut shop; none of them had been close to him since— but something had made his elbow bleed. He applied his iodine and prayed. Under stress, some men's mouths spewed obscenity, others Sunday-morning verse. In this case, the latter felt more appropriate as the sting of the iodine took hold.

φ

The cut had some angry red swelling around it by the time night fell and he walked, slowly and gently, down to the riverfront.

Two of the defunct casinos had electric light. Several had gigantic red crosses painted on their bargelike hulls, the universal symbol of help to whoever asks. Fire-gutted hotels lined the riverfront road. Valentine could picture the brilliant lighting above and around the multistory parking lots, the banners along the streets, the florid wealth of a gambling haven opening at the side of the Mississippi, beckoning like a Venus flytrap.

He kept out of the masses of somnambulists wandering under the lights, scooping handfuls of meal out of great troughs lining the streets.

Naturally, more food meant more piles of feces. And more rats eating the feces. And cats eating the rats.

He found an empty trough and passed a wet finger through it, sniffed the result. It smelled and felt like ground corn—hog-feed-grade corn, at that. Some rice and millet, too.

Valentine would rather eat the ants disposing of the leftovers.

"Val," he heard a hiss.

It came from the second floor of one of the hotels. He saw Duvalier's face in a window.

He floated into the shell of the fire-gutted building, a concrete skeleton.

She met him at the staircase with a hug, and they looked at each other's iodine-smeared wounds.

"Let's hope the vaccinations weren't just water," Valentine said. Rumor had it that ravies vaccine commanded a fantastic price in the Kurian Zone, and Southern Command had its share of the unscrupulous.

They crept upstairs. Cats (of the feline variety) scattered in either direction at their approach.

Duvalier and Everready had his pack and gun. Everready extended a piece of greasy waxed paper. "Cold chicken and a biscuit. From the Missions."

"What's next?" Valentine asked.

Everready threw a bone down the hall. A catfight started almost the second it landed. "I passed word to my contact in the Missions. He's going to get in touch with a trading man in Memphis, one of my sets of eyes in the city. Cotswald. Vic Cotswald. He'll take you in. Not the nicest man in the world, but reliable. He thinks I'm working for the Kurians down south, keeping tabs on things in Memphis. He knows me by the handle Octopus. Can you remember that? Octopus?"

"Great. What's my cover?" Valentine asked.

"I took care of that, Val," Duvalier said. "You're Stu Jacksonville, a new pimp on the Gulf Coast. We know the area from our time as husband and wife, so there'll only be a minimal amount of bullshitting."

"You sure you want to play a whore?" Valentine asked.

"Not whore. Bodyguard. Comrade in arms."

"Gay caballero?" Valentine asked.

"Lesbian, if you want to get technical."

# CHAPTER SEVEN

*M*emphis: *The dwindling number of old-time residents of this good-times city divide Memphis history into prequake and postquake. The destruction, the starvation, the Kurian arrival, the appearance of Grogs; all are linguistically bound together and organized by that single cataclysmic event.*

*When the New Madrid fault went, most of the city went with it. One of the few substantial buildings to survive the quake was the St. Jude Children's Hospital, whose grave granite now houses many of the city's Kurian rulers behind concentric circles of barracks and fencing.*

*The rubble left behind was pushing into piles. Eventually those piles were redistributed about the city, forming a fourteen-mile Great Wall of Junk in a blister based at the river that eventually had dirt piled on top of it to turn it into a true barrier. Now a precarious jeep trail circumnavigates the city atop the wall, except for three gaps to the north, east, and south.*

*The south gap is a subcarbuncle of its own, a fenced-in stretch of land between Memphis and Tunica full of livestock pens and grain silos, barge docks and coal piles, a supplemental reserve of food and fuel for the city in case events of war or nature cut it off from the rest of the Kurian Order.*

*Inside the wall, around the heart of the city, are the great bank camps, a temporary concentration of identical, wire-divided cantonments that stretch in some cases for miles. Once a tent city for those left homeless after the quake, the tents have given way to fifty-foot barracks, now wooden-sided, with windows and cooking stoves. Rail lines, sidings, and spurs stretch into the camp like the arteries, veins, and capillaries feeding the liver.*

*The residents go out of their way not to think about those in the camps.*

*Memphis still has some of its pre-2022 culture along Beale Street and in the "commons," the stretch of city bordering the waterfront. The commons are dominated by the ravaged and only partially glassed superstructure of the Pyramid. This mighty sports arena and convention center has canvas stretched over the missing panes, to admit air without the heat of the sun, giving it the appearance of an impossibly huge sailing ship squatting at the edge of the Mississippi, the trees of Mud Island separating its inlet from the main river.*

*The area around the Pyramid rivals Chicago's famous zoo as a center of dubious entertainments, though it is a good deal more exclusive, limiting its clientele to the River Rats, the men who work the barges and patrol craft of the great rivers of middle North America, and those brave enough to go slumming. The Pyramid itself sees a higher order of customer with appetites just as base. As a den where flesh is exchanged for goods or services, temporarily or permanently, the Pyramid has no rival on the continent.*

*While the city has any number of competing factions, captains of war and industry, mouthpieces both civil and Kurian, the commons and the Pyramid look to only one man for leadership. The great auctioneer Moyo has bought and sold more slaves in his forty years than many of the tyrants of old. Always to an advantage.*

*If anyone has gotten the better of him and lived to tell of it, even the old-timers of Memphis cannot say.*

φ

"You want to do what?" Vic Cotswald said.

Cotswald was a heavyset man, and puffed constantly, like an idling steam engine. He took up a substantial portion of the back cabin of his "limo"—a yellow-painted old Hummer.

"Learn about this fellow's setup," Valentine said. "Everyone's heard of Moyo. Why not do what he did, only somewhere else?"

They'd met at a roadside diner built out of a pair of old trailers fixed together and put up on concrete blocks. Duvalier looked a little wan and not at all herself. Valentine hoped it was just the pain of her wound and not the onset of ravies.

He'd know if she started trembling. That was usually the first sign. It might have been better to leave her with Everready in his casino-barge hideout, but she'd insisted on accompanying him into Memphis.

Valentine was dressed all in black. His costume was, in fact, a cut-down version of a priest's habit—it was the only well-made, matching clothing Everready could easily find at the Missions. Valentine had dyed the snake-boots to match on his own, and after cutting off the sleeves added a red neck cloth and a plastic carnation, scavenged from a discarded kitchen on one of the old gambling barges. He wore the gleaming pistol openly in its leather shoulder holster. The U-gun was zipped back up with the rest of their dunnage.

Cotswald wiped grease from his brow and sweat from his upper lip. "Of course everyone's heard of Moyo. Nobody moves deposits in or out of this town without him. The reason Moyo's still Moyo is that he doesn't let anyone get close to him who hasn't come up through his organization. He doesn't just hire Gulfies up to get a chance at the inventory."

Valentine had already learned two pieces of Memphis slang: deposits were the individuals in the bank camps waiting for trans-shipment to their probable doom; inventory was attractive women—and a few men and kids, he imagined—meant for the fleshpots, private and public.

"Octopus is a good guy. Pays well for the little scraps of information that pass my way. What are you offering?"

Valentine reached under his shirt and pulled up a simple lanyard that hung around his neck. A shiny ring turned at the end of the line.

Everready had taken it off a dead general.

"A brass ring? Is it legit?"

"It's mine. You get me in to see Moyo, talk me up, and I'll give it to you. I'm sure you have contacts who can verify its authenticity. If it doesn't check out, you can blow the whistle on me."

"A coast ring's no good here."

"But it is good on the coast. Ever think of your retirement? There are worse places than a beach in Florida."

Cotswald broke into a fresh sweat. "A ring. You better not be doing a bait and switch."

"A *real* ring and a friend named Jacksonville. The higher-ups are putting me in charge of Port Recreation. Got to keep the plebes happy."

"When's the end of the rainbow, Jacksonville?"

"I'm rebuilding a hotel down there. Furnishings are on their way. I just want to see about some—inventory."

"I'm your man," Cotswald said. "Just be warned, stay on the up-and-up with Moyo. He's a razor, he is."

ψ

As they drove through the city Valentine got a feel for the people of Memphis. For the most part they were drab, tired-looking, clad in denim or corduroys. Hats seemed to be the main differentiator between the classes of the city. The workers wore baseball-style hats, turbans, or various styles of tied kerchiefs. Those who gave the orders wore brimmed hats—a broad-brimmed variety called a planter seemed to be the most popular.

Cotswald's Hummer wove through horse carts and mopeds on the way downtown—they took a turn riverward to avoid the jagged outline of the old children's hospital. It had sprouted tulip-shaped towers since the advent of the Kurian Order. A communications tower next to the hospital supported ball-like structures, like spider egg sacks, planted irregularly along the sides, a strange fusion of steel and what looked like concrete—but concrete globes of that size couldn't be supported by the tower.

Cotswald stared studiously out the opposite window, reading billboards for birth-enhancement medications. Something called Wondera promised "twins or triplets with every conception."

OUR GOAL: TRANQUILITY AND JUSTICE FOR ALL read another. WHY SETTLE FOR VITA*MINS*? GET VitaMAX—GUARANTEED SATISFACTION (HIS AND HERS).

Once in the summit of the city—the ground rose at the edge of the river before falling away sharply into the Mississippi—Valentine saw men and women dressed with a little more flash. Some of the women even wore heels. Many of the men sported suits that would cause heads to turn and mouths to gape in the Ozarks: broad-shouldered, pinstriped suit coats with matching trousers and patent-leather shoes in a variety of colors.

"It's a party town," Cotswald said as the sharp notes of an outdoor jazz trio came in through the open windows of the Hummer.

The car turned north onto a well-paved road and shot down an avenue of impressive new homes looking out over the breeze-etched river. The car slowed and turned onto a broader highway that went down the steep hill to the river. Valentine looked up at the riverfront homes. All had balconies, some had two or more.

In the distance to the north, seemingly sitting out on the river, he saw the blue-and-white checkerboard of the Memphis Pyramid.

"That's my house," Cotswald said as they slowed below a brownstone monstrosity, pregnant with a glass-roofed patio thick with potted plants. "Should say, the top floor is mine. I rent out the bottom floor to a colonel and his family. Helps to have friends in the City Guard."

"I admire the neighborhood," Valentine said. Duvalier tapped her fingers on her walking stick.

"But I'm hardly ever there. I usually sleep at the office. Hard to make good when you don't have your own bank, but I couldn't manage it. The faces get to me."

Valentine marked Cotswald as one of the Kurian Zone survivors who made himself as comfortable as possible without hindering the regime. *Born in a different time and place, would I shuffle loads of rice and beans in and out of my warehouses? Trade in a few luxuries on the side?*

*Look the other way to avoid the faces?*

Docks with tethered small craft filled the riverbank. Valentine saw the soldiers of the City Guard everywhere, the russet-colored cotton uniforms and canvas-covered sun-helmets going everywhere in pairs. Pairs searching boats, pairs driving in small vehicles Valentine had heard called "golf carts," pairs walking along the raised wooden promenades.

They got out of the way for the Hummer.

"South end of the riverfront is strictly family fun," Cotswald said as they passed into an amusement park. Valentine marked a merry-go-round in operation and a Ferris wheel giving a good view of the area. Many of the other rides were motionless. "You should see it on Jubilation Day, or Peace Week. People camped out all over the hillside. Great time. Except for the Year Forty-three shelling. The vicious bastards across the river dropped artillery shells all over the place the last night of Peace Week. Killed hundreds. Hasn't felt the same since."

"That was—" Duvalier began.

"Horrible," Valentine cut in. "Macon radio carried the story." He'd heard some Wolves talking about it after the Kurian propaganda broadcasts. Evidently they'd hired mercenaries to do it, then killed the three gun crews. A patrol from Bravo Company found the bodies and shell casings.

The Pyramid grew larger as they approached. Valentine had underestimated its size at first glance. It too had a superstructure capping it, a tall, thin tower with a mushroomlike top, a tiny umbrella perched atop the great canvas-colored structure.

Valentine had never seen anything that more perfectly summed up what Mali Carrasca called *Vampire Earth*: a ruin from the old world, a pyramid of power, with a Kurian at the very top, looking down on the foreshortened, antlike inhabitants of his domain.

"That's some setup Moyo's got."

"It's an old convention center," Cotswald said, wheezing a little more. "Kind of a city to itself. Every riverman on the big three has his own story about his visits there. The Chicago or Vegas or New York girls got nothing on Moyo's; he takes his pick from the deposits across half a continent."

"I'm going to make Jacksonville compete," Valentine said.

"Moyo was young once too," Cotswald said, eyeing the gap in Valentine's shirt that showed the chain to the brass ring.

"What do you do for him?" Valentine asked.

"Run a little booze and high-grade beef."

"He pay you with parties?"

"No, I don't go in for that—not that I'm disapproving of your line of work, Stu. He's got his own clothing lines. When his girls aren't working they're sewing. Some of the fashions you saw downtown, they come from his Graceland label. I sell 'em to shops as far away as Des Moines and Chattanooga."

Duvalier had fallen asleep in the back of the Hummer. Her eyes opened again when it came to a stop.

Cotswald had brought them to the north edge of the commercial docks. A fresh concrete pier and wharves built out of what looked like rubble sat in the shadow of what must have once been a great bridge across the Mississippi. A low, tree-filled peninsula hugged the Memphis side. A rail line ran up into the city from its main tracks, running perpendicular to the old east-west interstate. Valentine saw platform cars being loaded with bags and barrels from the river craft.

"That's the river shuttle," Cotswald said. "My warehouses are at the other end of it."

A narrow pedestrian bridge jumped a few hundred feet of rail line and jumbled rubble separating the Pyramid from the rest of Memphis. Houseboats like suckling baby pigs lined up along the river side of the Pyramid in the channel between the tree-filled island and the Pyramid's plaza.

"You get a lot of boat traffic in Jacksonville?" Cotswald asked.

"A few big ships and a lot of small, intracoastal traders. Looks like you've got your share too."

"That big white one up against Mud Island is Moyo's yacht. Hey, your girl alright?"

Duvalier had sagged against the side of the Hummer.

"You okay, Red?" Valentine asked.

"Just a little faint," she said.

Spiders of anxiety climbed up Valentine's back. "Let me take the packs."

"Thanks."

"Mind if I check your pulse?" Valentine asked. He lifted Duvalier's wrist and watched her hand. Still steady—no, *was that a tremble?*

*She was bitten four days ago. She should be in the clear.*

Valentine threw the satchel of "traveling supplies"—the pseudo-Spam, chocolate bars, and a few detonators surrounded by fresh un-

146

derwear and toiletries—over his shoulder, along with the bigger duffel carrying their guns. She used her stick to walk down to the bridge.

"I think I've got a little fever," Duvalier said. Cotswald puffed ahead, almost filling the sidewalk-sized bridge.

Cotswald explained something to the City Guard at the other end ". . . here on business . . . show the big gear a good time . . ." as Valentine gave Duvalier a water bottle.

"Val, I don't want to be walking around naked in that pen," Duvalier said. "If I got it—"

"You've got an infection from the bite, I bet. God knows what kind of bacteria they have in their mouths."

"Everready says it mutates sometimes. Maybe it mutated so it takes four or five days . . ."

Cotswald waved at them impatiently and they stepped off the walkway. The City Guards smiled and nodded.

"Welcome to Memphis. Roll yourself a good time, sir."

Valentine felt around in his pocket for some of the Memphis scrip—Everready sometimes used the lower-denomination bills for hygiene purposes, he'd accumulated so much of it over the years—and tipped the City Guard. He'd learned in Chicago to tip everyone who so much as wished you a good afternoon.

The bill disappeared with a speed that would do credit to a zoo doorman.

The Pyramid island had obviously once been parkland, but a maze of trailer homes had sprung up around it, separated by canvas tents selling food and beverages.

"Remember, Cots, I've got to get a peek at Moyo's operation if you want your ring," Valentine said.

"Stay away from the Common," Cotswald said, indicating the trailers and tents with a wave. "You hear stories about men disappearing. Don't know if it's shanghaied or"—he jerked his thick chin upward toward the Kurian Tower, a gesture almost imperceptible thanks to his thick flesh. "No society types go there, not if they want to avoid the drip."

Duvalier stiffened at the word "society." "Bastards," she said.

Cotswald furrowed his eyebrows. "Seems a funny attitude for a bodyguard to—"

"Her mother died from complications of syphilis," Valentine said evenly.

"Visitors with gold buy themselves housing," Cotswald went on, pointing to the other side of the island, where the houseboats were nosed into the protective dike around the city.

"Not too expensive, please," Valentine said. Everready's gold would only go so far.

"I'll arrange something for a budget. Let's go down to the rental agent."

They walked along the flood wall. Like most Kurian civic improvements, it was a patched-up conglomeration of sandbags and concrete. The river wall made the dikes of New Orleans look like monuments to engineering. Too bad the river was dropping to its summer low. . . .

"Seems quiet," Valentine said, thinking of the towering white propane tank on the river flank of the Pyramid. Most of the activity around the colossal structure involved men pushing crates on two-wheelers into the convention center. Valentine wondered at the lack of Grogs; in both Chicago and New Orleans their horselike strength and highly trainable intelligence were used for loading and unloading jobs everywhere. "Don't you have Grogs on your docks?"

"Moyo hates them. As to the quiet, everyone's sleeping out the heat," Cotswald said.

Duvalier's face ran with sweat, and her hair hugged her head.

"Let's make this quick," Valentine said.

They followed a path up the side of the flood wall and went down to the docks. Cotswald spoke to an enormous man sitting beneath a beach umbrella near the entryway to the boats.

"He needs to see the color of your coin," Cotswald said.

After a little bartering—Valentine had some difficulty with the man's accent—through Cotswald's offices they arranged for an old cabin cruiser at the rock-bottom price of four hundred dollars a week. In gold. One week in advance, and after the first day the second week had to be paid for or the rate would go to five hundred fifty dollars.

Valentine nodded at the terms. *We'll be gone before then. Unless Duvalier . . .*

Valentine sacrificed one of Everready's coins and got a pile of devalued Memphis scrip in return.

"Let me make sure those are Memphis bills," Cotswald said before Valentine could turn away. He thumbed through the wad. "Hold it, this fifty's in Atlanta dollars."

"Sorreh-suh," the rental agent slurred back.

Cotswald arranged the money and handed it to Valentine. "There's a couple of little markets inside the Pyramid. I wouldn't buy anything from the carts in the commons unless it's fruit or vegetables. They'll sell you dog and tell you it's veal. And don't buy the sausages unless you need stink-bait."

"Thank you."

"I have to attend to a few things in town. I'll be back tonight to show you around."

"Maybe not tonight. My security's not well. How about tomorrow night?"

"Even better. It'll be the weekend."

"Fuck it!" Duvalier barked.

Valentine took her arm. She flinched, but settled down when she saw who he was. "She doesn't like it when I fuss. C'mon, Red. Let's get you in the shade."

She still wasn't trembling. Valentine wished he had listened to old Doctor Jalenga from Second Regiment talk more about ravies. All he could remember is that when they started to spaz out the safest thing to do was shoot—

He'd agreed not to let her suffer—but now he wondered.

Cotswald followed them down the wharf, puffing: "Our arrangement. The—"

Valentine quickened his step, looking at the numbers painted on the cement alongside the moored houseboats. "You'll get it. Once you get me a tour of Moyo's setup."

"I need a chance . . . to check out that ring . . . before you blow town."

"As soon as I'm in the Pyramid."

Number 28.5. This was their boat.

It looked like a frog sitting between two giant white tortoises. The two-level houseboats on either side of the spade-shaped cruiser looked as though they were using the craft as a fender. It had once been a dual-outboard, judging from the fixtures.

Cotswald shrugged. "It's a cabin."

A man who was mostly beer gut and sunglasses sat under an awning atop the port-side craft. "Yello, stranger," he offered.

"Hello back."

"You'll want to wash your bedding out good," their neighbor said. "Last time that cabin was used, it was by the president of the Ohio-Nebraska. He kept his bird dogs in there. They scratched a lot."

"I'll be back tomorrow," Cotswald said, perhaps fearing becoming part of a decontamination press-gang. Valentine nodded.

"Stu Jacksonville, Leisure and Entertainment," Valentine said. "Thanks for the tip."

"Forbes Abernathy. I'm a poor benighted refugee from Dallas, adrift in the world and drowning my sorrows in alcohol and Midway pussy. Or that's what the wife said before she took off with a Cincinnati general. Does this boat look adrift to you?"

Valentine threw the satchel down in the stern of his housing and helped Duvalier in. "Not in the least."

"Now, your putt-putt; a strong storm comes and you'll be blown downriver."

"Thanks for the warning." He tried the key in the padlock holding the doors to the front half of the cabin cruiser closed. After a little jiggling, it opened.

He could smell the dogs. Or rather, their urine.

"Sorry, Ali," he said. He went into the cabin—it had two bed-couches set at angles that joined at the front, and moldy-smelling carpeting that looked like the perfect place to hatch fleas—and opened a tiny top hatch to air it out. There was a tiny washroom and sink. He tried the tap and got nothing.

"Thanks, Forbes," Duvalier said to him as she almost fell into the cabin and plunged, facedown, onto the bench.

Valentine knelt beside her and checked her pulse again. It was fast but strong. Still no trembling.

Another piece of Doctor Jalenga's lecture rose from the tar pit of Valentine's memory. A few people had proven immune to the various strains of ravies virus, or fought it off with nothing more than a bad fever. He crouched next to her—crouching was all that was possible in the tiny cabin—and touched her back. It was wet through, wet enough to leave his hand slick and damp.

She stirred. "Got any water?" Duvalier asked, rolling over. Her hazel eyes looked as though they were made of glass.

Valentine poured her another cup from his canteen. Perhaps a half cup remained. He needed to get them some supplies.

"Why are we back, David?" she asked.

"We're not back. We're in Memphis."

"That's what I mean. Back in the KZ."

"We're trying—"

"We're trying to die."

He put his hand on her forehead. It felt hot and pebbly. "We're doing no such thing."

"That's why we keep going back in," she insisted. "Every time we get out of the KZ, all we can think about is the next trip in. Now why is that? We feel guilty. We want to die like them."

"Rest. I'm going to see about food and something to drink." He unbuckled the shoulder holster.

He went up on deck, feeling alone and vulnerable. Such a tiny piece of information measured against the vastness of the structure above him—

After a moment's thought he locked the door to the cabin with the padlock again. The orblike superstructure atop the Pyramid seemed designed to stare straight down into the back of his boat.

*Job at hand. Eat the elephant one bite at a time.*

His neighbor had a comic book perched on his bulging stomach.

"Excuse me, Mr. Abernathy," Valentine called. "Is there a market around?"

"Inside the Pyramid. Plaza north. Jackson, was it?"

"Jacksonville."

"Where you two from?"

"The Gulf." Valentine jumped up onto the wharf. "Excuse me, my friend's feeling a little sick."

"You two ever been to Dallas?"

Valentine pretended not to hear the question and waved as he walked down the wharf as quickly as he could. The boat attendant saw him coming and suddenly found something to do inside a rusted catamaran.

Valentine ignored him and crossed a wide plaza to the Pyramid. From close-in the base seemed enormous, flanked by concrete outcroppings with pairs of City Guard doing little but being visible.

A towering stone pharaoh, leaning slightly to the left thanks to the earthquake, Valentine imagined, looked out on the main parking lot with its hodgepodge of trailers from the bottom of an entrance ramp.

He walked up the ramp and noticed dozens of chaise lounges on the southwest outer concourse. Women and men, mostly in bathing suits or camp shorts, lounged and chatted and drank while waiters in white shirts and shorts dispensed food and drink from a great cart. It struck Valentine as similar to the lunches in the yard of the Nut.

No double line of fencing topped with razor wire separated these people from their freedom. Habit? The security of position? One deeply tanned man snored into a white naval hat with braiding on its black brim, a thick ring of brass around his white-haired knuckle.

Valentine paid them no more attention than he would a group of lakeside turtles. He passed through a set of steel-and-glass doors and into the Pyramid.

Moyo kept his realm cleaner than the zoo, Valentine gave him that. The impossibly cool interior smelled of floor polish and washroom disinfectant. He was on some kind of outer concourse, advertisements for alcohol, tobacco, women, games of chance, and sporting events hung on banners tied everywhere. As he walked tout after tout, mostly teenage boys Hank's age, tried to hand him flyers. Valentine finally took one.

Black letters on orange card stock read:

**Bloody "Cyborg" Action**
**Pulp Fontaine**
*(hook on right hand)*
*vs*
**The Draw**
*(solid aluminum left arm)*
*3 rounds or maiming*
**Friday July 22 9PM Center Ring**
*all wagers arranged by*
**Roger Smalltree Productions**
*"the pharaoh of fair odds since y37"*
• **Payouts are Moyo Bonded and Insured** •
*(Gallery of Stars Booth 6)*

The teen squeaked: "Listen, sir, my brother's a locker warden. He says Draw's long-shotted to pay off big. Do a bet and you can pay a whole week on the Midway, say?"

"Say," Valentine said and moved on. A woman thrust out a mimeograph of a ñude woman with snakes held in each outstretched arm. "Angelica the Eel-swallower!"

Four-color circus posters, bigger than life-size, screamed out their attractions as he followed an arrow to Plaza North.

**Tammy's Tigereye Casino—Fortune Level**
**Rowdy Skybox** • **Bring Your Attitude and Leave Your Teeth** •
**M-certified Tricks and Treats at Zuzya's—**
*You've tried the rest, now get sqweeffed by the best!*

Loudspeakers played upbeat jazz or orchestral renditions of old tunes Valentine couldn't quite categorize but which fell under the penumbra of rock-and-roll.

He found the food market using his nose. A lively trade from grill and fish vendors added to the aromas of cut melons, fresh berries, and tomatoes. At another stall fryers bubbled, turning everything from bread paste to sliced potatoes into hot, greasy delight, ready for salting.

His stomach growled.

He placed his hand on a pile of ice at the edge of an ice-filled bin holding two gigantic Mississippi catfish, resting on a semicircular counter, and felt the wonder of the wet cold.

"Mind! Mind!" yelled the woman behind the bins of freshwater food. "You buy? No? Shove off!"

Valentine settled on buying a five-gallon plastic jug full of water and some "wheat mix for cereals." Then he found a bottle labeled aspirin—it also smelled like it.

"You just bought that, son," the trucker-cap-wearing druggist said. He paid, glad that Memphis scrip was good in here.

Valentine sought out some food. The rotisserie chickens were reasonably priced and looked fresh—he had to buy a stick for them to put it on, and he topped his purchases off with a sugar-frosted funnel cake. He ate half of the last as he wandered, getting a feel for the layout of the Pyramid—or Midway, as the locals seemed to call it.

An area labeled the Arena seemed to be the center of activity; he heard a woman's voice warbling through a door as a pair of sandal-wearing rivermen exited. There were also two huge convention-center spaces, filled with wooden partitions turning the areas into a maze of tiny bars, tattoo parlors, and what he imagined were brothels or sex shows. Guards stood in front of the elevators, checking credentials and searching those waiting in line for a lift. Valentine guessed that Moyo's offices were somewhere upstairs.

Few visitors seemed to be around at this time of day; Valentine counted at least one employee for every tourist. Red-jacketed security supervisors ordered around men in black overalls with tight-fitting helmets; the footsoldiers bore slung assault rifles and shotguns, but twirled less-lethal-looking batons as they walked in pairs around the concourses, grazing from the food vendor stalls or being passed a lit cigarette by a marketer. Beefy old women pushed buckets and wheeled trash bins everywhere, their gray bandannas wet with sweat and PYRAMID POWER! buttons pinned to their sagging bosoms.

Valentine had done enough sightseeing and returned to the line of houseboats. His Dallas neighbor had disappeared. He hurried back to his small, rented boat, roasted chicken in one hand, water in the other. He set down the water jug and unlocked the cabin.

Duvalier came into the sunshine and reclined on the vinyl cushions—spiderwebbed with breaks exposing white stuffing threads—and drank almost her entire oversized canteen of water. Valentine mixed her up some of the cereal (IDEAL FOR CHILDREN AND SENIORS—ADVANCED NUTRITION! the label read) from the bag, and she ate a few bites with her field spoon.

"Gaw," she said, and tossed the rest to the Mississippi fishes. She leaned against the side of the boat and closed her eyes. He gave her two tablets of aspirin and she gulped them down, then gave him her cup to refill.

"Chicken?" Valentine asked

"You can have it. You get anywhere with this Moyo guy?"

"Haven't met him yet." He felt helpless against the heat coming up through her skin. "How are you feeling?"

"Weird dreams. Really weird dreams. Thought I was running in Kansas with a cop chasing me. He had giant bare feet with eyes in the toes. I know I'm awake now because you don't have flames coming out of your ears."

"I'm glad you're sensible. You were barking out profanity an hour ago."

"Give me a day or two. I'll be back up to strength—or I'll be . . . either way, you'll be on your way."

⚓

She slept, still sweating like a horse fresh from the track, in tiny doses all that night, waking Valentine now and then with brief cries. Not knowing what else to do, he stripped her and dabbed the sweat off her body. To add infestation to injury, both of them broke out in flea bites.

A firework or two went off outside, seemingly timed for the moments when she was sleeping. Forbes Abernathy made a noisy return to his boat about two A.M. with someone who communicated mostly in giggles.

Cotswald arrived the next day, dressed in a straw yellow linen suit. Valentine thought he had a ponderous elegance to him, but he still puffed and wheezed.

"Asthma," Cotswald explained. "Speaking of miseries, how's your bodyguard?"

"A little better," Valentine lied. Duvalier had visibly thinned as the fever wrung the water from her. Valentine, feeling almost as daring as the night he snuck into the general's Nebraska headquarters, had stolen a plastic bag full of ice from the fish vendor when her back was turned and used it to make a compress for her head. She now slept, perhaps a little more soundly thanks to ice and aspirin, in the flea-infested cabin.

He left her a note. Not knowing what the night might bring, he didn't lock her in the cabin. The only weapon he dared take was his little multiknife.

Cotswald puffed up past the stone pharaoh and into the cool of the Pyramid. The sun still seemed high, but the evening throngs were already milling around on the inside. The music played louder and livelier, and attraction barkers brayed. Rivermen in an assortment of outfits and assorted KZ thrill-seekers traveled in mutually exclusive clusters.

Women dressed so as to present décolletage, stomach, buttocks, and legs to advantage wandered through the crowd, selling shots of licorice-smelling alcohol called Mississippi Mud, or "party bead" necklaces of candy, aphrodisiacs, and Alka-Seltzers on a single convenient string, or hot pink Moyo-roses that could be presented to any working girl in tonight's theme costume—(Valentine overheard that it was a cheerleader outfit)—for a free tumble.

"Not that you really need one," a busty pimpette in a conglomeration of zippers and patent leather insisted to a young buck in a Mississippi Honor Guard uniform.

A faint cheer erupted from the arena as they walked the concourse toward the elevators.

"Fifteen-minute call for motorcycle jousting," a pleasant southern-belle drawl announced over the loudspeakers. "A reminder: The Jackson Rangers have gone all of July undefeated. Last year's finalists, Indianapolis Power, will challenge tonight. Ten minutes remain to get your bets in."

They shouldered past a group of off-duty soldiers extracting money from their socks and hats, and stepped into the line at the elevator.

"Destination?" a red-jacketed security man asked as he walked up to their place in the line. He had a bald head and the smooth-but-unenergetic manner of a headwaiter.

"Moyo's office," Cotswald said.

"You have an appointment, Mr. Cotswald?"

"Yes, we do. I made it through Anais."

The security man flipped through a three-ring binder. "Cotswald and Jacksonville. VIP visitor. Very good, sir." Two guards looked them up and down. "If I could just have you take off your coat, Mr. Cotswald," the security man said.

"Of course." Cotswald removed his coat and turned in a circle.

"Thank you. Excuse me, Mr. Jacksonville," the man said. "Step out of line and extend your arms, please."

Valentine submitted to a pat down from one of the guards. They extracted the folding knife. "I'm sorry, sir, no blades whatso-ever," the supervisor said. He placed it in a gridwork of cubbyholes like a mail sorter and gave Valentine a numbered chit, and each of them got red plastic badges on lanyards.

"Please wear these around your necks at all times, especially when upstairs," the supervisor said. "Gordon will take you up."

They rode in silence. Gordon advised them to watch their step when the doors opened. Valentine made a move to tip him but Cotswald shook his head.

They exited the elevator, went down a short hallway lined with paintings of irises and turned, then passed into a wood-paneled foyer. A red-blazered security man holding another binder waited on a chair. A man with the most neatly trimmed hair and nails Valentine had ever seen smiled from his wooden desk at a nexus of hallways.

"Mr. Cotswald, how are you tonight?" Asian eyes that re-minded Valentine of a picture of his grandmother crinkled in a friendly fashion.

"Keeping busy," Cotswald said.

"And this is?"

"Stu Jacksonville, Leisure and Entertaiment from the Gulf. This is Rooster. Stu's looking to upgrade his inventory."

"Excellent, just excellent," Rooster said. "You're wondering about the name. It's from my days looking for new talent in the rail yards. My hair used to stick up on top."

"Gotcha," Valentine said.

A voice shouted from behind leather-padded doors. "Christ on a popsicle stick, you're a fuckup. Rooster, I've got another ass that needs kicking in here!"

"Mister Moyo's having trouble with the lines up from Texas," Rooster explained. "Please excuse me. Won't you have a seat?"

"Oh, quit crying, you twat!" the same voice yelled. "Stuff the excuses!"

Rooster picked up a leather folio and passed through the double leather doors.

"I hate when he gets worked up," the security man said. "You want to go next?"

"You've got bad news too, I take it?" Cotswald asked, perhaps hoping for a piece of stray information he could sell to Everready.

"Desertions. Not of our people; the Memphis clowns. City Guard commander says we've got to start using our forces for exterior security as well as internal until they can get back up to strength. That means busting heads down in the commons, and no one much likes that."

"Maybe we should go first," Cotswald said. "Mr. Jacksonville is looking to spend a great deal of money."

"Then please, be my guest," the security man said.

One of the double doors opened again. A sullen-looking woman came out, holding the shoulder strap of her briefcase with both hands as though it were a lifeline in a hurricane.

Rooster had his arm gently touching her elbow. "Of course it's not your fault, Yayella. It's going to take a while for the reversals in Texas to be overcome." He guided her down the hall toward the elevators and Valentine followed the thread of the conversation by hardening his hearing. "We'll redirect traffic through New Orleans and coastal craft can get it to Houston. The deposits will arrive a little seasick, but they'll be safer."

Rooster glided back into the foyer. "We're next," Cotswald said, and the security guard nodded.

Moyo's office filled the entire east side of the Pyramid. Sloping glass looked out over Memphis' few remaining high-rise buildings and the gold-lit blocks of the former children's hospital in the distance.

Except for the striking slope to the glass, the office didn't look like a pimp's digs, full of exotic animal furs and silver barware, or a rail baron's throne room of oak and brass. Valentine was expecting some combination of the two. Instead Moyo's office seemed to be modeled on a small-town sheriff's: there was a battered wooden desk with a compact, easel-like computer on it, and a not-quite-matching credenza against a dividing wall next to the desk. A few tube-steel chairs were placed around the room, one opposite the desk and more against the walls. On the other side of the divider was a kitchenette where brewed coffee sat on a hot plate, a locked gun case, and dozens of aluminum file cabinets. The most esoteric features were fancy drop-lighting fixtures, throwing puddles of gold on the red carpeting and lending a warm tone to the room. The only personal touch was a curio cabinet filled with toy trains.

Two professionally dressed women played cards on a newsprint-covered table at the corner window. One had a diplomat bag with a laptop poking out of it, the other kept an old-fashioned steno pad at her elbow.

Opposite the women a corridor, complete with a steel-barred door better than anything Valentine had seen at the Nut, led to a darkened hallway that looked as though it went to the center of the Pyramid.

Moyo flicked off the computer screen as they entered.

Valentine thought Moyo had the junkyard-dog features of a man who bit down and kissed up, on the downslope of forty. A cigar that looked like it came with the desk protruded from the corner of his mouth.

"Mister Cotswald has a new associate, a buyer up from Florida," Rooster explained. "This is Stu Jacksonville."

"Jacksonville. Gene Moyo. Pleased." Moyo didn't look pleased, but placed the cigar carefully at the edge of the desk and came around the edge to shake hands. His hand felt like a wrench wrapped in desert leather. "Christ, Roo, at this rate I'm never getting down to the games. There's supposed to be a good match tonight."

"We won't be long," Cotswald said. "Just need a few permissions to look over your current inventory."

"Roo, call down to the box and tell them to hold dinner. Well, siddown, you two. Make it fast."

They pulled chairs as Rooster left.

Valentine wanted a look around the office, but didn't see how he could in his present circumstances. He surreptitiously felt around in his pocket.

"What's your line, Jacksonville? Pro or amateur?"

Valentine hazarded a guess. "My official title's Provisional Leisure and Entertainment Director. The port's growing."

Moyo put the cigar back in his mouth. "Learn something useful, son. No one with a title like that rises."

"It's a sinecure. I used to work coast security."

"Get the facial reconstruction doing that?"

"That would make a better story. It was an accident—I was careless with a rifle."

"What kind of numbers are you looking for?"

Valentine shifted in his seat to cover his hand's motion. "Thirty gals to start off. I'd like a seat at your auctions, too. I can see two, maybe three trips a year up here."

The cigar moved from the left side of Moyo's mouth to his right. "Payment?"

"Gold. I have enough for a substantial deposit."

"Let's see your color. Sorry, but you're a stranger to me."

Valentine placed a coin on the desk.

"Fort Knox mint. Very good."

"Mister Moyo, if you'd rather talk business at the game, I'm not averse to continuing negotiations down there."

"Anais!" Moyo barked over his shoulder.

The woman with the diplomat bag set down her cards. "Yes, Mister Moyo?"

"Get my weekly out. See if Rooster's got any last-minute additions, then you two can go home as soon as I'm done with my last appointment."

"Thank you, Mister Moyo," she said.

"Rooster!" Moyo yelled.

Rooster appeared quickly enough. "Take these gentlemen down to the owner's box. We have much inventory on hand?"

"New? Five or six girls at the most," Rooster said. "Sorry, Mister Jacksonville, a year ago we had half of Arkansas in here. At this rate there won't be another auction for some weeks."

"You can buy out of my joints, if you want, Jacksonville," Moyo said. "I've got a couple older gals who aren't half-bad managers, too. If the price is right you could hire one or two away from me."

"I appreciate your generosity," Valentine said, shifting his foot slightly.

Moyo put down his cigar again in the same wet groove. "Liquor in the box is on me, alright? Cots, you staying?"

"I need to see about my weekend shifts, and monthlies," Cotswald said. "Line In is piping the Sourbellies from Beal Street athenaeum tonight; thought I'd tune in."

"More ice for us, then," Moyo said, coming around the desk to shake hands again. "Rooster, take Stu down to the box and get him set up. Unless you want a quick look at the inventory?"

Valentine hated to think of the faces. "No, I'll check out your games. And your bar."

"Be down in an hour or so. I've got to go up and do my own reporting." Moyo inclined his head toward the barred corridor.

"You actually go up?" Valentine asked; no pretense was required for his incredulity.

"Just to an audience blister. You ever been in one?"

"No," Valentine said.

Moyo lost a little of his bristle. "My predecessor used to rub lemon zest inside his nostrils to keep out the smell. But it's the walls that get to me. That paste they use, it sucks water out of the outside air somehow. Everything on the inside's wet and dripping. When a big drop hits your shoulder . . . well, you jump. Feels like someone tapping you."

Valentine broke the silence that followed. "See you for a drink later, then."

"Sure. Whoa there, Stu, you missing something?"

"What's that?" Valentine asked.

"Looks like you dropped your roll." Moyo pointed. "It's right under the desk there."

*There goes the excuse to come back up here* . . . "Must have fallen out when I reached for my coin," Valentine said, flushing. "That would have been a pisser; that's my walking-around money." Valentine retrieved the bills he'd nudged under the desk moments ago.

"I'll forgo the ten percent finder's fee," Moyo said. "Rooster, give me the latest transport figures with destinations, then send in that ass Peckinsnow on your way out, would you?"

φ

Valentine slipped the brass ring to Cotswald on the way out as Rooster collected his carryall from his desk. Valentine wondered how long it would take him to have it "checked out." While a brass ring meant little to a Kurian or one of their Reapers if it wasn't on the actual owner's finger, it was still a powerful totem when waved in front of the groundlings. Valentine just had to hope the circumstances of the ring's loss were not so well known as to have everyone connected to it, including Stu Jacksonville, immediately rounded up for the Reapers.

"If you're into music, maybe you can show me around Beale Street tomorrow," Valentine said.

Valentine watched Cotswald touch the ring in his pocket, fingering it like an exploring teenager. "Sure," he said absently.

"You'll find that little thank-you—what did Mister Moyo say, 'finder's fee?'—useful if you ever get down my way," Valentine said.

"I'll have to do that before long," Cotswald said. Valentine felt sorry for the dreamy look in the man's eyes. Did confidence men ever feel guilty as they took their marks?

Valentine and Rooster exited on the "showcase" level. Cotswald continued down in the elevator.

Fresh paint covered the structural concrete here, and the lighting came from bulbs.

"Rooster, can I ask you a question?"

"Shoot, Stu. You don't mind if it's Stu, do you?"

"Not at all." Valentine liked using false names in the Kurian Zone. One more curtain between David Valentine and the vast darkness of the Kurian night. "Why the kindling up in Mister Moyo's office? My head porter has a nicer rig."

Rooster glanced up at the ceiling. "Affectation. He started out as a diesel mechanic. When they made him yard supervisor he got an office. It had that junk in it. To him, that first desk meant he made it. I don't mind—he gave me the previous director's outfit for my office. Solid mahogany and half a herd of leather."

"Do you intend to be the next director?"

"Almost there already. I run the day-to-day stuff, he gets the headaches. Personally, I like having him between me and them."

Valentine wanted to ask more about the day-to-day stuff, but they reached the box.

About a dozen people, not counting a food server and an impossibly beautiful young man tending bar, already lounged in the box. The wedge-shaped room was divided into a set of plush-looking seats arranged stadium-style and an entertainment area. A hot tub filled with ice prickled with the necks of beer bottles and sparkling wines. Harder liquors filled up a backlit case behind the bar.

A pair of televisions at each corner held scheduling information. "Closed-circuit TV," Rooster said. "Most of the skyboxes are wired. We've got a camera snafu so there won't be close-ups tonight. Getting replacement electronics takes practically forever."

Valentine looked over the attendees. One of the men had the look of an athlete, as big as one of the Razors' Bears, but his velvet skin had a far healthier sheen and only a neatly closed scar or two. Men and women in well-cut summer cottons were listening to the sportsman. Two obvious party girls eyed him hungrily from the bar.

Rooster introduced Valentine as a "hotel owner from Florida."

The box looked out over the three-ring circus at the center of the arena through tinted-glass windows. Valentine looked out on Moyo's entertainments.

The layout was familiar to anyone who had seen a circus. A

hard wooden track, black with wheel marks, surrounded three platforms. The two on either end were more or less stages—one had a band on it at the moment, furiously working their guitars and drums—and the one in the center was an oversized boxing ring shaped like a hexagon.

Two decks for the audience, a lower and an upper, held a few thousand spectators. Valentine saw motion in the upper deck to his right, just beneath the ring of skyboxes.

"Admission is free," Rooster explained. "Some of the bookmakers own skyboxes. If you bet heavy with them you can sit up here."

Valentine caught motion in the upper deck, not sure of what he was seeing for a moment. Yes, that definitely was a woman's head of hair bobbing in an audience member's lap.

"I've heard of seat service, but that's taking it to a new level," Valentine said.

Rooster laughed. "Some of the cheaper gals work the BJ deck. They're supposed to be selling beer and peanuts and stuff too, but a lot just carry around a single packet or can. Lazy bitches."

"Outrageous," Valentine said. He looked up at the gridwork above. And froze.

The lighting gantries had Reapers in them.

Valentine counted three. One sat in a defunct scoreboard, occasionally peering from a hole like an owl. Another hung upside down from a lighting walkway, deep in shadow, neck gruesomely twisted so it could watch events below. A third perched in a high, dark corner.

"They always here?" Valentine asked. He didn't want to point, but Rooster was sharp enough to follow his eyes.

"Oh, yeah. That dark box, there and there; you have a couple more in each of those. Memphis' own version of closed-circuit TV. They never bother anyone." He lowered his voice. "Sometimes a contestant gets badly hurt. The injuries end up being fatal."

"Then why do they fight?" Valentine asked.

"Look at Rod Lightning's finger back there. Nice little brass ring and a riverside house. He trains cage fighters now. Sight of beetles bother you?"

"Not unless they're looking at me," Valentine answered, honestly enough.

Moyo arrived with a small entourage of river and rail men. Valentine took an inconspicuous seat and watched events below. Something called a "bumfight" began, involving a half-dozen shambling, shabby-looking men clocking each other with two-by-fours. It ended with two still upright and the blood in the hexagon being scrubbed by washerwomen while a blond singer warbled from the stage near Moyo's box. He only had one brief conversation with Moyo.

"How do you like the Midway?" Moyo seemed positively bubbly; perhaps having another report over and done took a weight off—

"Better organized, and a lot less dangerous, than New Orleans," Valentine said. "There's nothing on the Gulf Coast like this."

"You checked out the inventory yet?"

"I've got a couple more days in town still."

"Rooster can set the whole thing up. I'm going to be on my boat this weekend."

"I think he's got a handle on what I need," Valentine said.

There was topless Roller Derby on the wooden ring—a crowd favorite, judging from the cheers. The metronome motion of swinging breasts as the woman power-skated had a certain fascination, Valentine had to admit. Then an exhibition of flame dancing. The first Grogs Valentine had seen on the Midway spun great platters full of flaming kerosene on their outstretched arms and heads. They arranged it so the liquid fire sprinkled off the spinning dishes and they danced beneath the orange rain. Valentine found it enthralling and said so to Rooster.

"God, I hate those things," Rooster said, on his third drink. "Stupid, smelly, ill-tempered. They're useless."

Attendants with fire extinguishers cleaned up after the dance as the Grogs cartwheeled offstage.

Then it was time for the main event. A cage descended on wires from the ceiling, ringing the hexagon with six wire barriers. He watched Pulp Fontaine turn the Draw's shoulder into a bloody ruin. *So much for long shots,* Valentine thought, as Fontaine accepted a victory crown from this month's Miss Midway.

"Ten thousand will get you her for the weekend, Stewie," Rooster chuckled. "Want me to set it up?"

"I don't roll that high," Valentine said.

The party in the box got louder and the stadium began to empty out. It was just after eleven. Rod Lightning left with the two bar girls. The announcer began to count down for kill-tally bets. Valentine wondered what that meant.

"Time to call it a night?" Valentine asked Rooster. "Thank you for your hospitality."

"Nope. One more special show," Rooster said. "Ever heard of a rat kill?"

"This have something to do with extermination?"

"In a manner."

Valentine watched twenty men of assorted sizes and colors being led into the center hexagon. Each had a black hood over his head. Some of the people on their way out hurried for the exits, but a good third of the audience stayed.

"What's this?" Valentine asked, a little worried.

"It's a rat kill," Moyo said from over his shoulder. "I'm going to watch this one. One of my yard chiefs is in there. Daniel Penn. He was screwing me on deposits, swapping out corpses for the healthy and smuggling them across the river."

Rooster made a note on a pad. "They're all criminals of one sort or another, or vagrants."

Some of the condemned men lost control of themselves as they stepped into the ring. Bladder, bowel, or legs gave way. Escorts in black uniforms shoved them into the cage and lined them up. Valentine saw a shot clock light up in the scoreboard—evidently one part of it still worked—set for sixty.

"And here comes the Midway Marvel," Moyo said.

"Jus-tiss. Jus-tiss! JUS-TISS!" the crowd began to chant.

Tall. Pale. Hair like a threadbare black mop. It was a Reaper, stripped to the waist, loose, billowing black pants ending just above its bare feet. It walked oddly, though, with its arms behind it. As it entered the cage he saw why—thick metal shackles held its wrists together.

"JUS-TISS JUS-TISS JUS-TISS!" the crowd roared, the attenuated numbers sounding just as loud as the thicker crowd had for the night's main event.

"The Marvel's got sixty seconds to off as many as he can. Record's fifteen for the year. All-time high is eighteen. Contest rules say that one always has to survive—even though we've never had a nineteen."

As they unshackled each man from his companions and removed his hood they read the crime, but no name. Number one was a murderer. Number two committed sabotage. Number three had been caught with a transmitter and a rifle. . . .

"Why no women?" Valentine asked.

"Haven't done women in a rat kill for years," Moyo said.

Fourteen, a currency forger, fainted when they took his hood off.

"Crowd didn't like it as well," Rooster said. "They booed when it killed a woman instead of a man. We have other ways of taking care of women. Would you—"

"No thanks."

A heavyset man in a black-and-white-striped shirt with a silver whistle entered the ring to more cheering. He wore a biking helmet and thick studded-leather gloves. The condemned men bunched up.

Valentine felt sick, suspecting what was coming. "Who operates the Marvel?" he asked.

"The one at the top of the Pyramid," Rooster said, lifting his glass a few inches for emphasis. "We only get to do one of these a month. You're lucky."

"You must have an unusually lawless town," Valentine said.

Moyo leaned in close. "I'll tell you a little secret. Only a couple are really criminals. The others are volunteers who took the place of a spouse or a relative in the fodder wagon. On a bad night only six or seven die, so they've got a better than fifty-fifty chance of making it back out."

*That's the Kurian Zone. A lie wrapped in a trap cloaked in an illusion.* "Jesus," Valentine said.

"Never showed up," Moyo said.

The referee held a black handkerchief high. Valentine was surprised to see that the Reaper's arms were still bound. Weren't they going to unleash it? Or would it simply break free at the right moment?

*Sixty seconds, Valentine. You can get through this.*

The referee let fall the handkerchief and backpedaled from between the Reaper and the trembling "rats."

As the fabric struck the floor the crowd cheered.

The Reaper sprang forward, a black-and-cream blur. It landed with both feet on the neck of the man who had fainted. Valentine almost felt the bones snap.

The referee blew his whistle.

"ONE!" the crowd shouted. Those still in the box counted along in a more subdued manner.

A convict grabbed another, slighter man by the arm and pushed him at the Reaper. Snake-hinged jaws extended and the stabbing tongue entered an eye socket.

*Tweeeeet.* "TWO!"

"Two," said the audience in the box.

The Marvel had a sense of humor. It head-butted the man who had thrown his companion into its jaws. Blood and grayish brain matter splattered across the damp canvas.

The whistle blew again. "THREE!"

"Three," Valentine said along with the others. The shot clock read forty-six seconds.

Another jump, and another man went down. The Reaper had some trouble straddling him before the tongue lanced out and buried itself in his heart. *Tweeeet.*

"Four," Valentine said with Moyo, Rooster, and the crowd.

"But it'll cost—"

Some of the men climbed the panels of the cage—not to get out, it closed at the top—but to make themselves inaccessible. The Reaper sprang up, jaws closing on a neck.

Whistle, cheers, and the shot clock read thirty-nine seconds. The Reaper threw the body off the way a terrier tosses a rat.

"SIX!" tried to hide behind the referee and got a leather-glove backhand for his troubles. "SEVEN!" was kicked off the fencing by another man higher up. "EIGHT!"

Valentine found himself yelling as loudly as anyone in the room.

Part of him wasn't faking. Another part of him was ready to vomit thanks to the previous part. . . .

Fifteen seconds left.

The Reaper hurled itself at the cage, and three men dropped off the fencing like windfall apples.

"NINE!" "TEN!" As the whistle and shot clock sounded, the Reaper lashed out with a clawed foot and opened a man up across the kidneys.

"Ten is the official count," the loudspeakers said. "Ten paid three to one. Check your stubs, ten paid three to one."

"About average," Rooster said. "Sorry you didn't get a better show, Stu."

The dripping Reaper folded itself onto the mat.

Eleven died anyway, screaming on the blood-soaked canvas.

Moyo said his good-byes. He looked exhausted as he drained the glass of whiskey he'd been nursing.

"How about a nightcap?" Valentine asked Rooster, who emptied his glass at the same time his boss did.

"Night's still young, and so are we, O scarred Stu." He refilled his glass.

"I've got a bottle of JB in my boat."

"Naw. Better liquor at my place," Rooster said. "You haven't really partied Memphis-style yet."

"Or we could hit some bars."

"I got something better than that."

"Better than the Midway?" Valentine asked.

"Better. I need to stop off at the security station first and check out some inventory. Meet at the big stone statue out front? Say in fifteen minutes?"

"How about I come with you?"

"No, you don't have the right ID for the security section. I'll be fast."

"See you there."

ψ

Valentine rode the elevator down—a more alert-looking guard worked the buttons after hours—and collected his pocketknife. He had to shrug off prostitutes—three women and a man, all with makeup headed south for the evening—on the way to the statue. The night had cooled, but only a little. The concrete seemed to be soaked with heat like the bloody canvas within.

*Please, Ali, be coherent when I get back.*

He caught sight of Rooster, leading a little procession of three individuals in oversized blue PYRAMID POWER T-shirts. All female, all teens, shackled in a manner similar to the twenty culls within.

"Got you a little souvenir, Stu." Rooster tossed him a black hood with the number ten on it. Valentine smelled the sweat on it.

"I had them tag it with the date. The one with the number the Marvel took is collectable."

Valentine wadded up the thin, slick polyester in his hand. "Who are these?" he asked, looking at the string of young women. Rooster held a leather lead attached to the first. A foot and a half of plastic line linked each set of ankles.

"I'm—" one began.

Rooster lifted a baton with a pair of metal probes at the end. "You wanna get zapped? No? Then shut it!"

"I just need to get a bag from my boat," Valentine said.

"Okeydokey," Rooster said.

"What's the plan for these three?" Valentine said as they walked.

"Inventory Inspecshun," Rooster slurred. "Fresh stuff, just off the train, that I picked out this week. Privileges of position and all that. They go back in the inventory hopper Monday morning." He glanced over his shoulder. "Provided I don't get a lot of lip," he warned. "Then it's back with the deposits."

"Three?"

"I don't mind sharing. I like to do one while the others watch."

Valentine looked at the trio. The youngest looked fourteen. He read silent pleas in their eyes.

"I think I'm going to bring my camera for this," Valentine said.

"Great idea!"

They walked slowly down the line of houseboats. Lights burned within some. Valentine heard moaning from the open window of another.

"Another Midway party!" Rooster said, as an orgasmic cry rolled out of the boat.

Valentine approached his boat. Their Dallas neighbor was apparently out for the evening.

"Red?" he called from the pier.

Duvalier popped out from the cabin like a jack in the box. One of the girls screamed. "The hell?" she said, gaping.

Duvalier had blood caked in her hair, under one eye, on her hand.

No time. Valentine brought his hand down, hard, on Rooster's wrist. He grabbed the butt of the club with the other hand, found the trigger, and released his grip on the wrist as he stuck the metal-tipped end against Rooster's breastbone.

A buzzing sound and the smell of ozone filled the riverbank air.

Rooster dropped, twitching, and he turned on Duvalier, expecting her to lunge, not knowing what he'd do to her. . . .

"Back off, Ali," he warned.

"Val, are you nuts? What's going on?" She sounded coherent, though her eyes blazed brightly.

"We're getting out of here."

"I was just going to suggest that."

"You want out of Memphis?" he asked the girls. Rooster moaned, and Valentine zapped him again.

"Yes," one said. The others nodded dumbly.

"Get in the boat."

He opened up the pocketknife and cut the bands between their legs, stuffed the hood in Rooster's mouth, and tied it down with the leather lead. He searched him, found a key to the girls' shackles, and transferred the restraints from the chicks to the cock.

"Who's the blood from?" Valentine asked Duvalier as they cut the lines from the little cabin cruiser to the wharf. Valentine made sure to leave a long lead at the front of the boat.

"Our Dallas neighbor," Duvalier said, pushing the girls into the cabin. "He insisted he knew me. I think he just wanted in my pants."

"Where is he?"

"Dead."

Valentine glared at her.

"Don't worry, I did him in his shower. Gave a blow job he never had time to forget. All the blood flowed into the boat drain."

"Except for what got on you."

"What's the plan now?"

"Thank God the river flows in the direction of Tunica."

Valentine hopped into the water and pushed the boat away from the wharf. The water was only four feet deep along the bank.

"Try and find something to use as a paddle," he suggested.

"Whaddya think you're doing, buddy?" someone called from another boat as they headed toward the river.

"Fishing!" Valentine yelled back. "Have a great weekend!"

The boat began to drift, and Valentine went around to the front and took up the line. He waded along the river, Mississippi mud, the real kind, treacherous beneath his feet. More than once his feet slipped on the bottom.

All Duvalier could find to use as paddles were dinner plates.

So he waded on, keeping close to the Memphis bank, until he passed Mud Island and got into the current. He fell into the boat as it slowly spun down the semi-intact bridge to the Arkansas side.

A few other pleasure craft were out, everything from ship-rigged sailcraft to linked lines of inner tubes, escaping the summer heat of the city but keeping well clear of the midchannel markers that evidently served as some kind of boundary. He parked the teenagers around the stern—their names were Dahra, Miyichi, and Sula, of Kansas, Illinois, and Tennessee respectively—and had them all hold plastic cups as though they were drinking. Valentine and Duvalier paddled with the dinner plates, weary work that required hanging off the side whenever the current threatened to carry them too close to a passing boat or the bank.

"The fever's down, I take it," he said to Duvalier as they caught their breath.

"Broke this afternoon," she said. "God, I'm tired."

Fewer and fewer craft were to be seen the farther south along the shore they drifted. They came to the second bridge. Only the piers nearest the shore were still connected with the road.

Valentine saw sentries on the empty bridge. It might seem odd to guard a bridge to nothing but a hundred-foot drop, but the vantage gave a superb view of the river south of Memphis.

"Ali, you get in the cabin with your shotgun. You three—pretend to be passed out," Valentine said.

After they passed under the bridge a spotlight hit them.

"You're coming up on the buoys," a megaphone-amplified voice called down. "Commercial and security craft only."

Valentine stood up, wavering. "My engine fell off," he yelled. "I need a tow!"

"Not our problem."

Sula raised her head and shielded her eyes from the spotlight. She jumped up on the front of the boat. "What unit y'all in?" she yelled, doing a thicker local accent than Valentine could manage convincingly.

"Bravo Company, Corsun's Memphis Guard," the voice called back, a little friendlier. "And you're about an eighth of a mile from being arrested."

"Well then, throw us a line," Valentine yelled.

"Bravo Company Memphis Guard," Sula yelled, raising her shirt. She hopped up and down in the spotlight. *"Whooooo!"*

"What's going on out there?" Duvalier asked softly from behind the cabin door.

"Distractions," Valentine said.

Approving yells broke out from above.

Then Sula sat down and hugged her knees, and they drifted until the spotlight went off.

"Nice improv," Valentine said. "Except it's likely to bring six patrol craft down on us."

Valentine knew vaguely that at the bend ahead a largish island divided the river. If they could reach it they'd be near the wall to the ravie colony.

A patrol craft even smaller than their boat plodded up the river on a single outboard.

"Are we in trouble?" Miyichi asked.

"Row toward the bank. Paddle!" Valentine urged. He leaned

over and dug into the water with a dinner plate. Someone on the bridge with a good pair of night glasses would still be able to distinguish individual figures.

The boat turned sharply their way. A small spotlight or a heavy-duty flashlight lanced out through the river night.

"Keep down, you three," Valentine whispered. Then, a little louder, "Ali, small boat. If one sticks his head in the cabin, you blow it off!"

Valentine stood up and waved with both arms. "Hey there. Can you give us a tow?"

"Where's Miss Midway?" a voice called from the boat.

Sula stood up. "I was just funnin' with the soldiers. Didn't mean any harm."

Valentine tried his drunk voice again. "I'm sorry about her not keeping the flotation devices properly stowed, sir."

"Hey, Corp, let's turn 'em in as vagrants and take the bounty," a shadowy outline next to the flashlight said, too quietly for Sula to hear. Valentine felt a little better about what he was about to do.

"Let me do the thinking," the corporal said. "Get the man on board and handcuff him. If he's a Somebody we apologize and bring him home to mama. Otherwise we'll take a little snatch break with the girls before we collect the bounty."

Valentine opened his pocketknife to the longest blade and climbed up on the front of the boat, where Sula had done her exhibition, and knelt. He made a move to tuck in his shirt and stuck the open knife in his back pocket. "Toss me a line, there, sir. I really appreciate this."

The police boat came alongside. It had a small trolling motor and a big inboard. A waterproof-wrapped machine gun was lashed to a platform on the retractable top. Unlike Valentine's craft, the front was open, with more seating.

A lean man with corporal's stripes in a blue-and-white shirt tossed Valentine a rope. His partner wore a black baseball cap with a Memphis Guard patch sewn to the front.

Valentine leaned forward to catch it and went face-first into the river.

"Grab onto this, you idiot," he heard as soon as he surfaced.

174

Sputtering, he grabbed onto the rope-loop boathook the corporal had extended.

"You're really racking up the fines, friend," the corporal said as he pulled Valentine into the boat.

*You two or us. You two or us. You two or us,* Valentine thought, working himself up for what had to come. He saw the other come forward with the handcuffs—

—and put his foot down—*hard*—on the corporal's instep. The knife flashed up and into the side of the man's throat. Valentine twisted his wrist as he pulled it out, opening the carotid artery.

The other dropped his cuffs and reached for his holster as his partner instinctively clapped a hand to the spurting blood. Valentine's fist seemed to take forever to cross the distance to the hat-wearer's face, striking him squarely between the eyes.

The gun quit coming up and spun off the stern.

Valentine threw himself after his fist and bodily knocked the man against the boat's side. The knife ripped into the Guard's crotch, digging for the femoral artery just to the side of the groin, then up and across the eyes.

A sirenlike wail and Valentine saw an explosion of light. He backed off, shaking his head, trying to think, to see. When his vision came back the man was on the deck, the blackjack he'd struck Valentine's temple with still in his hand. Duvalier was astride the railing, bloody sword cane in hand.

"Ali . . ."

"Not a bad killing," she said, nuzzling him. "But we have to go. Right now."

They transferred the people—including the bound Rooster—over to the police boat. Duvalier tossed over their dunnage bags as Valentine put on the river patrolman's baseball cap. They tied their now-empty boat to the transom on a ten-foot line. Valentine went to the control console and pushed the throttle forward. He didn't open it up all the way; too fast an exit might alarm the bridge watchers.

But they were still heading away from Memphis.

Valentine turned on the flashing police light. Perhaps the bridge sentries would think that the river patrol had spotted another craft and moved to intercept. They passed out of sight of the bridge behind the island, roaring down the river with a *V* of white water behind . . .

They rounded the island and rejoined the main channel of the river as it zigged back south again. "Ali, rig one of the cans with a timer," Valentine said. "We're into the ravies colony area now. We'll send this thing to the Arkansas shore and have it blow."

"Hope all this was worth it, Val," she said. "I don't think we're going to get another try at the Pyramid after this."

Valentine looked at the three girls in the bow of the police boat. "It was worth it."

ɸ

Twenty-four hours later they stood in a dark lower deck of one of the old casino barges. A single lantern threw just enough light off the remaining bits of mirror and glass to reveal just how big, dark, and empty the former gambling hall was. Rows of broken-open, dusty slot machines stood like soldiers on parade.

It reeked of bat guano and mold.

Valentine, Ahn-Kha, Duvalier, and Everready surveyed their handiwork. Rooster was tied facedown on an old roulette wheel, his hands solidly bound to the well-anchored spinner. The rather haggard-looking deposit-and-inventory man couldn't see anything; his head was enclosed in a bag with the number ten written on it.

A small bowl of foul liquid—blood and musk glands from a sick old tomcat Valentine had shot with his .22 an hour ago—rested on the wooden bar for the players' drinks.

"Money, then?" Rooster said. "Moyo's loaded. He'll pay to get me back."

Dahra, Miyichi, and Sula sat on the stools next to the wheel so they could see Rooster's face. Valentine took the hood off.

"Okay, Jacksonville, I give up," Rooster said. The man was crying. "You win. What do you want? What did I ever do to you?"

"No, this is purely professional," Valentine said. "I need to know about a certain train."

"I deal with dozens of trains a week, man. How am I supposed . . ."

"No, this is right up your alley," Valentine said. "It's a really special train."

"Look, I have a dog. No one to look in on him. He's dying—"

"Listen to the question. A train. A special train, not deposits. All women on board. Routed through Memphis. Some sort of medical test selected them. Maybe joining with similar trains."

Slight hesitation. "I don't know anything about a train like that. Let me go and I'll find out for you—"

Valentine turned to the young women. "Looks like you're going to get to watch after all. Bring it in, Smokey."

Ahn-Kha stepped forward from the opposite end of the table, snuffling and snorting. Rooster tried to look behind himself, but couldn't get his chin around his shoulder.

"What's that?"

Valentine walked to the end of the table and used the saw edge on the pocketknife to split Rooster's pants at the buttock line.

"A big, bull Grog, Rooster."

Valentine winked at Ahn-Kha. The Golden One snuffled and snorted around.

"I don't like this," Rooster said. "I think we sent a train like that north somewhere."

Valentine dipped his hand in the smelly cat offal. "You'd better dig deep in your memory, before our bullyboy gets deep into you, Rooster." Valentine smeared the bloody slime up Rooster's crack.

"You can't mean—"

Ahn-Kha began to paw at Rooster, his giant, long-fingered hands taking a grip on his shoulder. He whined eagerly, like a starving dog begging for dinner.

"He thinks you're a female in estrus, Rooster."

"Holy shit, that's big," Dahra said, as the other two girls' mouths dropped open. "Pimp, my forearm's got nothing on this Grog—"

"Stop him!" Rooster shouted.

"Where?" Valentine said, leaning down and looking him in the eyes. "You're about a minute away from a lifetime with a colostomy bag, if you don't bleed to death. Where?"

Something brushed up between Rooster's spread cheeks. "Laurelton, Ohio. Laurelton!" Rooster shrieked.

"Pull him back," Valentine said, and Ahn-Kha grunted as he came off Rooster's back. Valentine threw down the hood. "Show me on this map!" Valentine said, opening an old, rolled-up state atlas.

He did.

Duvalier lifted the eggplant she'd been working between Rooster's buttocks, sniffed the smeared end, and made a face. The teens giggled.

"There, you've helped yourself out of a jam, Rooster," Valentine said. "Sorry about your dog, but we'll have to keep you here a few months. Once we've checked your destination out, we'll let you go free."

Rooster sagged in his bonds.

"What do they do with the women there?" Valentine asked.

Rooster, his nose planted on 11 Black, said: "I dunno. It's just very important that they arrive healthy. A doctor accompanies each train."

"How many trains?"

"One or two a year. Maybe a hundred total bodies."

Duvalier and Ahn-Kha exchanged shrugs.

Valentine picked up the bowl of cat guts and sent it spinning into the darkness. "Girls, watch Rooster for a moment. Don't take advantage of a pantsless man."

They went to a stairwell where a candle burned. "Everready, you think you can take care of those girls and keep an eye on that prisoner for the summer?"

Everready nodded. "Be a nice switch from fresh Wolves with the milk still on their chins."

"If we're not back by New Year's, I'll leave it to your discretion," Valentine said.

"Everready's home for wayward girls," the old Cat said. "I kind of like the sound of that. Maybe this old Cat should retire and take up a new line of work."

"In your dreams, Gramps," Duvalier said.

"Looks like I'm Ohio-bound. You two want to go back?"

"Never," Ahn-Kha said. "Will Post is counting on us."

"It does occur to you that you're looking for a needle in a

haystack," Duvalier added. "Maybe a haystack that's been blown across half the country."

"You're going back, then?" Ahn-Kha asked.

"Maybe the ravies is finally kicking in," she said. "I'm game. But next time, Val, you're squatting under Ahn-Kha's junk and holding the vegetable, okay?"

# CHAPTER EIGHT

*T*he Tennessee Valley, August: Six former states lay claim to the Tennessee River, and benefit from the electricity it generates. Its tributaries are fed by the eighty inches or so of rain that drop on the Appalachian foothills, swelling the lakes behind the nine still-intact dams. Its total shoreline, utilized by man, bear, wildcat, ducks, geese, and wading birds, exceeds that of the entire Pacific and Gulf Coasts of the former United States.

The residents in the settlements around it pull pike, catfish, sauger, bass, and crappie from its waters, both to pan-fry and to plant alongside their seedcorn, a form of phosphate fertilization used by the Native Americans of the area three hundred years ago.

But there are still long stretches of river uninhabited and returned to the thickly forested banks of earlier times. The reason for the human flight: the skeeters.

Tennessee Valley mosquitoes are legendary for their numbers and virulence. With some stretches of the river overrunning flood control, swamps have formed, and the mosquitoes fly so thickly above the still water that they can resemble a buzzing fog. With them come malaria, bird flu, and some mutated strains of ravies—Alessa Duvalier could describe a bout with one strain in nauseating detail—so humans keep clear of certain stretches to safeguard their children and livestock.

There's still some river traffic in corn, soy, and grains (often concealing casks of white lightning and other illicit medications), and of course the quinine-gulping, citrus-candle-burning power plant workers and locksmen at the dams must be there. But the areas around the riverbanks and swamps belong to a few hardy individualists, fugitives, and *those who hunt them—"mad dogs and warrant men" in the vernacular of the Tennessee Valley.*

*David Valentine encountered both in the summer of '72 at the Goat Shack in south-central Tennessee.*

φ

The heat reminded Valentine of Haiti, which is about as much as could be said of any hot day, then and for the rest of his life. Even in the shade he sweated, the humidity about him like a sticky cocoon, turning his armpits and crotch into a swamp as moist as either of the bottoms flanking the peninsula of land projecting like a claw into the lower Tennessee.

Everready's map had been accurate, right down to the "friendly" homes along the way where they could trade news and a few bullets for food, a hayloft hammock, and washsoap. But the Old Black Cat's knowledge of the area ended at the dipping loops of the Tennessee. From there they'd need another guide to get them to Ohio. And he only trusted one.

"Trains are no good. There are checkpoints at all the major rivers," Everready said as they talked routes on the top deck of a defunct casino. "You'll have to go overland. Only man who knows the ground I know of is Hoffman Price. This time of year you'll find him at the Goat Shack on the Tennessee. He can't bear to hunt in August."

The name, but not the man, sounded vaguely familiar to Valentine, but he couldn't place it.

"What's he hunt?"

"People. Real criminals, not Kurian fugitives and whatnot. Though I'm not sure that's from morals, it's more that they don't bring enough warrant money."

"What about guerillas?" Duvalier asked.

"He sticks his nose into no war—or feud, I should say. He calls the whole Cause a big feud. He's brought in a freeholder or two. Like Two-bullets O'Neil; he and his posse were going around hanging Quisling mayors and whatnot along with their families."

"What are we supposed to bribe him with?"

"Give him this," Everready said. He took off one of his Reapertooth necklaces, and searched the string. After a few minutes of fiddling he extracted two teeth and passed them to Valentine. One had the letter *h* carved into the root, the other the letter *p*.

"Tell him Everready's calling him on his debts."

ψ

Valentine watched the Goat Shack through his Memphis river patrol binoculars. Except for the horse tails swishing under a barn's awning and ATVs parked around the outbuildings, he'd suspect the place was deserted.

The Goat Shack certainly looked dilapidated—even abandoned. Glassless windows, the front door laid out across the wide porch, a few holes in the roof. The road-facing side had fresh cypress boards nailed on horizontally to cover a pickup-truck-sized hole. A dock, divided into an aluminum half by the shore and a wooden extension out onto the lake, ended in a boathouse. Pilings for other docks, perhaps swept away in some flood, dotted the whole riverside behind the house.

Goats rested in the shade of the porch. Valentine watched a tired-looking billy plunge his head into a water trough fed by a downspout and drink.

Valentine suspected it had once been a bar and restaurant for pleasure craft on the river.

A few feet behind, Duvalier lay flat on her back, her feet up on her pack. Ahn-Kha sat cross-legged with his back to the chestnut tree shading Valentine.

The smell of goats reminded Valentine of his first day as a Wolf.

"It just doesn't feel right," Valentine said. "It's like the place is waiting for us."

"We could try going north on our own," Ahn-Kha said. "I don't think this country is muchly inhabited."

"No, we need a guide," Valentine said. "Oh, screw it. Ahn-Kha, cover us from out here with your gun, would you?"

While he changed into the cleaner cut-down black clothes he'd worn in Memphis, Ahn-Kha unstrapped the leather belts around the blanket rolls containing his gun. Duvalier picked up her pack and slung her pump-action shotgun, then handed Valentine his U-gun.

They wandered off the small hummock the chestnut shaded and walked the broken-up road, more potholes than grade.

"What if this Hoffman Price isn't here?" Duvalier asked.

"We find someone else."

"Reaper teeth won't do us much good."

"I have some gold left."

"Just enough to be robbed of and left for dead."

Valentine put his arm on her shoulder. "As if you'd let that happen."

She shrugged him off.

The nanny goats lying on the porch watched them walk past a pair of motorcycles and up onto the porch. A mutt watched them from the shade beneath a truck up on blocks. Duvalier wrung out her neckerchief in the water trough and wiped the sweat from her deeply freckled face and neck.

Valentine heard the clatter of a generator.

"Ready when you are, Val."

"Hello the house," Valentine called. "May we come in?" The brilliant sunshine made every crack in the repaired section of wall a black stripe. There were bullet holes in the door frame and around the windows.

"You a warrant-man?" a crackly woman's voice called back.

"No," Valentine said.

"Then you're not welcome here. Be off."

"We're looking for a warrant-man, actually." Valentine heard movement inside, chairs being pushed back from tables, perhaps.

"Who?"

"Hoffman Price."

"Then come in, friend," the voice said.

It smelled like vomit in the big, welcoming room. It took Valentine's eyes a second to adjust. He instinctively stepped out of the door, and Duvalier followed him in.

A mountain of a woman, gray-haired and with a washed-out red halter top, sat on a stool at one end of a chipped bar with an electric fan blowing on the back of her neck, talking to a bearded man wearing what looked like a bathrobe. Valentine looked around what was evidently a bar. Sandbags were piled around the door and windows, and circled the entire bar at least to waist height. The floor was thick with grit, the ceiling with spiderwebs. The furnishings appeared to have been pulled out of boats and cars. Two men in leather and denim and linked chain sat at a far table, biker boots stretched out in opposite directions toward each other like the tails of a yin and yang symbol.

"Good afternoon, Black and Red," the woman with the crackly voice said, horrifying Valentine with her teeth. "I'm Greta. What can I get you?"

Duvalier was examining the wallpaper, to which was glued an assortment of wanted posters, from cheaply printed ten by twenties to full-color photos to what looked like fax paper.

"What does the house recommend?" Valentine asked.

"I like him," Greta said to the man in the bathrobe, then turned back to Valentine. "Polite goes a long way with me. I do a real mint julep."

"You're kidding," Valentine said.

"I shit you not, Black," she said.

He looked at Duvalier and she shrugged. "Two then."

"Being strangers, please put the guns on top of the sandbags there. Take a seat," Greta advised.

They disarmed themselves, but sat next to their weapons.

Greta got up from her stool, revealing a .45 automatic lying on the bar. She tucked it into a leather back-waistband holster and waddled off to a door at the back, next to the far end of the bar.

"You two got someone you're looking to bring in?" the man in the bathrobe asked.

Valentine shrugged. "You're not Price, are you?"

"He ain't allowed in here."

Valentine wondered at that. "Then I'd rather not discuss it."

"Just asking, Black," the man said. "I wouldn't jump your claim. I'm retired, like." He shifted in his seat and revealed a conspicuous lack of underwear.

"Peekaboo," Duvalier said, rolling her eyes at Valentine. He heard a grinding noise from the doorway.

Greta returned with two tall, thin glasses, the outsides slick with moisture. Valentine looked at the drinks as she set them down.

"Ice!" Duvalier exclaimed, putting both hands around the glass.

"Only ice machine for fifty miles," Greta said.

"We don't come here for the decor, Red," the man said.

"Close up shop, George," Greta said. "It wasn't a prizewinner in your best days, and nobody's going to pin a blue ribbon on it now."

Valentine sipped at the sweet drink. The alcohol dropped and hit like a sledgehammer driving rail spikes.

"My bourbon does have a bit of a bite," Greta said, and Valentine heard chuckles from the far table with the bikers. "How about some food?"

"We'd like to see Hoffman Price."

"He was up early fishing. He'll be asleep now."

"What kind of payment do you accept? I have some Memphis scrip—"

She put her hands on her hips. "Strictly barter, Black. I'll take three shells for that twelve-gauge, or five rounds for your pistol. That'll include lunch and those drinks."

Valentine counted out pistol ammunition.

Fifteen minutes later she brought them fried slabs of catfish and hush puppies, wrapped up in old wanted posters. They read the greasy bills as they ate. "Wanted on Suspicion" seemed to be the most frequent crime, followed by theft and fraud.

When they were finished she added another oily wrap to their table. "Now that you're done, you can take Hoffy his dinner. Saves me the bother."

"I thought he was sleeping," Valentine said.

"I saw his tracking Grog up and around. Means he's up. The boathouse is at the end of the dock, just follow the ferry line. You can leave your weapons. No one's going to touch them. Shack rule."

Valentine picked up the still-warm bag and found the back door. What had been an extensive cypress patio now looked like a piece of modern art made of bird droppings. An assortment of canoes and motorized rowboats lined the bank of the inlet protected by the finger of land.

"And outhouses hanging over the river. Nice," Duvalier observed, looking at the shacks at the end of the deck.

"Could be worse. Could be upstream," Valentine said.

They walked down the dock, boots clomping more loudly than usual on the planking. If anyone wanted to sneak up on Price, they'd have to do it in a canoe.

A raft ferry built out of an old twenty-five-foot pontoon craft was attached to lines stretching to a piling in the center of the river. Another set of lines linked it to the other side. Valentine saw a turned-over rowboat there. Some kind of sign stood over the rowboat, but it was too far away to read, even with the binoculars.

Two great wet hands rose out of the river near the boat shack. A Grog, the simple gray variety distantly related to Ahn-Kha, climbed out. It was a female. She rapped something against the dock and then stuck it in her mouth. As she chewed she watched them approach.

"Hello," Valentine said.

The Grog hurriedly whipped a second crayfish against the dock, then dropped it in her mouth. She chewed and looked at them as if to say "you're not getting it now, flatface."

She let them pass to the door, which sat crookedly on its hinges. Valentine knocked. "Mr. Price?"

*God, something smells terrible. Is that the Grog?*

"Yeah," a clear tenor voice answered.

"My name's David. Greta gave me your lunch. Can I have a word?"

"Door's not locked, son."

Valentine opened the door to the little shack, got a good view of river through the open door, saw a tied-up canoe—

—and was hit by a wave of odor that almost brought him to his knees. It was BO, but of an intensity he'd never experienced before.

He saw a man standing at a workbench, a disassembled Kalashnikov spread out on an oil-smeared towel. Smoke rose from a short pipe with a whittled bowl.

Duvalier stepped in behind. "Oh, Jesus," she gasped. She backed out and Valentine heard retching. Her stomach had never been the strongest—

The filthiest man Valentine had ever seen stepped away from the bench. Hairy shoulders, black with dirt, protruded from mud-stained overalls that seemed clean by comparison. Two bright eyes stared out of a crud-dark face.

Dumbstruck by the man's hygiene pathology, Valentine could only stand and attempt to forget he had a nose.

"I always enjoy the reaction," Hoffman Price said, putting down the pipe. Valentine tried to fixate on the faint odor of the tobacco, but failed. Price smiled. His teeth were a little yellow, but clean and fairly even. Valentine tried breathing through his mouth. "Greta used to call me 'breathtaking.'"

Valentine counted blood-gorged ticks dangling from the region about Price's armpits and ears and stopped after six. "Everready sent me. From the Yazoo."

"How is that old backshooter?"

"Same as always," Valentine said, not sure if he'd be able to make it across the river, let alone across two states, with this stench.

"Haven't seen him in . . . it's three year now. You looking for someone?"

The Grog hooted outside, and Valentine heard Duvalier say, "No, thanks. I like them cooked."

"Just a guide," Valentine said.

"Uh-huh. To where?"

"Just across the Ohio River. A place called Laurelton. I'll show you on a map."

"That's quite a trip, son."

"That's why I need a guide. Myself and two companions."

"That little gal out there up for mileage like that?"

"I've been to the Rockies and back with her," Valentine said, which wasn't quite true by about two hundred miles but sounded good.

"I'm on my summer holiday. Hope you've got a wheelbarrow full of incentive."

Valentine dug out the Reaper teeth. "Everready said he was calling in your debts." He held out his hand with the teeth in his palm.

"I'll be damned," Price said. He took them. Valentine resisted the urge to smell his hand to see if the odor had transferred.

"Pretty," Duvalier said, and the Grog hooted.

Price cocked an ear to the sounds outside. "Nice young gal you got. Some of the titty trash that gets brought into the Shack, they scream at her. But I have to say no, son. Too far, too long since I've been over the Ordnance ground."

"Ordnance?" Valentine asked.

"Big stretch of ground between the Ohio River and the Great Lakes," Price said. "They make the Kentucky Kurians look like amateurs. Decent bounties, but I like to spend autumn and winter down here."

"But those teeth," Valentine said.

"I'd do anything for old Everready. But you aren't him. That particular debt isn't transferrable."

"Money, then. I have some gold."

"Hard to spend when you're getting gnawed on by a legworm. I'll put on the ol' thinking cap, son, and try and come up with someone crazy enough for a round cross Kentucky. But no names come to mind."

The Grog came back in, leading Duvalier by the hand. She deftly opened a tackle box and showed her collections of costume jewelry, interestingly shaped pieces of driftwood, and some old United States coins. The two men stood in silence at the strange, interspecies feminine cooing.

"I see Bee's making herself agreeable," Price said. "Nice to see someone being kind to her."

"Dzhbee," Bee agreed, looking up at Price.

"He doesn't want to do it, Red," Valentine said, wondering if Grogs operated on a different olfactory level.

"What about the teeth?"

"That deal's with Everready; you got nothing to do with it," Price said.

Duvalier looked at him sidelong, as though afraid to stare. "That makes you a welsher," she said. "As well as a skunk."

"Ali!"

"You've got no paper on me," Price said. "And nothing I want. The door's just behind, unless you want to swim outta here."

She put her hands on her hips. "When's the last time you had a woman, Price?"

Valentine felt the boathouse spin.

"What's that talk for?" Price barked.

"I'm talking about a bonus. You can have me for the duration of the trip. Interested?"

*She's gone nuts. What did that fever do to her?*

A tar-fingered hand passed through the knots of greasy hair. Valentine saw some things he guessed were lice fall out. "Get out of here, both of you. I've had my fill."

She passed her right hand down her breast, to her crotch. "We'll be up in the shack if you change your mind. Till tomorrow morning. I'm a limited-time offer. C'mon, Black, let's get out of here."

They walked back up the noisy planks.

"What was that all about?" Valentine asked.

"Don't tell me you're jealous? Oh shit, I think some of that smell got in your hair."

"And you were talking about sex with him?"

"Val, I let that pig Hamm drip all over me in bed. This guy's just dirty on the outside. That Grog's sweet. There's no way he can be that bad or she wouldn't be that way. He'll come round. He just needs to think about it."

"Just when I think I know you."

"Ah, but you didn't hear my conditions. I would have insisted that he take a bath, first. I'm not interested in hosting a flea circus in my crotch all the way to Ohio. I only just got rid of the Memphis brood."

ψ

They negotiated a room with Greta ("It'll be cool enough to sleep about three in the morning.") and then went out to bring in Ahn-Kha.

Which turned out to be a mistake.

"We'll feed and water him, but he can't stay inside," Greta insisted. "Grogs are strictly outdoor animals."

Valentine, watching flies buzzing in one window and out another, thought the distinction between inside and outside largely moot. Especially with goat droppings under one table.

"Sorry, Ahn-Kha. They're big on rules here."

"Your poet Kundera said 'Only animals were not expelled from Paradise,' my David. I am not an animal, save in the same biological sense as that woman."

"And this isn't paradise, old horse," Valentine finished. "I'll sit outside with you."

Duvalier joined them on the porch with the goats, drinking ice water from a pitcher that had to be refilled every half hour.

Valentine watched the Goat Shack's dubious clientele trickle in as the sun set. He heard the ferry wheels creaking twice. Greta disappeared, replaced at the bar by a gap-toothed relative who shared her peppery hair color.

Duvalier produced a deck of cards scavenged from the casino where they'd interrogated Rooster with an eggplant. The idle evening on the porch passed pleasantly enough. Muscles sore from weary days on the road stiffened.

Perhaps a dozen patrons now passed time and swatted flies in the bar. Precious little commerce seemed to be going on; most of the groups of tables were swapping drinks for tobacco, or old newspapers for a pocketful of nuts. Many of the men smoked. Peanuts and jokes cracked back and forth across the tables.

Valentine watched a man in deerskin boots swap a pipe for an unfinished bottle. A sheathed knife dangled from a leather thong around his neck, and his belt held no fewer than three pistols. Considering the clientele and the quantity of weaponry, the Goat Shack was surprisingly peaceful. Or perhaps it was due to the clientele and the quantity of weaponry. . . .

Valentine felt guilty lazing on the porch. He should be doing *something*. Arguing about the nature of promises with Hoffman Price, wandering through the barroom asking for stories about Kentucky—instead he was looking for another heart so he could lay down a flush and take the pot of sixteen wooden matches.

Two men wandered up from the riverbank, one bearing a dead turkey on a string. They wore timber camouflage, a pattern that reminded Valentine of the tall, dark, vertical corpses of buildings that he'd seen in the center of Chicago. The one with the turkey turned inside with a word about seeing to a scalding pot. The other, a pair of wraparound sunglasses hiding his eyes, watched their game. Or perhaps them.

"What manner of Grog is that?" he asked.

"We call ourselves the Golden Ones," Ahn-Kha said.

The bird hunter took a step back, then collected himself. "The who?"

"Golden Ones."

"Golden Ones?"

Ahn-Kha's ears went flat against his head. "Yes."

"Didn't know there was them who spoke that good of English of your sort."

"Likewise," Ahn-Kha said.

"Definitely see you later," he said, staring frankly at Duvalier. She ignored him. The hunter followed his friend in. Ahn-Kha squeezed out a noisy fart, Golden One commentary on the stink left behind by unpleasant company. Valentine heard a couple of welcoming hallos from the inside.

"The mosquitoes are getting bad," Duvalier said, putting down two pair and taking the pile of matches.

"I'll see about dinner and DEET," Valentine said, rising.

Greta's generator ran two lighting fixtures, both wall-mounted, both near the bar. One was the lit face of a clock—someone had broken off the plastic arms, and whether the remaining stubs still told the time Valentine couldn't say—and the other a green neon squiggle of a bass leaping out of the water, a bright blue line projecting from its mouth. Perhaps a dozen customers sat in the gloom, save for the two huntsmen, who were looking at a wanted poster under the clock-light.

Valentine felt the stares of the company. Because they were outsiders?

"You wouldn't have a bottle of bug repellent, would you?" he asked the slighter version of Greta at the bar.

She shook her head. "No, sir. You and your girl could come inside. The tobacco keeps them out."

"If you don't like the skeeters, you could relocate off-river, tag," a shaggy woodsman suggested. "Take your pet and go."

"Earl," the bartender warned. "Goat stew and biscuits will be up soon, mister."

A third man joined the other two by the clock, getting a light. He joined in the inspection of the bill.

"I'll buy four servings," Valentine said.

"There's only three of you."

"The Grog's got a big appetite."

"We've only got goat. No spitted youngsters," the man called Earl said. Valentine didn't like the way he kept his hand near his open-topped holster.

"You won't even get goat if you keep that up," the bartender said. "Greta hospitalitied them herself."

Valentine walked away.

"Hey, tag!" Earl called as Valentine walked away. The bar went quiet. "Tag!"

Valentine went out the door, glad to have the pile of sandbags and a cedar wall between himself and Earl.

"I think we'll spend tonight on the porch," Valentine said.

"See you in country, tag," Earl bellowed.

"Hey, Earl!" someone inside called. "Come over here and roll one. Calm down."

"Everready should have hooked us up with guerillas," Duvalier said.

"They're up in the mountains east of Nashville, for the most part," Valentine said.

"It's a place to get across this river," Ahn-Kha said. "Perhaps there are no Kur this near. Even a Reaper would have trouble with the crowd inside."

The crowd inside chose that moment to spill out the door. The two turkey hunters and Earl came out of the bar, pistols drawn. Duvalier made a move for her shotgun.

"Hold it," a voice barked from the repaired section wall. "I've got two barrels of buckshot on you."

Valentine stood up, hands up and away from his weapons. "Now hold on. I don't want—"

"You got a warrant on you, tag," Earl said, a flashlight clipped to his pistol shining into Valentine's eyes. "You and this lady here."

"Mister and Missus David Rowan," the turkey hunter read, despite his sunglasses. "He's even got that scar. It's two-year-old paper out of New Orleans, but a warrant's a warrant."

Other bounty hunters came out of the bar, forming a rough semicircle around the porch. They didn't pull their weapons.

"Fifteen thousand dollars Orleans each, it says," sunglasses continued. "Five thousand per bonus for live delivery. Payable at any Coastal Marine station. There's one in Biloxi!"

Valentine did a quick count. There were sixteen men around, if he counted the one covering them from inside.

"That's real good money," one of the leather-clad bikers said.

"Forty thousand dollars is," Valentine agreed. "If you're in New Orleans. How many of you have been there?"

None of the men said anything.

"Okay, you've got us. Let's say you take us to Biloxi, and collect your two thousand five hundred each, barring any bribes you might have to pay."

"Shuddup and face down, tag," Earl said. "We ain't all collecting this."

"Says who? Let him talk, Earl," one in the semicircle said, his hand resting on his gun belt.

Valentine continued. "Let's say you get us down there without soldiers hoping for a promotion taking us away from you. Biloxi'll pay you alright, in New Orleans dollars. They print that stuff like toilet tissue. It can only be spent in New Orleans, unless you want to trade it into a hard currency exchange at a third of the value. Boat fare Biloxi to New Orleans was four hundred dollars when I was down there. A bad bottle of Orleans gin was sixty dollars. A room's over three hundred, if you don't mind cockroaches. How far's that two thousand five getting you now?"

"It's not getting shared sixteen ways," Earl said. "Now—"

A gunshot from just behind the doorway interrupted him.

Greta stood in the door, her shotgun pointed to the sky. Valentine's ears rang from the shot, and he wondered what it had done to Earl's hearing.

"Earl, you owe me one shell and these people an apology. Nobody serves papers at my Shack. Nobody."

"They ain't warrant-men," Earl said.

"He's right, Greta," one of the spectators said.

"I knew that when I gave them my hospitality."

Greta lowered the gun and placed it against the back of his ear. The turkey hunters got out of the way of the potential blast. "Earl, holster your piece and say your good-byes. You're off my peninsula permanently."

Earl put away his gun. "I'll pay up and go." He stared at Valentine. "But you three can't retire here." He raised his voice. "Any man wants to call himself a warrant-man, kill the Grog—he ain't subject to hospitality. Later we'll track down these two and share the reward. Meet me at the old county sign."

"You just do that, Earl. You just do that," a deep voice called from the darkness. Hoffman Price stepped forward, his Kalashnikov tucked under his arm so his hands were free to work his pipe. He got it lit and sent out a puff of smoke.

"And another Grog-lover sounds off," Earl said. "You throw down on me, you skunk, and Charlie'll blow you in half with his ten-gauge."

"Bee!" Price called.

Valentine heard wood shatter and turned to see a warrant-man crash headfirst through the repaired section of wall, ten-gauge bent around his neck like a dress tie. Bee swung out through the hole, treading on the unconscious Charlie, and extracted a pair of sawed-off shotguns from her boot holsters.

"Earl, you better shut up before I've got your whole rig for damages," Greta said.

"Didn't you hear, Earl?" Price said. "These folks hired me for a little trip to Chattanooga. They're under my protection." He raised his voice. "Any man comes to serve papers on them will interfere with my ability to earn my fee. Bee's my accountant when I'm in country. I refer all financial difficulties to her."

"Let's everyone calm down. We're leaving right now," Valentine said. "Pretend none of this happened."

Greta lowered her shotgun. "You ordered four meals, Black. You and Red and your big friend eat first, then you can leave. You might as well—Earl's picking up the tab."

⊹

The warrant-men, save for Earl, trickled back inside.

They ate at the riverside. "Lots of bad blood gets built up in this business," Price said. He posted himself downwind of Valentine and Duvalier, but it didn't help much.

After some head bobbing and a mutual dental exam, the two Grogs sat down next to each other. Ahn-Kha ate a few bites of his stew, then passed her the bowl.

"She speaks northern slope dialect," Ahn-Kha said. "I only know a few words."

Duvalier was already mopping up her remains with a biscuit. Valentine marveled at her appetite. "You really taking us on, or was that just show?" she asked Price.

"I'm taking you."

"Not through Chattanooga, I hope," Valentine said.

"That was just in case Earl gets the second big idea of his life and goes to the authorities, such as they are."

"What changed your mind?" Valentine asked.

"I got to thinking that I don't have too many more years in me to pay Everready back. If I have to step off, I'll do it clean. Plus Bee got a look at your big friend when he came down to the river to hit the shitter. She got excited. Bee gets lonely for her own, I think."

"I've had my mating," Ahn-Kha said. "She is dead. Besides, we are not dogs. Our strains do not mix."

"But you share some customs, looks like," Price said.

"I've been among her kind. Do not misunderstand me. She is well formed and agreeable." Ahn-Kha broke a biscuit in half and gave it to her. "I just could no more be a male to her than you could."

"I want to put a few miles on across the river before dark," Price said. He clicked his tongue against the roof of his mouth three times. "I have a mule. Bee and I will go load him up."

Valentine kept the food close to his nose as he ate his stew. "Is there a chance that you'll take a bath before we set out?"

"What, and spoil my camouflage?"

Duvalier looked up. "You're hoping to pass as a feral hog, perhaps?"

"No. Everready explained it to me years ago. I never could hide lifesign for shit. All the critters interfere with the Hoods. I don't read as human at any kind of distance." He walked up to the back doorstep and returned his plate.

"You want your other biscuit, Val?" Duvalier asked as Price disappeared into the stable.

"You got used to him faster than I did," Valentine said. "How did you keep your dinner down?"

"Greta in there gave me a bottle of clove oil. It's good for more than mosquito bites. A dab'll do you—provided you put it under your nostrils."

# CHAPTER NINE

*The Kentucky Bluegrass, September: The bluegrass itself is only blue in the mornings, and even then for the short season when the grass is flowering. The rest of the time it is a rich, deep green.*

*Poa pratensis arrived in Kentucky by accident, used as padding for pottery on its way west to be traded to the Shawnee. Once thoroughbreds thrived on it. They have been replaced.*

*Land of the dulcimer and bourbon (invented by an itinerant Baptist preacher), home to the most soothing of all American accents, Kentucky raises more than just champion livestock. Perhaps it's something in the water, for the state produces fiercely individualistic, capable folk under its chestnuts and between its limestone cuts. Abraham Lincoln and Jefferson Davis were born there, approximately the same distance apart as their future capitals of Washington, DC, and Richmond.*

*In its earliest days, the wooded hills of Kentucky were called a "dark and bloody ground." That appellation applies to Kentucky of the Kurian Order as well. The state is divided into three parts, somewhat resembling an O between two parentheses. The western parenthesis is the usual assortment of Kurian principalities bleeding the country from their towers along the Ohio, Tennessee, and Mississippi Rivers. The eastern parenthesis is the mountains of Virginia, home to a scattering of guerrilla bands at war with each other when they're not fighting the Kurians or those in the center of the state.*

*The center is the most unique of all. Clans of legworm ranchers, some comprised of Grogs, some of humans, and some mixed follow their flocks. They cannot herd them; the legworms are too obstreperous and*

197

*powerful to be herded, but they can be tamed and controlled under the right circumstances.*

*The same might be said of the riders.*

φ

"I've never seen growth like this before," Valentine said.

"You're looking at snake trails," Price said.

They stood in southern Kentucky, on a little knob of a hill looking out over a meadow. Price knew about moving cross-country. Bee usually took the lead, walking with her eerily careful grace. Then the three humans, taking turns with the compass and map to avoid getting trail-stale, followed by the mule. The mule was unusually cooperative for its breed, perhaps owing to a jaunty knit Rasta cap it wore, complete with fly-scaring dreadlocks. Valentine didn't dare look to see if the dreadlocks were simply sewn in or if they were attached to a scalp, and the mule wasn't telling. Ahn-Kha brought up the rear. At least once a day they zigged on a different course, heading north the way a sailing ship might tack against the wind.

What caught Valentine's eye about this particular meadow was the strange furrowing. Lines of thickly weeded earthen banks meandered across the field like a drunken farmer's tilling. The banks were perhaps a foot high at most, ran down little open spaces clear of smaller trees.

"That's sign left by legworm feeding."

*Tchink tchink tchink*—behind them Duvalier knelt over a spread out *Byrdstown Clarion*. The newspaper, a weekly melange of property and equipment for sale and lease, with a few stories about the achievements of local NUC youth teams, wasn't being used for the articles. Duvalier was pounding together two ancient red bricks pulled from a collapsing house, collecting the fine dust on the paper to be poured into an envelope and used as foot powder.

Bee snored next to her in the sun, her short-but-powerful legs propped up on a deadfall. The mule, a cooperative beast named Jimi, cropped grasses and tender young plants.

"I've known ground like this," Ahn-Kha said. "Older, though, more evenly grown up."

"You see, Val," Price explained, passing Valentine's binoculars back. His odor lingered on them, but Valentine pressed the sockets to his eyes anyway—after a critter inspection. "Legworms move in small herds; I've never seen over a dozen together. They pull up the sod with their mouths. They eat everything, leaf, stem, and root, and of course mice and voles and whatnot that get pulled up, then they crap it out the other end more or less constantly. The waste is pretty sweet fertilizer, and their digestive system isn't all that thorough, quantity over quality, so in the wormcast there's a lot of seeds, living roots, stuff that comes back. It grows extra lush and you get these little walls of vegetation."

"They don't mess with big trees," Valentine observed.

Price pointed at a thick oak. "They'll climb up and take some low branches. That's why some of these trees look a bit like umbrellas."

"Those trails will lead us to them, if we find fresher leavings," Ahn-Kha said.

"Sure," Price said. "Except with legworm tracks it's hard to tell which direction they're going. If you're lucky you'll come across a partially digested sapling. The way the branches get pressed down makes it like feathers in an arrow, only reversed."

Valentine wondered if it would be like Nebraska, with different "brands" sharing the same area. "How do they feel about trespassers?"

"Depends if they can make a profit off you," Price said.

ɸ

They cut fresh worm sign two days later. After picking at the less-digested branches and shrubs, everyone agreed that the wide end of the cone was heading northeast.

"Five worms," Price said, counting the tracks. "Two big on the outside, three lesser in."

"Legworms mate in pairs?" Ahn-Kha asked.

"No, more like big orgies in the winter. Seriously," Price said, as Valentine raised an eybrow. "A legworm dogpile's a sight to see."

"What are we looking to get out of a bunch of worm-herders?" Duvalier asked.

Price whistled for Bee. "This is their land. I want permission to cross it. If we're lucky, they might bargain us up a mount."

"We don't have much to offer," Duvalier said.

"Your body is already spoken for," Price said.

"I've got some strong soap in my bag," she said. "Use it and I'll keep up my end."

"I thought humans made love face-to-face," Ahn-Kha said. Valentine wasn't sure he'd heard right until he looked at his friend. Even Price knew him well enough by now to know that one ear up, one ear out meant he was joking.

Catching up to the legworms wasn't as easy as having a clear trail made it sound. When moving without eating, a legworm goes at a pace faster than a horse's walk, similar to the Tennessee walking horse's famous six to twelve miles per hour run-walk. According to Price, they could pull up turf at a good three miles an hour, a typical walk for a human. A human on a sidewalk who isn't loaded down with pack and gun.

So they moved as fast as they could through the warm fall day, sweating and swearing at each new hill. Price and Valentine decided the course was arcing somewhat northerly, so they took a chance and tried to cut across the chord of the arc.

They never picked up the trail again. Other riders found them.

Bee pointed them out first. She dropped down on her haunches and let out a blue jay–like cry, pointing at a tree-topped hill. It took Valentine a moment to recognize what he saw. The legworm's pale yellow color was surprisingly effective camouflage in the shade of a stand of elms and oaks. Two figures sat astride it, probably human.

"Everyone wait here," Price said.

"Feels too much like a standoff," Valentine said. "Why not all go?"

"If you like, but as strangers we've got to approach unarmed." He unslung his Kalashnikov, held it up over his head, then placed it on the ground. He made a motion toward Bee and she sat next to his gun.

"Feel like showing off your famous charm school repertoire?" Valentine asked Duvalier. Behind them, Ahn-Kha kept a hand on Jimi the mule's halter.

"No. If there's a problem I like to disappear fast without anyone getting a good look at me."

"I shall stay back as well," Ahn-Kha said.

Valentine placed his U-gun on the grassy ground and set the pistol on top of it. He had to jog to catch up with Price.

"Let me do the talking, Val," Price warned as he lit his pipe. "They're tetchy around strangers."

"Any particular reason for it?"

Sweat ran lightly down the greasy dirt on his face. Price's filth was semiwaterproof, as impervious to rain as an oilskin. "Nobody likes them much. Most folks in the civilized world—beg your pardon, but that's how Tennesseeans see it, stuck between corn-likker-swilling guerillas west and east—avoid them like they carry a bad fungus.

"Even the churchies keep clear, except a few unreformed Jesus-pushers."

"Why do the Kurians let them be?"

"They get loads over the mountains, one way or another. Between the New York corridor and Chattanooga precious little moves by train; the lines are always getting attacked by guerillas, and you have to pay through the nose per pound. A legworm can haul as much cargo as a railcar. They and their brothers in Virginia are the main east-west smuggling artery for the whole Midwest. Not that they don't do legitimate runs too."

They hopped across two old wormtrails, little more than hummocks of summer-dried weeds, and entered the woods. Evergreens staked out their claims among the tough oaks and smooth-skinned hackberrys.

The two men astride the sixty-foot segmented worm wore black leathers fitted with an assortment of barbs like oversized fishhooks. A third had dismounted and stood near the front of their beast, a burlap sack of potato peelings and pig corn thrown under its nose. All three men wore their hair long, tied down in back and then flared out like a foxtail. All were on the grubby side, but didn't make an art form out of it like their guide.

Valentine had never seen a live legworm at rest. Its "legs" were hundreds of tiny, paired, black clawlike legs, running down the bottom of its fleshy hide like a millipede's. Oversized versions of the claws, growing larger even as the front of the worm grew thinner, pulled up the corn and the earth beneath, stuffing it into a bilateral mouth. Scimitar-like tusks, facing each other like crab claws, stuck out the front

"That's close enough, stranger," said the second man.

"Friendly call, high rider," Price said. "I'm Hoffman Price, friend to the Bulletproof, Worm Wildcats, and the Uttercross."

"We're Bulletproof."

"I know," Price said. "That's why I listed you first."

"Story!" the second man said. "And if it ain't, you know we don't like bums—"

"I know him, Zak," the one with the corncobs said, dropping his sack. He had a little gray in his red-brown hair, and a little more flesh around his middle. "He's no bum. He came and got that Swenson newbie. Maybe four years back. That Colt the Dispatcher carries, he got it from him."

"You wanna vouch for him, Cookie?" the one who'd been called Zak said.

"I'm just saying the Dispatcher knows him, is all."

"Where can I find the Dispatcher?" Price asked. "Is it still Dalian?"

Zak took a drink from a water bottle and passed it back. "Sure is. He's east. Soon as we've eaten we're moving on fast."

"Will you let us ride tail? Three human, two Grog. Mule in tow."

"You might be riding into trouble," Zak said. "One of our pods got jumped. The Dispatcher sent out a call."

"Our guns will secure the Bulletproof, as long as we enjoy the Bulletproof's hospitality," Price said. "You can count us on your side of the worm."

The man behind Zak pointed with a fingerless-gloved hand. "You know the words, but that don't mean much to me."

"He says he wants business with the Dispatcher, that's good enough for me," Zak said. "You can ride tail. Enjoy the music back there."

"Thank you, high rider," Price said. He touched Valentine and they turned.

"What did we just agree to?" Valentine asked.

"When you ride with the Bulletproof—any of the legworm tribes, really—you enjoy their hospitality. But you're expected to stand with them in any kind of a confrontation."

"You mean fight."

"Don't worry. When two tribes get into a feud they each line up on either side of an open field. There's a sporting match like lacrosse only with two contestants; all you have to do is cheer."

"What kind of feud?"

"Could be anything. Usually it's feeding ground. One group allegedly goes in another's area. It's hazy at best. About a third of Kentucky's divided up between the tribes. If they're caught, it's called an arrest but it boils down to being taken hostage. So they hold a contest. If the 'intruder' side wins, the hostages and their worms are released. If the 'intruded' side wins, a ransom and restitution are paid."

"Sounds rather civilized," Valentine said.

"Again, except for yelling, you won't have to do much."

Zac, Gibson—the man behind Zak—and Cookie gave them a quick legworm riding lesson, and issued them each a cargo hook and a climbing goad.

The cargo hook resembled a pirate's replacement hand, hanging from a chain whose links were wide enough for the attachment of lines. They used a pair to attach a long lead to the mule. The goad resembled a mountaineer's pickstaff, with a crowbarlike digger at one end and a long spike at the other. To mount the legworm, you plunged your goad into one of the many thick patches of dead skin—the worm's skin reminded Valentine of fiberglass insulation—and lifted yourself up to a height where a buddy could pull you the rest of the way up. Under no circumstances were you to use one of the longish whisker spikes projecting here and there from newer patches of skin in cracks between the dead material.

"They'll twist good if you grab a whisker," Cookie explained.

"Do they ever roll?" Valentine asked, though he knew the answer.

"Only if they're hurt," Zak said. "You abandon ship quick if that happens."

Bee went first. She plunged her goad hook up high, almost at the top of the worm thanks to her reach, then swung up on pure arm muscle. She accepted the rifles, then helped Price up, who then aided Valentine and Duvalier in their climbs. Ahn-Kha eschewed his goad; he stuck the implement between his teeth and jumped up, grabbing great handfuls of spongy skin, and clambered up with his toes.

"That's how the Grey Ones in the west mount," Ahn-Kha said. He attached his wood-framed pack, plunged the chained cargo hook into the creature's back, then casually gripped the chain with his long toes. Only the Grogs could sit astride the worm's broad back; the humans rode in a leaning sidesaddle fashion.

"Just like you're on a flying carpet," Cookie said. He looked at the strangers' faces. "None of you have heard of a flying carpet? Ignorants!"

"Everybody set?" Zak called back. His head was visible over the cargo netting holding down the trio's supplies.

"All-top and rigged," Price called.

"A lot of us don't say that anymore," Gibson said. "We just say 'yeah.' Try it, tender-thighs."

Zak reached back with a pole capped by something like an oversized legworm goad with a point on the end and stuck the hook down between the legs. That part of the legworm, right under Gibson, gave a little rise and they started ahead.

"You can stop bellyaching that people who aren't one of us aren't one of us anytime, Gib," Zak said, too quietly for anyone but Valentine to hear.

After the initial jerk of motion, the legworm ride made a believer out of Valentine. Whatever the legs were doing below, up top the creature simply glided as though riding on an air cushion. Little changes in the topography came up through the beast with all the discomfort of a cushioned rocking chair.

The mule was all too happy to follow behind without his pack.

Zak continued, "For all you know the gal's being brought to a tribe wedding, or the scarred guy's the Casablancan Minister of the Great Oval Office and Rosegarden traveling incognitpick. So be a good tribe or be silent."

Normally Valentine would be a little embarrassed at overhearing a dressing-down. Except he didn't like Gibson. But good manners won out and he diverted his hearing elsewhere: to the steady staccatto crunch of the fast-falling legs. He'd forgotten how strange legworms sounded. *Marbles poured out of a bag in a steady stream onto a pile of crumpled paper,* as Evan Pankow, a veteran Wolf, had described it in his first year of training.

The gentle motion of the legworm relaxed Valentine.

"You guys ever sleep up here?" Valentine asked.

"Only one at a time," Cookie called. "Other two have to keep each other alert."

The beast must have dipped its nose—if nose was the right word for the scowlike front end—and scooped a car-hood-sized divot from the earth with its tusks. Zak employed his legworm crook again and worked one of his three reins.

With the legworm in motion the "music" they'd been told to expect started. Like a massive balloon deflating, the beast dropped a cemetery-plot-sized mass of compost behind.

Valentine cautiously took a whiff. All he could smell was Price, and the other people and Grogs.

"Be thankful for small favors," he said to Duvalier as another colossal fart sounded like the horn of Jericho. The mule gave a start.

"It's always loud at startup," Price said. "Gas gets built up while it stands still. Give it a minute and you'll just hear a plop now and then as it makes a deposit."

Duvalier planted herself on the legworm's spongy back, holding her hook under her chin. "I don't mind at all if it means traveling off my feet."

Valentine wished he could see the reins better. The Grog's he'd encountered in Oklahoma used four, two set to either side. The men of the Bulletproof used three, one on each side and one up top. Valentine made a mental note to ask Zak about its utility.

φ

He learned that and a great deal more at the dinner break. This time Zak fed the legworm on bags of peanut shells and ground-up acorn. Price's mule liked the smell of the nuts and joined in, chomping contentedly but rather messily compared to the legworm, who took earth, sod, and shell together in a single gulp.

"If we have to move fast, most of what we carry is food for the mount," Zak said. His face and forearms had dozens of tiny scars.

"How do you make it turn?"

Zak pointed to the rein. A metal loop projected from the beast.

"Yes, but what does that do?"

"Oh, you want the science teacher version? Well, a worm's such a big bastard, there's not much we can do that'll influence it. So we make it think that all its motions are its idea. All those whiskers are wired, so to speak, to an organ under the skin on either side that looks a little like an accordion. When it turns, to keep from rubbing against a tree or whatever, the accordion contracts and it turns. That rein is attached to the accordion, and when we pull it closed the beast turns."

"And keeping the nose up?"

"It's got a balancing organ kind of like your ear in the top of its front end. A little jerk makes it feel like it's out of balance, so it'll stick its head straight forward until the organ feels back in equilibrium. But if they're fed regularly they don't graze all the time. They don't need all that much if it's fair-quality feed. All the dirt they pull up in the wild is a lot of wasted effort."

"How does it breathe?"

"That's something. Here." Zak's leathers creaked as he squatted next to it. "Look underneath. That lighter flesh? We call that the 'membrane' but it's actually a good two feet thick. That thing gets oxygen into its bloodstream. Water don't make much of a difference, but they get sluggish as hell and try to find high ground— though sometimes swamp water will kill them."

"I've never seen one this close."

"Where you from?"

"Iowa. Got out young. My dad worked for, you know—"

Zak nodded. "Me too. Indiana. Practically grew up under a tower. The P worked electricity. Cool stuff, but not if you're reporting to one of those pale-assed jumpers twice a day."

"I left home at eleven," Valentine said. "Ugly scene."

"So what does the flea-ranch over there want with the Bullet-proof?"

"I'm just trying to get from point A to point B."

"We'll be at camp a little after sundown. Don't fall off."

Gib drove the legworm a little faster through open country. After a few unheeded yawlps, the mule trotted behind to avoid being dragged. The rolling blue hills left off and they climbed onto the beginning of a plateau, where they gave man, grog, and mule a breather. Valentine saw wooded mountaintops in the distance.

"Keep your guns handy," Zak warned as night fell, looking over the landscape with a monocular. "There are guerillas in those mountains."

They struck a road and followed it to a waypoint town of a dozen empty homes, unless you counted barn owls and mice, a couple of hollow corner bars, and an overgrown gas station and market once dependent on the farm clientele.

Valentine marked fresh legworm furrows everywhere. Some ran right up to the road surface before bouncing off like a ricocheting bullet.

They passed up a rise, and a boy standing guard over the road and his bicycle waved them toward a commanding-looking barn. A pile of weedy rubble that might once have been a house stood close to the road, and a crisscross of torn earth emanated from it. Valentine guessed that from a low-flying plane the landscape would look like an irregular spiderweb. Legworms stood everywhere, pale blue billboards in the moonshine.

"Who's that with you, Zak?" a man afoot called.

"Visitors looking for the Dispatcher. I'm vouching, and I'll bring 'em in. Where is he?"

"Up in the barn."

Zak turned around, an easy operation on the wide back of the legworm. "We're here, folks. You'll have to leave your guns, of course."

"Um, how do we . . . ?" Duvalier asked.

"Get a newbie pole, Royd," Cookie called down.

"No, I'll help," Ahn-Kha said, sliding down the tapered tail. He lifted an arm to Duvalier. "Here."

Valentine jumped down, as did Bee and Price.

"Why not just jump?" Valentine asked Duvalier quietly. "I've seen you dive headfirst from two stories."

"Just a helpless lil' ol' thing without a big man around, Val," Duvalier said. "No harm in having them think that, anyway."

They got out of the lane and made a pile of their weapons and packs.

"Coffee's by the fire pit. Toilet holes are up in the old house," Zak said. "There's a lime barrel, so send down a chaser. Let me know when you're ready to see the Dispatcher."

"Bee—guard!" Price said to his assistant.

"Doesn't she have to use the toilet pits?" Duvalier asked.

"She's not shy," Price said. "And she always buries."

"I would just as soon not scoot my hindquarters on the grass," Ahn-Kha said.

Cookie stretched. "There's plenty of New Universal Church *Improved Testaments* up there. Help yourself."

Valentine wanted coffee more than anything. Duvalier took her walking stick and headed for the rubbled house.

They'd missed dinner, but a line of stretchers propped up on barrels still held bread and roast squash. Sweating teenage girls washed utensils in boiling water as a gray-haired old couple supervised from behind glowing pipes.

"Coffee?" Valentine asked.

"That pot, stranger," one of the girls said, tucking stray hair into a babushka. Valentine took a tin cup out of the hot wash water, choosing a mild scalding over the used cups tossed on the litters and plywood panels, and shook it dry.

It was real coffee. Not the Jamaican variety he'd grown regrettably used to while with Malia at Jayport, but real beans nonetheless. He liked the Bulletproofs even better.

The surge of caffeine brought its own requirements. He remembered to chase it down the hole leading to the unimaginable basement chamber with a ladle of lime.

McDonald R. Dalian, Dispatcher for the Bulletproof, was viewing babies he hadn't met yet when the Price-Valentine mission entered his barn.

The barn was a modern, cavernous structure that had survived its half century of inattention in remarkably good shape, thanks to its concrete foundation and aluminum construction. Small chemical lightsticks Valentine had heard called Threedayers in the Trans-Mississippi Combat Corps hung from the rafter network above.

Men, women, and children of the Bulletproof, most in their black leathers or denim, sat atop defunct, stripped farm machinery to watch Dispatcher Dalian hold court.

A half-dozen guitars, two banjos, and a dulcimer provided music from one corner. Another end of the bar had been turned into a food storage area; shelves had been cleared of odds and ends and replaced by sacks of corn and barrels of flour. A laundry also seemed to be in operation, with clothes and diapers drying on lines strung between stripped combines and the wall.

The Dispatcher had indeterminate features—a little Asian, and maybe a dash of Irish or African for curly hair, and a great high prow of a nose. Except for the curly hair, he reminded Valentine of his father, especially around the protruding ears and out-thrust jaw. He cooed over a sleeping baby as the proud mother and father looked on.

"She's grabbing my finger even while she's sleeping," the Dispatcher said. "Don't tell me she won't be a lead high rider some day."

The Dispatcher and the father of the child bumped their fists, knuckle to knuckle.

The flying buttress nose went up and turned. "Air strike! Only one living thing on the planet smells like that." He handed the baby back and turned. "Hoffman Z. Price has returned."

Price had his usual six-foot circle of solitude around him, even in the busy barn. "And grateful for the generosity of the Bulletproof, Dispatcher."

The Dispatcher opened a tin. "Tobacco?"

Price extracted his pipe and the Dispatcher took a pinch. "You picked your moment. We've got the better part of the tribe together."

"Is worm meat still profitable in Lexington?" Price asked.

"You're innocent of the ways of the trading pits as well as soap, brother. That den of moneychangers and Pharisees takes my meat and my belief in human goodness. I kid, I kid. But if it weren't for

209

the Grogs in Saint Louis I'd be bankrupt. So I hope you're feeling generous. If I have another fugitive in my tribe I'll drive a harder bargain."

Valentine found himself liking the Dispatcher, even if he could be categorized as a Quisling and had a touch of tentpole-revivalist singsong to his words. There was no "step into my office," and as far as he could tell no retinue of subordinates and bodyguards one might expect of a feudal lord. The man carried out his business in the center of his people; any interested eye or curious ear could hear the latest.

A boy brought a spittoon made from an old motorcycle helmet.

Price pointed to Valentine. "I'm looking for a ride to the Ohio for five. We need food for same. Myself, Bee, David here, his friend Ali, and another Grog, an emissary from the Omaha area named Ahn-Kha."

Ahn-Kha didn't claim any titles, though in Valentine's opinion he deserved many. Valentine had to hand it to Price for adding a lot of sizzle to what was probably a very unappetizing steak.

"What does the job pay?"

"Two gold justices. Fort Knox mint."

"Hard currency. Lovely. But it won't pay for the kind of numbers you'd need to get up there safely. There are towers along the Ohio. That could be a dangerous trip, and the Bulletproof have no friends north of Lexington. I'll have to see if I can find you a lead rider willing to hazard a one-worm excursion."

"You seem to have most of them here. That man Zak seems capable."

"He is. I'll speak to him after tomorrow's challenge. He's a bit distracted at the moment. His sister was the lead rider for the leg-worm that started all this."

"Where should we camp?" Price asked.

"Bed down where you like, but keep clear of the campfires around that farm across the fields to the east. That's the Wildcat camp."

"May we use your laundry, sir?" Valentine asked. Everything he owned was long overdue for more than just a streamside rinse.

"Of course, umm, David," the Dispatcher said. "Our soap is yours. Did you hear me, Hoffman?"

As they walked back to collect the others Valentine had one more question for Price.

"I didn't know you could eat legworms. Even in the Ozarks we couldn't stomach it."

"You have to butcher them fast. The meat can be ground into pig feed. But there are other ways. Didn't you ever have a Ribstrip?"

Valentine remembered the preprocessed barbecued meat from his days masquerading as a Coastal Marine and in Solon's short-lived TMCC. Placed in a hard roll with onions and pickle relish, it was a popular sandwich.

"You don't mean—"

"Yeah. You put enough barbecue sauce on you can hide the taste. Ribstrips are ground and pressed legworm."

φ

Human instinct is to join a crowd, and Valentine gave in to it the next morning. Everyone in the party save Duvalier came along to watch events.

At breakfast, mixing with the Bulletproofs, he'd learned a good deal about what to expect out of the contest. The challenge was fairly simple, a mixture of lacrosse and one-on-one basketball.

The two sides lined up at either end of an agreed field, roughly a thousand yards apart. At the Bulletproof's side, a line of short construction stakes with red blasting tape stood about ten yards out from the crowd, and the only one at the line was the Dispatcher.

Valentine decided there was probably an interesting story having to do with the rifle range of an experienced marksman behind it, but didn't press the issue. The two contestants each went to the center of the field, carrying only a legworm starting hook. The referee, usually either a medical man or a member of the clergy, would be in the center of the field with a basketball. He or she would toss it high enough in the air to dash out of the way before it came back into crook-swinging distance, and the contest would end when one contestant brought the basketball to his side.

"Why a basketball?" Valentine asked a Bulletproof rider who was also explaining the rules to his young son. Nothing was happening yet. The Dispatcher and some of his riders were meeting their opposite numbers in the Wildcats, presumably negotiating the recompense that would be paid.

"You know the answer, Firk. Tell him," the father suggested.

The boy shook his head and shrank against his father. Valentine turned away to save the boy embarrassment and looked out across the dew-spangled field, recently hayed. Opportunistic spiders had woven their webs on the stalks, creating tiny pieces of art like cut glass in the lingering summer sunshine. Some operational farms still existed in this part of Kentucky. Valentine wondered how they ran off grazing legworms.

"It's about the size of a worm egg," the father explained. "That, and basketballs are easy finds."

"No other rules?" Valentine asked.

"I see where you're going. You can't bring anything but the crook. You're stripped down to your skivvies to make sure. Not even shoes."

"Does one ever try to just brain the other and then walk back to the home side with the ball?"

"You get that sometimes, but both sides hate a plain old brawl. Slugging's no way to pump up your mojo, or your tribe's."

A stir of excitement broke out in the crowd when a wandering wild, or unreined, legworm dug a feeding tray toward the challenge field. A pair of legworms with riders hustled out at full speed for a legworm, about the rate of a trotting horse. By judicious use of the mount's bulk, the furrow was redirected.

By the time that ended the two parties had returned from the center of the challenge field. The Dispatcher looked downcast.

Valentine edged closer to the center of the line of people, but many others had the same idea.

He couldn't hear through the babble. "What's up?" people called.

Word passed quickly in ever-expanding circles. "The Wildcat challenger is a Grog! Some kind of import!"

"Ringer!"

"Damn them."

"Take a knee, everyone!" someone bellowed.

Everyone but the Dispatcher sat down. He looked around, nodded to a few, and spoke out to the squash field of foxtailed heads.

"Yes, you heard right. They've got a big Grog they're using in the challenge. Biggest one I've ever seen—even standing on all fours he's bigger than me."

Valentine judged the Dispatcher at about six-three. Ahn-Kha's size. Could there be another Golden One wandering the Cumberland Plateau?

"I saw a man challenge a Grog when I was eight," a well-muscled, shirtless man said, presumably the contestant, as everyone else had jackets or knits against the cool of the morning—warming fast as the sun rose.

"I remember that one," the Dispatcher said. "Fontrain died from his injuries. There's bad blood for this one. According to their Dispatcher, Tikka killed a man when she got taken into custody. Could be they're looking for payback.

"We're going to forfeit," he continued. "It's a hell of a ransom, but I'm not risking Tuck's head over a challenge."

"Might be a bluff," the shirtless man, presumably Tuck, said. "They're trying to get you to fold up by showing you a big, mean Grog. I'll go out there. It's my skull."

"And end up like Fontrain?" the Dispatcher said. "No."

"That means a feud," a craggy-faced woman sitting cross-legged next to Valentine said to everyone and no one. "Oh Lord, lord."

Valentine stood up. "Sir, I'll take a whack at this Grog."

Hundreds of heads turned in his direction. The Dispatcher straightened.

"You ever even held a legworm crook, son?"

"I've played grounders with Grogs," Valentine said, which wasn't quite true. He'd whacked a ball around with a cross between a hockey stick and a cricket bat a few times as Ahn-Kha taught him the fundamentals of the Grog game, and ended up bruised at all compass points.

Consternation broke out in the crowd; much of it sounded approving. "What do we have to lose?" "Leastways if he gets his head bashed in, it's no feud."

"Can we trust you, um, David?" the Dispatcher asked.

"I don't see how you can lose. You're ready to forfeit. Worst thing that could happen is that you pay the ransom anyway and get your riders back."

"Let David do it," the woman next to him called. "Let him take that Goliath."

The crowd liked the sound of that.

"Okay, boy, strip down and grab your crook."

"I've got one request, Dispatcher."

McDonald R. Dalian's eyes narrowed. "What's that?"

"Can I borrow a pair of underwear? Mine aren't fit for public display."

The crowd laughed.

φ

Valentine stood behind a blanket held up by Ahn-Kha as he stripped.

Zak held out a white pair of shorts. "They look a little odd but they're the best thing for riding. They're military issue up in Indiana for their bike troops. Everything stays tucked up real tight."

"Thank you."

As he tried on the shorts Ahn-Kha spoke. "My David, let me try my luck at this."

"I'm from Minnesota, old horse. Born with a hockey stick in my hand."

"Then you will be careful out there."

"Since when am I anything but?"

"In what year were you born?" Ahn-Kha asked, ears askew.

"Be careful. If it is a Grey One, when they are on all fours and running they cannot turn their heads, or hear very well behind. He will not see you if you come at him from the side."

*Neither would a freight train,* Valentine thought. *Doesn't mean I can bodycheck it off its course.*

"Understood," Valentine said.

Price paced back and forth as Bee pulled up and chewed on

dandelion roots. Valentine wondered where Duvalier had gone. But then a sporting event, even one as deadly serious as this, probably wasn't of interest to her.

The shorts were snug-fitting, running from his waist to mid thigh. The padded white pouch at the groin made him feel like one of the come-hither boys that strutted on the streets of New Orleans.

"Oh, that's cute," Price said.

"Better than the ones with three weeks of trail."

Ahn-Kha dropped the blanket and walked with Valentine, Price, and Bee to the center of the line of spectators. Valentine walked barefoot, testing the field's soil. Some murmured about the burns on his lower back and legs. The Dispatcher stood at the center of the line with the twelve-foot legworm crook, looking like a warrior out of some medieval tapestry.

"I can still order it called off," the Dispatcher said, the words just loud enough to travel to Valentine.

"I can't resist a challenge," Valentine said.

"Well, you look fit enough, 'cept for the limp. Hope you can run."

"I can run," Valentine said.

He tried the crook, an all-wood version of the one he'd seen Zak use. Its hooked end had a rounded point.

"Using metal isn't considered sporting," the Dispatcher said.

*Damn, it's awkward. Like a vaulting pole.*

"Any rule on length?" Valentine asked.

"Yes, it can't be over fifteen feet."

"How about, say, seven?"

"You must be joking. A Grog can already outreach you. You'll just be cutting yourself shorter."

"I'd rather swing a handy short crook than an awkward long one."

The crowd broke out in consternation when Ahn-Kha buried his old TMCC utility machete into the haft of the crook where Valentine indicated, and broke it over his knee.

Valentine tried the crook again. Now he could run with it.

Five hundred yards away, in the center of the field, the Grog waited. He looked huge even at this distance.

"Good luck, David," the Dispatcher said.

"Is anyone taking odds?" Valentine asked.

"You don't want to know," Price said.

"All you have to do is get the ball back to our line," the Dispatcher said. Valentine marked the stakes, stretching a hundred yards to either side, with the crowd spread out behind. "How you do it's up to you."

Valentine looked at Ahn-Kha. The Golden One's ears twitched in anxiety, but one of the great limpid eyes winked.

Valentine raised his arm to the crowd and turned to walk into the center of the field, stretching his arms and legs as he went. The legworm ride yesterday had tasked his muscles in a new way, a trace of stiffness which gave him a good deal more cause to doubt. He wondered how the Bulletproof would feel about a valiant try . . .

The "referee" wore taped-up glasses and a modest crucifix. He carried a basketball under his arm, and leaned over to speak to the Grog as Valentine approached the halfway point. Valentine noticed a pistol in a holster, with a lanyard running up to the referee's neck.

The Grog rivaled Ahn-Kha in size, almost as tall and a good deal wider of shoulder and longer of arm. Pectoral muscles like Viking roundshields twitched as he shifted his half ton of weight from side to side. The Grog's legworm crook lay before his massive hands as though to establish a line Valentine would never cross.

"You're Tuck?" the referee asked.

"Change of programming," Valentine said. "I'm David."

"David, your Wildcat opponent is Vista. Vista, your Bulletproof opponent is David. Don't touch me or you forfeit. Interference by anyone else also results in a forfeit for the interfering side. This mark"—he indicated a pair of flat river stones—"is the center of the field, agreed to by your respective Dispatchers."

The Grog yawned, displaying a mellon-sized gullet guarded by four-inch yellow incisors, capped with steel points, top and bottom. The great, double-thumbed hand picked up the long crook.

The referee held out the basketball. "The object of the contest is to get this ball to your own line. The game begins when the ball hits the ground, and ends when the winner brings it home to his own goal line. I'll fire my pistol in the air to indicate a victory."

Valentine noted the hook on Vista's crop had been chewed to a sharpened point, and hoped that his intestines wouldn't end up draped over the loop at some point.

"Any questions?" the referee finished, stepping to the two stones in the center.

Neither said anything. Vista glared at Valentine. Valentine stared back. The referee held out the ball between them, and when he lowered it for the bounce-toss the Grog was looking away.

"May the best . . . ummm . . . contestant win."

The referee tossed the basketball straight up into the air and backpedaled out from between man and Grog, quickly enough that Valentine felt air move.

Valentine heard a faint sound like a distant waterfall and realized it was cheering, cut with a few whistles. He felt not at all encouraged, and took a few steps back out of clobbering range as Vista raised his crook—*No sense getting my head knocked off the second the ball hits*.

The damn thing took forever to fall. Was it filled with helium?

The ball struck. Valentine's brain registered that it took a Wildcat bounce, helped along by a quick swing of Vista's crook that Valentine didn't have the length to intercept.

But Vista went for him instead of the ball. The Grog leaped forward, using one of his long arms as a decathlete might use a pole, and upon landing swung his crook for—

The air occupied by Valentine. If Vista didn't want the ball, Valentine would take it. Valentine sprinted after the ball, now rolling at a very shallow angle toward the Bulletproof on its second bounce.

The instinct to just go toe-to-toe with Vista and decide the contest in a brawl surged for a moment. But he'd lose. Valentine looked back to see Vista galloping toward the ball, crook clenched at the midpoint in those wide jaws. Grogs running on all fours looked awkward, but they were damn fast—

Valentine cut an intercepting course.

*Vista, you messed up*—the Grog's crook had the hook end on Valentine's side. Taking great lungfuls of air, Valentine poured it on. He reached forward with his own hook, Vista's head invisible behind the mountainous shoulders—

—and latched his hook to Vista's. Valentine planted his feet to bring the racing Grog down the way a cowboy would turn a cow's head.

The field smacked Valentine in the face as he landed, yanked off his feet by five times his weight in charging Grog. The crook slipped away like a snake.

By the time he looked up again Vista had retrieved Valentine's crook, and used it to give the ball a whack, sending it farther toward the Wildcat line. Vista left off the contest. Instead of following the ball to a likely victory he advanced on Valentine, long crook in his left hand, held hook out, and Valentine's shorter one looking like a baton in the right. Apparently the Wildcat Dispatcher wanted to teach the Bulletproof a lesson.

*You wily gray bastard. You suckered me!*

Animal triumph shone in Vista's eyes. Valentine tasted blood from a cut lip. The referee ran across the periphery of Valentine's vision, moving for a better angle on events.

Valentine stood up, swiping the dirt from his knees as he watched Vista advance, and ran his tongue along the inside of his teeth.

Vista raised his twin weapons and bellowed, stamping his feet and banging the crooks together.

Valentine raised his middle finger in return.

The Grog knew what that meant. It charged, wild-eyed.

Valentine ran away.

He felt the long crook tug at his hair and ran harder. Vista couldn't sprint with weapons in his hands, so the Grog paused. Valentine used the precious second to achieve some distance, then settled into his old, pounding Wolf run, pretended his aching left leg didn't exist.

Vista gained on him, slowly, but only by sprinting full tilt. And the Grog couldn't breathe as well with two crooks crammed into its bear-trap-like mouth. Valentine slowed a little, listening to the footfalls behind, but didn't dare look back; a trip and a sprawl would be fatal.

Vista slowed. The Grog's eyes no longer blazed, but were clouded by new doubt, and it came to a halt perhaps a hundred yards from the Bulletproof line.

A shout from somewhere in the line: *"Hrut ko-ahhh mreh!"*

Valentine glanced back and saw Ahn-Kha, making a sawing motion with one of his mighty arms.

Vista screamed back, words or pure rage, Valentine couldn't tell. Vista dashed off at an angle southward, running an oblique course for the Wildcat line.

*Got you now!*

Valentine's crook spun past his nose and he sidestepped—and caught it as it bounced in the air. This time he heard the cheers clearly. With fresh energy he tore toward the Wildcat side and the distant ball, hidden by a gentle fold in the earth.

*Sorry, Vista. You'll keep your temper next time.*

But the Grog had unguessed-at reserves. It pounded up behind Valentine, sounding like a galloping horse. Valentine risked a glance over his shoulder and saw Vista running in a two-leg, one-arm canter, the long crook raised to catch him—

Vista swung and Valentine blocked. Valentine shielded his back against another blow and hurried on, then got a painful rap on the knuckles that opened his hand, and he lost his crook for the second time.

He could run better without it anyway.

Now for a real burn.

Valentine ran, extending his sprint. Were he still a fresh Wolf of twenty-two with an uninjured leg he would have left Vista gaping behind. As it was he increased the distance, but only just.

The ball would be an awkward thing to carry. Under his arm he wouldn't be able to run with a proper stride; held in each hand he'd be running upright, not a natural human motion. He could kick it, but what if he mistimed an approach and missed? If only he had a satchel . . .

Valentine spotted the ball and changed his angle. Vista slowed behind him, perhaps conserving his wind to intercept Valentine on his sprint back. Even more distance yawned between them.

The referee caught up on both of them.

Valentine reached the ball and the Wildcats booed. He ignored the catcalls.

Vista pulled up, perhaps forty yards away, and blew air like an idling train engine. He left ample room to cut an intercepting course.

Valentine dropped his shorts. Someone on the Wildcat side had enough of a sense of humor to whistle, a twittering wolf whistle.

He picked up the ball and stuffed it into the elastic waistband, then closed most of the waist in his fist. The ball was too big to go out the leg holes.

Vista cocked his head, oddly doglike with ears outstretched.

Holding the ball in the improvised sack, Valentine ran straight at him.

The Grog, perhaps fearing another trick, widened his stance and rocked back and forth, crook held loosely in his right hand.

At three strides away Valentine feinted right, away from the crook—then leaped.

He tucked the ball into his belly as he flew through the air, not wanting it batted away as he went over Vista's head in a great Cat leap.

It swung its crook where Valentine should have been.

Valentine landed lightly on his good leg, had a bad split second when Vista's thrown crook struck him in the ankle, and ran, feeling rapidly growing pain from the blow.

Valentine managed to open the distance between them, and Vista let out a strangled, winded cry.

The Bulletproof danced and shouted behind their markers, some urging him on by circling their arms in wheels toward the red tape.

Valentine crossed the line—a gunshot sounded, and old instincts made him flinch—and fell into a mass of Bulletproofs. He felt a sharp slap on his bare buttock, and looked to see the craggy-faced woman giving him a gap-toothed grin.

Valentine turned to look at his opponent. Vista collapsed to his wide knees, pounding at the turf with great fists. He took the basketball out of his underwear, gave up trying to reach the Dispatcher, and tossed the ball in the air.

Limping, Valentine went out to Vista. The Grog jumped up, snarling.

Valentine offered his hand.

The Grog snatched him up by the arm and lowered his head with mouth gaping to bite it off at the wrist. Another shot sounded and the Grog pulled back, a bleeding hole in its cheek.

Valentine spun out of reach.

The referee trotted up, pistol held pointed at the Grog. "Back to our side! Back!"

The Grog emptied a nostril at the referee and turned away.

The referee lowered his gun, looked at Valentine from beneath a sweat-dripping brow. "You, sir, are one dumb son of a bitch. Congratulations."

"Thank you," Valentine said, rubbing his wrist.

Ahn-Kha loomed up. "My David!"

"I'm fine. A little bruised."

The Dispatcher and Zak joined them, the former with the basketball, the latter holding Valentine's clothes.

"What did you yell?" Valentine asked, remembering the scream from the sidelines. "He forgot all about me."

"I accused his mother of the lowest-caste choice of mates," Ahn-Kha said. "Such an insult can only result in a duel. He started to answer me when you ran."

"Maybe you'd better stay in camp when David goes to collect his share."

"Share?" Valentine asked.

"You won. A portion of the recovered herd is yours."

"And I owe you a great debt," Zak said. "Dispatcher, may I go along and collect my sister?"

"Go in my place. But keep away from the Grog. One blood contest a season is enough."

φ

The Wildcats fell back from their side of the field as they crossed, Valentine holding the basketball up as though it were a torch per Zak's instruction.

A huge legworm, longer than the one Valentine had ridden into the Bulletproof camp, led six unreined worms onto the contest field. Valentine watched them pull up soil, weeds, and hay stubble like plows.

Three riders sat astride the broad back, in the "flying carpet" sidesaddle-seat Valentine was beginning to recognize.

"That's Tikka, she's the reiner," Zak said.

Tikka had sun-washed, caramel-colored hair, plumed into a lusher version of the foxtail her brother wore, and the tan, wind-burned face of a woman who seldom knew a roof. The man behind her was shirtless, with bandages wrapped around his midsection. The third rider, a beefy, gray-haired woman, evidently kept the tradition of the third rider being older.

"Watch the whiskers on the unreined legworms," Zak advised Valentine. "Tikka! Look at the trouble you caused," he called.

She dismissed him with a wave. "Talk to the herd."

Zak turned to Valentine. "The Dispatcher won't allow us to ride together. Too many brawls."

"I thought it was cousins who liked to fight in these parts."

Zak winked. "Fight . . . or kiss. Fact is, I don't feel guilty about either. I'm adopted."

φ

Valentine spent the day mildly worried. Duvalier had tucked a note in his pack

> Checking out the other camp
> Back tonight
> —Meeyao

and had not returned.

Valentine found himself a minor celebrity in the camp. As he limped around on his sore ankle, Bulletproof children came up and bumped him with their fists and elbows. He explored the camp with Price, trying to stave off the coming stiffness by keeping his muscles warm. He looked at some of the carts and sledges the leg-worms towed. Many held loads of fodder, or sides of meat, but one, under guard near the Dispatcher's tent, had a generator and racks of military radio gear.

"There'll be a party tonight," Price said. "Weather's nice and the herders will disperse."

"The little contest this morning," Valentine said. "Does anyone ever not pay up when they lose?"

"That's why they bring together as much of the tribe as they can. Sort of like wearing your gun at a poker game."

Valentine and Ahn-Kha did laundry at the washtubs. The other Bulletproofs doing washing insisted on giving them soap flakes and the outside lines for drying their clothes. A woman carrying six months of baby under her tie-front smock hinted that Valentine would be getting some new clothes that night. "They're going round for donations," she said.

By nightfall a raucous throng of legworm herders surrounded the barn like a besieging army. Their rein-pierced mounts stood along the road ditch in lines, eating a mixture of grains and hay dumped into the ditch.

Valentine didn't feel much like joining. His legs had been filled with asphalt, his ankle had swelled, and his shoulder blade felt like a chiropractor had moved it four inches up. He stayed out in the warm night and ate beans from a tin plate, scooping them onto a thick strip of bacon, and watched Ahn-Kha make a new pack for Bee out of a legless kitchen chair the Golden One had traded for somewhere.

"Everyone wants to see you," Zak said, coming out of the darkness. "Dispatcher himself asked for you."

"I'm tired, reiner."

"Just for a moment. You're Bulletproof now. You've got to have a sip."

"A sip?"

"It's where we get our name. What did you think it meant, Kevlar? We've got some char-barrel-aged Kentucky bourbon."

Valentine scraped off his plate into the legworm-feed bucket.

EVERY BITE ADDS AN INCH was written on the side. "You should have opened with that, Zak. I'd have been up there already."

Inside the barn, a wood-staved cask big enough to bathe in stood upon two sawhorses near the band, each of whom had a sizeable tumbler tucked under their chair as they scraped and strummed and plucked away. Tikka, in a fringed version of her brother's leathers, gave him a welcoming hug that allowed Valentine a whiff of leather-trapped feminine musk, then took Zak's hand and pulled him away. The Dispatcher poured drinks into everything from soup bowls to elegant crystal snifters, with the help of Cookie at the tap.

Valentine entered to applause and whoops. He kept forgetting he was supposed to hate these people. Perhaps they'd bred the legworms that destroyed Foxtrot Company at Little Timber Hill. But they'd carved out a life, apparently free of the Reapers. He had to give them credit for that.

"Our man of the night," the Dispatcher said, his nose even more prominent thanks to its reddish tinge. "How do the victory garlands feel?"

"They're turning purple," Valentine said, accepting a proffered thick-bottomed glass from Cookie. A quarter cup of amber liquor rolled around the bottom.

"Some Bulletproof will take the edge off."

"Just a splash, please, sir. I—don't hold my liquor well."

"It's that cheap radiator busthead you flatties brew in the Midwest, is why," Cookie said. "Bulletproof's got aroma and character."

"It blows your damn head off," Tikka said. "That's why we called it 'bulletproof' in the first place."

"Enjoy," the Dispatcher said, raising his own glass and bringing it halfway to Valentine.

"Bad luck not to finish your first taste," someone called from the audience.

Valentine touched his glass to the Dispatcher's, and several in the crowd applauded.

The liquor bit, no question, but it brought an instantaneous warmth along for the ride. Cheering filled the barn.

"He's Bulletproof now," the Dispatcher called to the crowd, noticing Valentine's wince. "Bring out his leathers!"

A parade of Bulletproof wives and daughters came forward, each holding a piece of leather or armor—a jacket with shoulder pads sewn in, pants, boots, gloves, a gun belt, something that looked like spurs . . .

Valentine stood a little dumbly as they piled the gear on his shoulders and around his feet. It was a dull gunmetal color, and made him think of a knight-errant.

"Zak," the Dispatcher called. "Where'd he get to? *Zak!*"

"Right here," Zak called, coming in from the gaping doorway to the barn, Tikka in tow, both looking a little disheveled.

"Zak, show David here how to wear his leathers."

Valentine, Zak, and Tikka picked up pieces of his new outfit and went outside. He'd seen breastplates like the one they strapped on before. They were an old army composite, hot as hell, made you feel like a turtle, but they could stop shrapnel. "You got ol' Snelling's rig," Zak observed. "He was a good reiner, if a bit flash for the Bulletproof. Dropped stone dead of a heart attack one hot summer day while climbing his mount. You never know."

"No, you don't," Valentine agreed, glad this Snelling hadn't been felled by a sniper working for the Cause.

"Zak says you're a flattie?" Tikka asked. She had a siren's voice, and her melodious accent begged a man to sit down and stay a while.

"Iowa," Valentine said. "But I left when I was young. I spent a lot of time in the Gulf."

"That where you picked up those scars?"

"Pretty much. What's this on the sleeve?" A series of hooks, reminding Valentine a little of sharpened alligator teeth, ran down the outside seam of the forearm of the jacket.

"Serrates," Tikka said. "They're for digging in when you mount, or hanging on to the side."

Zak showed him how to fix the spurs, which were a little more like the climbing spikes utility linemen wore to reach their wires. They could be flipped up and locked flush to the inner side of the boot. Locked down, they projected out and down from his ankle.

"Some guys put them on their boot points. I think that looks queer," Zak said.

Valentine explored the padding in the jacket shoulders and elbows. Military Kevlar plates were buttoned into the back and double-breasted front. The pants had stiff plastic caps on the knees and shins.

"You can take the bulletproofing out, but we generally wear it. Can be a lifesaver."

Valentine felt a bit like a porcupine. His old Cat claws would fit right in on this outfit. He could wear them openly and they'd just look like another set of spikes.

"How do you two kiss without harpooning each other?" Valentine asked.

A smile split Tikka's tan face and her eyes caught the firelight. "That's just part of the fun."

"Don't make fun of the leathers," Zak said. "A lot of effort goes into each one."

"Fine stitching," Valentine said. He wondered about the hides, though; they were thicker and pebblier than cowhide.

"I don't mean that. That's legworm egg-casing, stretched and dried. Getting it is trickier than threading a full-grown legworm for reins. You have to go into a breeding pile and get the egg right after it hatches, because it rots fast if you don't get it scraped out and dried. You have to help the little bugger inside out of it, or he'll eat almost the whole thing, and if you hurt a legworm grub doing that the adults stomp everything in sight."

"It's kind of a rite of passage for our youths," Tikka said. "They have to go into the winter dogpiles and check on the eggs. When they come out with a hide, they're considered full-grown members of the tribe."

"Thank you for skipping that step with me," Valentine said. "I'll wear it with pride."

"But be careful, Dave. There are lots in town that look down on riders. You'll get called a hillbilly and a Grogfucker and worse.

Some think riding herd on a legworm's the same as cleaning up after a gaunt."

"He looks too fine for that kind of talk, Zak," Tikka said.

"How do you do the foxtails in your hair?" Valentine asked.

"Easy," Tikka said. "There's a cut-down pinecone attached to the tie. Some braid their hair around it. I can show you. Now that you've got a few worms, you should look the part."

"Zak, I want to talk to you about that. I'm passing through. Hoffman Price brought us up here in the hope that we'd get a guide to the Ohio River, up around Ironton or Portsmouth. I'll swap you my share of the recovered beasts for a ride."

Zak shook his head. "I've got a bigger string a little to the west. I'm leaving early tomorrow to get back to them."

"Then I'll drive you," Tikka said. "That way I'll get my string back."

"He's already got a girl, Tikka," Zak said. "You'll have to excuse my sister, Dave, she's man-crazy."

"Any girl who doesn't want a husband by twenty and babies after is man-crazy, in my brother's opinion," Tikka said. "Zak, you know you're the only one for me."

" 'Only one' when I'm around, that is. And that's just 'cause I keep saying no to a train."

She tried to stomp him with her heavy riding boot but Zak danced out of the way. "You're a fresh piece of wormtrail, Zachary Stark."

"What in the hell are you wearing, David Black?" Alessa Duvalier asked from the darkness. She wore her long coat, black side turned out, and carried her walking stick.

"And that's the girl, Tikka," Zak said, grabbing for her long hair. She dodged out of the way and got behind Valentine.

"Apparently I'm Bulletproof now," Valentine said, striking a Napoleonic pose. "What do you think?" Tikka played with his hair.

"I'm tempted to get your pistol and test you. Starving, is there any food left?"

Valentine smelled blood on her. "Sure. I'll show you. Excuse us."

"Let's hurry. Starved."

Valentine led her up to the food tables, and she cut open a loaf and filled it with barbecue. They went back to their camp in the empty field. Ahn-Kha and Bee were wrapped up in a fireside game that involved piling buttons on a rounded rock.

"Price is walking his mule," Ahn-Kha said. "Did they offer us transport, my David?"

"Oh, he's got a ride. Count on him," Duvalier said.

"What have you been up to?" Valentine asked.

"I didn't miss your performance this morning. I just watched it from the Wildcat side. I was checking out these camps. There's some bad blood between these, um, tribes."

"You've made it worse?" Valentine asked.

"Of course. We might want to shift a little more to the west. When it got dark I offed a couple of the Wildcats and left a note warning them not to use Grogs in any future contests. They were already stirred up because someone got shot when they captured those Bulletproofs. When they see what I did to the bodies it ought to put them over the edge. A lot of their riders were upset that they let it go with just a contest. This should put them right over the edge."

Ahn-Kha sent a cascade of buttons down the side of the rock and bowed to Bee. He got up and went over to the wrapping for his oversized gun.

Valentine rose and looked across to the ridge with the Wildcat campfires. Had some of them gone out? He should have counted. Captain Le Havre would have taken a piece out of his ass for that kind of sloppiness. He picked up his U-gun.

"Wait here," Valentine said. "If shooting starts, let's meet at the creek we crossed just before we turned in here."

"Val, what are you doing?" Duvalier said.

"I'm going to warn them."

"Why? The Bulletproof will probably win; there're more of them. It'll get a good war started between these assholes."

"There are kids all over the place."

"Nits make lice, Val," Duvalier said.

"Is that who you really are?" Valentine asked.

"Whose side are you on, Ghost?" she called after him. "I know the answer: your ego's."

Valentine hurried up to the barn, the new leather pants creaking as he trotted. His ankle hurt, but seconds might count.

"Yes, you look fine in your leathers, Bulletproof," a woman called from the door of the barn. The party was still in full cry, and Zak and Tikka were stomping the concrete with bootheel and toe in syncopation, another quarrel forgotten. Valentine ignored his greeter and went straight for the Dispatcher.

The crowd parted, alarmed at the U-gun. Valentine carefully carried it pointed down, his hand well away from the trigger area. Zak stepped in at his rifle arm. "Dave, there's no need—"

"Watch that weapon, David," the Dispatcher said. "What's going on? Pants too tight and you're looking for the tailor?"

A few laughed.

"Dispatcher," Valentine said. "Our Grogs were down looking at the contest field. They went off to some bushes to—you know—"

"And?" the Dispatcher asked.

"They saw the Wildcats. Some of them on their worms, armed, others gathering."

"Coming this way?" the Dispatcher asked.

"The Grogs just ran back. Armed riders is all I know."

The Dispatcher upended his glass of bourbon onto the concrete. "Carpenter, get to the herd riders, have them try to lead the wild worms west. Mother Shaw, take the children out to the cover-field. Everyone else who can shoulder a gun, get to the rein-worms. Lead riders Mandvi, French, Cherniawsky and McGee, with me. David, you and your people with Zak; Zak, get them clear."

"You might see some fancy riding after all," Tikka said.

The crowd dissolved, and the musicians cased their instruments, if not sober at least sobered.

Zak brought Valentine to his legworm at the road trough. Other riders were climbing on board, bawling orders to the teenage boys watching the mounts—

—when a rocket cut across the sky, leaving a sparking trail. It exploded overhead with a *BOOM* that rattled Valentine's bones.

The legworm reared but Zak settled it.

Zak extended a hand, but Valentine found that with the hooks and spikes in his costume, climbing the side of the legworm was possible without assistance, as long as another shell didn't fire.

"What the hell was that?" Valentine asked, the boom still echoing in his ears.

"A big firework, sorta. Scares the worms. They're trying to make the mounts bolt."

Valentine saw one worm humping as it headed down the road, a rider raising dust as he was dragged. The others had their mounts under control, more or less, and turned them toward the barn.

Another rocket exploded, but it only served to hurry the legworms in the direction they were already going. Zak reached their campsite.

"Get on!" Valentine called. "We've got to ride out of here. Where's Price?"

"I don't know," Ahn-Kha said. "Still off with his mule." Valentine helped the others up.

Bee looked alarmed, and refused to mount. She let out a shriek into the night. Ahn-Kha barked something at her and reached out, but she slapped his hand away and ran off toward the road.

"I'll drop you off with the kids in the cover-field," Zak said. "You'll be safe there."

"Take us to the fight," Valentine said.

"The Dispatcher—"

"The Dispatcher's going to need every gun," Valentine said. "We've got three. Right?" He looked over his shoulder at Duvalier and Ahn-Kha.

Anh-Kha nodded. He had his cannon and Price's Kalashnikov. Duvalier patted her shotgun. "I'm happy to plant a few bobcats."

"Wildcats," Zak said.

"Then let's get online."

Valentine looked down at his U-gun. The only ammunition he had for it was Everready's 5.56mm. He wished he had a real sniper load. He looked at Duvalier's shotgun. The Mossberg would be useless in anything but a close-quarters fight. "Ali, take Price's rifle."

"Be sparing," Ahn-Kha said. "There is only one magazine."

"Where's the rest?"

"In boxes." Ahn-Kha rummaged around in the battle satchel that contained spare bullets and gear for his gun, and handed him the box.

Cookie and Gibson joined them and the legworm slid quickly down the hill to where the other riders were gathering. Cookie had his ear to a headset, coming from a handcrank-charged portable radio.

Another rocket exploded over the massive barn. Yellow-white sparks ran down the tin roof.

"They're good with the fuses over there. Probably been cutting them all day. So you're a brother rider now," Gibson added to Valentine.

"Seems like," Valentine said. Zak lined up his legworm behind another. Just behind them, in the center of the column of legworms, the Dispatcher waved a flashlight. The column turned and the legworms went single-file up toward the barn.

"If we go to battle line you, the girl, and the Grog can cling to the cargo netting," Zak said. "Keep your heads down."

Valentine learned what battle line was as soon as they crested the hill and turned their line north. Another sky-cracking explosion over the barn sent a legworm humping over from the other side of the hill, its riders hanging on for their lives. The line of battle-ready legworms twitched, but stayed in station front to back.

"They're coming. Flank facing offside," Cookie called, listening to his headset.

Zak and his team slid off the top of their worm, as did riders all along the battle line, digging their hooks, goads, and spikes into the thick patches of dead flesh. Women and teenage boys with rifles, hooks looped around their chests and attached to their ankles, joined the fighting line, adding their guns.

The column moved in the direction the fleeing legworm had just abandoned. Valentine readied himself for what would be on the reverse slope of the hill when they topped it.

Cookie slapped his thigh, headset to his ear. "Zak, we got 'em. They're in the field, not halfway across, in open order."

Cheers and foxhunting hallos broke out all across the Dispatcher's line of legworms as the news spread.

Zak's mount crested the hill and came down the other side, turning slightly as it followed the worm directly ahead.

Twenty or more legworms crept—or so it looked in the distance—in three columns across the contest field toward the Bulletproof camp.

Valentine took comfort in the thick length of legworm between him and the Wildcats. It was like shooting from a moveable wall. He thought of stories he'd read of fighting warships, their lines of cannons presented to each other. In naval terminology, the Bulletproofs were "crossing the T" against the oncoming Wildcats.

The Dispatcher's legworm followed theirs, and the one behind his let loose with a whooshing sound.

"The pipe organ's firing!" Gibson yelled. "Yeeeah!"

Streams of sparks cut down the hillside and exploded in the earth among the columns. The Wildcat legworms began to turn and get into line to present their own bank of rifles to the Bulletproofs, but the mounts kept trying to get away from the explosions.

Machine guns from the front Wildcat legworms probed their line, red tracers reaching for the riders. Another Wildcat firework burst above and Valentine felt the legworm jump, but it had overshot.

The Bulletproof column accelerated. Zak employed his sharpened hook to urge the legworm along and close the gap that opened between his mount and the one ahead. Zak still had his rifle slung; his job was to keep his beast in line, not fight.

Now the two masses of legworms, the Bulletproof's tightly in line and moving quickly, the Wildcats' in an arrowhead-shaped mob, converged.

Ahn-Kha sighted and fired. "Damn," he said, loading another shell. He shot again. "Got him."

A legworm in the Wildcats turned and others writhed to follow or to avoid its new course. Ahn-Kha picked off another driver.

"That's some kind of shooting," Cookie said. Ahn-Kha ignored him, fired again, swore.

The front end of the Bulletproof column began to fire. It had run ahead of the Wildcats; the marksmen got an angle on the exposed riders clinging to the right sides of their mounts.

The Wildcat column dissolved into chaos. Each legworm turned and hurried back toward their camp as fast as the hundreds and hundreds of legs could carry their riders.

Cheers broke out all across the Bulletproof line.

"That's how you win a scrap!" Gibson said. "Tight riding. Damn if Mandvi can't point a column."

"It's because we were ready for them," Zak said, nodding to Valentine.

"Cease fire," Cookie shouted, radio headset still to his ear—though no one but Ahn-Kha was shooting. The Wildcats retreated in disorder.

Valentine hadn't used a single bullet.

⚓

More rounds of Bulletproof were being issued as riders danced jigs. Other legworms, still with armed riders, circled the barn at a distance, though the scouts had claimed that the Wildcats were decamping and heading for higher ground to the east.

"Zak, I take it you're willing to give our friends a ride north, now," the Dispatcher said. "And if you aren't, I'll make it an order."

"Of course I'm willing. I'm willing to dig a hole to hell if that's where they want me to drive my worm."

"Your sister can go watch your string," the Dispatcher said.

"Wormcast." Tikka kicked a stone.

Duvalier hung on Valentine's arm, but it was play; she felt stiff as a mannequin. "Better luck next time."

"What's your destination over the Ohio?"

"We're trying to find an old relative," Valentine said. "She's come up in the world, and we're going to see if she'll set us up."

"Take Three-Finger Charlie, Zak," the Dispatcher said. "He's got connections with the smugglers. Tell him to trade egg hides if he has to, I want these folks set up so they can pass through the Ohio Ordnance in style."

Hoffman Price led his mule into the circle of revelers. "I was

233

scavenging for mule shoes. He found a mess of wild carrots, and they were fat and sweet so I pulled up a bushel."

"You missed—" Zak began.

"I know. I saw it from a couple miles away. You Bulletproofs throw one hell of a party. Fireworks and everything."

Price looked at the bourbon-sloppy smiles all around. "What? Don't y'all like carrots?"

# CHAPTER TEN

*T*he Ohio River Valley, September: North of the bluegrass in the upper reaches of the Ohio River lies a stream-crossed country of woods and limestone hills. Rust-belt ruins, dotted with an occasional manufacturing plant, line the river. North of the river is the Great Lakes Ordnance, a network of Kurian principalities in a federation of unequal ministates huddled around the middle Great Lakes. South of the Ohio are coal mines and mill towns, under wary Kurians who have staked out claims bordering on the lands of the legworm ranchers.

No one much likes, or trusts, anyone else. But this is the industrial heartland of the eastern half of North America, such as it is, producing engines, garments, footwear, tires, even a bush-hopping aircraft or two, along with the more mundane implements of a nineteenth-century technology. Their deals are made in New York, their "deposits" are exchanged in Memphis, and their human workers are secured by mercenary bands of Grogs hired from and directed by the great generals of Washington, DC. As long as they produce, even slowly and inefficiently, the material the rest of the Kurian Order needs, and keep the Baltimore and Ohio lifelines open, their position is secure.

It was here that David Valentine lost his forlorn hope of a trail.

φ

Valentine, Price, Bee, Ahn-Kha, and Duvalier stood at the Laurelton Station a week later in a blustery rain.

Zak and the other Bulletproofs departed after depositing them in the care of a man named McNulty, a River Rat trader and "labor agent" friendly to the tribe on the south bank of the Ohio.

They'd ridden into a shantytown right in the shadow of a grain-silo Kurian Tower—only the most desperate would resort to such real estate in broad daylight—with Price's mule happily munching hay in a flatbed cart being towed by the powerful legworm. After introductions at the River Rat's anchored barge-house and one last round of Bulletproof bourbon in farewell, Zak turned over six full legworm egg hides, cured and bound in twine. Valentine only parted with them after McNulty gave them Ohio ID cards, ration books, and an up-to-date map of the area. The map was annotated with riverbank areas that were hiring and cheap lodgings—all with the password "BMN."

McNulty probably took a cut of any business he referred.

With a week's familiarity, Valentine could see why the legworm-egg leather was so valuable. It breathed well, and though it became heavy in the rain the wet didn't permeate to the inside.

They followed the riverside train tracks to the turn-in for Laurelton. Price told them what he could about the north side of the river. He had returned fugitives to the Ohio authorities once or twice, but had never been much beyond the river. Bee stuck close to him here under the somber sky—autumn had arrived.

The residents kept to their towns. Patrolmen on bicycles, most armed with nothing more than a sap, rode the towns and highways. The officers looked at Price's Kalashnikov as they passed—the rest of their longarms were wrapped in blankets on the mule—but made no move to question them. Valentine saw only one vehicle, a garbage truck full of coal.

The ground reminded Valentine of some of the hills near the Iron Range in Minnesota, low and jumbled and full of timber. But where the forests in the Northwoods had stood since before the Sioux hunted, the forests in Ohio had sprung up since 2022, breaking up and overrunning the little plots carved out by man.

So when they cautiously turned the bends nearing Laurelton, only to find more windowless houses and piles of weed-bearing brick, he couldn't help feeling deflated.

There was a station, if a single siding counted as a station. The track continued north, but the height of the weeds, trees, and bracken suggested that a train hadn't passed that way in years. Valentine even checked the rust on the rails to be sure. In his days as a Wolf he'd seen supply caves hidden by saplings and bushes specifically pulled up and replanted to discourage investigation.

Deep oxidation. He could scrape it off with a thumbnail.

"Fool's hope," Valentine said. "Rooster either lied or didn't have correct information from the Kurians. Maybe they divert the trains to keep the final destination secret."

Price unloaded his mule to give the animal a breather. "The debt is settled. I feel for you, David. Long way to come to find nothing. It's happened to me."

Post would know he'd tried his best. How many vanished a year in the Kurian Zone? A hundred thousand? A half million? But how do you laugh in a legless man's face and tell him the last rope he's clinging to isn't tied to anything but a wish?

The narrow road bordering the track was in pretty poor condition. It certainly wasn't frequently traveled.

*Why here?*

Price filled the mule's nosebag and Bee rooted inside one of the abandoned houses for firewood. Duvalier stretched herself out next to a ditch and took off her boots.

The hills around Laurelton were close. A hundred men, properly posted, could make sure that whatever transpired here couldn't be seen by anything but aircraft or satellites.

Ahn-Kha poked around the road, examining potholes. "Strange sort of road, my David," Ahn-Kha said.

Valentine joined him. Like the tracks, it ended in weeds to the north. The south part—

—had been patched.

Valentine trotted a few hundred yards south.

There was a filled gap in the road at a washout, recent enough for the asphalt to still be black-blueish, rather than gray-green. The Kurians weren't much on infrastructure maintenance even in their best-run principalities; they didn't like anything that traveled faster than a Reaper could run. . . .

Valentine examined the weeds and bracken bordering the station. Sure enough, there were three gaps, definite paths leading from the tracks to the road. Quick-growing grasses had sprung up, but no brambles or saplings, though they were thick on the west side of the tracks.

"A farewell feast," Price said, revealing a sausage wrapped in wax paper and a loaf of bread. "Unless you want to come back with us."

Valentine handed him Everready's Reaper teeth. "More than earned. If I had another set I'd give them to you, with my initials written on them."

"If you see the old squatter again, let him know I appreciate being able to repay the debt. What are you going to do next?"

Valentine rubbed his chin. He needed a shave. "You said you'd brought in men to the Ordnance?"

Price consulted a scuffed leather notebook and extracted a card from a pocket. "Yup. I'm 31458 here in Ohio." He passed it to Valentine.

The card had the number, and some kind of seal featuring a man in a toga holding one hand over his heart and the other outstretched, over a pyramid with an eye at the top. "Meaning what?"

Price shrugged. "Dunno. They always recorded my number when I brought a man in, though."

"How hard is it to get one of those?"

"I didn't even know I had to have one. They gave it to me when I brought my first man in. I was going to stop at one of the cop stations and look at what kind of warrants are out. Long as I'm up this way, maybe someone's hiding out in Kentucky I can bring in. Make the trip profitable in more than a spiritual sense."

"Mind if I tag along?"

"Not at all."

"Let's walk along the road on the way back to the river."

After lunch they walked single file down the side of the road. Valentine stayed in the center of the road, crisscrossing it, checking blown debris, the patchwork repairs, anything for some kind of sign. He found a few old ruts that he suspected were made by heavy trucks, but they were so weathered that he could only guess at the type of vehicle.

"So we did all this for nothing?" Duvalier asked when they took a rest halt. "We're just going back?"

There was a welcome tenderness to her voice; she'd been cold since Valentine had turned the mutual slaughter she'd tried to start into a victory for the Bulletproof.

"Wherever they take the women, it has to be pretty close. I want to start searching. Seems to me it's got to be within a few miles. Otherwise they'd bring the train somewhere else, or right to where they want them. We'll just start searching, using a grid with the station as a base point."

"Why are we still with Stinky, then?"

"To set us up as bounty hunters. It's not far from what we're really doing, and it would explain us poking around in the woods."

"I don't like it here. These hills and trees, all wet and black. It's like they're closing off the sky. I haven't liked this job; just one misery after another."

Valentine looked up from yet another worthless mark that wasn't a track. "I'm glad you're here. I'd have been hung months ago if it wasn't for you and Ahn-Kha, most likely."

"The Lifeweavers were watching over us all back there. But they don't know about us being here. How can they know we need their help?"

Duvalier's worshipful naivete when it came to humanity's allies took strange forms sometimes. "Not sure how they could help us now," Valentine said.

"Something would turn up. A piece of luck. Like the general's train showing up in Nebraska."

"After we crisscrossed three states looking for him. Would have been better if the Lifeweavers had arranged our luck to hit when we passed a dozen miles from his headquarters without knowing it."

She planted her walking stick. "You think everything's chance."

"No. If it were, I wouldn't still be alive."

⚓

After Price flagged down a patrolman on the riverside highway, they stopped in the little Ohio-side town of Caspian. An Ordnance Station, part police house, part customs post, and part post office had the latest warrant flyers posted in a three-ring binder.

Valentine and Price went inside while the rest visited a market to buy food.

"Look what the river washed up," an Ohioan with a package said to his friend as they passed in on their way to the postal clerk.

Price helped Valentine select a handbill. Valentine wanted a female, thirtyish. "Not much to choose from. Guess Ohio women are law-abiding. Except for Gina Stottard, here."

"Stealing power and unauthorized wiring," Valentine read. "A desperado electrician."

"She's all there is."

"What do I do next?"

"Follow me."

Price took three handbills of his own—the top man had killed a woman while trying to perform an illegal abortion—and went over to a blue-uniformed officer behind a thick window. She blinked at them from behind thick corrective glasses.

"Copies of these, please," Price said, sliding the handbills under the glass along with his warrant card. "And—"

"Gimme a moment," she said, and went to a cabinet. She got a key and disappeared into another room. Ten minutes later—perhaps she'd worked in a coffee break—she returned with the copies. They were poor-quality photocopies, but still readable. "Six dollars," she said.

"My associate needs a bounty card."

"That makes it sixteen dollars. You could have said so. Have to make another trip to get one."

"I tr—I'm sorry."

Fifteen minutes later she returned with the form. It had a numbered card on it similar to Price's. Valentine filled it out using his Ohio ration-card name—Tarquin Ayoob, not a name Valentine would have chosen on his own; it came off his tongue like a horse getting wire-tripped—and passed it back under the partition. She counted the money, stamped both the document and the bounty card, then took out a scissors and cut the card free.

"What's the number for?" Valentine asked.

"If you got a prisoner in tow you can get free food and lodging at any NUC door, they just need the number. Counts as good works for the Ordnance Lottery. Bring in a man or even a useful report and your number goes in that week. You can buy tickets, too. This week's pot is half a million. Care to enter?"

"Doubt we'll be in the Ordnance long enough to collect," Price said. "I thank you, officer."

They left the station and reunited with Duvalier and the Grogs at the riverbank, sharing a final meal. Apples were growing plentiful, making Valentine think of Everready. Price pulled up the mule's feet and inspected them one by one as Bee held the animal.

"This is really good-bye," Valentine said.

"Watch your curfew around here, son," Price said. "Folks button up really tight. If you're solid-silver lucky, the police pick you up and throw you in the clink for breaking.

"I'm going to be poking around in Lexington for a bit. Ohio fugitives head there, more often than not. There's jobs at the processing plants, and the West Kentucky Legion isn't too choosy about who it takes on. I'll check in at the depots."

"Can I come back with you that far?" Duvalier asked.

Valentine almost dropped his apple. "You want to give up?"

"This led nowhere, David. I don't want to stumble around ground I don't know. I feel like we stick out here. Everyone talks different, wears different clothes."

"Give me three more days," Valentine said.

"How far away will you be in three days?" Duvalier asked Price.

"I could dawdle along the river here for a bit. I never got my vacation in at the Shack. I owe myself some fishing."

"Three days' worth?" Valentine asked.

"Three days."

"Lots of people here on bicycles," Valentine said. "Price, where do you suppose we can rent some?"

φ

Price treated himself to a motel room. He found one with a distinctly nondiscriminating owner when it came to personal hygiene, Grogs, mules littering the weed-covered parking lot, and where the occupants poured their night soil.

241

It turned out you couldn't rent bicycles, and no money would buy a bike capable of supporting Ahn-Kha. By parting with yet another gold coin to a bike and moped dealer under a canopy of festive plastic bunting, he and Duvalier each got bicycles with tires, functioning brakes, storage baskets, even clip-on flashlight headlamps that charged by pedaling.

After some exploring with Ahn-Kha they found a house deep in the woods, not quite a cabin and not quite a shack. While it rested at a tilt thanks to the absence of a foundation, there was a functioning well and Ahn-Kha got water flowing into the house again with a little tinkering and a lot of root cutting.

The weather turned fair again and Valentine and Duvalier bicycled together, almost unarmed—he brought the .22 pistol, she her sword-carrying stick—starting at the nearest crossroads to the end-of-the-line station and working their way outward, following roads heavy enough to support trucks.

Valentine kept turning them to the north and east, into hillier and more isolated country. He couldn't say what drove him into this particular notch of Ohio. Perhaps it was a line of three legworms patrolling a ridge, glimpsed as they crept through the trees at a distance. Or it was the one true military convoy that passed them coming out of it; three tractor trailers, with Grog troops in supporting vehicles and venerable five-ton cargo trucks.

They were only questioned once, by a pair of policemen also on bicycles. Valentine showed his card and the warrant for the renegade electrician, explaining that he'd learned she had a cousin who lived out in these woods.

"Don't think so, Ayoob," one of the patrol said. "Even during deer season most around here know to avoid the point country. You're better off searching the other side of the river."

So on their third day they risked a predawn ride along the river road to get into the hills early. Other than the good condition of the roads in the region, he couldn't point to anything but a feeling.

"Another feeling. Is it because you can't go back?" Duvalier asked. "Is that why you won't let this go? You need something to do, even a ghost chase?"

Valentine chewed a wild bergamot leaf and tossed its purple-pink flower to Duvalier. "You've been good company. After today you can go find the Lifeweavers. But be sure to tell them about this."

She nuzzled his cheek. The half quarrel had faded.

"Wish we could find out where that's going," Valentine said as they breakfasted on bread and cheese. A green-painted military truck turned off from the river road and approached their position. Black smoke belched from its stack as the truck shifted up.

"Can do," she said, putting the flower between her teeth and picking up her bicycle. "Watch my coat."

"Ali—"

She pedaled madly in the same direction as the truck, and brought her bike alongside. She reached out and grabbed a tie for the cargo bed's canvas cover.

Valentine watched her disappear.

He had little to do over the next three hours but refill their water bottles and worry. When she came coasting down the hill again she had a huge smile.

"I've got a date for tonight," she said, pulling up her bike and accepting a water bottle. "Nice guy from New Philadelphia. Lance Corporal Scott Thatcher. He plays the guitar."

"Thought you were leaving tonight."

"Don't you want to know what I found?"

The jibe Valentine was working on died half-formed. "You found something?"

"It's big, it's well-guarded, and Thatcher didn't offer to take me to lunch inside, even with a lot of hints. You wanna see?"

Valentine picked up his bike as Duvalier shoved her coat into the basket on the back of her bike.

"What is it?" Valentine asked as they pushed up the hill.

"I'm not sure. It looks kind of like a hospital. There were ambulances out front, military and civilian. Big grounds, double-fenced."

They topped a hill; another loomed on the other side of a narrow gully. The road took a hairpin turn at a small stream. "I don't suppose your Corporal Thatcher illuminated you?"

"He said he was just a delivery boy."

A truck blatted through the trees. They pulled their bikes off the road and watched it negotiate the gulley. It was an open-backed truck, filled with an assortment of uniformed men, some in bandages, some just weary-looking.

"Okay, it is a hospital," Valentine said as they remounted their bikes. "Why all the security, then?"

They finally saw it from the top of the next hill.

"This is probably as far as we should go," Duvalier said. "There's a watch post at the end of the trees."

Valentine couldn't see much through the trees, just a few salmon-colored building tops, at least a dozen stories tall. The ground leveled out past the hill, flat ground and a straight road to a guarded gate beyond a half mile or so of open ground. Valentine looked through his minibinoculars. Yes, there was a little watch station, about the size of a lifeguard's house at a beach, near the break in the trees.

"Three layers of fencing, with a road between," Duvalier said. "Outer layer is electrified. Innermost layer is just a polite six feet of glorified chicken wire. He dropped me off at the gate. The gatehouse looks normal enough, but ten yards out to either side there's tenting over something. I'm guessing heavy weapons."

Valentine did some mental math. This place was perhaps twenty minutes from the train tracks, in trucks driving forty miles an hour.

"Oh, Thatcher gave it a name."

"He did?"

"He called it 'Zan-ado.' "

"Xanadu?" Valentine asked.

"Yeah. Mean anything to you?"

"I've heard the word. I don't know what it means. A fairyland or some such. You hanging around for your date?"

"I'm meeting him in Ironton."

"Ahn-Kha and I will check this out. Tonight."

φ

They said good-bye to Price while Duvalier biked off to keep her appointment. Valentine decided he could trust Price with a message to Southern Command. Someone needed to know about Xanadu.

If Price was willing to act as courier.

Valentine insisted on a farewell drink. Their supply of Bulletproof had been much reduced in trading, but they still had a few stoppered bottles.

They drank it inside the filthy motel room, windows and doors wide open to admit a little air.

"Price, you ever run into any guerillas?"

"I avoid them if I can. I've had my guns commandeered off me. They've threatened to shoot Bee, too."

"If you could get a message through to the Resistance, you'd really help the Cause."

"*The Cause*. Not that shit again."

"It's the only—"

"No! You don't tell me about the Cause, boy." Price took a drink. "I know your Cause. I know Everready's Cause."

"How did you come to know Everready? What happened with those teeth?"

Price took another long swallow. "Don't suppose you ever heard of a place called Coon County?"

"No."

"Won't find it on your old maps. Nice little spot, up in the mountains near Chattanooga, north of Mount Eagle. Called it Coon County because of Tom Coon, roughest son of a bitch you ever met. I bet he killed near as many Reapers as Everready. Ol' Everready was our liaison officer with Southern Command. Got radio gear and explosives through him.

"We had a bad scrape and lost twenty-six men, captive. Colonel Coon, he had some Quisling prisoners of his own. We kept them around pulling plows or cutting wood, that kind of stuff. He went in, alone, to negotiate. We figured they hung him, since he vanished for a month. But wouldn't you know, he came back with twenty-four. Said two had been killed before he could get there, and he exchanged the survivors for twenty-four of our prisoners.

"A few weeks later this big operation got under way, Rattlesnake I think it was called. Lots of guerillas involved. I missed it because I had Lyme disease. Tick bite. Put me on antibiotics and finally got a transfusion from old Everready.

"Then Colonel Coon came back. He looked tired, but he took the time."

He stared out the window, looking at his mule grazing in the field across the road. Valentine wondered what visions he really saw.

"Coon sat by each bed in the hospital, told a few jokes. He asked me how my wife was doing, if the baby had come. He had that kind of memory.

"Then the Reaper showed up.

"It wasn't any kind of a fight, any more than pigs in a slaughter pen put up a fight. Doc Swenson tried to get to a gun; he went down first. A nurse ran. I remember Coon wounded her in the leg. Kneecapped her.

"The Reaper took a friend of mine, Grouse, we called him. The woman next to me blew air into her IV and died rather than have the Reaper take her. I just froze up. I couldn't move a muscle. Not even my eyes, hardly. It killed the nurse right at the bottom of my bed.

"It fed and Coon started staggering around. He was speaking so fast—you ever hear someone speaking in tongues, David? Like that, words coming out as fast as voltage. The Reaper started dancing, doing this sorta waltz with the nurse's body as it jumped from bed to bed. Some of her blood and piss got on me as it swung her around, hit me right in the eye.

"That's when Everready came in. He gave it a face full of buckshot and stuck a surgical knife in its ear. Then he drowned Coon in the slop bucket where they emptied the bedpans. He picked me up like I was a six-year-old girl and ran.

"Well, there were Reapers everywhere. Coon had led them right in. They got everyone in Coon County, even—even my wife."

Price passed the bottle back to Valentine.

"Everready told me about how he'd heard from the Lifeweaver what a seductive thing it was, to feed on another man's spirit like that. He said humans could do it same as the others with the right training—kind of like what the Lifeweavers do to men like Everready. I thought they got to Colonel Coon when he went to bargain about those twenty-six men, but Everready said it was probably even before that. I felt dirty, living when Na—everyone else died."

"What's Coon County like now?" Valentine asked.

"Just another Kurian Zone, David. I gave up the war then. How are we supposed to win when they can grant a man immortality for joining in? The Kurian Zone ain't so bad. The Reapers feed behind closed doors, it's like it's not even happening. A person gone now and then, like they walked off into the country and never came back."

Price looked at him sidelong.

"Even the end's not so bad, they tell me. The Reapers, they look into your eyes and you see pretty meadows full of flowers and sunlight, or everyone you know who's dead welcoming you, urgin' you on, like. You don't even feel the tongue going in. That doesn't sound so bad. A good Christian doesn't fear death."

"He doesn't hasten it, either," Valentine said.

"Young and idealistic. You want to talk 'hastening' death—you've been in battles. Who's got the better deal, the man in the Kurian Zone has plenty of food on the table, leisure time to spend, a family if he wants—children, even grandchildren if he keeps his nose clean—compare that to you boys in the Ozarks. Get drafted, what, sixteen is it now? Break your back in labor units until a rifle becomes available, and then you're dead by twenty. How many virgins you buried, David? What kind of life did they have?

"Only people I'm setting myself against are those that want to make other people's tiny slice of life a misery. Murderers, rapists, child touchers, swindlers. That's my cause."

"You're forgetting the biggest murderers of all."

"You say. I say all they're doing is making it sensible and orderly. You get an orderly birth, an orderly life, an orderly death. I've come across dozens of folks running from the Kurians. Or at least they started out that way. Two, three days later they're hungry and cold and they ask me to lead them to food and shelter, thank me for putting them back in the Order, even if it's an NUC waystation with a Reaper in the belfry. They want the Order."

"Keep telling yourself that, Price, if it makes you feel better. Wish I'd known the man Everready saved."

"You missed him," Price said. "I don't. Let's talk again in ten years and see if you're still so sure of your Cause."

ф

Valentine rode his bicycle and Ahn-Kha loped along, his gear tied to Valentine's handlebar and on the back of his bike. A distant whistle sounded curfew as the sun disappeared, and Valentine walked the bike off the road.

They slept for three hours, long enough to give their bodies a break, then moved through the hills more cautiously. Valentine kept his lifesign down, and hoped that his old ability to feel the cold presence of a prowling Reaper hadn't been dulled by disuse. Sure enough, there was one in the gully with the hairpin turn on the road, keeping watch.

They put earth and trees between themselves and the Reaper, threw a wide loop around—

And Valentine sensed another one, a dark star on his mental horizon.

It reminded him of the installation he'd come across with Gonzo in Wisconsin, before their disastrous encounter with a sniper.

He and Ahn-Kha backed off, put another half mile of woods and wildlife between themselves and the sentry Reaper.

"I might be able to get through them alone, old horse," Valentine said. "You don't make human lifesign, but you make enough for them to get curious."

"I could go first. When it comes to investigate, you—"

Ahn-Kha was no fool. The Golden One knew exactly what he was saying, that he was willing to draw a prowling Reaper and trust Valentine to dispose of it before it killed him.

"No. A Reaper goes missing and they'll know someone's poking around. Go back to the house, keep to thick cover, and wait for me. Or Duvalier."

"What will you do?"

"I'm going to get past the Reaper sentries. Then keep down until the day watch comes, if any. If I'm lucky, I'll be inside the sentry line and outside the wire, and I can get a real look at the place by daylight. At dusk I'll creep out again."

"If you're not lucky?"

"You and Ali get back to Southern Command. Hopefully they'll try again with a better-prepared team."

"I remember having this conversation before. We only just found you. Would it not be better to look around from inside the wire, my David?"

"Of course. How do we do that?"

"It is a hospital. One of us just has to be sick enough."

Valentine nodded. "I know a couple of old tricks. One or two can even fool a doctor. Let's get back to Ali first. If this blows up in our faces, I have a feeling we'll never get outside that wire again."

ψ

Valentine, Ahn-Kha, and Duvalier stood at the crossroads. The river road stretched off east and west, the road leading to the well-guarded hospital branching off.

She didn't discuss her "date" the previous night—save to deny that she got anything of use out of the soldier. "He's going on a long patrol. He offered to see me again in four days."

"Are you going to wait for him?" Valentine asked.

"Depends if you and the jolly gold giant here go through with this insanity."

"It will work," Valentine said.

"Price left us a bass boat," Duvalier said. "And I've still got our Spam. How much action do you want?"

"Just a little fire or two on the other side of the river. Tonight. Nothing too hard."

"And your illness?"

"A little ipecac and other herbs with unfortunate pharmacological side effects."

"Will that be convincing enough?" Ahn-Kha asked, scanning the road and woods. "I think I see your dinner, Alessa. My David, may I see your pistol?"

Valentine handed over the gun. Ahn-Kha checked it over, then pointed it at his neck.

"Ahn—"

The gun went off with a sharp crack. Valentine and Duvalier

249

stood dumbfounded. Blood and flesh flew from the Golden One's neck. He lowered the gun to his elbow and shot himself through the arm. Then again, at the hip point.

Valentine tried to wrestle the gun from Ahn-Kha's grip, burning his hand on the barrel, but the Grog was too strong. It fired again.

"Urmpf," Ahn-Kha grunted, releasing the gun.

"What the hell, man?" Duvalier asked.

"No need for insults," Ahn-Kha said. "I just decided—"

"You wounded yourself to get into the hospital?" Duvalier asked.

"Why not just shoot yourself once?" Valentine asked, putting the gun back on safety and digging for his first-aid kit.

"One bullet wound with powder grains around it might be self-inflicted. How many desperate cowards avoid combat by shooting themselves four times? But I fear the last penetrated my intestines."

"I'm sorry," Valentine said. "I thought you'd gone mad."

"I knew what I was doing. Pass me that disinfectant."

"You should get going," Valentine told Duvalier. "If you pass some of our local constables, have them send an ambulance."

Duvalier gathered up her stick and pack, and wheeled her bicycle over to Ahn-Kha. She kissed him on the ear. "You taste like a muskrat. Don't let him leave you."

Valentine glared at her.

"I'll hang around at Price's motel," Duvalier said. "They made him pay for a month because of the Grog. If you make it back out you can find me there. Unless, of course, I get the feeling I'm being watched. Then I'm gone."

ψ

Valentine applied dressings, then sat Ahn-Kha on the saddle of the bike. The tires immediately flattened, but it served as a convincing conveyance for a wounded Grog, with one long arm draped around Valentine's shoulder. Birds called to each other in the trees; they both could lie down and die and the birds would still sing on.

"How you doing, old horse?"

"The wounds burn."

"They'll get you patched up. Hope that supply truck passes soon."

"I can walk all the way there if I must."

No supply truck came, but a white ambulance snapped dead-fall twigs as it roared through the riverside hills. It didn't employ a siren, but there was no traffic to hurry out of the way.

Valentine sat Ahn-Kha on the weed-grown shoulder and stood in the roadway, waving his arms. The ambulance, tilted due to a bad suspension, came on, unheeding, lights flashing—

Then swerved and braked, stalling the motor.

The driver spoke through the wire grid that served as his window. "You almost got yourself killed, quirt." His associate used the stop to light a cigarette.

"We're trying to get to the hospital. My friend's wounded."

The clean-shaven pair in blue hats exchanged a look. "A Grog? Try the—"

"I'm hurting too. Can we—"

"On a call, sir. We'll radio back and have you picked up." He nodded at his associate, who touched a box on the dashboard.

"Thank you. Thank you very much."

"Don't move. Another ambulance will be along." The driver got the engine going and moved off.

"Curbside service," Valentine said, taking out his pocketknife.

"My David, what are you going to do?"

"We're both going in wounded."

Valentine raked the knife twice across the outer side of his left hand. He'd been anticipating the pain, which made it all the worse.

"Defensive wounds," Valentine said.

"I hope we have no need for a real dressing. This is our last one," Ahn-Kha said.

"Just give me some surgical tape and a scissors. I'll close them with butterfly dressings. Those two in the ambulance might have noticed that I didn't have a big dressing on my hand."

"I will cut the tape. You're bleeding."

Valentine spattered a little of his own blood on his face to add to the effect.

Ahn-Kha deftly cut notches into each side of the surgical tape and handed the pieces to Valentine one at a time. A butterfly bandage used a minimal amount of tape directly over the wound, gripping the two sides of skin with its "wings." Valentine splashed on stinging disinfectant, then used three bandages on one cut, two on the other.

It took twenty minutes for the second ambulance to arrive—a gateless pickup truck painted white. The driver was a single, older man with a ring of flesh adding a paunch to his chin.

"You two're the walking wounded, I'll bet."

"That's us."

"Hop in the back. There's a water jug there, don't be afraid to use it. Bring your bike if you want."

A yellow plastic cooler with a cup tied to a string was stuck in one corner of the pickup with a bungee cord. Valentine put the bike in, then he and Ahn-Kha climbed into the bed. The truck sagged.

"Hoo—he's a big boy, your Grog. Now hold on, I'm going to drive gentle but I don't want to lose you when I turn."

The driver executed a neat three-point turn.

Valentine spoke to him through the open back window of the pickup. "I'm Tar Ayoob. What's your name, sir?"

"Beirlein, Grog-boy. I never seen his type before. He some special breed?"

"They got them up in Canada," Valentine said. "They're good in the snow. Big feet."

"Oh, Sasquatches is what he is, huh? What do you know."

"I'm told this is the best hospital south of Columbus," Valentine said. "Hope they're right. My friend's got a bullet in him."

"We'll patch him up. Don't worry."

The pickup negotiated the hairpin turn, climbed out of the gulley in second gear, then came out of the trees and Valentine finally saw Xanadu.

It filled all the flat ground in a punchbowl ring of wooded hills. Most of the structures were salmon-colored brick or concrete, save for some wooden outbuildings.

Duvalier was right; a triple line of fencing, one polite, two lethal, surrounded the campuslike huddle of structures. Guards at the gate made notations on a clipboard and handed Valentine and Ahn-Kha stickers with red crosses on them. In the farther corners of the expanse of grass between buildings and fence Valentine saw dairy cows. There looked to be a baseball diamond and a track closer to the gate.

The four biggest salmon-colored buildings looked like apartments Valentine had seen in Chicago, except those had been built with balconies, and large windows. Each one was as long as a city block, rectangular, and laid out so they formed a square. Valentine counted twelve stories.

A long, low, three-story building of darker brick extended from the four, and was joined to a concrete jumble, tiered like a wedding cake, that had ambulances and trucks parked in front of it.

The ambulance didn't stop in front of the hospital. It continued to drive around back, past what looked like three-story apartments.

"Hey, what about the emergency room?"

"Your Grog goes out to the stables. Don't worry, our vet's treated Grogs before."

The pickup drove to a pair of barns, giant old-fashioned wooden ones with an aluminum feed silo between. The truck pulled up to a ranch house with a satellite dish turned into a decorative planter. Valentine saw another, distant barn. Fields with a group of Holsteins and a group of Jerseys were spread out to the wire. A guard tower, hard to distinguish against the treetops, could just be seen.

Xanadu's footprint covered several square miles, perhaps the size of downtown Dallas. If it was a concentration camp of some kind, it was a pleasant-looking one.

A blond woman in a white medical coat, a stethoscope around her neck, came out on the porch of the ranch house and walked to the back of the truck. A man in overalls followed her out, holding what looked like a set of shackles. "This is Doc Boothe, Tar."

Doc Boothe had one of those faces that hung from a broad fore-

253

head, progressing down from wide eyes to a modest nose to a tiny, dimpled chin. "How cooperative is he?"

"Extremely," Ahn-Kha said. The vet let out a squeak of surprise. "Unless you try to put manacles on me."

"A patient who can talk. You're a DVMs dream. What's your name?"

"Ahn-Kha."

"I'm Tar," Valentine said. "We're out of Kentucky, Bulletproof tribe."

"And another Kentucky quirt shows up looking for Ordnance medical attention," the man with the shackles observed. "They need to patrol the river better."

The vet ignored both her helper and Valentine, except to say, "Leave your guns in the truck for now. We've got a safe inside. Ahnke, come into the operating room."

She led them in past kennels filled with barking German shepherds and pointers. She unlocked and opened a gray metal door. The tiles inside smelled of disinfectant. Dr. Boothe checked to see that they were following, then turned on a light in a big, white-tiled room. A heavy stainless-steel berth, like an autopsy table, dominated the center of the room.

"It's not right to treat him in a vet office," Valentine said.

"I've got experience tranquilizing large animals. And I'm comfortable around them. I know you're worried, but he's in better hands here than in the main building. They slap bandages on and send everyone to the sanitarium in Columbus. Okay, Ahnke, on the table. Do you want to lie down? Make it easier for me to reach. You ever had a reaction to pain medication?"

"I've only had laudanum," Ahn-Kha said.

"This is better, it takes the edge off." She opened a cabinet and took out a box of pills, shook three out, and poured him a cup of water. "Pepsa!" she called. "Gunshot tray."

Ahn-Kha swallowed the pills.

A plump woman in blue cotton brought in a tray full of instruments. Valentine recognized a probe and some small forceps. The doctor removed Ahn-Kha's dressings.

"Pepsa, take a look at the legworm rider," Boothe said. "He's got some cuts on his hand. Unless you object to being treated by a vet assistant."

"I'd rather stay with my tribemate."

Pepsa gestured into a corner, and Valentine took a seat. She took up Valentine's hand and looked at the self-inflicted wounds, then got a bottle and some cotton balls.

"Does that hurt?" Boothe asked Ahn-Kha as she cleaned the wound on his neck.

"I'm not worried about that one."

"We'll get to your stomach in a moment. Neck wounds always worry me."

"He has a lot of neck," Valentine said.

"Must have been some brawl. You've got some graining."

"We walked into the wrong room," Valentine said.

"It happened in Kentucky?"

"Yes. A few hours ago."

"Uh-huh. I can still smell the gunpowder on you, Bulletproof. You two didn't get drunk and get into a fight or anything?"

Pepsa professionally dressed Valentine's wound without saying a word. By the time she was done the doctor had a light down close to Ahn-Kha's stomach, injecting him just above the wound.

"You've got a lot of muscle in the midsection, my friend," Dr. Boothe said. She probed a little farther and Ahn-Kha sucked wind. "Uh-huh. I think we can forget about peritonitis. I don't want to dig around without an X-ray."

Xanadu had no shortage of medical equipment.

"Is Pepsa a nickname?" Valentine asked as the nurse gave him his hand back. She nodded.

"Pepsa's mute, Tar. You done there, girl? Get him the forms. Put down whatever bullshit you want, Bulletproof, then we'll talk."

Valentine liked the doctor. Her careful handling of Ahn-Kha impressed him. That, and the fact that apparently she gave a mute a valuable job in a land where disabilities usually meant a trip to the Reapers.

Pepsa led Valentine to a lunchroom. A quarter pot of coffee— real coffee according to Valentine's nose—steamed on a counter in a brewer. Above the poster a placard read "FALL BLOOD

DRIVE! *They bleed for you—now you can bleed for them!* Liter donors are entered in a drawing for an all-expense-paid trip to Niagara Falls." Valentine filled out the forms, leaving most of the blocks empty—like the eleven-digit Ordnance Security ID, which occupied a bigger area on the form than name.

The vet dropped in and sat down, rubbing her eyes. "Calving last night, now your Grog. He'll be fine, but I will have to operate."

"Will it be a hard operation?"

"Toughest part will be opening up those layers of muscle. But no. Kentucky, since you're not Ordnance you'll have to pay for these services, cheap though they are. What do you have on you?"

"Not much."

She stared at him. "I know there are a lot of rumors about this place. That it's some kind of Babylon for high Ordnance officials. Or that strings of happy pills get passed out like Mardi Gras beads. I've heard the stories. I'm not saying you two jokers tried to get in here by doing something as stupid as putting some small-caliber bullets into each other. But Xanadu's no place you want to be.

"What it is, in fact, is a hospital for treating cases with dangerous infectious conditions. Anti-Kurian terrorists got it in their heads to try a few designer diseases lethal to the Guardians, and there's been some weird and very dangerous mutations as a result. That's why we've got all this ground and livestock, the less that passes in and out of those gates, the better. Just in case. Do you know how diseases work, microorganisms?"

"Yes, little creatures that can fit in a drop of water. They make you sick."

"Uh-huh. So every breath you take behind these walls is a risk, and the closer you get to the main buildings, the more danger. So you should thank your lucky stars you were treated out here."

Valentine nodded. *Interesting. Is it all a cover? Or is there a project I don't know about?*

"After I operate we're going to keep your friend here for three days of observation. Don't worry, you'll have a bed, but you'll work for it. Consider it paying off your debt for your partner's medical treatment. Once you're out of here, go back to Kentucky and tell your buddies. This isn't a drugstore, it's not a brothel, and it's not a place to come get cured of the clap with the Ordnance picking up the tab. It's a scary lab full of death you can't even see coming. You understand, or should we start writing it on the sides of the leg-worms you sell us?"

"I understand," Valentine said. "Thank you."

# CHAPTER ELEVEN

$\phi$

*Xanadu, October: Summer lingered that year between the Great Lakes and the Appalachians. In eastern Russia and Mongolia the bitter winter of '72 came hard and fast, leading to starvation in the Permafrost Freehold. In the Aztlan Southwest El Niño blew hot, making a certain group of aerial daredevils licking their wounds in the desert outside Phoenix ration water. Florida, Georgia, and the Carolinas drowned under torrential tropical storms hurtling out of the mid-Atlantic one after another, ushering in what came to be known as the mud fall.*

*Ohio could not have been more idyllic, with cloudless days reaching into the midseventies and cool nights in the high fifties, perfect weather for sleeping under a light blanket. There was plenty of time for apple picking and blueberry gathering, and the turkeys had grown extra large in that year of plenty.*

*David Valentine always remembered that first fall of his exile as a grim, disturbing business under a kindly sky. Perhaps if he'd been lazier, or argumentative, or a thief, he and Ahn-Kha would have been thrown out of Xanadu with the Golden One's sutures still weeping. But after his first day in the fields he found the biowarfare scare story implausible, and became determined to find out what lay behind the neatly tuck-pointed facade of those reddish bricks.*

$\phi$

The job offer didn't come as much of a surprise. It happened over dinner in the "field house"—a small apartment building that reminded Valentine of Price's motel, essentially a line of tiny rooms, two sharing one bath, that housed the lowest of the low of Xanadu's laborers: the "hands."

Up one step from the hands were the service workers, who mixed with the hands at their shared recreation center just behind the hospital. The fixtures made Valentine think it had originally been built to be a large-vehicle garage, but now it held Ping-Pong tables, a video screen and library (full of dull-as-distilled-water New Universal Church productions), and a jukebox ("Authentic Vintage MCDs").

The service workers performed cafeteria and janitorial duties inside the main buildings. Valentine learned his first night there that they expected the hands to do the same for them. He learned how to cook "factory food,"—washtub-sized trays of pastas, vegetables, and sweet puddings. Every other night there was meat from the Xanadu livestock. Beef predominated, which Valentine found remarkable. Even during his hitch as a Coastal Marine he'd only been fed chicken; beef was saved for feasts before and after a cruise.

A step above the service workers was the security. There weren't many of them, considering the evident importance of the facility. Enough to man the two gates (there was a smaller one to the east) and the towers, and to keep guard at all the main building doors. Valentine could have stormed the place with a single company of Wolves, had he been able to get the company that deep into the Kurian Zone.

And made it past the cordon of Reapers.

The security forces lived and worked from the long building almost connecting the hospital with the salmon-colored apartment blocks.

That was all Valentine could learn about the self-contained community in his off hours. During the day he worked on the plumbing for a fourth barn, stripped to the waist and digging the ditch for the piping. He recognized make-work when he saw it; a backhoe could have completed the digging in a day.

"You ever think of joining the Ordnance, Tar?" Michiver, the chief hand, asked him over his plate of stew at one of the long cafeteria tables in the rec center. Michiver had a nose that looked like an overgrown wart and ate slowly and stiffly and with a bit of a wince, like an old dog.

"I like the soap and the flush toilets," Valentine said, truthfully enough.

"When I saw you pull up with your big Grog in that leather outfit, I thought you were just another Kentucky quirt. But you put in a real day's work and stay sober at night."

"That's not hard when the nearest liquor store's ten miles away."

Michiver's eyes puckered as he leaned close. "Ordnance duty is nice, if you put in the hours. Three hot meals a day, good doctors and dentists, Lake Ontario cruises for your vacation."

"I'm not much on the Church, though."

Michiver rested his head on rough hands. "It's just one day a week. I've gotten good at sleeping with my eyes open. Heard one lecture about the importance of recycling, heard them all."

"So are you offering me a job, boss?"

"For you and your Grog, assuming he's willing to work. When that new barn goes in I'll need a supervisor, you could be it."

"I was thinking of joining up with the Kentucky Legion."

"And get your head blown off? Chasing guerillas up and down the hills is alright for some, but you've got character and intelligence. I see it plain. We could use you here."

"Doc Boothe warned me off about diseases."

"Hands work outdoors; you're not cleaning up after the patients inside. I've been here fourteen years and I've never seen anything but colds and flu and a bit of pneumonia in the winter. Don't concern yourself with what's going on up at the Grands."

"You sure seem eager to have me. That means there's a catch."

"I'm no spring chicken, Tar," Michiver said, rolling a lock of gray hair between thumb and forefinger. He had an I GAVE MY LITER button on his shirt. "If there's a catch, it hasn't caught me."

"Do I have to sign a contract or anything?"

"Ohio's booming. Hard to find reliable men these days; everyone wants city work under the lights. You Kentuck aren't so hot for jump joints and dazzle halls. Don't worry about contracts, you can quit whenever you like. Forget about your tribesmen. No one in Kentucky's in a position to say boo to the Ordnance. Stay the weekend at least. Saturday's a half day and we're having a dance in town at the NUC hall. The Church is bringing down some husband-hunters from Cleveland and the beer's all the way from Milwaukee, if you're partial to that poison." Michiver made his points poking the table, each poke nearer to Valentine as though trying to herd him into saying yes. "Great way to end your week here, either way—what you say?"

"I say fine."

φ

Ahn-Kha watched him get dressed for the dance—leathers on the bottom, freshly washed blue chambray workshirt up top—and offered only one piece of advice: "Don't drink. Doctor Boothe says Michiver doesn't touch a drop of alcohol."

Valentine wished he had something other than work boots to put on his feet. "I'm more interested in getting friendly with the security staff. There's one odd thing about this place; except for the people in charge of the various departments, and that vet's nurse, seems like no one here's worked here longer than a year or two. Except friend Michiver."

Ahn-Kha gave that a moment's thought. "Perhaps you either get promoted or rotated out."

"I get the feeling Michiver's offer is a wiggling pink worm inside the mouth of a very big snapping turtle."

"It gives us time to look down the turtle's throat, my David."

φ

Valentine waited in front of the staff apartments, a little apart from the crowd of off-duty hands and service workers waiting for the buses into town. A last bottle of sealed Bulletproof was tucked inside a plain paper bag he cradled. He watched those waiting to go to the dance. A few passed around a silver flask, more smoked. The women wore golden metallic eyeshadow and heavy black liner, apparently the current style in Ohio.

A dozen of the security staff all waited together in a line against the wall, like the schoolkids too cool to be out on the playground.

Doctor Boothe rode by in her little four-wheeler—an electric golf cart tricked out for backcountry. She used it to get from animal to animal on Xanadu's horizon-spanning acreage. She stared at Valentine for a moment, then picked up her bags of instruments and turned indoors.

Three buses took them into the riverside town. Valentine managed to take a seat next to one of the security men, but he either stared out the window or spoke to the two of his class in the seats just ahead during the half-hour trip. The church hall turned out to be a quasicathedral with attached school; the dance was set up beneath raised basketball backboards in what had been the gymnasium. A raised stage was built into one end of the gym.

Red and blue streamers formed a canopy overhead and decorated the refreshment tables—provided by the Ohio Young Vanguard, Actualization Team #415, according to a sign and a jar accepting donations. A teenage girl, eyes bright enough to be the result of Benzedrine, thanked him for his five-dollar donation and offered him a four-color pamphlet.

The Ordnance and NUC thanks its Health Security Workers of Xanadu read the banner over the raised platform at one end of the gymnasium. Dusty red curtains half closed off a stage, hiding the lighting gear for the musicians. At the other end folding tables and chairs had a few balloons attached.

A nostalgic hip-hop dj-backed band ("lame" pronounced one of the security staff) laid down a techno beat as they entered, and the chief bandsman started exhorting the crowd to enjoy themselves as soon as the workers trickled in. The music echoed oddly in the high-ceilinged, quarter-lit gym, making Valentine feel as though he'd just stepped inside a huge kettledrum.

Valentine knew a handful of names and a few more faces, and once he'd nodded to those he knew he sat down on the basketball stands and read the tri-fold pamphlet the Young Vanguard girl had given him.

**7 Civic Virtues we grow inside, as our bodies grow outside:**
1. *Humility—we understand that mankind has been pulled back from the brink of self-destruction by wisdom greater than ours, giving us hope.*

2. *Hope for the Future—we know we can build a better world if we just listen to the quiet voice in our hearts.*
3. *Hearts that know Compassion—to act for the better of all, we pledge our minds, and the mind's servant, the hand.*
4. *Hands Busy in Labor—we pledge to work and sacrifice so that the following generation may live happier lives.*
5. *Heroism—we stand for what we know to be right and pledge our lives to the future; our word is our bond.*
6. *Honesty—we must be honest with others, for only then can we be honest with ourselves.*
7. *Healthy Bodies and Minds—we pledge to refrain from partaking of any substance that might cloud mind or pollute body.*

Pictures of particularly outstanding Vanguards and their Ordnance sponsors filled the back. Valentine more than half believed it all. The Churchmen knew how to keep their flocks all moving in the same direction—straight to the slaughterhouse.

The male-female ratio equalized a little when a pair of local Churchmen arrived with a contingent of single women. Their clothes and stockings marked them as city girls, looking like peacocks dumped in a headwater barnyard, and smelling of desperation. Or perhaps that was just the name of the perfume. The Churchmen divided the group in two parts and led their subflocks around, making introductions.

"Take a heck of a lot more than applejack to get me to take a run at one of those boxies," one of the security men said to his mate.

"Try a blindfold," another agreed from behind a thick mustache.

Valentine sidled up to the trio. "I've got an untapped bottle of Kentucky bourbon, if you like."

Thick Mustache sneered. "Take a hike, cowpuncher."

"My—" Valentine began.

"Get lost, quirt," the one eyeing up the women said. "You're not making yourself look good, you're making us look bad."

Valentine felt the room go twenty degrees warmer. "We could talk more outside, if you like."

"I'll share your liquor, new man," a female voice said in his ear.

Valentine startled. Six feet of creamy skin stood barefoot next to him, her heels dangling loose from one hand and a clutch purse in the other. She was at least a decade older, but high-cheeked and attractive in a shoulder-padded dress. Or simply more skilled with makeup and clothing than the rest of the women in the gym. Valentine wondered if she'd come in by a different route—she'd neither arrived on the buses nor been escorted in by the Churchmen.

"Looking hot, Doc P," the security man who'd called Valentine a "quirt" a moment ago said.

The woman cocked her head, an eyebrow up. Even Valentine, thirty degrees out of the line of fire of the stare, felt a chill.

"C'mon, you 'bot," Thick Mustache said, pulling his companion away.

"What's your name?"

"Tar. Tar Ayoob."

"Tar? Like in 'nicotine and . . .' "

"Short for Tarquin," Valentine said.

She transferred her shoes to her purse-holding hand. "Fran Paoli. I work up at Xanadu too."

"I'm liking it better and better there," Valentine said, shaking her offered hand. She laughed, but lightly.

Valentine showed her the bottle.

"That's real Kentucky Bourbon, I believe," she said.

"Care for a snort?" Valentine asked.

"With water," she said. "About 5ccs."

"How much is that?"

"A shot glass."

When Valentine returned from the refreshment table with two ice-filled plastic cups of water, she stood next to a paper-covered table festooned with balloons reading "Happy Birthday."

Valentine set his glasses down and held out the chair for her. "Why did you take your heels off?" he asked.

"I can be sneaky that way. Besides, it makes me feel sexy."

*It also makes you two inches shorter than I am,* Valentine thought. "I didn't know we'd have any doctors in attendance."

"I'll be it. Oriana and I came down to the waterfront to do some shopping."

"And you just couldn't resist the music and the decor?" Valentine passed her drink to her. She sipped.

Fran rolled the liquor around in her mouth, and swallowed. "No. I wanted to meet you."

"You're very direct."

She looked up as the liquor hit. "Whoo, that takes me back. I did a term with a field hospital down your way."

"Wanted to meet me?" Valentine insisted.

"When you get a few more years' . . . oh . . . perspective on life, let's say, you run short on patience for gamesmanship."

Valentine watched more uniforms flow in. Couples began dancing, doing curious, quick back-and-forth movements, one part of the body always touching. Hand gave way to arm that gave way to shoulder that gave way to buttock that turned into hand again. He felt like a scruffy backwoodsman at a cotillion.

*Good God. Ali's here.*

She wore a plain woolen skirt and a yellow blouse that flirted with femininity, but went with her flame-colored hair. Lipstick and eye makeup were making one of their rare appearances on her face. A soldier who looked like a wrestler's torso on a jockey's legs was introducing her to one of the Churchmen. Valentine wondered if he was looking at an infatuated boy or a dead man.

"Do you want to dance?" Valentine asked.

"You don't look like the slinky-slide type."

"Is that what that dance is called?"

"It was when they were doing it in New York ten years ago. God knows what it's called out here." Her thin-lipped mouth took on a grimace that might be called cruel.

Valentine tried a tiny amount of bourbon, just enough to wet his lips and make it appear that he drank. "So how did you know you wanted to meet me?"

"Moonshots."

"Is that something else from New York?"

"No," she laughed, a little more heartily this time. "Have you been in the Grands yet?"

"The four big buildings? No."

"I have a corner in Grand East. Top floor." She said it as though she expected Valentine to be impressed. "Apartment and office. I've got a nice telescope. Myself and some of the nurses have been known to take a coffee break and check out the hands. We call a particularly attractive male a 'moonshot.' It's hard to get a unanimous vote from that crew, but you got five out of five. The hair did it for Oriana—she's the tough grader."

"There's not a bet having to do with me, is there?"

"Admit it. You're flattered."

"I am, a little." He picked up his drink. "Don't go anywhere." He took a big mouthful of his drink, headed for a corridor marked "bathrooms," and turned down a cinder-block corridor. He found the men's. An assortment of student- and adult-sized urinals stood ready. He went to the nearest one and spat out his bourbon, thinking of an old Wolf named Bill Maranda who would have cried out at the waste.

Alessa Duvalier tripped him as he exited. He stumbled.

"You're a rotten excuse for the caste," she said, keeping her voice low and watching the hallway. "Have you found her?"

"No. Just as tight on the inside."

"So how do you like pillow recon?" she asked. "Is she tight? Or is the bourbon loosening her up?"

"Haven't had a chance to find out, yet."

"According to my date she's big-time. You be careful. I've moved to the NUC women's hostel, by the way. My would-be boyfriend was horrified by my accommodations. Bed checks."

"I've got a chance at an upgrade too, methinks."

She pressed a piece of paper into his hand. "Phones work around here, but you get listened to," Duvalier said. "If you need to run, leave a message at the hostel that your migraines are back. I'll get to the motel as soon as I can and wait. Do they allow inbound calls up there?"

"I think there's a phone in our rec center. I'll call with the number."

"Good luck." She made a kissing motion in the air, not wanting to leave telltale lipstick. She dived into the women's washroom, and Valentine went to the bar for more ice.

He chatted with Fran Paoli for thirty minutes or so, learned that she'd been born in Pennsylvania and educated in New York. She found the Ordnance "dull enough to make me look forward to *Noonside Passions*," evidently a television show, and wouldn't discuss her work, except to say that it required specialized expertise but was as routine as the NUC social. But it promised her a brass ring and a Manhattan penthouse when she completed her sixteenth year at Xanadu.

She couldn't—or wouldn't—even say what her area of medical expertise was.

Paoli waved and another woman approached, with the purse-clutching, tight-elbowed attitude of a missionary in an opium den.

"Oriana Kreml, this is Tar, our moonshot babe. Tar-baby! I like that."

"The market was a joke. 'Fresh stock in from Manhattan' my eye. Are you done presenting in here?"

"Oriana's a great doctor but a greater prig," Fran Paoli laughed. "Would you like a ride back, Tar-baby?"

"Thank you," Valentine said.

"Then let's quit the Church. Crepe paper gives me a rash."

They took Valentine outside to the parking lot. A well-tended black SUV huffed and puffed as its motor turned over. It was a big Lincoln, powered by something called Geo-drive.

"Would you like to drive my beast, Tar?" Fran Paoli asked.

"Would you forgive me if I wrecked it?" Valentine said. "I'm not much with wheels." Valentine liked cars, the convenience and engineering appealed to him, but he didn't have a great deal of experience with them.

He climbed into the rear seat. The upholstery had either been replaced or lovingly refurbished. A deep well in the back held a few crates of groceries. Valentine smelled garlic and lemons in the bags. The women in front put on headsets.

Fran Paoli turned on the lights and the parking lot sprang into black-shadowed relief. Music started up, enveloping Valentine in soft jazz. She turned the car around and drove down a side street until she reached the river highway. Two police pickup-wagons motored west. Valentine wondered how many unfortunates they carried to the Reapers. Two each? Three? Nine? Valentine stared out the window as the red taillights receded into demon eyes staring at him from the darkened road. They blinked away.

"You and your hobbies," Oriana said quietly.

Fran Paoli turned up the music, but Valentine could still hear if he concentrated. "So I like to go to bed with more than a good book."

"Someday it's going to bite you."

"Mmmmm, kinky. But don't fret. I can handle this hillwilly."

"He's after status and that's it. Don't fool yourself."

ψ

Valentine looked for Reapers in the woods as the truck approached Xanadu, but couldn't see or sense them. The security guard hardly used his flashlight when the SUV reached the gate. Fran Paoli waggled her fingers at him and he waved twice at the gate, and the fencing parted in opposite directions.

She drove up a concrete, shrub-lined roadway and pulled into a gap under the south tower. "Two-one-six, entering," she said into her mouthpiece, working a button on the dashboard, and a door on tracks rolled up into the ceiling. The SUV made it inside the garage—just—and parked in the almost-empty lot. A few motorbikes, a pickup, some golf carts, and a low, sleek sports car were scattered haphazardly among the concrete supporting pillars like cows sleeping in a wood. A trailer with an electric gasoline pump attached was set up on blocks near the door.

"You'll like the Grand Towers. You mind helping with the groceries?"

Valentine took two crates, Oriana one.

They walked past a colorful mural, silhouettes of children throwing a ball to each other while a dog jumped, and Fran Paoli passed her security ID card over a dark glass panel. An elevator opened. It smelled like pine-scented cleanser inside. Soft music played from hidden speakers.

"Home," Fran Paoli said, and the elevator doors closed.

"You don't have to hit a button?" Valentine asked.

"I could. It's voiceprint technology. A couple of the techs on the security staff like to tinker with old gizmos."

"I wish they could get an MRI working," Oriana said.

Valentine looked in his boxes on the ride up. Foil-wrapped crackers, a tin of something called "pâté," a bottle of olive oil with a label in writing Valentine thought looked like Cyrillic, artichokes, fragrant peaches, sardines, a great brick of chocolate with foil lettering . . .

The elevator let them out on a parquet-floored hallway. If there was a floor higher than twelve the elevator buttons didn't indicate it. Lighting sconces added soft smears of light to the maroon walls.

Fran Paoli held Oriana's groceries while she let herself in. "Good night. Call if you want your rounds covered."

"Thanks, O."

Oriana thanked Valentine as she took her box of foodstuffs—slightly more mundane instant mixes and frozen packages with frost-covered labels. Her door had a laminated plate in a slide next to it: ORIANA KREML, MD.

"I'm at the end of the hall, Tar-baby," Fran Paoli said.

She led him down, putting an extra swivel in her walk. Valentine clicked his tongue against the roof of his mouth in time to her stride. She twirled her keys on their wrist loop.

The door at the end read EXECUTIVE MEDICAL DIRECTOR. She opened it and Valentine passed through a small reception office—a computer screen cast a soft glow against a leather office chair—and a larger meeting room with an elegantly shaped glass conference table. Floor-to-ceiling windows reflected only the darkness outside and their faces. Lights came on as she moved through the space to a frosted-glass partition. Valentine marked a telescope at the glass corner she passed.

A casual living space and then a kitchen. Valentine set the boxes down on a small round table, and extracted the fresh fruits and vegetables.

"Stay for a drink?" Fran Paoli asked.

φ

Fran Paoli snored softly beside him in postcoital slumber.

Her makeup was on the sheet, him, and the oh-so-soft pillowcases, and she gave off a faint scent of sweet feminine perspiration and rose-scented baby powder. She made love like some women prepared themselves for bed, following a long-practiced countdown that evidently gave her a good deal of pleasure.

Valentine thought of "Arsie," the professional he'd met at that Quisling party in Little Rock. Was this how it was for her? Did she feel like her body was an apparatus as her customers took what they wanted?

Valentine engaged in the lovemaking with—perhaps clinical detachment was the right word. It had been fun; Fran Paoli's hunger for him, the way she discovered his scars and touched them, licked them, gently as though drawing some mixture of the pain they represented and taking pleasure from them, both motherly and sexual, healing and arousing; while he'd become instantly erect at the first touch of her full, falling breasts and flesh-padded hips. She touched his erection, squeezed it as though testing its tensile strength, clawed and gasped and bucked out her satisfaction with its quality, and then brought him back again after he spent himself into the black-market condom—a thin-walled novelty that made Southern Command's prophylactics feel like rain ponchos.

"You can get a shortwave radio easier than these," she said, and she passed him the second plastic oval.

But he'd learned little, other than Fran Paoli's expertise with a bathtub razor, from the "pillow recon." She still wouldn't talk about what she did.

ϕ

She woke him briefly when she got up, though she tried not to. Valentine dozed, feeling the sun change the quality of the light in the apartment, heard a vague whirring sound, remembered that he'd seen some kind of pulley-topped treadmill. Then she woke him for sex; sweaty, clean-faced, with her hair tied in a ponytail and her muscles hot from exercise. In the morning light the dark circles under her eyes showed, along with the sags at the backs of her arms, and the topography of the deposits on her thighs, but he came erect and she rode him like a final exercise machine.

"Tar, you are a treat for sore thighs," she said, and collapsed backward, still straddling him. He felt her hair on his ankle. He couldn't see her face, and had the strange feeling he was speaking to her vulva.

She pulled herself up. "I need a shower. There's another bathroom right next to the outer office if you need to use it. You can help yourself to anything you like in the kitchen. No homesies for your Aunt Betty, though. Poppy-seed crackers and Danish Havarti are too hard to come by."

"I should check in at the barn," Valentine said. "The livestock don't take days off."

"If I'm still in the shower when you're dressed, feel free to just leave. When I got up I phoned down to the security desk and let them know you were my guest last night. Just take the yellow card on the counter for the elevator."

He investigated the kitchen, and found bananas and orange juice. The "orange" juices Southern Command issued had a grainy taste, but this had real pulp in it. Valentine ate two bananas and explored the apartment. There was an office off the conference room, but it was locked. He could jimmy or pick it easily enough with something from the kitchen, but after she walked naked from the bathroom to go to her bedroom dresser for clean underwear he decided against it.

Fran Paoli didn't keep much that revealed anything about herself as a person in her apartment. He saw a photo in the bedroom of her as a teenager, atop a horse, in a khaki uniform with a peaked cap tipped saucily on her head. A gray-haired man in a tweed sport coat, with a forced smile, hung in a frame on the wall. A sad-eyed china spaniel sat on top of what might be a candy dish on the kitchen counter. It was chipped and scratched, but the dish contained nothing but a couple of bands for her hair.

He looked out the windows. The conference center looked out on the grounds, barns, and wire in the distance. The living room was set so you could look at the other three "Grand" buildings. All had the tall windows at the top, and he saw a few desks and living room furniture in the others. The rows of windows below were darkened and many were shaded. They told him nothing except that if there were one room per window, that made a lot of rooms, over three hundred per building. Twelve hundred rooms.

Between the four "Grand" buildings was some kind of common space, nicely laid out with lots of bistro tables around the edges near trees and planters, and a long pool at the center under greenhouselike glass. People were swimming what looked like laps, but in a leisurely fashion. He couldn't tell much about them thanks to condensation. Others were sitting at the bistro tables, enjoying what remained of the soft fall air, but from so high up he could tell little by the tops of their heads. All were wearing either blue or pink scrubs.

Pink and blue. Pink and blue.

He set his glass of orange juice down on an end table. Valentine strode into the conference center and looked at the telescope. He tried lifting it. He could stagger, just, with it. He looked at the smaller "finder" scope—it could be detached from the larger. He twisted a screw, freed it, and went back to the living room. He looked from pink to pink down in the plaza.

The patients were all women. He'd expected that. They were thin, some sickly looking, most with tired, limp hair. He'd expected that too, as he'd seen it often enough in the Kurian Zone.

Almost all were pregnant. Some bulging, some with just a swelling.

He hadn't expected that.

The shower turned off. Valentine picked up his orange juice and drained it as he returned the spotting scope to its rest, lined up with the telescope. He hoped he hadn't screwed up the alignment too badly. He pointed the large scope at the barn, adjusted the counterweight, and made it clear that he'd been screwing with the optics.

When Fran Paoli came out of the bathroom, her hair in a towel, he was washing his glass in the sink.

"Just leaving," he said.

She gave him a kiss on the neck.

"I don't suppose you'd like to come to my place, next time," he said.

"You're cocky." She unwrapped the towel and began to work her scalp with the dry side.

"No next time?" he asked.

"Of course there will be, Tar-baby. You're so tight. I don't feel like I've begun to unwrap you yet."

"I'm in room—"

"While there's a certain thrill in those old, stained mattresses down there, I'm a bit worried about fleas. How about we meet halfway? I might work in a picnic tomorrow—I've got a spare afternoon. You can tell me where you got those hot-assed pants. I would love to have a skirt of that leather. Is it kid?"

"More like bug."

"Is Michiver still running things out in the fields?"

Valentine tried to read her brown eyes, but failed. "Yes."

"I'll get you the afternoon off tomorrow, if I can make it."

"Great."

"And tell that old knob we need a golf course, not more cows. I'm really sick of the one-hole wonder on the north forty."

"I'm the bottom man in the totem pole in the barns, Fran-tick."

She laughed. *Frantic*. Tar-baby, I love it. You'd better go, or you'll really see frantic. I'm due on my rounds."

Valentine slapped her thin-robed bottom as he headed for the door. She stopped him with a whistle and passed him a yellow piece of plastic. "Here. Elevator won't work without this. Just slide it into the slot above the buttons. There's a diagram."

"Thanks."

He winked as he closed the door behind him and walked down the hallway. The lighting had been altered; it was brighter and cheerier this morning. He went to the elevator, feeling like a male black widow spider who's crossed the female's web and inexplicably lived.

He swiped the card in the reader according to directions. As an experiment, he hit the button for the sixth floor, but the elevator took him to the ground floor.

Valentine exited at a high-ceilinged lobby. Cheerful, primary-colored murals of square-jawed agricultural workers, steel-rimmed medical men, and aquiline mothers told him that those who passed through this lobby were

CREATING A BETTER TOMORROW

and that

PROGRESS COMES WITH EACH GENERATION

A rounded, raised platform held a few of the security staff. Two women in blue scrubs, one holding a plastic water bottle, the other a Styrofoam coffee cup, chatted near a bank of wide-doored elevators that evidently didn't go all the way to the top floor. Valentine walked toward the doors leading to the patio and pool area.

"Hey, hand!" one of the security men called.

He couldn't pretend not to have heard. He turned. "I'm sorry?"

"Your yellow building card. Turn it in."

Valentine fished it out of his pocket, reached up to place it on the desk. "Here you go."

He went back toward the doors, pretending not to see the other exits.

"Am I getting smarter or are they getting dumber?" the security desk said to his friend. "Hand!"

But Valentine was already passing out the doors.

He headed across the slate bricks. The intertower area smelled like flowers and cedar chips, which were spread liberally around the landscaping. Two women in pink, both copiously pregnant, nibbled at ceramic bowls, eating some kind of breakfast mix with beat-up spoons. Valentine's nose detected yogurt. Both were rather pallid and looked as though they needed the morning sun.

Another group of four, no visible swelling inside the loose pink outfits, kept company by one in blue, worked on each other's hair and a pitcher of tomato juice. Valentine passed through the greenhouse doors and down a short ramp to the swimming pool deck. Chlorine burned his nostrils. Two dozen heads bobbed in the wide lap lanes. Others were lined up at one end of the pool, talking, waiting their turn.

No two swimming suits were alike; there were hot pink bikinis and big black one-pieces. Maybe the pool was the one place the women got to express themselves with clothing.

"Come on, ladies," a man in shorts with a coach's whistle exhorted from a short diving board. "Keep swimming. Gets the blood flowing. Gets the bowels moving. I want to see healthy pink cheeks—yo, can I help you?"

The last came when he spied Valentine.

But the words barely registered.

Gail Foster, formerly Gail Post, waited at one side of the pool with the next group.

Her hair and cheeks were thinner, but the big green eyes and delicate, upturned nose were unmistakable. With her hair wet and flat, idly kicking the water as she talked to the woman next to her, she appeared childlike, so unlike the ID photo from Post's flyer where she stared into the camera as though challenging the lens to capture her. She didn't even look up as the man with the whistle hopped off the board to approach Valentine.

"Just taking a shortcut," Valentine said, tearing himself away from Gail's face.

"Don't disturb the expectants. Turn right around and—"

"Right. I'm going." Valentine retreated back up the ramp.

He walked around the greenhouse to the east side of the patio, looking for a hose, a rake, anything. But there were no groundskeepers or tools in sight. He removed his work boot and went to work on the leather tongue with his pocketknife, tearing it. If questioned, he could say that he was trying to get rid of an irritating flange.

He managed to idle away a half hour. A new group of women marched out of the south tower in single file, white robes held tight even in the warm morning air. Valentine looked at the knobby knees and thin legs, and wondered what kind of diet the women were on. They looked like gulag chars who hadn't been on full rations of beans for weeks. Once they passed in another group walked two-by-two back into the tower, led by one of the medical staff in blue scrubs.

Valentine went to work relacing his boots so the laces presented fresh material to the eyelets.

Like clockwork, another group came out, this time from the west tower, and Gail Foster's exited. It was hard to tell under the robes, but all seemed to have about the same level of swelling in the midsection. Same routine, led like chicks behind a blue mother hen.

*Damn. West tower.*

Valentine put his boots back on and hurried back to the road leading to the pastures.

A faint beep sounded from behind. The vet, Dr. Boothe, sped up on her little four-wheeler cart. "Want a lift?"

*My weekend to be offered rides by women.*

Valentine hopped into the seat next to her. The trail tires kicked up gravel as she set the electric motor in motion again. "What did I tell you about falling for the bullshit here?"

"I like being indoors every night. I've seen too many bodies in the woods."

She looked at him and away again, quickly. "Impolite to bring up such matters."

"It's all the same bullshit, Doc. Depends on how much you want to shovel off."

"Give me a break. You're part of it now. You were, even in Kentucky."

"There's being a part and taking part. Your assistant, for example. How'd she get past the genetics defect laws?"

"Pepsa? She wasn't born that way. She's from a tough neighborhood in Pittsburgh. She complained once too often, and that's what happens to complainers there. They ripped out her tongue. She still complains—just does it on that little pad of hers."

"So what's with all the pregnant women?"

She took a breath. "They're highly susceptible. You know how the Ordnance is about birthrate."

"I don't, actually."

"They're here so the babies can be saved."

"Don't want anyone going before it's decided. Nice and orderly." Price had that right, anyway.

"Don't talk to Michiver that way, Ayoob. I wish you weren't talking to me."

She pulled up to the veterinary station. The guard dogs in their kennels barked a welcome.

"I imagine you're supposed to turn me in," Valentine said.

"If it comes to protecting my position, don't think I won't. You and the Grog are nothing to me. Nothing."

"Except someone you can be honest around."

"You want honest? I don't like people. That's why I'm a vet. Now get out, I've got some cows to inseminate."

Valentine got out and went over to greet the dogs. He nodded to Pepsa, busy cleaning out the kennels. Dr. Boothe stared at him for a moment, then drove away.

ψ

Michiver seemed to know more than he was willing to say as he greeted Valentine at the farm office. "Heard you had a good time after—err, at, the dance, buck." Out back a feed truck clattered as the winter's stores were transferred to the silo. A group of hands ate sack lunches on the porch.

"A lively night," Valentine agreed. "Where do you want me today?"

"You can have the afternoon off. Be back for evening milking. Let the machines do the titty-pulling for a change."

"I give him a month," one of the other hands said to his lunch mates.

"He's colored," a big piledriver of a man named Ski said as Valentine left. He didn't bother to lower his voice; Valentine hardly had to harden his ears at all to pick up the commentary. "And a Grogfucker to boot. She'll keep him around to show off to the other doctors at the holiday parties. He'll get his dismissal papers right before New Year's."

Valentine seethed. He took a walk to let the anger bleed off. Watching cows had a magical soothing quality to it, something about the tail swishing and contemplative chewing always put him in a better mood.

The cows of Xanadu were rather scrawny specimens. Compared to the fat milkers in Wisconsin or the small mountains of beef he'd seen in Nebraska they looked fleshless and apathetic—despite the good grass and plentiful water.

Of course, with characters like Ski taking care of them, anything was possible. He probably left nails or bits of wire lying

277

around. Cows aren't overly bright in their grazing, and they're never right again once a wire is lodged in one of their stomachs.

Valentine found Ahn-Kha scooping grain. The Golden One was alone, and the cascade of grain going onto the conveyor as it went up to the silo gave a lot of covering noise. He hopped up onto the side of the truck.

"I met a doctor last night and got inside the towers. I saw Gail."

To his credit, Ahn-Kha didn't miss a stroke with the shovel. "I knew this would be the end of the trail. I am surprised she is still alive."

"Give me that. You shouldn't be pushing."

Ahn-Kha passed him the shovel. It felt good to move the mix of corn and feed grain. "This is some kind of baby factory. I've heard stories of women otherwise unemployable just being warehoused while they gestate. Once they recover they go through it all over again."

"Then why all the security?"

"Remember the Ranch? The Kurians might be tinkering with the fetuses. I've wondered why they don't make their own versions of Bears."

"Too hard to control, perhaps. My David, where were you born?"

"The lakes in the Northwoods. You know that."

"But do you? You've told me before it was a strange childhood. Never seriously ill. Never a broken bone. Healing from cuts overnight."

Valentine shoveled harder. "Bear blood, passed down. Like Styachowski. If someone was breeding a more pliable human, it didn't take."

ψ

Fran Paoli continued to see him on her strange schedule as the weather turned sharply colder.

Valentine loved autumn up north, the bannerlike colors of the trees, the wet, earthy smell of leaves falling and rotting. He found excuses to work near the wire where he could see the trees, smell the woods.

They saw each other strictly on her terms. Her duties some-times left her with as much as a whole day free, and she would tear up the roads in her big Lincoln to get them to a show in Cleveland and then back down again. Once she brought him to the south Grand and they made love in an empty conference room on the top floor where a few spare mattresses were stored, for medical staff working long shifts to take breaks.

Valentine never asked her about putting him to work in the towers. He never asked her for so much as a ham sandwich. She bought him two sets of clothes, a fine-material suit with a double-breasted jacket—he feigned ignorance with the necktie knot, since the only one he really knew how to make was the tight Southern Command military style—and some casual, slate-colored pants with a taupe turtleneck made of an incredibly soft and lightweight material she called cashmere.

"You need more than cash to get that these days," she said, ob-serving the results when he put it on and stood in front of the framed floor-length mirror in the corner of her bedroom. "You need connections."

"My whole life I've never had a connection."

"Which is why you're milking cows. I'm not even that great of a doctor, but I'm running a whole department here thanks to con-nections I've made. Why haven't you asked me for a better job? Every guy I've dated wants me to set him up in an office."

Preguilt flooded Valentine before he even said the words. "You're not like any woman I've ever known, Fran. I didn't want you to think I was . . . what did Oriana call it . . . 'after your status.' "

"You're so young."

Valentine let that rest.

"A brass ring won't just fall into your lap, you know. You're smart. Haven't you figured out that you need to be angling for job security?"

"If I don't like it in the Ordnance I'll just go back into Ken-tucky, or sign on as an officer in a Grog unit."

"That's a waste. Any stump-tooth can fill out requisition forms for Grog infantry. You need to get yourself into a field Kur needs here. Something not just anyone can do. That's why I chose obstetrics. Kur looks ten thousand years into the future, and about the only certainty is that you need babies to get there."

"The kind of education I have doesn't lend itself to medical school," Valentine said. The bitterness came of its own accord, surprising him.

"There's nursing. You could put in a year here, then go off to Cleveland or Pittsburg for classroom work."

"You could arrange that?" Valentine said.

"I'll speak to the director. Be right back." She turned her back to him, then turned around again and sat on the bed.

"She said you might fit an opening," Fran Paoli said, patting the spot next to her. "Let's do a follow-up interview to be sure."

ψ

Valentine managed to wheedle a job for Ahn-Kha out of it as well. Ahn-Kha went to work in the laundry of the main hospital building—the amount of clothing and linen generated by the hospital and the four Grands was formidable. Ahn-Kha discovered two other well-trained Grogs, the simpler Grey Ones, working in the bowels of the hospital, also filling and emptying the washers.

They left the grotty little hand housing and moved into the cleaner, but smaller, apartments for the service workers.

"Less than two weeks in Xanadu and already you're improved," the housing warden said. He carried an assortment of tools at his belt and a long-hosed can of bug spray in a hip holster. "I want your Grog to shower outside, though, or you're outta here. He can use the hose. First sign of fleas and you're outta here."

The room had a phone, and even more amazingly, it functioned. Valentine couldn't remember the last time he'd stayed in a room with a working phone.

They put Valentine to work in the South Grand to begin. His "nursing" duties involved bringing food and emptying the occasional urine bottle, and endless tubes of breast milk.

He learned a little more of the "baby factory" routine. The women had their children at an appointed date and time, always by caesarian. Up until that time they were two to a room, with high cubicle walls in between giving the illusion of individual apartments.

After giving birth, they were "rotated" to a new building and given a new room. If they hadn't had a window before, they got one the next time.

Each room had a single television.

A modicum of deal-making took place having to do with television choice and the window side of the room The television had four channels; channel three exhibited a parade of tawdry dramas including the staple *Noonside Passions*. Would Ted turn Holly in to gain the brass ring he'd so long wanted, though he did not yet know she was carrying his child, and would her sister Nichelle ever get out of the handsome-yet-despicable black marketeer Brick's webs? Channel six showed a mixture of quiz shows, courtroom contests where curt, black-robed Reapers impassively heard evidence and assigned monetary damages, divorces, or inheritances, then self-help or skill-improvement sessions in the evening; channel nine broadcast children's programming in the day and then music, either with the musicians or with relaxing imagery at night; channel eleven was the only station that broadcast twenty-four hours a day, providing nothing but propagandistic Ordnance newscasts and bombastic documentaries about mankind's past follies.

Valentine worked four floors in his new blue scrubs, madly during mealtimes, slowly at other hours. Two days of twelve-hour shifts, then a day off, then two more days of twelve-hour shifts, then a day off and a half day—though the half day usually consisted of either training or NUC lectures or some kind of team-building make-work project. His charges were all in their second trimester. Though the women looked wan and drawn thanks to their pregnancies, they were cheerful and talkative, or spent long hours on sewing projects for Ordance soldiers (rumor had it the semen that fertilized them came from decorated combat veterans). He wondered if Malita Carrasca had been this upbeat during her pregnancy. He wondered at the weight loss; the mothers to be he'd met over the years had mostly put on weight.

"It's the quick succession of pregnancies," another nurse, an older woman with years of experience, told him as she lit up in the emergency exit stairway, the unofficial smoking lounge. Valentine had taken to carrying cigarettes, and even smoking one now and again—it was the easiest excuse to get away from his duties for a few minutes. "They have six and then they retire to the Ontario lakeshore and run a sewing circle or a craft workshop. Nice little payoff. But hell on the body while you're cranking them out."

"Diet, Tar," the hefty nurse who counted off meals as they went on Valentine's cart said. She was his immediate supervisor for mealtime duties. "These doctors are all protein-happy. Throwing pregnant women into ketosis. Protein, fats, fiber, and more protein is all they get. And enough iron for a suit of armor. Liver, onions, supplements."

"It gets results," Valentine said. "They're happy enough."

"That's the medication talking. Every woman here's buzzier than a beehive."

φ

Valentine got a chance to test his supervisor's opinion the next day. Every time Valentine got a chance, he looked out one of the windows facing the patio area and the greenhouse below, trying to get a feel for the rhythm of Gail Foster's schedule. Other than a trip to the pool every other day, she never seemed to join the other groups of pink mothers to be.

He wondered if there was a reason for that.

Then one day, as he served lunch, he saw her again, sitting at a table with a book open before her. She had one of the thick, white robes around her body and a towel around her neck.

Valentine finished passing out his meals to the women who ordered food delivered to their rooms—most ate on the second floor, in the cafeteria—and then hurried to the elevator and went outside, ostensibly for a smoke.

Gail Foster sat wrapped up in her book and white terrycloth. He tried to read the title, but it was in a cursive script hard to see at a distance. He walked up at an angle, getting out of the mild fall breeze so he could strike a match.

The smell of the match lighting reminded him of that long-ago escape from Chicago's Zoo.

It looked like the elaborate cursive script of her book read *A Dinner of Onions,* but Valentine couldn't be sure. Gail studied the pages before turning, as though she had to learn the first chapter for a test.

"Good book?" he asked.

She didn't respond. Valentine watched her eyes. When she got to the bottom of the right-facing page, instead of turning it she went back up to the top of the left-side page again. Was she memorizing the novel?

"Not many patients here like to read," Valentine tried again. He took another step forward, blocking her light. "What's it about?"

She turned, looked up at him. "I'm sorry?"

"Your book. What's it about?"

"Some people. I don't know."

"You feeling alright?" Valentine asked. She seemed distant.

"Very well. Doctor says I'm doing very well. But I need some sun, you see?"

Valentine took that to mean he should get out of her light. "Your accent, where are you from?"

"Down south."

*Nothing to be gained by waiting,* though he felt as though he were having a conversation with a child. "Do you ever want to go back?"

The words slid off her like the water in the pool. "Back where?"

"Down south?"

"No. I have to stay here so the baby can come. It's part of being a healthy mom. There are four parts to being a healthy mom, did you know? Diet, Exercise, Care, and Attitude. I had to work on my attitude most of all, but it's much better now."

"Obviously," Valentine said, giving up. "Do you ever wish you could be with your child after it's born?"

Her eyes grew even larger. "Oh, no. Our children go to special schools. They learn, from their very first weeks, how to lead mankind out of darkness. The Long March to the Future. It would be selfish of me to want to keep my baby from that. That would be a very bad attitude to have."

"Absolutely," Valentine said, finishing his cigarette. Post had once told him that he and Gail had their falling out over an abortion. She did not want to bring a child into the world just to be disposed of at some future date by the Kurian Order.

Was there anything left of that woman?

ɸ

On off days Valentine and Ahn-Kha went out to "the grotto"—a low pond ringed by trees on the southwestern perimeter of Xanadu—and plotted out how an escape might be engineered. They would eat and talk, then throw a fooball back and forth when they needed to think. At the next break they would talk again. The escape had to buy them enough time to get across the river before an alert was sent out and a pursuit organized.

They developed a plan, but it was like a string of Morse code, a group of dots and dashes with gaps in between. The biggest problem was the security system. Thanks to some postcoital perusals of Fran Paoli's file cabinets—he turned the television on after shutting her door to allow her to sleep in peace—he had learned that Gail was in room 4115 of Grand West, and that she was scheduled for her caesarian in early December. Valentine's ID would get him into his building and onto his assigned floors, plus the common areas for staff, but he couldn't even get access to a floor above or a floor below his levels, let alone a different building. Ahn-Kha could bring laundry into the basements of any of the four Grands, but couldn't access the elevators.

His conversations with Alessa Duvalier grew increasingly anxious. She wanted to know how his head felt.

"Go back home if you like," Valentine said. "Or are things getting heavy with Lance Corporal Scott Thatcher?"

"Soon to be Sergeant Thatcher. He's talking about getting married, said it makes a big difference in how the officers look at you when promotion time rolls around."

"That's wonderful," Valentine said.

"I'm counting the days until he pops the question. I hope your schedule lets you come to an engagement party."

Cooperation from Gail would make all the difference in the world. During daylight hours the women were free to visit their outdoor patio, or even a strip of park bordering the north tower.

But how to get cooperation from a woman who had to think long and hard over whether she'd finished a page in her novel or not, and what action to take about it once she did?

"We need someone who can drive. Drive really well," Ahn-Kha said as the days began to run out in October. There was frost on the ground most mornings now.

"That might be doable," Valentine said. "You think we could trust the doc?"

"Your lover? No—"

"I meant Doctor Boothe. I've seen her with pickups and that little ATV. She says she hates people. Maybe she means she hates the system."

"She is risk-averse," Ahn-Kha said. "She does her job, wraps herself in it like a cloak, my David."

"There's one bit of skin showing. That assistant of hers, Pepsa, she's protecting her, hiding her. I wonder if she'd get her out with us."

"And why are we leaving?" Ahn-Kha said.

"I'll come up with a reason."

⌀

Evenings at the rec center were typically a bore, and that night was no different. The cavernlike garage had a few games of cards going, an almost-unwatched video, a pickup basketball game, and a "reading circle" where a group of nurses took turns reading a novel—a tattered old gothic about some siblings locked in an attic by a cruel grandmother—and performing the different voices. The only things new were several taped-up orange flyers for the Halloween Dance at the NUC hall, and a table where some of the workers were sewing together odds and ends and adding colored feathers or glitter to masks and hairpieces. The result was more Mardi Gras than Halloween. Valentine wasn't planning on attending. Since he had been to the previous dance, and his lover didn't feel the need to go trolling again, he offered to work that evening.

He opened a "coke" and took a swig of the syrupy concoction with its saliva-like texture. Xanadu cokes had never seen a cola nut but they did give one a brief rush of caffeine-charged glycemic energy.

The pickup basketball game had a lot of noisy energy. Valentine watched Ski, the hand who liked to call him "Grogfucker," sink a three-point shot over the heads of the other hands. An easy man to dislike. Valentine counted heads, nerved himself.

"You've only got five players. Need a sixth?" he asked.

They ignored him.

Valentine set down his bottle and moved around under the basket.

"Clear out, Nursey," Ski said. "Boys only." The jumble of arms and legs shifted back to the basket to the beat of the bouncing ball. Ski tipped it in and Valentine reached out and snatched the ball. He gave it an experimental bounce.

"How about a little one-on-one?" Valentine asked, looking at Ski. The others lined up next to Ski.

"How about you fuck off," Ski said. "Before I bruise up those pretty little eyes."

*Let's get it over with, big boy.*

Valentine bounced the basketball off Ski's forehead, feeling oddly like he was facing Vista again. He caught the ball on the rebound.

"Naaaah"—Ski let loose with a scream, charging at Valentine with fists flailing. He was big, but a sloppy fighter. It would have been so easy for Valentine to slip under his guard, take his elbow, and use the big hand's momentum to tip him over the point of Valentine's hip. Instead Valentine put up a guard as Ski rained blows on him. He put his head down and rammed it into Ski's stomach. Ski gripped him by the waist and they locked.

A couple of the others saw Ski winning and joined in. Valentine felt himself pulled upright, took the better part of a punch on the temple, a grazing blow to his chin, then another in the gut. Air— and a little coke—wheezed out as his diaphragm contracted. He tasted blood from a cut lip—

Then they were pulled apart, Ski by two of his fellow hands, Valentine by a burly blue arm. Valentine realized it was one of the security staff, talking into his radio even as he put him on the ground with a knee across his back.

Xanadu's security arrived faster than he would have given them credit for—perhaps they were better than they appeared—and didn't let the fight go with a simple "shake hands." Valentine, Ski, and a third hand all made a trip to the long security complex between the hospital and the Grands, where they were put into white-washed cells to cool down. Valentine gathered from the exchanges at the admissions desk that Ski had caused trouble before, and Valentine had been scooped up in the administrative overkill. Almost as an afterthought they fingerprinted him.

Valentine sat in his cell with a rough brown paper towel, wiping the ink off his hands, wondering—

He'd been printed before in the Kurian Zone. A set of fingerprints existed in the Great Lakes Shipping Security Service, inserted there as part of the long-ago operation that brought him to the Gulf Coast with a good work record that could survive a detailed background check. He imagined the Ordnance had some kind of connection with the GLSSS, and he just might be able to explain away a connection if the old "David Rowan" identity pinged.

But if the connection was made to the renegade officer of the late *Thunderbolt* . . .

Valentine felt a Reaper's presence in the building. Somewhere above.

A warty, one-eyed officer had the three brawlers brought up a level so they stood before his desk. The Reaper lurked somewhere nearby, not in the room. Valentine felt cold sweat on his belly and back, and his eyes searched the desk and file cabinets for something, anything, that could be used as a weapon.

"Brawling, eh?" the officer said from his paper-littered desk. His desk plate read LIEUTENANT STRAND.

"Hot blood, Strand," Ski said. "Nobody was aiming at murder."

"Little too much hot blood. You didn't join in the blood drive this fall."

"I get woozy when they—" Ski said as his companion winced.

"Corporal!" Strand said. "Take them over to the hospital. Liter each, all at once. They won't feel like fighting for a while."

"I get spells—" Ski's accomplice said. Valentine felt only knee-buckling relief. Anything was better than the hovering Reaper.

They were marched over to the hospital under a single-security-officer escort. The security man had a limp worse than Valentine's. Perhaps a sinecure at Xanadu security was a form of payoff for commendable Ordnance service.

"A nice, big bore. Right in the leg," the security man told the nurse.

*Noonside Passions* was on in the blood center. Valentine concentrated on it as they jabbed the needle into his inner thigh. Ted's evidence against Holly had mysteriously disappeared, and the episode ended with Nichelle's revelation that she'd stolen it—not to protect her sister, but to force her to steal gasoline for Brick's smuggling ring . . . even as Brick started seducing a virginal New Universal Church acolyte named Ardenia behind Nichelle's back.

"That bastard," the rapt nurse said as she extracted the needle. Valentine didn't know if she was referring to Brick or the guard, who was holding a hand-mirror up to Ski to show him how pale he was getting. "One liter, Ayoob. You're done. You'd better lie for a while until I can get you a biscuit. Coffee?"

"Tea. Lots of sugar."

"All we have is substitute. How about a coke? That's real syrup."

"Great," Valentine said as he passed out.

ɸ

Footsteps in the hall. A blue-uniformed, mustachioed security man turned a key in Valentine's cell. "Ayoob. You're being released to higher authority."

Valentine found he could stand up. Just. Walking seemed out of the question at the moment.

"C'mon, Ayoob, I don't have all night."

Had the fingerprints been processed?

The guard led Valentine out from the catacombs, up some stairs, each step taking him closer to the Reaper, past a ready room, a briefing area, and out to the entryway.

*Away from the Reaper!*

Valentine caught a whiff of familiar perfume.

"Tar-baby," Fran Paoli said, from across the vastness of the duty desk. "Your face! You need to see a doctor."

ɸ

The damage wasn't as bad as it looked.

She took him back up to her apartment, dressed the small cut on his cheek, and gave him a pair of cream-colored pills that left him relaxed, a little numb, and with a much-improved opinion of Kurian Zone psychotropics.

"There's a little halloween party tomorrow night at the top floor of Grand North. You won't need a mask."

"I might be working."

"I'll get you off," she said, snapping the elastic waistband on her scrubs. He liked Fran Paoli better in her plain blue scrubs than in any of her more exotic outfits that were designed to impress.

"Undoubtedly. But I don't know that I should miss any shifts. I think I have to keep my nose clean here for a while. If they even let me keep my job. Otherwise it's back to Kentucky."

"Let me worry about your reputation. And your job. Besides, it's going to be a fun party. North has this beautiful function space, and even Oriana's going to get dressed up."

Valentine found it easier to talk with his eyes closed. He felt as though he were drifting down a river on a raft, and opening his eyes might mean he'd have to change course. "I don't have a costume."

"Yes, you do. That biker getup of yours. I've been working on something to match all those spikes."

"Easily done."

"You nap. I have to get back to the wards—I'm missing an operation." She left.

Valentine didn't nap. He wondered—agonized—about the efficiency of the fingerprinting procedures. Would it go in an envelope, off to some central catalog for a bored clerk to get around to? Or would it be scanned into a Xanadu computer, which would spit out a list of his crimes against the Kurian Order as fast as bits of data could be shuffled and displayed? How long before that long, low building, resting at the center of Xanadu, a crocodile keeping watch on his swamp, woke up and came for him? The Kurian Order, like a great slumbering dragon, could be tiptoed around, even over, by a clever thief. Make too much noise, though, rouse it through an attack, and it would swallow you whole without straining in the slightest.

The sensible thing would be to blow this operation, tonight; take Ahn-Kha, find Ali, and be across the river in Price's bass boat before the next shift change.

Could he face Post, tell him his wife was a drugged-up uterus for the Kurian Order? Better to lie and tell him she was dead.

He wouldn't even be able to bring the news himself. He was an exile, condemned by the fugitive law. Ahn-Kha or Duvalier would have to find him in whatever rest camp was helping him adapt to an artificial leg and a shortened intestine.

Getting her out, hopefully in time to beat the fingerprint check, would mean he'd have to bring more people in on the effort. Could he trust the doctor?

Madness. He was right back where he started.

*Would William Post do the same for you? How much can one friend expect of another?*

*No, that's a cheat. The question here is what is a promise, hastily issued from beside a hospital bed, a tiny promise from David Valentine, worth?*

ψ

Doctor Boothe yawned as she came to her surgery door. "Ayoob. What happened?"

He tried to show the good half of his face through the strip of chained door. "A fistfight with Ski and a few hands. Can I come in?"

"It's eleven at night."

"It's important enough."

She shut the door and Valentine heard the chain slide. He looked around. The cool night air was empty.

She brought him into the tiled surgery and turned on a light. "What's so important, now?"

"I'm leaving the Ordnance. Going back to Kentucky."

"Good for you."

"I was wondering if your assistant might like to come. Anyone with veterinary training would be welcome there."

"Pepsa? A rabbit-run? Why should she do that?"

"She's mute. I'm surprised she hasn't been culled out of the herd before this."

"How dare—"

"Just cutting through the bullshit, Boothe. Or are you the type who only likes to see half the truth? I know people. We could get her somewhere safe from the Reapers, a lot safer than your dog kennels and dairy stalls."

"We?"

"Me. Ahn-Kha. You. Someone on the outside. I don't want to say more."

"You just offered your heart up, you know that. You'd be gone tonight if I told security. I'd get a seat at the head table at the next Ordnance Gratitude Banquet."

Valentine didn't want to kill this woman. But if she moved to the phone— "If you're such a friend of security, why haven't our guns ever left your office? Or have they?"

She couldn't help but look over her shoulder at the corridor to her storage room.

Boothe seemed to be fighting with something lodged in her throat.

"You could come along," Valentine continued. "Disappear into the tribelands, or relocate into Free Territory."

She frowned. "Free Territory's a myth. Some clearing full of guerillas does not a nation make."

"I've been there."

"As if it's that easy."

"I didn't say anything about it being easy."

She lifted her chin. "Let me talk to Pepsa."

Valentine followed her with his ears and listened from the surgery doorway as she went into a back room and spoke to Pepsa. The quiet conversation was one-sided; Valentine couldn't see what Pepsa communicated back on her kiddie magic tablet. This would be an all-or-nothing gamble. Every person added to a conspiracy doubled the risk.

Dr. Boothe, with Pepsa trailing behind in a robe, joined him in the surgery. Pepsa looked at him with new interest in her gentle eyes.

"You have people who can help us get all the way to Free Territory?"

Valentine thought it best to dodge the question. "There are plenty of animals to take care of there. Herds of horses."

Pepsa wrote something on her board.

"But you do have people outside Xanadu to help us get away?"

"Absolutely."

Boothe and Pepsa exchanged a look. Pepsa wrote again.

"What do you need us to do?" Boothe asked.

"We need some food that can be preserved. Pack some cold-weather clothing and camp-mats, and have it all ready by tomorrow afternoon. Make some excuse for not being available until November first or second. And one more thing. I need a quick look in your pharmacy."

φ

Valentine walked all the way back to the rec center to use the phone there. He could have used the phone in Boothe's office, but just in case she or Pepsa turned on him, he could warn Duvalier.

The phone rang fourteen times before a gravelly voice at the hostel answered it. "Yeah?"

Valentine asked to speak to Duvalier's Ordnance ID pseudonym.

"No calls after nine."

"It's urgent. Could I leave a message?"

"She'll get it in the morning, Corporal."

The attendant must have thought Valentine was Duvalier's would-be boyfriend, Corporal Thatcher.

"Tell her my migraine is back. I'll come by tomorrow night, then we can get to the party."

"Migraine?"

Valentine spelled it.

"She'll get the message at a decent hour. Reread your phone protocols, Corporal—dating doesn't give you special privileges to disturb me."

"Tell her some new friends will be along. We'll have transport."

"I'm not a stenographer, son. Call her tomorrow."

Valentine thanked him and replaced the receiver. Next he'd

have to wake Ahn-Kha. He looked at the craft table with the Halloween costumes.

ϕ

Xanadu had its share of children, and while it was still light out they paraded around in their costumes from building to building, collecting treats from the security staff at the doors.

The kids sang as they collected their candy.

> *A Reaper, a creeper*
> *Goes looking for a sleeper*
> *Wakes him up, drinks him down*
> *And packs him in the freez-zer.*

Valentine, dressed in his Bulletproof "leathers" and carrying a large brown market bag full of costuming, was a little shocked to hear the realities of life in the Kurian Zone expressed in nursery-rhyme fashion. He watched one young child, dressed in the red-and-white stripes of a frightening, bloody-handed Uncle Sam, pull his cowgirl sister along as they sang. He'd been at sea during his other Halloween in the Kurian Zone, so he couldn't say if it was a widespread practice. Or maybe on this one night mention of the real duties of the Reapers was allowed.

Valentine passed in to Grand East and nodded to the security staff. They were used to him by now.

"Nice costume, Tar. You really rode those things?"

"Sure did," Valentine said, trying to put a little Kentucky music into his voice.

Valentine went to the smaller of the elevators, the one that went to the top and garage floors, and rode up.

He couldn't help but pat the syringes stuck in the breast of his legworm-rider jacket. His .22 target pistol was tucked into the small of his back, held in place by three strips of surgical tape. Hopefully he wouldn't need it.

Fran Paoli just yelled "come in" at his knock. He hurried in, wondering just how—

And he had his answer when he saw her.

293

She stood in the doorway of her bedroom, a gothic queen spider in thigh-high boots thick with buckles. Black eyeliner, spider earrings, a temporary tattoo of a skull on one fleshy, corset-enclosed breast.

"Sticks and stones may break my bones, but leather and chains excite me," she quoted.

"What on earth do you use boots like that for?" Valentine asked.

"Turning men on. Is it working?"

"I'll say. Come here, you naughty girl."

She giggled, and came up and kissed him. She tested the hooks on his forearms, and looked down at the spurs.

"You're dangerous tonight," Fran Paoli observed.

"You've no idea."

He sat on the arm of her sofa and threw her across his knee, raising the torn, black-dyed taffeta miniskirt. A black thong divided her buttocks. He gave her backside an experimental slap.

"Ohhhh!" she cooed.

"I may just have to tie you up so other men don't get a chance to see this," he said, snapping the thong. He hit her again, harder.

"Nothing I could do about it," she said.

He hit her harder. She gave tiny giggle-gasps at each swat.

"My, what a strong arm you have," she said, lifting her now-splotched buttocks a little. Valentine extracted the syringe from his jacket, pulled the plastic cap off with his teeth, and held it in his mouth while he spanked her again, even harder. He felt both ridiculous and a little aroused.

"Uhhh—" she gasped. He transferred the syringe to his hand and injected her, threw it across the room behind her, and struck her again.

Six more swats and she was limp and moaning. The large-animal tranquilizers had their effect.

She slurred and tried to caress him as he transferred her to the bedroom. He kissed her several times, gagged her with her bathrobe belt, and tied her up in the closet using pairs of pantyhose and leather belts.

She offered no resistance save a dopey-eyed wink.

"Now you just wait there for a little while," he said, and kissed her on the forehead. He shut the closet door.

Valentine took her keys from the dresser, and her blue ID card. He pocketed them and rode the elevator to the basement.

He'd worked out every move in his mind, gone over it so many times a sense of unreality persisted. Was he still lying in bed, planning this? Was it his real hand reaching for the big Lincoln's door, his bag he placed on the passenger seat, his foot on the accelerator as he backed toward the fuel pump?

The pump clattered loudly enough that he wondered that the whole building didn't come to investigate. He topped off the tank, and filled the two spare twenty-liter plastic containers she kept in the back. He climbed into the driver's seat, and put on the seat belt and com headset. He started the SUV and turned it toward the garage door.

"Two-one-six, leaving," he said into her mouthpiece, pressing the com button on the dash.

"Dr. Paoli?"

"Tar Ayoob, running an errand," he said.

"Two-one-six, leaving," the voice acknowledged. "Enjoy the party." The garage door rose.

Valentine pulled the SUV around to the west tower, parked it in plain sight under a roadside light, and trotted over to the basement door with his bag. He knocked, and Ahn-Kha, in his laundry overcoat, answered.

"Here," Ahn-Kha said, and passed Valentine some blue scrubs.

The boots looked a little funny under them, but he'd pass. Once Ahn-Kha checked the basement hallway, thick with conduits and junction boxes, Valentine went to the larger, gurney-sized elevators and pressed the up button.

Ahn-Kha brought a wheelchair out from around a corner. They were easily found all over the building, but it never hurt to be prepared.

He pushed Fran's blue card in the slot and went up to the fourth floor.

Halloween decorations, traditional orange-and-black paper, festooned the hallway over the honor-in-childbearing propaganda.

Vague noises of something that sounded like a Chevy with a bad starter came from the central common room. Valentine walked behind the wheelchair to Room 4105.

The outer cubicle was empty. A woman lay in the next bed, sleeping—but it wasn't Gail.

He knew Gail Post's schedule by heart. She'd already been fed, and it was getting to the point where the women were usually expected to be in their beds, asleep.

He crossed the building to the common room. Twenty-odd women watched spacecraft blow up a model of long-ago Los Angeles. Vacant, tired eyes reflected the sparking special effects.

Gail Foster sat right in the center.

A nurse popped up at the door. "Can I help?"

"Gail Foster. Follow-up X-ray."

She glanced at Valentine's ID badge, but didn't examine it closely. "Follow-up to what?"

"Not sure. Dr. Kreml's orders. They should have called. She wants it taken tonight."

"That one," the nurse said, pointing.

Valentine tapped her on the shoulder. "Gail, I need you for a moment," he said.

"Sure," she said absently. Valentine helped her to the chair by the door. A few of the other patients exchanged looks, but most watched the movie.

The nurse who had questioned Valentine was at the center console, speaking into the phone.

No choice.

He wheeled Gail to the station. The nurse turned to watch him.

"Is there a problem?" Valentine asked.

"Just checking with central."

"Should I wait?"

"If you don't mind." She turned and checked a clipboard again.

Valentine hated to do it, but he took out the horse tranquilizer. With one quick step, he got behind her and jammed it into her neck. He pulled her down, one hand on her mouth, and waited until her legs quit kicking.

"You certainly got her cooperation," Gail said.

"Let's not have any attitude tonight, okay, Gail?" Valentine asked as he pulled the nurse into a file room. He found a length of surgical tubing and tied the door shut.

Gail offered a *wheeeee* as he raced her down the hall to the elevator. On the ride down he stripped off his scrubs.

"I've never been here before," Gail observed as they entered the basement corridor. Ahn-Kha helped her get dressed. "Oh, pretty," she remarked, as Valentine slipped a feathered mask on her.

They walked her out to the Lincoln, Ahn-Kha half carrying her across the road. The Golden One climbed in the back cargo area where his disassembled puddler waited, along with Valentine's weapons.

"Keep her quiet back there, and out of sight," Valentine said.

He drove the Lincoln around the building perimeter to the veterinary office. "Glad you remembered the heavy coat," Valentine said as Dr. Boothe slipped into the passenger seat.

"You give good instruction. Is this Paoli's rig?"

"I like to make an exit," Valentine said.

Pepsa's eyes widened as she saw Ahn-Kha in back.

Valentine passed out masks to Dr. Boothe and Pepsa. "Just on our way to a party, okay? Once we're past the gate, you'll be driving."

As they rolled around the hospital the headlights illuminated a figure at the roadside in harsh black and white, gleam and shadow. A pale face, exaggerated and immobile as a theatrical mask, held them like a spotlight.

A Reaper.

Boothe sucked breath in through her teeth. Valentine's heart gave a triple thump. The Reaper could upend the Lincoln as easily as it might lift a wheelbarrow. Then what chance would they have, still within Xanadu's walls. If it moved he'd have to—

But it didn't.

After they passed it crossed the road behind them. How could it not know they had an expectant mother inside the SUV? Of all forms of lifesign, a pregnant woman's was the strongest, and Valentine had one experience involving a Kurian and an infant's lifesign that he'd rather die than repeat. Perhaps the Kurian animating it was sick, or sated, or . . .

297

Someone was letting them go.

The gate warden hardly looked at them as they followed a bus full of Halloween partygoers out of Xanadu. Ahn-Kha lay flat in the back cargo space, holding down Gail Foster. "Have a good time, Dr. Paoli," the sergeant said. Valentine nodded and Boothe waved in return.

Pepsa tapped her hands against the leather seats as Valentine pulled away from the gate. "We've done it!" Boothe said.

"We've done it, alright," Valentine demurred. "Now what are they going to do about it?"

# CHAPTER TWELVE

*E*scapes: *Nearly every part of the Kurian Zone is traced with "pipelines," or channels for escapees to reach safety. Other networks supply guerillas and underground information distributors, and a few do double, or even triple duties as criminal organizations involved in smuggling and black-market trading. In the better-run networks, each person at a pipeline junction only knows her links in the next stage of the operation, making it harder for a pipeline to be rolled up. Generally, the less that is known about a pipeline the safer it is to travel.*

*This has a drawback, however. Without careful preparation work, operatives who venture into unfamiliar territory will have no idea who to trust and who not to, as the man next door in the New Universal Church hostel might be the local pipeline operator or a Kurian informer.*

*A grim vocabulary exists among those who shuttle material, human or logistical, through the pipelines. Shutdowns and spills are bad, involving loss of a route, and a penetration is the worst of all, indicating that the Kurians successfully uncovered a line and cleaned it up after their "mole" crept its way through. A "rabbit" is an escapee that makes a try for freedom without any guidance whatsoever. Rabbits are useful in that "rabbit runs" divert resources that might otherwise be used to uncover a real pipeline.*

*Like a cottontail's dash for cover, most rabbit runs are fast, panicked, and quickly finished.*

ψ

Valentine switched places with Boothe as soon as they passed out of the light of the gates. It was a cloudy evening and the woods were black as a mine shaft. Only with wide-open Cat eyes could he distinguish a tree trunk or two. He relaxed a little once they passed where he had sensed the Reaper pickets on his reconnaissance and made it out of the hairpin-turn gully—if Valentine had chosen a spot to ambush the big-framed Lincoln, it would have been there.

The Reapers, if they were out there, hadn't caused the "Valentingle"—but with his blood loss, and nervous exhaustion after the strain of the past few days, his wiring might have loosened.

Boothe drove skillfully, just fast enough to choose the best way to negotiate the patched road without bouncing her passengers around too much. The rugged suspension on the truck helped. In the rear cargo area, Gail counted the bumps, but lost track at sixty-seven.

As they took the river road into town Valentine saw what looked like bonfires in the hills, on both sides of the river.

"What's all this?"

"Hell night," Boothe said.

"Meaning?"

"Kind of a tradition. Old, emptied houses get burned to the ground on Halloween night. Farther out it's grain silos and barns."

On this one night the town sounded lively. People crisscrossed the streets burning everything from road flares to candles in grimacing, fanged pumpkins. Valentine wondered at the pumpkins—Reapers had pale skin, not orange in the slightest, and a yellow squash might better reflect both skin tone and their long, narrow skulls.

They pulled up on the street leading to the NUC hostel. It, too, was burning. Firefighters and police fought the blaze with hoses.

"I thought you said only abandoned buildings?" Valentine asked.

Boothe stopped the four-wheeler well away from the conflagration and its attending crowd.

"Could be some drunk got carried away. I should see if anyone—"

"No," Valentine said. "Stay here."

He got out of the vehicle. A man in football padding sat on the curb, drinking from a bottle within a paper bag.

Valentine heard a high-pitched whistle from the other side of the street. Duvalier and a man in the shale-colored uniform of the Ordnance, old US M-model rifle over his shoulder and a duffel in his hand, ran across the street and to the Lincoln.

"You weren't kidding about transport," Duvalier said. "Tar, meet Corporal Scott Thatcher."

Valentine remembered him from the dance. Thatcher had a bony face, but everything was pleasantly enough arranged.

"You sure about this?" he asked. He meant the question for Duvalier but Thatcher spoke up.

"I want out, sir. Passage all the way if it can be arranged." He lowered his voice. "Free territory."

Valentine didn't like it. The boy could win a nice position in the Kurian Zone by turning them in. He was certainly armed heavily enough to take control of the escape, with a pistol at his hip, an assault rifle over his arm . . .

*Is that what you really think? Or is it Alessa finding someone?*

Valentine's first escape from the Kurian Zone, leading a few families of refugees with a platoon of Zulu Company's Wolves, had been betrayed to the Reapers. He wouldn't let it happen again.

On the other hand, an Ordnance uniform, stripes, and knowledge of the region—assuming Thatcher could be trusted—would come in handy.

"He's okay, Val," Duvalier said. For her to use his real name like that must mean something. "He knows the ground. I trust him. So can you."

"We'll see."

"Says the man who manages to come out the gates with three, count 'em, ladies and gentlemen, three women. New personal best?"

Valentine ignored the jibe. "You'll have to put your duffel up top," he said to Thatcher. "The rifle can go in back. Give me that pistol."

Thatcher passed him the weapons. Valentine handed the assault rifle back to Ahn-Kha in the cargo bay.

"Take shotgun," Valentine said. "And remember, another shotgun's in the seat right behind you."

Valentine wondered how they'd all fit. Duvalier crouched in between the driver and passenger seats, next to Thatcher, with Valentine and Pepsa in the seats behind.

"Fire your doing?" he asked Duvalier as they pulled away from the fire and the growing crowd.

"Yes. But it's just a diversion. In another half hour the police headquarters is going to lose their fodder-wagons and fuel depot."

Pepsa took a startled breath. "I had a feeling you were more than just a boy heading home, Tar," Boothe said.

"You thought of everything," Thatcher said. "But it's not the police we have to worry about, it's the Ordnance."

"A girl has to keep busy," Duvalier said.

In the back, Ahn-Kha assembled his puddler.

"West on the river road," Valentine told Boothe.

"Where you planning to cross?" Thatcher asked, excitement bringing his words fast and hard.

"Route ten bridge," Valentine said. "Just a mile ahead here. Saw it when we were biking. It gets a lot of traffic."

"Yeah, 'cause it's open to civilians," Thatcher said. "You'll at least get a flashlight sweep. Go up five more miles and cross at Ironton Road. That's an Ordnance checkpoint. There's a Kentucky Roadside popular with all of us up a ways there. Better all around."

"Well?" Boothe asked.

"Ironton Road it is," Valentine said.

Duvalier gripped Thatcher's hand and nodded, but Valentine felt like it was a mistake. He handed her a party hat.

φ

The old, rusty trestle bridge had been blown up at some point. New girders and railroad ties had been cobbled together to close the gap.

"Don't worry, we've taken trucks over it," Thatcher said as Boothe slowed. Valentine checked the magazine of Thatcher's 9mm, then chambered a round.

They made it over the gap with no more than the sound of tires rumbling across the ties.

A lighted guardhouse at the other end had a couple of uniformed men in it. The Lincoln's headlights revealed two chains, running from either side of the bridge to a post in the center, more of a polite warning than a serious obstacle. Yellow reflective tape fluttered from the center of each length, looking like a dancing worm in the headlights' glare.

"I'm supposed to be asleep now," Gail announced, an angry tone in her voice.

"Oh great, we have a med-head," Duvalier said.

"Keep her quiet in back, there," Valentine said to Ahn-Kha. He heard a squeak.

Boothe rolled down her window as they approached the checkpoint. She swerved into the left-hand lane to pull up to it.

"Hey there, Cup," Thatcher called. He passed over an ID card. Valentine didn't know if it was Ordnance slang or a nickname, but the man's shirt read "Dorthistle." "Five and a lost Grog going to Beaudreaux's. Back by sunup."

The sentry looked at the card, then placed his flashlight beam on Thatcher.

Boothe began to glance around and Valentine stiffened. If he was on the ball, the sentry would notice the fight-or-flight tell. She was looking for a direction to run. Valentine yawned and returned his hand to the butt of the pistol next to his thigh.

Valentine heard the phone ring in the guardhouse.

"Line's up again," the man inside said. "That was quick."

*Shit shit shit.*

"You going to unhook or what, *Private,*" Thatcher said. "It's Halloween and we need to raise some hell."

A soldier inside picked up the phone.

The private went around to the center post and placed his hand on the chain.

"Border closed, alert!" the soldier with the phone shouted from inside the guardhouse.

"Ram it," Valentine shouted. Boothe sat frozen, her hands locked on the steering wheel.

The guard by the chain stepped back, fumbling for his rifle as the butt hit the post.

"Christ, go!" Duvalier said.

Valentine opened his door and aimed his pistol through the gap at the white-faced guard, lit like a stage actor by the Lincoln's beams. A whistle blew from somewhere in the darkness.

*Pop pop pop*—the flash from the pistol was a little brighter than the headlights; the guard spun away, upended over the chain.

The noise unfroze the gears in Boothe's nervous system. She floored the accelerator.

The Lincoln hit the chain, bounced over something that might have been the post going down, or might have been the guard, and Valentine heard a metallic scream that was probably the front bumper tearing.

The Lincoln gained speed.

"Turn the lights off," Ahn-Kha boomed as he looked out the back windows. "Don't give them a mark to aim—"

Bullets ripped into the back of the Lincoln. Ahn-Kha threw himself against the back of the seats, wrapping Gail Foster in one great arm and Pepsa in the other.

"Agloo," Pepsa yelped. Gail screamed.

Valentine felt the Lincoln head up a slight rise, then turn, putting precious distance, brush, and trees between them and the checkpoint.

"Everyone okay?" Valentine asked.

"Some glass cuts," Ahn-Kha said. "Post's mate is hit in the foot. Let me get her shoe off."

Gail yelped again. "I want to go home," she wailed.

"I believe a toe is missing," Ahn-Kha said.

Pepsa nodded at Valentine.

"Pepsa, take my bag. See what you can do," Boothe said.

Ahn-Kha shifted to give her room to get in the back. Valentine heard his friend wheeze.

"Glass cuts?" Valentine said.

"I fear it may be more than that, my David," Ahn-Kha said.

"Who's David?" Boothe asked.

"Just drive, please."

"I could go faster if I turned on the lights."

"No," Valentine and Thatcher said in unison.

"Go left here," Thatcher said. "Good road."

Valentine, smelling blood, his stomach hurting as though he'd been mule-kicked, saw a distant patch of flame; a house burning over by the river. Somewhere there were people dancing in firelight. Somewhere Reapers were asking questions. Boothe made the turn, heading south.

The bumper ground as it scraped the road surface.

Ahn-Kha let out a gentle cough. "My David. I saw headlights hit the clouds far back. I believe we are being followed."

How far would the Ordnance chase them into Kentucky?

"Stop the car. I'll drive," Valentine said. "Doc, check out Ahn-Kha. Do what you can for him."

Valentine slipped into the driver's seat, and got the sport-utility vehicle moving as soon as he heard the back door close. Boothe switched places with Pepsa in the cargo area. Ahn-Kha kicked out a bullet-starred window.

*You can do this. Nothing to be afraid of. You've driven before. Badly, but you've driven.*

He could see farther than Boothe, and pushed the engine up past forty miles an hour. They ate miles. Every now and then the Lincoln hit a pothole with a resounding thump.

A flash blinded him. "You need help," Boothe said.

"Watch the light back there," Valentine said. Boothe had been using a flashlight to look at Ahn-Kha. Sudden increases in light gave him an instant headache.

Valentine spotted a legworm trail, the distinctive rise and thick vegetation cutting across a field.

"I'm going to go off-road," he told Thatcher.

Thatcher pushed a button on the center console, engaging the four-wheel drive. "Slow down. They'll see tire marks otherwise."

Valentine applied the brake, felt the Lincoln change gears. Automatic transmission made a huge difference in driving effort.

He turned onto the legworm trail. Any tree big enough to stop the Lincoln was avoided by the creature. The ground looked easier to the east, so he followed another legworm trail leading that way. He listened to the car cutting through weeds and grasses.

"I've done all I can," Boothe said. "The external bleeding's stopped, for now."

Valentine found another road, got on it, and took it for a mile until it intersected with one in even worse condition, but at least he was heading south.

"We're still being followed," Duvalier said. "Looks like a motorcycle."

Valentine didn't need the confirmation. He felt them behind, a presence, the way you felt a thunderstorm long before its first rumble.

"Stop the car, my David," Ahn-Kha said. The Golden One hoisted his puddler, then waited until they could hear the faint blatt of the motorcycle engine.

"Cover your ears," Ahn-Kha said.

The gun boomed. Gail screamed. Valentine watched the motorcycle light shift, wink out.

"That'll learn 'em," Duvalier said.

Valentine put the car in gear again. He watched the colon blink on the dashboard clock. Had all this happened in only twenty minutes?

He pushed the Lincoln, daring himself to wreck it, locked on to a distance a hundred yards in front of the car as if watching for downed tree limbs was the be-all, and end-all of his life. Which it might be, if he struck a big enough object in the dark.

"They're still behind," Ahn-Kha observed ten minutes, or six hundred or so clock flashes, later. "Gaining, it would appear. Perhaps they have Hummers."

"Shouldn't have shot that poor Cup," Thatcher said. "They wouldn't be after us like this otherwise. I bet there's a locator in this rig."

"You people are crazy," Gail said. "They say I'm the one who causes problems. They must have never met you." Her voice sounded raw and tired.

Valentine crossed legworm trail after legworm trail, recent mounds with just the beginnings of growth on them.

Ahn-Kha coughed again. "My David, I have a suggestion."

"I don't want to hear it," Valentine shot back.

"They are going to catch up with this truck sooner or later. Would it not be better if we weren't all in it when they did?"

"Ahn—"

"Let him talk," Duvalier said.

"I cannot walk far. Let me lead them on a wild Grog hunt. When they catch up, I will grunt and pretend that I am simple. They will think a trick has been played, that a poor dumb Grog has been put at the wheel to lead them away."

"Lots of Grogs know how to drive. They're good at it," Thatcher said.

Valentine looked at Duvalier, but she wasn't listening, or was only half listening. Her lips were moving in steady rhythm.

"Four minutes behind," she said. "I marked that hilltop."

She began to fiddle with her explosive-packed Spam cans, a detonator, and a fuse. She threw one out on one side of the road, and then the other went into the opposite ditch.

"You'll have to get royal-flush lucky to take one of them out," Thatcher said.

"I'm not trying for that. I just want to fool them into thinking they've been ambushed."

Valentine drove past a burning barn, collapsed down to the foundation and mostly sending up smoke by now. The Lincoln plunged into a thicket and he had to slow down. He found another legworm track and cut off the road again, splashing through a stream. The wheels briefly spun as they came up the other side, then they were out into broken country again. Following the legworm trail, he found yet another farm service road running along a rounded, wooded hill. They were in real back country now. It would be dangerous to go off-road—not that the roads in this part of Kentucky were much better.

"They're still behind," Duvalier said.

Valentine wanted to wrench the steering wheel free of its mount, throw it out the window, turn around, and smash the Lincoln into their pursuers—

"Enough, my David," Ahn-Kha said. "Let me take the wheel."

"Val, it's the only way," Duvalier said.

"Alright. But I'm coming with you."

"No," Ahn-Kha said. "You've kept faith with me. You must still see Gail back. I may be able to fool them. With you, there will be too many questions."

Valentine stopped the Lincoln in the middle of the road. "We have to hurry. Everyone out. Thatcher, don't forget your gun and duffel."

Ahn-Kha climbed out the back and came around to the driver's door, helping himself stand up by putting his long right arm on the side of the Lincoln, puddler cradled in his left. He was a mess, his back peppered with bandages and streaked in blood, a thick dressing on the back of his firepluglike thigh. Duvalier stopped before him, then stood on tiptoe to kiss one whiskered cheek. She looped her oversized canteen around the Golden One's neck. "I want this back, you hairy fuck. You hear me?"

Ahn-Kha murmured a few words into her ear.

"Oh, dream on," she laughed, wiping away tears.

Valentine could only stand, tired and fighting his headache, fiddling with his gun. Would it be better for their pursuit to come upon all their bodies, stretched out next to the flaming Lincoln? Perhaps with every dead hand posed with middle finger extended?

"We'll meet another dawn, my David," Ahn-Kha said as he reclined the driver's seat all the way so he could squeeze up front. He tossed the puddler onto the passenger seat.

"If we live to see another dawn," Valentine said.

"If not, we'll meet in a far better place," Ahn-Kha said. One ear rose a trifle.

"Good luck, old horse," Valentine said. He placed his forehead against Ahn-Kha's, hugged him, felt the rough skin and the strangely silky hair on his upper back.

Ahn-Kha squeezed the back of his neck and the Lincoln drove away.

"Off the road! Fast," Valentine said. Issuing orders in his old command voice, then picking a route up the hill, kept him from staring after the receding Lincoln. The best friend Valentine ever had, or would ever have, left only a little blood on the road. "Thatcher, lead them up that hillside."

Duvalier pulled the whining, pregnant Gail Foster into the bush, opening a gap in the bramble with her walking stick. Dr. Boothe and Pepsa followed her, Pepsa searching anxiously down the road for their pursuers. Valentine spotted one of Duvalier's Spam cans, unopened and unwired, left in the center of the road, and picked it up with a curse.

Valentine closed the gap in the brush behind them by forcing a few tree limbs down, and limped after his party, giving his tears their time.

Halfway up the hill they froze and counted the pursuit. A column rolled up the slight incline: another motorcycle, two Hummers, a pickup with dogs in it, and two five-ton trucks. A platoon of Wolves or a team of Bears could knock hell out of them, but he and Duvalier would waste themselves against it.

Without Ahn-Kha's reliable strength alongside him, he felt like a piece of his spine had been plucked out.

"He did it," Duvalier said as they saw the pursuit convoy crest another rise in the distance.

They crested the hill, and thanks to its commanding view Valentine went through Thatcher's inventory. He'd brought some good topographical maps of Kentucky, and between the two of them they made a good guess as to where they were. Several lights could be seen between the hill and the northern horizon, but they were so distant he couldn't tell if they were electric or burning homes.

"What do you suppose that is?" Duvalier asked, pointing southwest.

"I don't see anything," Boothe said, but she couldn't without Cat eyes.

*A garbage pile, perhaps?* It looked like a plate of spaghetti the size of a football field.

"That's a legworm dogpile," Valentine said. "Look at all the tracks."

"What, that hump down there?" Thatcher said, squinting to try to make out what they were talking about. "I saw three of them all tangled up once after a snowstorm."

"Let's get off this ridge," Valentine said. "Take a closer look. Maybe some of their tribe is around."

Valentine pointed out a tree at the bottom of the hill, and had Thatcher find a path toward it. Gail's breathing was labored and Duvalier gave her the walking stick. Valentine hung back to check the rest spot, and waved Duvalier over.

"You dropped this in the road," Valentine said, giving Duvalier back her can of explosive-filled meat.

She looked at it, puzzled, and whipped her bag off her back. The wing locks were still clicked shut. "Then it jumped out on its own."

"Someone left it?"

"Everyone was in a hurry to get out of the truck. Maybe it got kicked out in the confusion."

Valentine only remembered the sound of feet hitting the ground. "Let's not leave anything to luck, good or bad," he said.

They caught up to the others at the bottom of the hill, and walked out into the horseshoe-shaped flat with the legworm dog-pile roughly in the center. What might have been utility poles at one time could be seen against the horizon, a few miles away. The peak of a funnel-topped silo and a barn roof showed.

Legworm trails crisscrossed the ground everywhere, but none looked or smelled fresh. Maybe their minders were on the other side of the valley.

Gail collapsed, crying. "Legs won't hold me up anymore."

Boothe listened to her heart and breathing with her stethoscope. "She's healthy, just out of condition."

"We can rest for a little," Valentine said.

Then need came, terrible need. Valentine felt them on the towering hill behind, moving like an angry swarm of bees.

*Reapers.*

They'd home in on the lifesign—he had a pregnant woman, and bitter experience told him that Kurians hungered for newborns like opiate addicts sought refined heroin; he might as well be running with a lit Roman candle—and that would be the end of them.

"We're in trouble," Valentine said.

"What—" Duvalier began.

"No time," he snapped. He handed her his rifle. "You and Thatcher head for those telephone poles. Doc, you and Pepsa go into those woods and find low ground. Lie flat, flat as you can." He tossed her Thatcher's 9mm.

"Reapers?" Duvalier asked.

"Coming down the hill." Boothe went as white as the cloud-hidden moon. "Hurry." He grabbed Gail's wrist. "I'll lead them off. Maybe I can lose them."

*You won't. Too long until sunup.*

"How?"

"Interference." *Price's critter camouflage, writ in sixty-foot letters.* Valentine took Gail's wrist and pulled her to her feet.

"Hate this," she said. "I want to go to my room. Please? This endangers the baby."

He could feel them coming, but caution had slowed them, stalking lions reevaluating as the herd they'd been stalking scattered.

Gail's legs gave out. Valentine picked her up in a fireman's carry, hoping it was safe to carry an expectant woman this way.

"Those chain things sound like wind chimes. I like wind chimes," Gail said. "Are we going back to the Grands soon?"

"Very possible," Valentine said as he ran.

From a hundred feet away the legworm pile looked like a gigantic lemon pie with a lattice-top crust—baked by a cook who was stoned to the gills. The legworms had pushed banks of earth up into walls, forming the pie "tin," and had woven themselves at the top.

Valentine reached the bank and climbed up it, sending dirt spilling. He went down on one knee, set Gail on churned-up ground, and caught his breath.

They were coming again. After him. Fast.

"I don't want to run anymore," Gail said.

"Good. We need to crawl."

He pulled her beneath a smaller legworm's twisted body, back set to the elements, shaggy skin flapping in the wind like an old, torn poster. They descended into the dark tangle, and perceived a faint aqua glow from within.

Valentine felt like he was back in the ruins of Little Rock, negotiating one of the great concrete-and-steel wrecks of a building downtown. Legworms lay on top of each other everywhere, a sleeping pile of yellow-fleshed Pickup Sticks.

The air grew noticeably warmer as he pulled Gail deeper into the nest.

The legworms were not packed as tightly at the bottom. Valentine felt air move. He followed it, and the glow.

"Don't like this," Gail whispered.

"Don't blame you."

And came upon the eggs. The legworm bodies arched above and around, making a warm arena for their deposits.

About the size of a basketball, the eggs had translucent skin. The glow came from the growing legworm's underside; the soft "membrane" had blue filament-like etchings of light, transformed into aqua by the greenish liquid within the eggs.

"Smells like old laundry in here," Gail said.

"Shhh."

Valentine saw deep pock marks in the skins of the larger legworms at the center. The eggs must have dropped off. Black lumps, like unprocessed coal, lay scattered between the living eggs. Evidently only a few eggs made it to whatever stage of the metamorphosis they now enjoyed.

Stepping carefully, Valentine crossed the egg repository, hoping the baby legworms were giving off enough lifesign to confuse the Reapers' senses.

He heard-felt-sensed motion behind.

A string of Reapers entered the egg chamber, clad in their dark, almost bulletproof robes, the first staring about as if to make sense of the small glows and vast shadows.

Valentine shoved Gail toward an A-shaped arch in a legworm's midsection. She turned around to protest, and her big eyes grew even wider, until they seemed to fill her face.

Gail shrieked. She instinctively reached for him, putting his body in between herself and the others.

As one, six Reaper heads turned in their direction. Valentine drew his .22 target pistol.

The lead Reaper dismissed the threat with a wave, a grotesque wigwag of its double-jointed elbow. It had a burn-scarred face, making its visage that of a badly formed wax mask.

Valentine pointed the gun at Gail's head. She squeaked.

The Reapers spread out, but came no closer.

*"keep calm, brother,"* the leader said in the breathy voice that always brought Valentine back to the terrors of the night Gabriella Cho died. *"no one need die tonight. be warned: hurt her and we will peel off your skin and leave you raw and screaming."*

He switched the sights of the pistol to the Reaper's yellow gimlet eye.

Valentine tried to still his hand.

*"you believe you can stop me with that?"*

"Not me," Valentine said.

And shot.

He aimed at an egg, shot, switched targets, and shot again, as quickly as he could pull the hair trigger. The gun felt like a cap pistol in his hand.

But the bullets had an effect.

They struck the eggs and tore through them, sending fluid flying, splattering the Reapers. The egg chamber suddenly smelled like old milk. He stifled a gag.

Evidently Reapers didn't get nauseated, or had poor noses—they just wiped at the fluid in disgust.

All around, legworm digits twitched like fluttering eyelashes.

Valentine dropped the empty gun as he ran, pulling Gail along behind. Tons of legworm righted itself and he threw her under it, dove, rolled, felt its legs on his back as he made it to the other side. Snapping noises like garden shears came from the egg area.

Valentine drew his legworm goad, buried it in the back of one as it began to roll, and pulled Gail tight to him as they ended up on its back.

The earthen bowl writhed with searching legworms.

Valentine anchored one of his cargo hooks in the loose skin atop the legworm, and looped a chain around Gail. Her white fingers gripped it while the legworm's back rose and fell as it negotiated the lip of the crater.

A Reaper flew through the air. Well, half of one. Its waist and legs were still on the ground.

Another jumped atop the back of a moving legworm and ran toward them like the hero of a Western on top of a train, arms out and reaching.

Two legworm muzzles rose from either side, one catching it by the head and arms, the other by its waist.

"Make a wish," Valentine said. Gail shifted position so that she wasn't resting on her belly, and gasped at the scene behind her.

The Reaper parted messily.

More legworms carefully stabbed down with their muzzles, lifted them covered with black goo and shreds of black cloth, then stabbed down again.

"Help!" Gail screamed.

A bony, blue-veined Reaper hand gripped her leg, pulling her off the legworm.

She clutched at Valentine and the securing chain. He shifted his grip on his legworm goad. He brought down the crowbarlike shovel edge on the Reaper's head. Skin peeled back, revealing a black, goo-smeared skull.

The Reaper made a sideways climb, more like a spider than a man, still pulling at Gail so hard that Valentine feared both she and the baby would be divided between the antagonists in Solomonic fashion.

Valentine crossed the shimmying legworm back, jumping as the Reaper swung its free arm. He buried the goad in the forearm holding Gail, and the Reaper released its grip.

Stars—a ringing sound—pain.

The Reaper had struck him backhand across the jaw. Something felt horribly loose on the left side of his head; bone held only by skin sagged at the side of his face. Valentine blindly swung with the goad as he backpedaled, then lost his balance. This time Gail screamed as he clutched at her to keep from falling off.

Valentine's vision cleared and he saw, and worse, felt, the Reaper straddling him. The goad was gone, his pistol was gone. He put up a hand against the tongue already licking out of the Reaper's mouth. It pulled his shirt open.

Valentine groped at his belt. He had another cargo hook. . . .

Gail struck the Reaper across the back of its neck with her hands interlocked, but it ignored her the way it would a butterfly alighting.

Valentine brought up the cargo hook—feeling the pointed tongue probe at his collarbone—and buried the hook into the Reaper's jaw, returning pain for pain. He pulled, desperate, and the black-fanged mouth closed on its own tongue.

The Reaper's eyes widened in surprise and the tongue was severed. The cut-off end twitched on Valentine's bare chest. Valentine slid and gripped the Reaper by its waist with his legs. It brought up its bad arm to try to pull the hook out, fumbling with the chain.

Valentine pulled, hard, putting his back muscles into the effort, straining—God, how his jaw hurt as he gritted his teeth—the Reaper looking oddly like a hooked bass with eyes glazed and confused—*hurt it bad enough and the Kurian shuts down the connection?*—and the Reaper's jaw came free in a splatter of blood. The Reaper swung at his eyes but Valentine got a shoulder up. He punched, hard, into the open wound at the bottom of its head and groped with his hand wrist-deep in slimy flesh. He dug with fingers up the soft palate.

The Reaper's eyes rolled back into its skull as he squeezed the base of its brain like a sponge.

Gail whacked it again and it toppled off the back of the legworm. Valentine sucked in air and pain with each breath.

"You look funny," Gail said.

"I bet I do," Valentine said, though it hit his ears as "I et I oo." Valentine examined his chest. The tiny wound from the Reaper's tongue had a splattering of Reaper blood all around it. It itched. He tore up some of the fiberglass-like legworm skin and blotted the tarry substance away.

The legworm they rode waved its snout in the air as it hurried around the perimeter of the pushed-up earth. When it slowed to re-descend into the pit, Valentine removed his first cargo hook, used it to lower Gail, and dropped off himself. He retrieved his goad and the other cargo hook.

This time she clung to him as he carried her, running for the telephone poles.

φ

Valentine heard voices, and turned toward the sound.

"I can't believe you used me as bait," Thatcher said.

"I got it, didn't I?" Duvalier chided.

"A second later and it would have popped my head off."

"Uh-uh. I never leave less than a second and a half to chance, sweetie. Wait—"

The last was at the sound of Valentine setting Gail on her feet again.

"It's us," Valentine said, holding his jaw. He came into what might pass for a clearing—thick grasses rather than trees—around an old barn. The telephone poles lined a road like the Roman crucifixes on the Via Appia.

Duvalier knelt down, working.

Valentine stepped up and found what he expected, a headless Reaper.

"Hell, Val," Duvalier said.

"Uf igh," Valentine tried. "Rluff nigh."

Thatcher seemed lost in his own thoughts as he stared at the Reaper corpse. "You should have seen it—the Reaper was coming for me. I tried to fire but my gun was on safety, and before I could even flick off it reached, and there she was behind it."

"Big tactic," Duvalier said, examining the robe she had stripped off the Reaper for black—and poisonous—subcutaneous fluid. "Lying in the grass like a snake."

"You're one of those . . . one of those Hunter-things," Thatcher said.

"You have a problem with that?" Duvalier asked.

"Offerz," Valentine garbled. "Oturs."

"The others?" Duvalier said. "I dunno. I didn't hear any screams."

316

"Are there any more around?" Thatcher asked.

"Ope nog," Valentine said.

Thatcher took a better grip on his gun and looked warily around. "How do you know?"

"He knows," Duvalier said. "He just knows. Leave it at that." She gave him his rifle back, as though glad to give up an unpleasant burden.

"Can we sleep soon? How about in that barn?" Gail asked.

Valentine waved tiredly. "Attitude, Gail," Duvalier said.

"Stick the attitude. My feet are killing me," she said hotly.

"I think she's getting better," Thatcher said.

⚬

It took them a while to find the trail of Dr. Boothe and Pepsa. Valentine found their marks in the long grasses. They'd cut over to a legworm trail and followed it up the hillside.

"What are they going back in that direction for?" Thatcher asked.

Valentine shrugged, resolved to communicate with hand signals. Gail groaned as they started up the hill.

They caught up to the pair, Boothe hiking along behind Pepsa carrying the gun in one hand, her medical bag slung.

Valentine elbowed Duvalier, pointed, and made a T with his hands. She nodded and slipped into the bushes, gripping her walking stick like an alert samurai carrying his sword.

"What's the matter?" Thatcher asked, keeping his voice low.

Valentine found he could whisper coherently. He spoke into Duvalier's ear.

"Something's wrong," she said. "Somebody's been giving us away."

Back in the legworm valley, Valentine heard hoofbeats. Two legworms and perhaps a dozen men on horseback were investigating events in the pit. They looked like native Kentuckians intermingled with Grogs.

"Let's catch up," Duvalier said.

They went up the hill as quickly as Gail's weary, unsteady legs would allow.

317

The vets must have heard them coming. Both turned around. Pepsa looked frightened.

Boothe brought up the pistol and pointed it between them.

*Shit. Guessed wrong. Why didn't I just shoot the pair of them?*

*Because they might not be in it together.*

"Hey, Doc, it's us," Thatcher said.

"Guns! Drop them," Boothe said. The gun shook in her hands as she pointed. Tears streamed down her face.

*Tears? Why would a Kurian agent cry?*

"Epsah!" Valentine shouted, shouldering his rifle, sighting on the first Kurian agent he had ever looked upon.

The U-gun burned. Its stock burned him, the trigger guard; he felt the flesh on his hands cook; the agony of the steam in the Kurian Tower redoubled and poured through his nervous system. Drop it, all he could do was drop the gun.

Don't~think~so, a voice in his head said.

Thatcher brought up his rifle—*what the hell?*—the burning agony left, relief and wonder at freedom from pain but why was Thatcher shouldering his rifle with the barrel pressed to his collarbone and the butt pointed at Pepsa

*Krrak!*

Blood and bone flew from Thatcher's shoulder, the gun fell, the spent cartridge casing spun

and before it completed its parabola Duvalier was out of the Kentucky grass, sword held up and ready

Stupid~bitch!

Duvalier screamed, dropped her sword, jumped back from it as though it were a snake striking—

Valentine grabbed his short legworm pick, lunged up the hill

Boothe turned her gun at Pepsa, no, not at her, at a patch of dark shortleaf pine behind her, and fired.

Behind him Thatcher screamed. Valentine was still three strides away, the pain came, the legworm pick lightning in his hands . . . no, fire, hot blue flame that burned—

*Lies. They fight with lies. Lies can't change steel to flame.*

He raised the pick, screaming in agony, fighting the pain with sound.

You~dumbfuck~terrorists, Pepsa said between his ears.

And he threw, sent the pick spinning at her, watched it hit, saw the point bury itself in one fleshy breast, a gurgle, went to Boothe, took the hot gun from her shaking hand, pointed and fired

Where~are~you~lord?

Another shot, HEEELP~the~burn! the gun clicked empty, even as she toppled over he straddled her, hitting her with the pistol butt, silencing the screaming from between his ears by caving in her skull and the awful warble of her tongueless mouth, but nothingness yawned beneath him like a chasm, he felt himself tottering at the edge of an abyss.

Duvalier picked him up off her corpse, pulled him out of the darkness. Hoofbeats. The loom of riders in the darkness. Words, Boothe bending over Thatcher, applying pressure as Duvalier waved the riders over. Finally the strange emptiness in his head left, and he could distinguish faces again.

"Haloo, Bulletproof. You're far from home. What hospitality can fellow tribesmen offer?"

φ

They bartered the Reaper's robe for transport and found their way back to the Bulletproof. In a few days they again knew Kentucky hospitality in a chilly, Z-shaped valley fed by artesian springs, his jaw braced and bandaged with baling wire by Boothe. Valentine learned to appreciate smashed cubes of legworm flesh, slathered in barbecue sauce sucked through a straw. He also got mashed squash, pumpkin, and corn, eating out of the same pot as the resident babies.

A giggling nursing mother offered him a spare teat after feeding her daughter. It hurt to laugh.

Once his jaw knit he borrowed an old-fashioned horse, loaded up a second with grain and dried meat, and rode out to where he had last seen Ahn-Kha. He left a stoppered bottle of Bulletproof bourbon at Grog-eye level with a note to his friend, telling him where they were wintering until warmth allowed travel again. He tried to learn what had happened to Ahn-Kha and his pursuing column, but only found some shattered glass and debris that might have been from a motorcycle eight miles away.

The fruitless search left him moody and depressed. His tender mouth troubled him every time he spoke and ate, and a fragment of mirror showed that his jawline now had an uneven balance to it thanks to the break. The only bright spot was Gail Foster's transformation into a convivial, charming woman, though she remained a little pallid, even on the hearty Bulletproof cooking. She looked as though she were about to have twins. He couldn't remember the last time he'd seen a woman with such a wide belly after the baby dropped.

The baby came on December 22.

Duvalier woke Valentine and passed him a hot cup of grassy-tasting tea. "Gail's water broke. Our vet is attending. Suki's there too."

She brought him to a modest, pellet-stove-heated home that served as a sickroom for the local Bulletproof.

Suki was a Bulletproof midwife. She was young, perhaps a year or two older than Valentine, but had a calming effect on Gail brought about by nothing more than her quiet voice and cups of the honey-filled silvery cinqefoil tea she brewed. Gail had given birth once before, but remembered nothing of the event but gauzy business on the other side of her screened lap.

Valentine went in and saw Gail lying on her side with her knees drawn up and buttocks at the edge of the hammocklike "birthing bed." He gripped her hand through a contraction, sponging the sweat from her forehead when it was over. She'd soaked through her shirt even in the winter cool.

"I wish Will was here," she gasped. "He always . . . " The words trailed off.

Valentine wrung out the sponge. "Will never forgot about you for a moment. Your husband wasn't the man you thought. Or he was. You'll understand when you see him again."

She smiled and nodded.

"First we have to get your baby into the world. Can do?"

"Can do," she agreed.

*But you can't be there to see it. This trip, the risks. You'll never see a payoff. You could just as well have driven away with Ahn-Kha. You can never walk down an Ozark highway again. You're condemned by your own actions, an exile.*

"She's quit dilating," Boothe said, bringing Valentine out of his thoughts with a flash of guilt over what Gail must be experiencing. She had a short flashlight attached to her forehead: a medical unicorn. "I'm going to C-section. Pe—Suki, get me the tray I laid out in the kitchen."

Valentine got out of the way as the midwife came in with the tray.

"Suki, keep her chin up."

Boothe poured a shot glass full of Bulletproof, then added a couple of drops of ether to it. She tipped it into a fist-sized wad of cotton.

"Have her breathe this," she said, handing the mask to Suki. Gail inhaled the mixture.

"Christmas baby. You were almost a Christmas baby," Gail said as the ether took effect.

"Enough," Dr. Boothe told Suki. "Gail, keep looking at the ceiling. Over before you know it." Valentine watched her focus on Gail's belly, steadying the scalpel.

Valentine watched, relieved and fascinated at the same time, as the scalpel opened Gail just above the pelvis.

"Coming now. Your baby's doing fine," Boothe said.

Valentine couldn't help but think about Malia. What had Amalee's birth been like? The sweet, burning scent of ether in the air, along with blood, sweat, and amniotic fluid?

*God, do they all look like that?*

Boothe pulled out a froglike creature, narrow, legs drawn up tight, arms folded like a dead insect's, brachycephalic skull all the more unreal as the doctor held it upside down. "Oh, Christ."

A baleful yellow eye, slit-pupiled, peered at him from a face pinched by internal agony. It hissed, fought for breath.

Gail Foster Post had given birth to a Reaper.

Suki backed away, hand over her mouth.

"Boy or a girl?" Gail said, then, when there was no reply, "What? What?"

321

Boothe showed her.

"Get it away from me!" Gail screamed. "Bastards! Lying bastards!" Her words trailed off into sobs.

"Stay still," Boothe ordered. "Suki, put three more drops in another shot glass."

"Give it to me," Valentine said, extending a towel. He took the struggling infant—cleaned its sexless body.

"What a mess. Tearing everywhere in the uterus," Boothe said. "I hope I can fix this." She turned her light on Valentine. "Just pinch its nose and mouth shut. Bury it outside."

Valentine took the infant out into the December air, instinctively holding it close against the chill. He looked at the blood-smeared face, purple and green and blue, crisscrossed with veins, horror in miniature. Black nails, impossibly tiny, gleamed wetly as it moved its hand.

The future death machine coughed.

*Did yellow eyes make you evil? A pointed tongue?*

"Do you have a soul?" someone asked, using his larynx, tongue, and mouth.

Valentine wondered if he'd directed the question to the newborn or to himself. Tiny nostrils, long little jaw; he could smother it one-handed.

*My DNA is 98% identical to a chimpanzee. How much code do I share with you?*

However much, a tiny amount of it was Kurian. Evil.

Or Lifeweaver. The *Dau'weem* and *Dau'wa* shared however many gene pairs they possessed, thirty thousand or three million. They differed only in their opposition over vampirism.

Could he say a creature fresh from the womb deserved to die, thanks to its appearance?

*Not appearance, design.*

A newborn, innocence embodied in what felt like ten pounds of sugar. Harmless. But experience told him otherwise.

*Songs of Innocence and Experience*. William Blake.

*Did he who made the Lamb make thee?*

Valentine closed up the towel, protecting the newborn tyger

against the chill. The Reaper's head turned, sensing something it liked in Valentine's wrist.

Valentine pushed his pulse point a little closer, offering.

Its mouth opened, latched on, and Valentine felt the prick of the sharp tongue. The penetration only hurt a little.

Softly, the Reaper fed.